The Heir

The Armor of God

Book 3

The Heir

JEFF BOLES

ISBN: 978-1-6653-0773-4 - Paperback
ISBN: 978-1-6653-0774-1 - Hardcover
eISBN: 978-1-6653-0775-8 - eBook

These ISBNs are the property of BookLogix for the express purpose of sales and distribution of this title. The content of this book is the property of the copyright holder only. BookLogix does not hold any ownership of the content of this book and is not liable in any way for the materials contained within. The views and opinions expressed in this book are the property of the Author/Copyright holder, and do not necessarily reflect those of BookLogix.

Library of Congress Control Number: 2023920658

⊗This paper meets the requirements of ANSI/NISO Z39.48-1992 (Permanence of Paper)

1 0 2 5 2 3

Prologue

The great castle stood tall and proud, the majesty of its ramparts and walls hidden by the dark of the moonless night. A heavy mist slowly rolled across the landscape, a reflection of the cloud-filled sky that blocked out even the brightest of heaven's lights. The bare whisper of a breeze moved across the glass-like lake, pushing the white veil across the water and into the forest, giving an ever-so slight rustle to the leaves. Though normally enveloped by a chorus of the creatures of the night, the lake and forest were oddly silent. The only sounds that drifted across the water came from within the castle's grand walls.

Sounds of music and laughter bounced through the halls, filling nearly every corner of the castle and spilling out into the grand courtyard where an occasional shadow or two would weave its way from one building to another. The dimly lit corridors seemed cold and lonely despite the jubilant echoes that grew louder and louder deeper in the castle. Though there were but a few candles along the walls to provide just enough light to navigate the hallway, the darkness was chased away as the glow of a thousand candles and torches spilled into the corridor from a massive banquet hall.

It was a grand celebration, a royal feast, of such magnitude as to be worthy of lore. What had to be three hundred men and women were gathered eating, drinking, and dancing. The walls of the great hall were decorated with large, elaborate tapestries and silks. A band of a dozen musicians threw out song after song that energized the partiers, moving many to dance and others to sing along. Table after table was covered with fruits, vegetables, meats, and breads. There were so many pitchers of drink that it appeared every person could have his or her own without the need for sharing. On a stage in the middle of the room were eight extremely attractive young women dancing with and around each other, and surrounding the stage were easily twenty men enjoying the rhythmic gyrations. It was a scene of excess rarely seen.

Toward the back of the room was a large rectangular table with two dozen people sitting along its borders. At the far end of the table, facing the rest of the room, was an extremely large man who easily weighed over three hundred and fifty pounds. Though everybody at the table was dressed more elegantly than the other people in the room, this man had no equal in adornment. His dark-green, silk-like shirt was covered with gold stitching that created intricate, eye-catching patterns. His blemish-free leather boots were partially covered with what appeared to be leggings made of wolf fur. His dark-burgundy robe, fresh from the tailor, was lined with fur that matched his leggings. A large gold medallion hung from his neck and rested on his massive stomach. Despite the excessive quantity of food and drink that he had consumed, the man's clothes contained not a single stain. His boisterous, contagious laugh seemed to rise above the chaos of the room. When he spoke, those seated with him listened. When he laughed, they laughed. When he drank, they drank.

A young servant girl, tightly holding on to a ceramic pitcher, gingerly approached the large man. She waited for one of the rare pauses in conversation, then spoke to him in a soft, if not nervous, voice.

"Your Majesty, would you care for more wine?"

The man turned and looked at her, his deep blue eyes appreciating her delicate features and his warm smile, though nearly hidden by a thick, blond beard, easing some of her nervousness.

"My dear, asking me if I desire more wine to drink is nearly as irrational as asking me if I would like more air to breathe. Though

I cannot be sure of which I could live longer without, air or wine."
His chest and stomach bounced heavily as he let out one of his
deep, mighty laughs and slammed the table with his massive
right hand. His fellow diners obediently laughed with him, two of
them nearly choking on the wine they had just swallowed. The
servant girl smiled politely and patiently waited for the laughter
to die down. After thirty seconds the king, his face a deep red
from his outburst and still smiling, looked at the girl again.

"Yes, lass, we would care for more wine. Leave the pitcher on
the table. And you may bring another pitcher every two songs
until one of us falls over, and then make it a pitcher every three
songs." He let out another bellow-like laugh and on cue, his
table-guests laughed with him. The young girl smiled again,
bowed her head to the king, then turned and left.

"My lord, I do not believe the servant girl quite appreciated
your sense of humor," the man to his right observed.

"True, James, but then again, I do not believe she has been
drinking the finest wine in the kingdom for the past four hours
like you have, either," the king aquaint responded jovially.
"What a thing wine is," he continued, lifting his chalice and peering
into it as though there was some great secret contained within.
"Take a man who seems fearful that his face should break lest he
smile or laugh and give him a few glasses of this red liquid, and he
becomes the happiest and most entertaining person in the room.
Take a woman whose heart is as cold as the stones we walk on
and let her consume a share of this drink, and she becomes as
warm as the sun on a mid-summer's day."

"Hmph," another man grunted. "Not to impugn your
wisdom, your majesty, but I have known women whose cold
hearts were immune to the warmth of wine."

"Calvin, I did not realize you knew the queen that well, God
rest her soul," the king replied. There were a few unsure snickers
around the table. "On a good day she was about as warm as a
gravestone in the dead of winter and on a bad day, well, let us just
say that she could send a chill throughout the entire castle with
but one of her icy glares."

"But she did give you two strong, smart sons, heirs to your throne," a woman at the table offered, trying to lighten the conversation.

"Aye, Meredith, she did at that," the king answered. "To my sons, Thomas and William DuFay!" he said, lifting his chalice of wine. The others at the table followed his lead, raised their cups, and cried in unison, "To Thomas and William DuFay!"

King Robert DuFay looked around the room, breathing in the exuberance of his guests. Truly, little made him as happy as seeing the people closest to him enjoying such a celebration. Their smiles and laughs warmed his heart. These were the lords and ladies of his kingdom, the noble landowners, the people he could always count on to support him. At his table were the wealthiest of the wealthy and while most of the people in the room were barely more than acquaintances, these were the people whom he considered to be his friends. His eyes fell on a man standing against a wall not too far off, by himself, observing the crowd. He was neither eating nor drinking, and he certainly was not smiling or laughing. The man was just over six-foot tall, not too lean but not quite husky, and around forty years old. He was wearing a modest, dark-blue robe tied at the waste and wore a short necklace with a small gold cross attached to it. His face was cleanshaven and his dark-gold hair was cut short. His greenish eyes surveyed the room, and a look of disapproval covered his face.

"It would seem that our esteemed holy man is not quite enjoying the celebration," the king noted to his guests.

"Speaking of a man whose social skills could benefit from a few cups of wine," Calvin said.

"You could pour an entire barrel of wine into that man, and he would still not know how to have an enjoyable time," Meredith offered bitterly.

"You speak as though you know from experience," Calvin responded teasingly. Meredith shot him an icy glare but said nothing.

"Well, this just will not do," the king said, motioning to a nearby servant. "Tell Reverend Knox that I would speak with him," he instructed the servant. The young boy bowed quickly and ran over to the man, relaying the king's message. The minister did not move immediately but instead, took a moment to survey the king's table. He did not wish to speak with the king at that moment, considering the excessive consumption by the king and his guests, but to refuse to do so would have been a great insult to the king. Reluctantly, he left his spot away from the commotion and approached the king's table.

"Your majesty," he said with a voice that was deep and smooth, almost soothing.

"Matthew, I do not know if you noticed, but there is a grand celebration in progress tonight," the king said as he looked up at the churchman. "Do you hear the music and laughter, and do you see the people dancing and eating and drinking?"

"Yes, my lord," he replied, "I see quite well that which fills this room tonight."

"Yet there you stand, not eating, not drinking, not speaking a word to anyone as though to do so might shut heaven's own gates against you. These musicians are playing some of the finest music to be heard and while it seems nearly every other person here cannot help but dance or at least move in some fashion to the music, I would wager that you have not so much as tapped a single toe once."

"Your majesty is quite observant," Reverend Knox replied drily.

"Do your holy vows forbid you from the enjoyment of celebrating the gifts of food, drink and music?" the king asked.

"No, my lord, they do not. I am no stranger to the pleasures of a hearty meal, or a stout ale or fine wine, or the sweet melody of music played by those given gifts to do so. However, such things are to be enjoyed in...moderation."

"Ah, come now, Matthew, the good Lord surely will not deny you entrance into glory should you indulge this tasty wine in a bit more than a moderate fashion," Meredith offered, eyeing the clergyman with a bit of a teasing smile.

"That may be true," he answered, "but I would not want my

mind clouded by the fruits of the vine to such a degree that I miss the opportunity to show those who need it the path to the gates of glory." The woman's smile quickly faded and was replaced by a scornful glare before she turned her attention elsewhere.

"So, you do not approve of our feasting and celebrating," the king stated, "for in truth there is little being done in moderation here this evening. Which reminds me," he turned his head to locate the young lady who had brought him the wine just a few minutes earlier. "Girl! More wine!" he shouted to the servant girl. His table guests laughed at his outburst.

"I would say that it is God who does not approve of this show of gluttony, drunkenness and other things being partaken of tonight which I shall not give mention to," the holy man stated. "You say you are celebrating. What is it that you celebrate?"

"Life, my boy, life!" the king replied, raising his chalice. "To life!" he toasted and took a long draw from his cup.

"We were not given the breath of life to be used as an excuse for nights such as this," the reverend replied. "Life is not something to be celebrated in and of itself. It is a gift for which to be thankful, to be sure, but the celebration of it is to be found in the use of it. A life of indulgence and excess is a waste of breath and a slap in the face of He who gives life. If you truly desire to celebrate life, then use your life to build the kingdom of God."

"No, reverend, the building of the kingdom of God is your duty," King DuFay replied. "It is that for which you have been trained, for which you have been taught. For the rest of us, it is our duty to enjoy the blessings of God and the fruits of life."

"It is the duty of every one of us to build the kingdom of God, Your Majesty," Matthew answered. He looked around the table and around the room. "You have been given much, my lord," he added. "It would be wise to use what God has given you for His glory and not your own. To whom much is given, much is required. That which the Lord gives, he also can take away." An uncomfortable silence fell over the table. The man of the cloth had all but rebuked the king, in public, and that was an offense for which men had lost their freedom, and in some cases, their lives. The king's eyes locked onto the minister's eyes and held them for an extended period. Neither man would look away.

"Since this joyous environment of over-indulgence and celebration is an offense to your sanctification, perhaps you should return to your prayers and meditation, in private," the king said none-too-friendly, dismissing the pastor.

"As you wish, my lord," Matthew replied. With a respectful bow of his head, he turned and left the room.

"Well, what are we to do now that the life of the party has left the room?" Calvin asked sarcastically.

"We shall eat and drink and dance, and we shall do so in excess!" the king shouted as he drained the wine from his cup. His guests were all too eager to follow their king's example.

It was well past midnight when King Robert DuFay, citing old age as the culprit, made his excuses and retired to his chambers. The celebration continued well into the night and in fact, it was closer to dawn than dusk when the last glass of wine was swallowed, the tables were cleared, and the banquet hall fell silent. The once-roaring fires in the pits surrounding the room slowly died out, and the chill of early morning soon crept into the great hall.

There were few stirrings in the castle as the faint glow of the morning sun appeared over the mountains to the east. The fog that enveloped the fields and trees began to lift, and the mist over the lake dissipated. The captain of the guard, a tall, muscular man named Gerritt Hanson, began his morning rounds to check on his men. Many were asleep at their posts, which had become an all-too-common occurrence. There was a lack of discipline in the ranks, something he would have to address. He suspected that most of them had participated in many of the smaller parties that had popped up around the castle the prior night for those who were not "regal" enough to join the king's private party. He would give them a firm kick in the side or a slap against their helmet, scold them, and move on to the next sentry. He had arrived at one of the posts near the front gate and was waking the guard when he glanced out over the wall. At first, he did not believe what he was seeing, but it only took a second for the reality of it to sink in. His eyes widened in horror. He slapped the drowsy guard several times. "Wake up, you imbecile!" he shouted at the man. "Wake up! Take to your post!"

Hanson leaned over the wall and looked down into the courtyard. There were but a few men slowly walking about, appearing to still be half-asleep. "Sound the alarm!" he shouted to the closest man, a sentry preparing to relieve one of the night guards. "Sound the alarm!" he repeated when the man looked up but did not immediately move to comply with the order. "All sentries to their posts! I want every man fully dressed, armed, and ready for battle ten minutes ago! Station archers along the battlements and at the arrow loops. Load the ballistas and prepare them for firing. Lower the second gate and double the guard behind it. Load the catapults. Do it now!"

As the sentry sprang into action, Hanson ran down the stone stairway and across the courtyard. He burst into the castle and rushed past the two guards who did not appear the least bit alarmed at their captain's sudden entry. "Prepare to protect the king!" Hanson shouted over his shoulder as he bolted through the foyer. "We are under attack!" He did not pause to see if his men complied but continued across the open floor and down one of the side corridors. He did not slow down until he reached the king's chambers and even then, he barely reduced his momentum as he threw open the door and rushed in, leaving the guard outside the door with a puzzled look.

"Your Majesty! We are under attack!" Hanson called out as he ran to the side of the king's massive bed. The king barely stirred.

"Your Majesty! Did you not hear me? We are under attack! You must dress and come with me!"

"Under attack?" the king repeated, still not fully awake and his senses still dulled by the night's excessive consumption. He rolled over onto his back and looked up at Hanson. "What do you mean we are under attack?"

"My lord, there is an enormous army, the likes of which I have never seen, gathered outside the castle. There must be three thousand men, dozens of trebuchets, and platforms stretched across the moat."

"Have the castle's walls or gate been breached?" the king asked, coming to his senses and rolling out of bed.

"No, my lord, they have not. In fact, while the army appears fully ready for attack, they have not advanced."

"Why do they wait?" the king mused, getting dressed. As if on cue, a messenger appeared in the doorway to the king's chambers.

"Your Majesty, I beg your pardon, but there is a courier at the gate claiming he has a message from his leader that he is to deliver to you," the young man said.

"That is interesting," DuFay said, looking inquisitively at his captain. "Perhaps he wishes to surrender already?" he said sarcastically.

"My lord, this is not an army formed for surrender," Hanson replied. "It is bred for one thing: destruction. And with our army all but disbanded... "

"I know, I know," DuFay replied with a wave of his hand. "Perhaps it was not such a wise idea after all to reduce our troops. It seemed such a waste of money at the time considering there has not been the need for an army in nearly two hundred years." The king looked at Hanson, who appeared ready to speak. "You do not need to remind me that you were against the decision, Gerritt. I remember quite clearly your passionate arguments against a limited military. It would appear your objections were well placed."

"That is of no matter now, my lord," Hanson replied, taking little pleasure in the king's admission. "Let us see what this man has to say. Perhaps battle can be avoided altogether." Hanson turned to the messenger. "Give entrance to the courier, but him alone. Ensure that he is not armed. Bind his hands behind his back and bind his feet. Place four guards around him, weapons at the ready. We will be there shortly." The messenger nodded and quickly left the room.

"Not exactly a hospitable welcome for our guest," DuFay said as he pulled on his boots. "But a necessary precaution, I know. Shall we see what lies in store for us this day?" Captain Hanson nodded and led the king out of the bedroom and down the hallway.

Twenty minutes later, after grabbing a piece of bread and sausage from the closest kitchen and having ascended one of the castle's four main towers to view the enemy, the king and his captain entered a small room off the large foyer near the main entrance to the castle. A man sat in a chair at one end of a six-foot long wooden table, his hands and feet bound, with four fully armed guards standing by him at the ready. King DuFay took a moment and looked the man over before saying anything. Finally, he pulled out the chair at the other end of the table and sat down. Captain Hanson moved to the king's right side and stood, glaring at the visitor.

"I must say, this is the last way that I would have envisioned my morning starting," DuFay said, addressing the bound man. "I certainly do not appreciate being awoken from one of the soundest sleeps I have had in some time. Therefore, let us not waste time with insincere pleasantries. Deliver your message."

"As you have seen, your castle is surrounded by my lord's army," the messenger started. "There are three thousand men stationed outside your main gate, just beyond the reach of your strongest weapons, and another thousand in the woods that you cannot see. Another two hundred are stationed on barges on the lake, again just beyond the reach of any of your weapons. There are two dozen catapults spaced in such a manner that there is no corner of your castle beyond their range. Four wooden bridges now stretch across your moat rendering that defense all but useless."

"Yes, yes, I have seen all of this," DuFay said, an uneasiness forming inside of him that he kept hidden from the man across the table. "Say what you came here to say."

"My master is feeling unusually generous this morning. Ordinarily he takes what he wants by force without preamble, but today he is willing to come to an agreement that will avoid unnecessary bloodshed. You and your sons will surrender your castle, and yourselves, to my lord. The three of you will be executed in public, quickly and painlessly. All others will be spared."

"I thought you said the agreement would avoid unnecessary bloodshed," DuFay replied.

"Unfortunately, some bloodshed is necessary," the man replied matter-of-factly. "You cannot be allowed to live, nor your sons, lest you seek to rally the people and reacquire your throne. All others will be spared. That is, as long as they swear allegiance to my master. If they refuse to do so, well, their fate shall be the same as yours and your sons."

"This is your master's definition of generosity?" DuFay asked incredulously.

"To be certain," the man replied. "Otherwise, you would all be dead already."

"I hardly think so," DuFay countered. "It is your master and his army that will be dead soon enough. Word has been sent to my army that is stationed but a few hours from here. With nowhere to retreat to, you and your friends will be decimated before the first one steps foot inside these walls."

"You have no army," the man replied dismissively, calling the king's bluff. "You have not had one for years. The rag-tag group of men you like to call your army, all five hundred of them, are poorly trained and in no condition to fight. In truth, considering how you have treated them, it would not be surprising if they turned against you altogether."

DuFay knew that the man was right. His only defense against this horde was there with him now, fewer than three hundred men, most of them never having been in any kind of fight beyond a tavern brawl. The scenario of them trying fend-off three thousand well-armed, well-organized barbarians was not a pleasant one. It could end in only one way.

"Come with me," DuFay instructed Hanson as he rose from his chair and left the room. The two men walked into the large communal area, well away from the small room, so the messenger could not hear them conversing.

"How long could we hold off an attack?" the king asked.

"A few hours," Hanson replied grimly, "perhaps a day at most. With their numbers, with their weapons, with our limited fighting resources…" He shook his head. "Every man will fight to the death to defend this castle, to defend his king, and the enemy will suffer greatly, I can promise you that. However, I fear the outcome is inevitable. Without an army to protect us, we cannot be victorious."

King DuFay knew that his captain was right. The minister's words from the night before came back like a slap in the face. *That which the Lord gives, he also can take away.* He solemnly looked around at the walls forming the great foyer and the beautiful tapestries hanging from them. He walked over to the closest one and ran his hand over it, feeling its silky smoothness, admiring the intricacies of its design. "You know, I do not believe that I have ever actually taken the time to appreciate the artistry of this tapestry, or any of them truth be told. I feel as if this is the first time that I have laid eyes on them. What a sad commentary." He took a few steps over and ran his hands over a life-sized marble statue of a lion that looked to be stalking prey. "So beautiful. So majestic." He knew what he had to do. He returned to the interrogation room, but this time he did not sit down.

"It would appear your master leaves me with little choice," the king said. "How much time will he grant my sons and I to surrender?"

"As I said, my master is feeling generous this morning. He will give you and your sons until midday to offer yourselves as sacrifices for the sake of your people. You will remove all your sentries from the walls and disarm them. At noon, you will raise your gates and lower your drawbridge. You and your sons, and only you and your sons, will walk across the bridge and present yourselves to my master."

"What guarantee does your master offer that he will not decide to renege on his end of the agreement and slaughter all of my people?" DuFay asked.

"Guarantee?" the messenger replied. "There is no guarantee but his word. Do as he commands, and your people will live. That is, as long as they swear allegiance to him."

DuFay paused and looked deeply into the man's eyes, looking for any hint of insincerity. However, the man's eyes betrayed nothing. After a few more moments of stalling, the king provided his answer.

"Tell your master that I agree to his terms. At noon, I will order my sentries to stand down. The gate will be opened, and he will have his sacrifice." He looked at one of the guards. "Untie him and escort him to the side door near the gate. Ensure that no harm befalls him. Then return to your post."

DuFay strolled confidently from the interrogation room and Hanson followed without a word. After walking down three corridors and flights of stairs, DuFay entered a room and lit several torches stuck in sconces around the room. It was a small room with only a few pieces of furniture, a tall cabinet along one wall, and a table with six chairs.

"I have never been in this room," Hanson said as he looked around.

"There has been no need for this room for many years," the king replied, looking around. "This is my war room, where battle plans are created."

"You intend on engaging this horde in battle?" Hanson asked in disbelief.

"The desire to fight this evil, to at least engage it and look it in the eye, is quite strong to be sure. What more glorious death is there but the one brought forth in battle? Yet I know that to engage in battle would be certain death for every person within these walls."

"Your majesty, you do realize that there is every possibility that this man is lying and that despite you agreeing to his terms, after murdering you and your sons he will execute every man, woman, and child upon whom he can lay his hands?"

"Yes, I suspect that is his plan. This is likely no more than a game to him, a venture of his ego. Imagine what pleasure he would derive having a king and his sons bow down before him, offering their necks to his sword," DuFay answered. "That is why I do not intend on honoring this so-called 'agreement' of his. No, I do not intend on engaging him in battle. Nor do I intend on offering my sons to him. Here is what I want you to do: First, find my sons and bring them to this room. Have them pack only a few changes of clothes. Go to one of the kitchens and find enough provisions to last them several days at least. They will need weapons, but nothing heavy, nothing that will encumber or slow them down. Second, find every servant, every woman, every non-military person you can locate and have them begin taking down every tapestry they can find. I want every item that has any value at all taken down to the dungeon level and stored in the largest room down there. Two men will then remove the door and enclose the doorway with block and mortar to blend in with the walls of the corridor. You will then collapse the ceiling in the corridor up near the main entrance to the dungeons. I will not have these barbarians laying their hands on the treasures of my fathers. Finally, you will gather the people and lead them to this room. Like my sons, they are to pack lightly."

"I do not understand," Hanson replied. "Why lead them to this room? There is no defensive advantage here. If anything, it makes it that much easier for them to be slaughtered."

"You will see," DuFay replied. "Now go and do as I have instructed. You have much to accomplish and little time to spare."

"And what of you, my lord?" Hanson asked.

"There is something I must do," the king replied. "Go, now."

With a final look of puzzlement, the Captain of the Guard obediently turned and left the room. After he was gone, DuFay stood in silence and looked around the room that he had not visited for many, many years. His eyes locked on the tall cabinet for a few moments then he, too, turned and left the room.

"Have you come to beg God for salvation from your enemies?"

King DuFay did not rise nor turn to meet the eyes of the minister as the man entered the small sanctuary. The room was about twenty-five feet long by twenty-feet wide. Ten wooden, padded benches provided room for up to fifty people to sit comfortably. At the far end of the room a beautiful stained-glass window stretched from two feet off the floor to the fifteen-foot-high ceiling. In front of the window was a simple wooden podium and a small wooden table with a two-foot tall, jewel-embossed silver cross centered on it. On either side of the cross was a silver goblet, decorated with intricate carvings and numerous emeralds, rubies, and sapphires. Several tapestries hung on the walls depicting various people and events straight out of the Bible. DuFay sat stoically in the middle of the first bench, staring at the stained-glass window.

"No, Matthew, I have not come to beg God for salvation from my enemies. I know that there is no deliverance from what is about to come," the king answered rather quietly. Sensing a change in the king, the minister pressed.

"Then what brings you to this place of worship after all of these years?"

"My life," the king whispered.

"So, it is not salvation from your enemies you seek but salvation from death?"

"I know there is no deliverance from that, either," the king replied. "You of all people know the life I have lived. It has been full of selfishness and pride. I have indulged with little restraint my appetite for food, drink, and women. I have amassed a great fortune during my life and have used it to feed my impulses. I have two sons raised by servants and teachers instead of their father. I have a wife who died of loneliness and neglect. My best friends are bought and paid for with land and titles and while at any given time there are at least three dozen servants and attendants surrounding me within these walls, I could not tell you the names of five of them. And now this day comes when everything I have, even my life, will be taken from me. This is the very warning you expressed to me last night but looking back I know it was a warning you gave me many, many times. I just did not want to hear it, to believe it could happen." The king turned and looked at the minister who stood silent, listening to the king's confessions.

"I have not come to this place to seek salvation from my enemy, nor have I come to seek salvation from death," DuFay continued with tears rolling down his cheeks. "I have come to seek salvation for my soul, if that is even possible."

The minister walked over and sat down beside the king. "That, my lord, is the one salvation you can be sure to attain this very day."

"Why would God be willing to spare my soul?" DuFay asked. "I cannot remember ever speaking a word to Him. I have ridiculed Him, and you, at every turn. What is there about me that is worthy of saving?"

"That is just it, your majesty. There is nothing in you that is worthy of saving. There is nothing in me that is worthy of saving. There is nothing in anybody that is worthy of saving. We can do no good in and of our own that is pleasing to God because none of us are good. Left to ourselves, we all would lead lives of selfishness, indulging every desire that came into our heart without a second thought. That is what makes the graciousness of God that much more glorious. Despite our rebellious hearts, despite our filthiness, He still chooses to rip out our cold, dead hearts of stone and give us warm, living hearts of flesh."

"What can I do to be saved?" the king asked, bewildered. "What can I do?"

"Confess that Jesus is the Son of God," the minister answered. "Confess your life of rebellion to Him, ask for forgiveness, and rely only upon the blood that He shed on the cross for the salvation of your soul. Do this and you will be saved, you and your household."

The king sat in silence, a whirlwind of emotion coursing through him. He thought about his life, from his earliest childhood memories to this very morning. He saw a life of wanton indulgence, of waste. As a child he had been given everything he had ever asked for and could not remember a time when his mother or father had denied him. When his father had passed away and he had ascended to the throne, there was nothing to stand in the way of what Robert wanted. He took and took from his own people to support his lavish lifestyle. Nobody dared say a word of rebuke or reproof to him because if they did, he would arrest them for challenging his God-given authority. Yes, he believed in God, of that there was no doubt. God had been nothing more than a distant thought, though, a nearly forgotten relative in a land far, far away whom he had never seen. But now God was here, outside of his gates, ready to pass judgment on him. And the thought of eternal suffering terrified him.

"I confess," the king said, the tears continuing down his face. The two men sat there in near silence for what seemed hours, speaking and praying in the softest of voices. To the king the world had become silent and he all but forgot about the army of barbarians just outside his gates. A sense of peace that he had never known washed over him and he no longer feared the certain death he would be facing in but a couple of hours. He looked up at the minister.

"There is one more thing I need to ask of you, Matthew," he said, and proceeded to tell him of his plans.

The sun had risen high in the sky and was but an hour from reaching its apex. There was very little movement outside the gates of the castle as the invading army waited patiently for the gates to open and for the king and his son to venture out. They knew the chances of battle were extremely slim and even if DuFay decided to go back on his agreement, whatever battle came would be swift. Inside of the castle's gates, there was little activity to be seen in the courtyard. Many of the sentries along the castle's walls had been pulled back and there were only a few remaining to keep an eye on the enemy. Within the castle's walls, in the great banquet room, nearly two hundred people were crammed, waiting for a promised address from King DuFay. They knew that a siege was imminent and were anxious to see what plan their king had for their safety. The king appeared on a balcony overlooking his people.

"My people," he began, "my beloved people. As you know, an invader is poised outside of our gates, ready to lay siege to this castle and slaughter every living soul to be found." There was a great groan from the crowd, and many started crying out in panic. The king lifted his hands in a quieting gesture. "Be not afraid, my people, for you shall suffer no such fate. In a few minutes you will be guided to an escape route and soon you will be far from harm." That seemed to calm most of the people. King DuFay looked them over, sorrow covering his face. "I have failed you, my friends. I have failed you as king and as protector. I have not upheld the faith that my fathers did, that the great King Reginald DuFay had, which made him such a magnificent king and in whose honor six glorious pieces of armor were made. I am not worthy of that armor. I did not seek to imbue within me that which the armor represented, the armor of God. I see that now. There shall come a day, though, when another DuFay shall be worthy of that armor and that for which it stands. If not my son, then his son, or his son's son. On that day, when the six pieces of armor are brought together again and placed in the hands of my worthy heir, peace and prosperity will once again return to the land. Reginald DuFay will once again govern a land of freedom, justice, and righteousness! Look to that day, my friends! Look for Reginald DuFay and the armor of God, and you will know the time has come!

"Now, you must leave and not look back. You will be led by men who will take you to safety, to places where you can make new homes and new lives. But never forget your home, never forget Durinburg, for one day, your posterity shall return and continue the lives that you are being forced to leave. Farewell, my people. Farewell, my friends." With that, the king retreated from the balcony and into darkness.

Only a few minutes later, his time running out, King DuFay was in his war room, sitting at the small table, looking at the cover of an old book he held respectfully in his massive hands. He gingerly opened the cover and scanned the first few pages, not really reading them. Spread on the table were six objects tightly wrapped in burlap, some rather small, others somewhat large. Six heavily armed and very tough looking men stood behind the king. The door to the room opened and Gerritt Hanson entered with the king's sons behind him. The sound of many concerned voices poured into the room. Only a few paces behind the three men was Matthew, who entered the room and closed the door.

"Father, what is happening? Why are we here?" Thomas DuFay asked his father nervously. Thomas was fourteen years old and possessed a stature that was normal for a boy his age. His hair was dark, like his mother's had been, and his complexion was borderline olive. He had chestnut brown eyes, which again were a reflection of his mother. In fact, there was little if any resemblance between father and son. This had given rise to doubts and rumors around the castle as to the boy's true father, but such rumors were never given to more than a whisper. Kenneth, his brother, though a year younger, was larger in stature than Thomas and to a stranger would appear to be the older of the brothers. While Thomas' nature was more of a negotiator and thinker, Kenneth was much more aggressive and at times, reckless.

"We are here because you must live," the king replied, looking at both boys in turn. "Outside of our gates is a man who is intent on taking over our kingdom, and there is nothing we can do about it."

"We could fight," Kenneth replied quickly.

"Yes, we could fight, but there are so many more of them than there are of us that our defeat would be certain. But if we choose not to fight, then there is no need for anybody to die. This man has agreed to let everyone live if we surrender to him."

"Surrender like cowards, without a fight?" Kenneth asked in astonishment.

"Not like cowards," the king answered. "To be brave does not mean to fight every fight that comes our way, and to avoid a fight does not mean that one is a coward. Sometimes it is best to preserve one's life rather than give it up needlessly, when nothing will come of it. Sometimes, though, it is necessary to give up one's life when so much will come of it."

The king stood up. "I am going to have to leave you for a while. It is not what I want to do, but it is what I must do. Matthew is going to take care of you. You must listen to him and do whatever he says. It is especially important that you listen to him. Do you understand?" The young boys nodded. The king reached over to the table and picked up the old book. He offered it to Thomas, who reached out hesitantly and took it.

"This is a book written by an incredibly wise king, and other incredibly wise men, many, many years ago. It is a book that I should have read to you, and a book that my father should have read to me. Read it with Matthew and let him explain it to you. In this book is wisdom, my sons, and it will help you greatly as you grow into men. Read it and memorize it. Teach it to your children and your grandchildren."

"Yes, father," the boys replied together. Thomas looked at the cover of the book, on which was written, "The Psalms and Proverbs."

"Kenneth, you must help protect Thomas. Being the first born, he is the rightful heir to my throne. Should anything happen to me, he will become king. He will need you in many ways. You are a fighter, and the two of you are going to need to fight to survive. Do you understand?"

"I understand completely," Kenneth said, though his tone was anything less than submissive.

"My lord, the time is drawing near," Hanson urged the king. "We must hurry."

The king looked from his captain to his minister to his sons.

He wished with all his might that there was another way, but he knew there was not. It was the only way to give the people enough time. He walked over to the cabinet along the wall and putting his weight against it, moved it several feet. A large hole in the stone wall revealed a dark, dank hole.

"Matthew, you and Gerritt will guide my sons and the people outside in the corridor through this tunnel. It will take you more than an hour to navigate through it. The tunnel ends in a rock wall a couple of miles from the castle. The opening is covered with brush so hopefully it has not been discovered by the enemy and you will not encounter any of the barbarians. You will take my sons far away from here, to the town I previously described to you. As I explained to you earlier, these six men will follow you through the tunnel, each one carrying one of these packages," the king said, gesturing to the items on the table. "They are the most trusted of my personal guards, and I have knighted them. It is their duty, along with yours, to ensure that these packages do not fall into enemy hands and that one day, a DuFay shall once again sit on this throne. Over the course of the next few weeks, you will rendezvous with the men at the predetermined locations. Once you have all these packages in your possession, you will hide them until the time is right. Do you understand? It is the only hope we have of carrying on the DuFay line, taking back the land, and restoring hope."

"I understand, your majesty," Reverend Knox replied.

The king reached over to the table and picked up a twelve-inch long, quarter-inch round metal rod that had an intricate, two-inch diameter design on one end. He held the end of the rod over the flame of the candle on the table for several minutes, then called Thomas over to him.

"Thomas, I know this is going to be very painful, but it is very necessary. This will be a sign of your lineage, of your right to sit on the throne of DuFay which is being taken from us today. This, along with those items on the table, will prove who you are and that you, and you alone, are heir to my throne. You will pass this on to your son one day, and he to his son, and on throughout their generations. This will forever be the sign of DuFay. Should anything happen to you, then my throne shall pass to Kenneth, and he will bear the sign. Do you understand?" Thomas nodded nervously but did not say a word.

With a slight hesitation, the king reached out and grasped his son's right arm. With a final look of reassurance, he pressed the hot end of the brand onto Thomas' forearm. The boy screamed in pain but did not jerk his arm away. The king pulled the brand away and Reverend Knox quickly moved over to the boy and wrapped his arm with a medicated bandage. Tears streamed down Thomas' face, but he did not make another sound.

"There is one more thing," the king said, reluctantly. "From this day forward, our name will be a hunted one. There are those who will stop at nothing to ensure that neither I nor my descendants will ever sit on the throne of this land again. The name 'DuFay' will be the target of many arrows and spears and conniving schemes. Until the time comes when you, or your son, or his son, is ready to retake the throne long sat upon by our fathers, the name 'DuFay' must be left behind. Until that day comes only this scar shall bear witness to your true identity. Until that day comes you both take the name of the Reverend Knox and be like sons to him. When you pass beyond the walls of this castle you shall no longer be Thomas and Kenneth DuFay. Your family name shall be Knox. Do you understand, my sons?"

"I understand, father," Thomas said, his voice barely more than a whisper. Kenneth did not respond but only looked at his father with a hint of anger.

King Robert DuFay knelt once again and wrapped his arms around his sons for the last time, tears streaming down his own cheeks.

"Remember, my sons, I love you very much. We will see each other again someday, I promise. Remember who you are and remember where you are from. Matthew has sworn to protect you, and I have no doubt that he will do so to the end of his days. Listen to him, follow his instructions, and you will be better men than I have been. You will be a better king than I ever have been." The king, reluctantly, stood up and moved aside. He reached out and grasped Matthew's hand. "May God protect you. Now go, save my sons."

"God be with you," the minister replied. He grabbed two torches that had been stockpiled in the room. He lit one and gave the other unlit one to Thomas to carry. With little hesitancy he stepped into the dark cavern. Thomas was reluctant at first to follow, hesitating at the black hole, but after a nod from his father, he followed Reverend Knox. Kenneth followed Thomas and cast a last, less-then-loving look at his father.

King DuFay looked at Gerrit. "These men know their duty," he said, indicating the men behind him. "They have sworn to protect these packages to their death. They are to be spread out amongst the people. I do not want them bunched together. It is imperative that the packages do not fall into the wrong hands. Do you understand?"

"Yes, my lord."

"Very well," the king said, giving the dark cavern a final look. "Make sure that the door is locked and bolted after the last person leaves and move the cabinet as best you can to hide the hole. If they do find it, our people will be long gone anyway. Catch up with my sons and Reverend Knox. Protect them with your life. Now I must go and buy as much time as I can. Farewell, my captain, my friend."

"Farewell, my king," Gerritt said, shaking the king's offered hand. The king turned and left the room, issuing words of encouragement to the people waiting in the hall.

At exactly noon, without any additional warning, the invaders began launching their missiles at the castle. Most hit the stone walls and caused no damage, but several made it over the walls and slammed into the less-fortified buildings surrounding the courtyard. The barrage continued as the king made his way calmly and slowly across the courtyard. Finally, he reached the gate and ordered the half-dozen sentries who volunteered to stay behind to open the gate and lower the drawbridge. It took five minutes for the bridge to be lowered and as it began its descent, the barrage stopped. King DuFay calmly walked across the bridge. The barbarian army was eager to rush the castle but was held in check by their fear of their leader. They would not move until he said move, for to do anything else would be certain death. DuFay raised his arms out from his sides to indicate that he had no weapons. His stride was slow and deliberate. Two men rushed forward and grabbed his arms, pulling the king forward to the point that he nearly lost his balance. They stopped when a towering, beastly-looking man stepped forward. He stood just shy of seven feet tall and was covered with animal hides and fur. The hair on his face was as thick, if not thicker, than the furs covering his body and he looked as if he had not bathed in a year. His odor matched his look. The two men holding DuFay searched him for weapons and when they were sure he had none, they stepped aside.

"Such a coward," the man growled at DuFay. "You should have fought like a man. At least you would have died with honor."

"Death is death," the king answered, his eyes not wavering from his enemy's.

"Where are your sons?" the man asked, looking beyond the king. "The agreement was that you and your sons would surrender."

"They are far from the reach of your sword," DuFay answered with a wry smile. "Call me pessimistic, but I did not believe for an instant that you intended on keeping your end of the bargain. Therefore, there was no reason for me to keep mine."

"You are correct in that," the man replied with a vicious grin. "Every soul inside those walls shall taste death this day."

"If that were true, then there would be no more than six men who would meet such a fate," DuFay replied.

"What do you mean?" the barbarian asked angrily. "There are easily three hundred people within those walls."

"There WERE three hundred people behind those walls but thanks to your generosity, you have given all of them time to flee. Your blood lust will have to be satisfied with my head and my head alone this day."

The giant of a man let out a primeval scream of rage and delivered a mighty blow to the king's head. DuFay fell to his knees, barely clinging to consciousness. Turning his head slightly, DuFay could see the drawbridge being lifted back up and the gates being lowered. He looked back at the barbarian who was also looking at the castle, his face full of evil fury. "No unnecessary blood shall be spilt this day," the king said, looking up at the beast in front of him. He pulled his hands together as if in prayer.

"The blood that shall soon spill from your body will come with great pain, I can assure you that, and your life shall not end too quickly," the man growled down at DuFay.

"What I can assure you of," DuFay replied with a smile of victory on his face, "is that your life will end quickly, and it will also end in great pain." Before the barbarian could fully comprehend the meaning of DuFay's words, the king lashed out with his right hand and buried into the man's thigh a needle that had been hidden in one of his rings. The barbarian looked down at DuFay with a questioning look. Almost immediately the man began feeling a burning sensation in his leg. The pain quickly grew and soon it felt like a thousand knives were being thrust into his leg. The pain quickly spread to his other leg, and then up to his waist. Realization suddenly hit the barbarian, and he knew that he had been poisoned. In a final act of rage and defiance, with mere seconds left in his life, the barbarian lifted his mighty sword and with a powerful down stroke, sent Robert DuFay to the gates of heaven.

Chapter 1

The merciless drizzle from the gray sky turned into fanciful snowflakes as the temperature dipped below freezing. It did not take long for the ground to become blanketed with a light white dusting and small icicles to form on the bare tree branches. A lone horse and rider trudged along the narrow pathway that wound its way through forest and meadow. The horse and rider were also soon covered with a thin layer of snow and just as with the branches of the trees, the horse's tail soon sported small fingers of ice. It was difficult to tell the exact time of day since the sky was the same grayish color from morning until evening and the sun had not been seen in a week. But it was easy to tell that the days were getting shorter, and colder.

Lawrence Morecraft led his horse off the trail and into a small clearing where two covered wagons were parked. One was dark, but light was emitting from the second one. Lawrence dismounted, tied his horse's reins to the first wagon, and walked to the back of the second wagon. He pulled the canvas flap aside and stepped into the relative warmth of the shelter. Andrew, Marie, Heather, Annette, Steven, and Ian were crowded inside the wagon around a small campfire contained within a metal tub. While the others were sitting, Heather was lying on the floor of the wagon with several blankets covering her body from her chin to her toes. A wet cloth was stretched across her forehead, and she appeared to be sleeping.

"How goes it with Heather?" Lawrence asked, removing his saturated outer coat and squeezing as close as he could to the fire.

"Not well," Ian replied, glancing down at the still figure. "I cannot get her fever to break, and she has barely opened her eyes today."

"She has barely opened her eyes for the past three days," Annette, Heather's mother, added, looking at her daughter with much worry. "And when she does wake, what little we can get her to eat does not stay down very long."

"Is there nothing more you can do?" Andrew asked.

"Not with the resources available to me," Ian replied. "I have no medicine and have tried every herbal remedy known to me. If I had access to proper medicine and facilities, even different herbal treatments, I could at least ease her discomfort if not remove this malady for good. But out here, in the wilderness? I am afraid that there is truly little more that I can do for her, and her condition will continue to worsen. In truth, I do not see her recovering."

"There must be something more we can do!" Annette said, tears filling her eyes. "We have come so far, having barely escaped our homeland with our lives. I cannot, I will not, believe that I may lose my daughter to some illness, out here in the wilderness. We have to do something."

"There is a village not far from here," Lawrence said, looking at Heather. "Stanwyck it is called. I saw it this morning. Perhaps there we can find what we need to treat Heather's illness."

"A town?" Annette said hopefully, looking up at Lawrence. "How far is it?"

"Perhaps a half-day's ride," he replied.

"Then we must leave immediately!" Annette said, becoming excited. "We have to get there as quickly as possible."

"I would recommend that we wait for morning before anyone leaves," Andrew replied. "We are all very tired and traveling at night is not very advisable. Lawrence has been riding all day and he needs his rest."

"It would not be the first time that I have slept while riding my horse," Lawrence replied. "Besides, once we get there, we will all be able to rest comfortably for several days while Heather recovers."

"I have been to this village," Andrew continued, not acknowledging Lawrence. "Several years ago. I do not believe it is a place where we should tarry."

"But if there is help for Heather, a chance to end her illness, surely we must go there," Marie said, having to this point remained silent.

"Ian can tell you and Lawrence what is needed, and you can go into the village tomorrow and get what is needed and bring it back," Andrew replied.

"But Heather's condition continues to worsen," Marie argued. "We cannot afford to wait that long. We need to take her there, and we need to leave now."

"I have to agree with Marie," Ian said. "The more time that passes before we find proper medicine for Heather, the dimmer her chances of recovery."

"We cannot wait," Annette said anxiously. "Andrew, you said you have been to this village. Surely you know somebody there who can aid us."

Andrew paused a moment before replying. "My stay was not long, and I did not befriend any of the people. My departure was," Andrew paused, "not entirely under the most positive of circumstances."

"Be that as it may, we will leave this evening, as quickly as possible," Annette said firmly. "I will not delay in making every effort possible to save my daughter's life. And you, Andrew MacLean, I cannot believe that you would even hesitate for a moment in moving whatever mountain necessary to save Heather's life."

"I will do whatever is necessary to save her life," Andrew countered emphatically, feeling insulted at Annette's accusation. "We shall leave as soon as we can break camp and hitch the horses to the wagons." With that, Andrew left the warmth of the wagon. Lawrence was quickly on his heels.

"I take it your experience with Stanwyck was not exactly a pleasant one," Lawrence said as they headed to the other wagon. Andrew did not reply.

"That bad, huh?" Lawrence pressed.

"It is not one that I wish to discuss," Andrew replied. "The sooner we get there and get the medicine Heather needs, the sooner we can continue our journey."

"When we left Durinburg just four weeks ago, you would never have hesitated a moment to do anything for Heather and more than that, you would have been the one to insist on leaving tonight and getting to Stanwyck as quickly as possible," Lawrence said, as if contemplating a riddle. "And yet now, you seem to hesitate. Why is that? Is it truly Stanwyck that gives you pause?"

"What do you mean by that?" Andrew asked, although this was a conversation he did not truly wish to continue.

"I have noticed over these many days of our travels that your time spent with Heather has gradually decreased to the point that you seem to barely speak to her at all. I cannot help but wonder why that is."

"I have a lot on my mind," Andrew answered unconvincingly. "We are heading to a land from which I was driven years ago with nothing but my horse and this sword that I truly now feel is cursed. There is no doubt that Gallard has a company of men chasing us and every moment of every day, I fully expect to turn my head and see them within an arrow's flight of us. Furthermore, I must somehow explain to my nephew that his father is dead, and now he is the heir of Reginald DuFay and the rightful ruler of some far-away land even though there is now no throne from which to rule. I have a lot on my mind," Andrew repeated.

"Indeed, those are compelling arguments," Lawrence replied. "But having such a beautiful woman at your side to distract you from those burdens, and one who is quite willingly sharing in those burdens, should provide some comfort."

Andrew did not respond but continued breaking down their encampment and moved to hitch the two horses that were standing stoically in the snow, trying to benefit from whatever meager shelter the overhead trees provided.

"You are no longer in love with her," Lawrence surmised when Andrew failed to respond.

"I have never been in love with her," Andrew replied.

"I thought..." Lawrence started, surprised at Andrew's response.

"I have never said that I loved her," Andrew cut him off. "Everybody believes that we are in love, but the truth of the matter is that while I cannot deny that I have had feelings for Heather, and I do care for her, I am not in love with her."

"Does she know this, for there is little doubt in my mind that she would not be saying the same thing about you."

"It is likely that she suspects," Andrew admitted.

"I do not understand," Lawrence continued as if trying to put a puzzle together. "Are you saying that it is too soon in the relationship for you to be in love, or that you do not believe that you will ever be in love with her?"

"Sometimes I question whether I will ever truly be in love with anyone," Andrew said thoughtfully. "I used to know what I wanted, or I thought I knew what I wanted. A wife. A family. A peaceful life. So much has happened in the past six years of my life that now I am only certain that I desire a peaceful life. I have been a loner for most of my life and am used to being like that. I truly do not know that I want that to change."

"That sounds like a pretty lonely existence," Lawrence countered.

"Perhaps to some," Andrew answered.

"Here is what I think," Lawrence offered. "Let us find your nephew. You tell him about his father, and you tell him about his heritage. You give him this sword. You tell him to be a good boy, to obey his mother, and grow up to be a good man. Then you decide on how you wish to live the rest of your life. You do not need to make that decision here and now, and for sure you do not need to drive away from you a woman who genuinely cares about you."

"I think it is a bit more complicated than that," Andrew replied.

"Only if you make it so," Lawrence countered. "But first things first. Let us get Heather to town and get her well. I am sure the town cannot be as uninviting as you remember it to be."

"We shall see," Andrew said under his breath.

Chapter 2

I t was just before dawn when the two wagons and their occupants reached the outskirts of Stanwyck. The snow had stopped during the night and the temperature had held steady in the upper 20's. Andrew led them to a small grove near a brook where they once again set up camp, just as they had every evening for what seemed like an eternity but what had only been four weeks. Andrew and Lawrence had taken turns at the reins so they could both get some sleep during the all-night journey. Ian had remained in the wagon with Heather and her mother and Steven, while Marie had transferred to the first wagon with Andrew and Lawrence. The horses for the second wagon had been tied to the first wagon, so there had been no need for anyone to drive the second wagon. Sleeping had been difficult along the rough road, so it was a great relief when they finally stopped.

"Any change in Heather's condition?" Andrew asked Ian as they finished unhitching the horses and went to the brook's edge for some fresh water.

"She did come awake for a while and managed to drink some water and keep down a few pieces of an apple, which is a particularly good sign. But her fever persists. She still needs proper medicine and plenty of rest. She needs to stay-put for a few days at least, especially in this freezing weather."

"We cannot afford to stay in one place for more than a day," Andrew protested. "It is vital that we reach Nordham and contact my brother's family as quickly as possible. Also, we can be assured that Gallard has sent his men to track us down. The only reason that we have not been captured is that we have, for the most part, stayed off the most heavily traveled roadways. It is only a matter of time before we are discovered."

"And it will only be a matter of time before Heather's health decline reaches the point of no return if we continue pushing forward," Ian countered. "In truth, I am amazed that the rest of us have managed to stay healthy this whole time. We are all exhausted, not one of us has been getting fully rested each night, the weather has been wet and cold for the past week, and our nutrition on this trip has suffered greatly. We should all be ill."

"Then let us count our blessings that we are not," Andrew answered. "We should all get some much-needed rest for the next few hours and then you, Marie and I will go into the village and get the medicine along with more supplies."

The sun was shining brightly, and the temperature had risen a respectable fifteen degrees by the time Andrew, Ian and Marie ventured into the village. With the glowing sun and the rising temperature, the snow was quickly melting and the trail into the village was muddy and slick. The trio stopped near the center of the village, surrounded by both buildings of residence and buildings of commerce. It was close to mid-morning and the town square was busy. People milled about as they conducted their business, completed errands, and performed chores. Nearly a dozen carts containing food and other items were parked along the sides of the main thoroughfare where people traded for and purchased various necessities.

"Yes, I can see why you hesitated to come here," Marie said to Andrew as several people walked by them and offered smiles of greeting. "Who would want to stay in a place such as this, where the people smile at strangers?"

"Let us get what we need and get back to the wagons," Andrew replied, ignoring Marie's smart-aleck attitude. He scanned the area several times, as though he was looking for someone. "We should not tarry longer than necessary."

"Do you recall if there is an apothecary in this village?" Ian asked. "That would be the best place for me to start searching for what is needed to treat Heather's condition."

"If I recall correctly," Andrew answered, "there should be one several buildings down the street ahead of us, on the right. It used to have a sign hanging over the door."

"Very good," Ian said. "I will head that way. What about you and Marie?"

"We will stay here in the square and purchase the remaining supplies we need to continue our journey," Andrew replied. "We will meet back here in thirty minutes."

"Thirty minutes?" Marie repeated. "That just will not do. That is not nearly enough time for me to find new shoes and new trousers to replace these that have been destroyed by this foul weather," she said playfully.

"Then we shall find some soap and you can make use of the brook," Andrew replied testily. "We are not here to update your wardrobe. We are here to find medicine for Heather, food, the basic necessities for us all, and to get back on the road as quickly as possible. Thirty minutes, Ian."

The physician, eager to get away from what appeared to be a tense situation arising, said nothing and hurried off. Marie stood silent, taken aback at Andrew's terse words. Andrew took a final look around the town square before pulling the hood attached to his cape over his head and heading towards the closest food cart.

"Somebody certainly woke up on the wrong side of the wagon this morning," Marie said, finally finding her voice. "Was your prior visit here so foul that simply being here is an offense to you? Judging by the hood pulled over your head on the nicest day we have seen in a week, your insistence on such a short shopping trip, and your completely dour mood, I would venture that your primary concern, or better yet fear, is that of being recognized."

"Venture what you will," Andrew replied. "I know what best serves our purposes in this place and spending more time here than necessary does not serve our purpose well."

"If getting away from this place will chase away your bitter mood then by all means, let us finish our business and make a hasty retreat," Marie said caustically. She followed Andrew as he retrieved an empty, unused two-wheeled cart from beside one of the merchant wagons.

"Somebody might miss that," she said, an accusing tone riding her voice.

"We will bring it back when we are done," Andrew replied assuredly. "It is the way around here."

The next fifteen minutes went without conversation as the pair moved from wagon to wagon and even visited a couple of indoor merchants, gathering their supplies. The cart was full of food, warm clothing, blankets and other items. They were picking out some bread and going through some bags of wheat when they heard a young, feminine voice call out to their left.

"Gustaf?" the young woman cried out, her tone one of surprise and hopefulness. Andrew and Marie continued shopping, ignoring the girl, although Andrew tensed slightly.

"Gustaf is that you?" the stranger called out again, taking several steps towards Andrew. Marie turned her head out of curiosity to see who was calling out. Andrew, on the other hand, turned slightly to his right as though he was trying to hide his face from the girl. The girl continued approaching them and came to a halt beside Andrew. Andrew tried to turn away from her, but she would have none of it. She grabbed his arm and turned him toward her. A look of surprise and excitement crossed her face, and her eyes flew open wide.

"Gustaf, it is you!" she exclaimed as she wrapped her arms around him. The young woman looked to be seventeen years old, give or take a year, and was dressed in commoner clothing. She had brown hair and brown eyes with a frame that was a bit larger than average. She had pleasant facial features and was moderately attractive. Andrew stood still as a statue and did not return the girl's embrace. His eyes were closed, and his facial expression was one of disappointment and resignation. Marie's expression was one of confusion mixed with amusement. This was one explanation that she could not wait to hear.

The young girl released Andrew from her embrace and took a

small step backwards. She then proceeded to slap Andrew on the chest none-too gently.

"THAT is for leaving without even saying goodbye!" she said in a chastising manner. "How could you leave in the middle of the night like you did without a word to anybody? And do not excuse yourself by saying you left a note. That does not count."

"Naomi, what a surprise," Andrew replied sheepishly.

"That is an understatement," Naomi said. "I did not think I would ever see you again."

"I did tell you that I would not be able to stay very long and would have to leave," Andrew answered in defense.

"Aye, that you did," Naomi conceded, "but after having spent nearly three months here working and living with my family, one would think that a small word of farewell would have been in order."

"You are correct," Andrew replied, "and I apologize for having left so abruptly. However, certain circumstances dictated a hasty departure, and I could not pause to wake your family for a sendoff."

"I am sure they will forgive you once you apologize to them in person."

"Oh, I am afraid that will not be possible," Andrew said quickly. "I am traveling with several others, and we must continue our journey with the utmost haste. We only stopped for some much-needed supplies." From beside Andrew, silent to this point, Marie cleared her throat.

"Ahem. Gustaf, how about an introduction?" she said with a devilish grin on her face. Andrew shot her a glare of annoyance but complied.

"Naomi, this is my friend Marie," he said, his hand gesturing towards Marie. "Marie, this is Naomi. I spent some time with her and her family during my prior visit here a few years ago."

"Naomi, what a lovely name for such a lovely young woman," Marie said as she reached out to shake Naomi's hand. "It is such a pleasure to meet you."

"Thank you," Naomi replied graciously. She looked at Marie and then at Andrew, then back to Marie with a look that bordered on disappointment, and finally back to Andrew. "Is she your...?" she asked, as if afraid of the answer. Andrew was not sure what Naomi was asking but Marie immediately recognized the look and tone of Naomi's question.

"Oh, goodness no, I am most certainly not," Marie replied in as reassuring a tone as possible. "We are simply friends and traveling companions."

"Oh," Naomi said, her face brightening-up once again with a smile of renewed hope.

"Gustaf has somewhat exaggerated our need for such a hurried departure," Marie said with a sideways glance to Andrew. "In fact, it would actually be best if we stayed for a few days. You see, one of our traveling companions has fallen ill and getting her proper medication is the primary reason we have come to town. Our physician, who is traveling with us, has recommended that we delay our journey to give her time to properly recover."

"Then you must stay!" Naomi said eagerly. "Where are you sleeping this evening?"

"We are camped by the brook just outside of town," Andrew replied with resignation, knowing where events were headed.

"That will not do," Naomi said. "Your friend needs a house and warmth to properly recover. You will bring her to the house right away and there will be no discussion about it. I will inform Mother and Father that you have returned and that you and your traveling companions will be our guests for a few days. You can apologize to them this evening, in person, over dinner."

"I look forward to the hospitality and the opportunity to express contrition for my prior actions," Andrew said, his choices all but taken from him. "We will bring my friend by this afternoon."

"Excellent!" Naomi cried, her face erupting in joyous triumph. "The whole family will be so excited to see you again!" Naomi turned and all but ran through the town square, heading home with the exciting news.

"Well, Gustaf, that was quite interesting," Marie said, smiling at Andrew. "I can certainly understand your desire to stay away from such an inhospitable place as this."

"It is a long story," Andrew sighed in resignation.

"A bit young, is she not?" Marie asked teasingly. "Although I must admit, there is something about her personality that I do find quite appealing."

"It was not like that," Andrew replied in a defensive tone.

"Then please, indulge my curiosity," Marie pressed. "Otherwise, I will be left only to my imagination and, well, you know my imagination."

Knowing all too well how persistent Marie could be, Andrew gave in.

"It was my intention to rest here only a couple of days," he explained. "I had been on the road for several months straight and needed to rest, both my body and my mind. I happened up-on Naomi, who had been to the market, and a wheel on the cart she was pushing home had fallen off. She was trying desperately to repair it, but the chore was beyond her abilities. I repaired the wheel for her, and she insisted that for her to properly display her appreciation for my help, I would have to accompany her home and have dinner with her family."

"So, rescuing damsels in distress and wrangling a meal out of it is something of a pattern for you," Marie teased.

"I accepted her invitation and accompanied her home," Andrew continued. "Her family had a reasonably-sized farm, large enough to provide comfortably for the family and then some, but small enough that her family could run it. However, her father had recently sustained an injury to his leg and but a month before, her older brother had died when his horse was spooked and threw him. It was harvest time and they needed help to bring in the crops and provide a stockpile of food and wood for the winter. Her father offered to pay me to stay and help. I would have done it for room and board, but he insisted that a day of work be equaled by a day of wages. My two-day rest period became a three-month work period."

"Quite the altruistic one you are," Marie said. "Based on

Naomi's reaction at seeing you, your assistance was greatly appreciated. Or was it more than that?"

"Of course not," Andrew replied, taken aback at the implication. "I will confess that Naomi had developed a fondness for me, though I certainly did not encourage her in any way. I attempted to stay as aloof as I could without being rude, but that only seemed to embolden her."

"Is that what motivated you to leave so abruptly?"

"Partially," Andrew admitted. "More than that, though, I felt there were eyes upon me, unfriendly eyes. Perhaps it was nothing more than paranoia on my part. I felt it best that I leave in such a manner that I would not be seen or followed. I truly regretted leaving such a fine family, one that I had grown close to in such an abbreviated time, but I knew it was what I had to do. I could only leave a brief note expressing my gratitude for them taking me into their home and that I would always remember them fondly. And that was that. End of story."

"And what of the name Gustaf?" Marie asked.

"Being a hunted man, I did not feel it prudent to give them my true name. So, to them, I was Gustaf Anderson."

"Well, it certainly was not that long of a story, Gustaf Anderson" Marie said.

"What is a long story?" Ian asked as he approached Andrew and Marie. "And who is Gustaf Anderson?"

"I am sure Gustaf would love to fill you in as we head back to camp," Marie said, not able to suppress a slight laugh. Ian gave them a quizzical look but said nothing.

Chapter 3

T he disappearance of the sun over the western horizon brought
back the chill to the late-autumn evening, but inside the stone
walls of the house a large fire kept the coolness at bay. It was not an
exceptionally large house, but large enough in which a family of six
could live comfortably. Crowded around a large table near the fire,
preparing to feast on the nightly meal, were nine people. Andrew,
Lawrence, Marie, Ian, Steven, Naomi, her father Patrick McKenzie,
her mother Alison, and Naomi's younger sister, Leslie, circled the
table. Annette had elected to stay with Heather, who was resting in
Naomi's bedroom, while the others had dinner. Andrew's
appearance had indeed been quite the surprise to the family and
despite his unannounced departure three years ago, the family
eagerly welcomed him back as though the prodigal son had
returned home. While it was going to be a tight squeeze, room had
been made inside the house for the travelers to rest comfortably.

"You can sit here, by me," Naomi said to Andrew, indicating
a seat to her left. "It is where you always used to sit."

"It would be my pleasure," Andrew replied with a courteous
smile as everybody sat down.

"It is so good to see you again, Gustaf," Alison said as she began
to fill plates with food and pass them around the table. "When you
left, it was as though a member of the family had disappeared."

"Naomi cried for three days straight after you left," Leslie said,
eager to participate in the conversation. She was four years
Naomi's junior and as a younger sister, she was always looking for
an opportunity to needle her older sister.

"That is not true!" Naomi cried out in defense of herself. "Mother, tell Leslie to be quiet!"

"Now, now, girls," Alison said reprovingly, trying to calm her daughters. "I am sure we all shed a few tears when Gustaf left so suddenly. We all missed him."

"As I have missed your family," Andrew replied. "And again, I would like to apologize for the way I left last time. I know I did not give you many details regarding my travels but suffice it to say that I believed there were some very unfriendly people with some very unfavorable intentions following me and it was best for me, and this family, that I make my departure as quietly as possible."

"No explanation needed," Patrick said as he passed a plate of food down the table. "You are an honorable man, Gustaf, and whatever your reasons were, they too were honorable."

"Please, call me Andrew," Andrew said, tired of the name game. "Gustaf is actually my second name, which was my mother's father's name. My first name is Andrew, which was my father's name. I ceased using Gustaf as my name some time ago to aid in continuing to evade those who were after me. My friends here know me only as Andrew."

"Very well, Andrew," Patrick said.

"Where have you been these past three years?" Naomi asked, eager to get past her sister's embarrassing accusation.

"I have traveled quite far and wide," Andrew replied, "and explored many lands. Most recently I was in a place called 'Durinburg' with these fine friends of mine, which is a four-week journey from here. I spent around six months there, but the village fell on challenging times and there was an outbreak of illness. When I decided to return to a village farther north, where I had lived for a lengthy period of my life many years ago, my friends chose to accompany me."

"Durinburg," Patrick said, reflectively. "Rumors are floating around that there was a great battle there recently and the kingdom was overthrown. Is there any truth to that?"

"Unfortunately, yes, that is the truth," Andrew replied. "The kingdom was attacked and fell."

"So, when you say the village fell on challenging times and there was an outbreak of illness, it was your way of saying it was invaded and conquered," Patrick said somewhat suspiciously.

"I did not know that word had spread so quickly," Andrew replied, not directly addressing Patrick's statement. "It was certainly a terrible time for all. Thankfully, we were able to flee in time and avoid the worst of the confrontation."

"Was there anybody else in your group when you left, someone who perhaps got separated from you?" Patrick inquired.

"No, we are all still together," Andrew replied, his guard coming up. "Why do you ask?"

"I am sure it is just a coincidence," Patrick answered with a wave of a hand.

"Please, indulge me," Andrew said, a tingling rising in the back of his neck.

"Two days ago, a man came through town, a stranger. He spent most of the day walking around town, as if he were searching for something. I happened to be in town at the time and began conversing with him, to see if I could be of assistance. He said that he had been traveling with some friends but had become separated several days prior and could not find them. He asked if any strangers had passed through town recently. I told him I had not seen any such people, but then again, I am away from town more than I am in town. After speaking with several more people, he continued riding north."

"Yes, that is a remarkable coincidence," Andrew stated, his guard now turning to alarm. He stole a glance at Lawrence and could see his friend's concerned expression, the same expression he was sure was plastered on his own face.

"The ironic thing is," Patrick continued, "he described one of his friends and that description pretty much fits you exactly."

"How interesting," Andrew said. "And here I was thinking that I was one-of-a-kind," he joked.

"You are one-of-a-kind," Naomi said, smiling brightly at Andrew.

"How would you describe this man?" Andrew asked, trying to ignore the fact that Naomi had slid a little bit closer to him.

"Your height, perhaps a bit taller," Patrick answered. "Very broad shoulders. Dark hair, almost black, with a long, dark beard. Not a friendly looking soul, that one. Oh, and he had a scar on the left side of his face." When Andrew did not respond, Patrick continued.

"You said that three years ago you felt as though you were being followed. Is it possible that this man was following you back then and continues following you today?" Patrick asked.

"I do not believe that it is the same person," Andrew replied, "but I feel confident that his purpose is the same."

"Does that mean you will be leaving again?" Naomi asked, disappointment in her voice.

"I am afraid so," Andrew answered with a slight smile. "I cannot place your family in danger."

"What could possibly be the reason for these men to be pursuing you for such a long time?" Alison asked.

"It is rather complicated to say the least, however, suffice it to say that I came into an inheritance that they desire quite passionately, and they vowed to follow me to the ends of the earth to steal it from me."

"That is putting it mildly,' Marie said under her breath, but not so quietly that Andrew failed to hear her. He gave her a sideways glance but said nothing.

"Will it ever end?" Patrick asked. "Will you ever be free from looking over your shoulder every day?"

"Someday," Andrew replied. "Someday."

"Well, tonight let us not think of such things but instead dwell on the past, for though your stay here was short, it was not without some very memorable moments," Alison said.

"Yes, Gustaf, let us be entertained with some of those very memorable moments," Marie said, her eyes twinkling.

Chapter 4

T his is not good news," Andrew said to Lawrence and Marie. They had stepped outside after dinner on the pretense of retrieving some belongings from their wagons to discuss the recent revelation in private.

"You know the man Mr. McKenzie described?" Marie asked.

"There is no doubt in my mind that the man he described is none other than Walter Brewster, Gallard's chief military advisor," Andrew replied. "That scar Patrick described? I gave it to him the day I was chased from my homeland, when he and two of Gallard's men tried to take the sword from me."

"So, I take it you two are not on good terms," Lawrence half-joked.

"He would take immense pleasure in relieving me of the DuFay Sword, and my life. I am not surprised that Gallard sent him to track me down," Andrew answered. "Of all people, Walter would be the most motivated to find me. My strike to his pride was more painful than my strike to his face."

"If Gallard sent this man to find you, he would have had to have known that you survived the battle. How could he possibly have known that?" Marie asked.

"Do not underestimate Gallard's hatred of me and his desire for the DuFay Sword," Andrew replied. "He would be willing to personally view every corpse on that battlefield to verify whether or not I was among the dead. No, he knows well that I escaped the battle."

"What course of action do we now take?" Marie asked,

concerned. "For all we know, while Walter is ahead of us, more of Gallard's men chase us from behind. We could be captured any day now."

"Staying in one place for any length of time is not an option," Andrew replied. "We will have to leave here much sooner than desired."

"But what of Heather?" Marie asked. "You know she needs much more than one day, even two, to recover her health. Ian said that he found in town the treatments to restore her health, but it would all be in vain if she was not given the opportunity to rest for at least a week."

"We cannot stay here a week," Lawrence said matter-of-factly.

"No, I cannot stay here a week," Andrew said. "I am the one for whom Walter is searching. He does not know the rest of you."

"Ahem," Marie cleared her throat. "Lest you forget, I spent a little time myself as a guest within Gallard's encampment and I am pretty certain that Walter knows who I am."

"He will not be looking for you," Andrew countered. "Nobody will be looking for you. You are not important to them."

"You have such a way of making a person feel special," Marie retorted with feigned hurt feelings.

"My point is that whether it is for the sword or for my life, I am the one being hunted, not you. Not any of you," Andrew replied.

"I disagree," Lawrence said. "Why else would Walter tell McKenzie that he had become separated from his traveling companions and was seeking them?"

"Perhaps he thought it would be suspicious if he said he was looking for just one man," Andrew guessed. "Walter described just me, not anybody else. He said two women and two men were his traveling companions. That is hardly an accurate description of our group."

"Accurate or not, we cannot assume anything but that we are all targets," Marie said. "The question remains, what is our course of action?"

"Patrick said that Walter continued north," Andrew replied.

"Therefore, I shall continue north. Perhaps I can turn Walter from predator to prey."

"Is it possible that he knows of your brother's son and that he is now the heir of DuFay?" Lawrence asked. "Part of his mission could be to find and dispose of the boy."

"I do not see how he would know," Andrew replied. "It is apparent that he did not know that Donald was the heir of DuFay for if he had, there is no doubt in my mind he would not have allowed Donald to live. Regardless, for all Gallard knows, Donald is still alive and therefore Alexander is of no importance."

"Why else would Walter have chosen to travel north in his pursuit of you?" Lawrence argued. "There is no way that he could possibly know for certain in which direction you chose to travel after escaping the battle."

"We can only assume that someone saw us depart the valley and reported back to Gallard," Andrew guessed. "Gallard surmised it was me, possibly trying to hide within a group of people."

"That would explain why Walter said he was looking for a group of travelers and not just one man," Marie surmised.

"True," Andrew admitted.

"So, you intend on continuing to Nordham by yourself and along the way, hopefully run into Walter so you can...what exactly would you do if you found him?" Marie asked.

"That would be entirely up to him," Andrew replied. "His life is not mine to take lest he tries to take mine from me. I think a bit of rational discussion would be in order. Perhaps I could convince him of the futility of seeking the DuFay Armor."

"From what you have said, I doubt that this man would be agreeable to a casual conversation," Marie noted.

"Well, you are certainly not going alone," Lawrence stated firmly. "If you believe for one second that you are going to leave me in this boring little hamlet while you ride on, you are sadly mistaken."

"You should stay here and watch after the others," Andrew

advised. "Marie was not being paranoid in proposing that Gallard has men on our trail. He is cunning enough, and determined enough, to have sent two groups in pursuit of us several days apart."

"Not going to happen," Lawrence replied, shaking his head. "You need someone to keep you from rushing head-long into trouble. I am with you and that is the end of the discussion."

"I am going too," Marie said. "Who knows what trouble the two of you are capable of getting into, and you may need someone with a great deal of common sense to talk you out of trouble."

"And why would you be going, again?" Lawrence joked.

"Marie, you need to stay here," Andrew said. "The Bergmans are going to need you. You are Heather's best friend after all."

"Oh, they will be fine," Marie argued. "The McKenzies seem to be very hospitable people and I am sure they would not mind helping the Bergmans assimilate into the village. And do not forget Ian, he is incredibly wise, very capable, and they know him well."

"We will be traveling at a very quick pace with little sleep," Andrew informed her. "There will be no wagon for you to sleep in, and little shelter if any along the road. There will be few if any hot meals. It will be extremely uncomfortable, even for Lawrence and me, and we are no strangers to discomfort. It is best that you stay here."

"I believe I can determine what is and what is not best for me without anybody else's assistance," Marie retorted, angered that Andrew was trying to make her decision for her.

"Not in this case," Andrew countered. "Besides, it could be that in this instance, the importance is not in what is best for you, but what is best for your friends. You should think of them first."

"And you should…" Marie started with a tone that bordered on venomous and a piercing glare that was nothing but pure poison, but Lawrence was quick to interrupt her.

"So that being settled, Andrew, when do you and I leave?" Marie shot Lawrence a penetrating scowl, but Lawrence ignored it, and Marie did not continue the argument.

"We shall leave at first light, after the first and probably last decent night of rest we shall know on this grueling journey. We will take what we can of the goods we purchased today, which should last us perhaps a week before we have to resupply."

"Perhaps this time you will be able to offer the McKenzies a word of gratitude and farewell before you take your leave," Marie said bitterly.

"I shall take care of that courtesy right now," Andrew replied unphased as he turned and walked back into the home.

Chapter 5

H ow is your friend?" Patrick asked Marie as she closed the door to the room in which Heather was resting. It was late in the afternoon and Patrick McKenzie was kneeling by the wood stove, stacking several split pieces of wood for his wife to use for cooking the evening meal. The bedrooms were immediately adjacent to the cooking and living area of the house.

"It appears that she is well on her way to recovery," Marie replied as she took a food bowl over to a pan that held several cooking utensils, all waiting to be cleaned. "Her appetite has finally returned as you can see from the empty bowl. Her color is back to normal, and she no longer looks as though she had not seen the sun in several months. I would venture that in another day or two, she will be quite ready to get back on her feet and visit the town center."

"That is good news," Patrick said as he stood. "These past two days of rest and warmth, along with your physician's skills, are just what she needed. In truth, when you first arrived and brought her into the house, I was not confident that she would recover. Your journey must have been exceedingly difficult and uncomfortable."

"Yes, it has been," Marie answered.

"'Has been,' meaning that you intend on continuing your travels?" Patrick asked in as non-prying a tone as he could muster. Marie hesitated a moment, not sure how to answer.

"I do not believe that a final decision has been made," she replied as the main door to the house opened and Patrick's wife entered.

"What decision might that be?" Alison asked as she set a bucket of fresh water on the dining table.

"Whether we will be continuing our journey to our original destination," Marie answered.

"And where might that be?" Alison asked.

"Nordham," Marie replied. "Andrew has family there and has not seen them in a number of years. He wishes to return and visit for a time."

"Nordham, you say?" Patrick repeated.

"Yes," Marie confirmed. "You know of this place?"

"It is another week from here, give or take, to the north," Patrick replied. "While ordinarily not a hard journey, as you can see the weather is turning and winter is on our doorstep. There is a lot of open land between here and there with little shelter from the elements. It could make for an even more difficult trek than you have had from Durinburg to here."

"It would be a terrible idea to subject Heather to such conditions," Alison said protectively. "Although she is doing better, her system will remain weak for some time. She could easily fall ill again if she continues on and the weather turns foul."

"We shall certainly put Heather's health above all other considerations," Marie replied.

"Good. Now, Patrick, there are a few things I need to properly prepare dinner this evening. We are out of potatoes and carrots. The girls are off who knows where. Would you be kind enough to run into town and get some from Mr. Varden?"

"Of course, my dear," Patrick replied. He opened the front door and paused. He turned to Marie. "Would you care to accompany me to town?" he asked. "That way, if Alison is not pleased with the potatoes and carrots I choose, I will have someone to share in the blame."

"While I have never held myself out as an expert in the

vegetable realm, I will be happy to lend whatever assistance I can," Marie answered with a smile as she followed him out of the house.

"What do you think of our little hamlet?" Patrick asked as they walked down the road leading to the village, which was a little over a mile from his home.

"Very welcoming," Marie answered. "Andrew was not very generous in his description of your village, I must confess, and was resistant to coming here, but I am happy to see how warm and friendly the people are. Of course, considering the circumstances under which he left last time, I can understand his hesitancy in returning."

"Yes, his departure was quite sudden and unexpected," Patrick said as he recalled the morning on which his family awoke only to discover Andrew's absence. "He must truly have felt he was in danger. How long ago did he arrive in your village?"

"A little more than six months I should think," Marie answered. "It was late spring, at the time of the first harvest."

"Yes, that would make sense. Durinburg is far enough south of here that its first harvest comes sooner than ours," Patrick stated. "Speaking of Durinburg," he continued almost as an afterthought, but with predetermined intention, "I am curious as to why Andrew attributed your leaving there to an illness in the land instead of to the war that ravaged it."

"That is a question for which only Andrew has the answer," Marie replied, not entirely sure of the answer herself. "However, not long before we were invaded, we were warned by our scouts of a plague north of our village, and travel to and from that direction was prohibited by my father." As soon as that final word left her mouth, Marie cringed inside.

"Your father?" Patrick repeated in question. "Your father is King Richard Talbot?"

"He was my father," Marie acknowledged. "Unfortunately, he was killed during the siege."

"I am sorry for your loss," Patrick said gently. "I heard good things about him."

"He was a good man," Marie replied, holding back the tears that wanted to trickle down her cheeks. "He was kind, loving and gracious. I shall miss him terribly."

"I cannot help but wonder why King Gallard pushed his army to near exhaustion to invade your father's kingdom, a kingdom that was never a threat to him."

"How did you know it was Gallard that invaded our land?" Marie asked, perplexed. "I do not believe we ever mentioned his name."

"Come now, Lady Talbot. Our village may not be large, but it does border one of the main travel routes from north to south. Gallard's army passed through here three months ago. They took much of our food and livestock, and not in such a friendly manner. Upon hearing that Durinburg had been laid siege to, there was no mystery as to who the invader was. However, the mystery remains as to why he invaded your homeland. There was never any rumor or word that Gallard was looking to expand his kingdom such a great distance. Indeed, there are many villages and towns between Nordham and Durinburg that have no allegiance to Gallard, and one would assume that he would first take control of those places before heading so far away. So now, being the daughter of King Richard Talbot, surely you would have some idea for the motivation behind the assault?"

"I was simply his daughter, Mr. McKenzie. I was not privy to the politics of our country or military strategy," Marie answered innocently.

"But unless I am mistaken, you were his only child and heir to this throne," Patrick countered.

"That is true," Marie replied. "Perhaps he was waiting for the opportune time to instruct me in such matters, or perhaps he was waiting for me to marry so the throne would be occupied by a more traditional monarch and not a fragile, weak woman."

"You, my lady, are anything but fragile and weak," Patrick responded with a friendly grin. They were approaching the outskirts of the town center when a man slightly older in appearance than Patrick met them.

"How goes it, Victor?" Patrick asked, reaching for the man's hand to shake it.

"Well enough," the man replied, grasping Patrick's outstretched hand.

"What brings you to this side of town this fine day?" Patrick asked.

"I was out to pay you a visit. I have not seen you in several days."

"Ah, yes, I have not been to town recently. I have been seeing to the comfort of my guests," Patrick replied.

"It seems it is our week for visitors," Victor said, glancing at Marie.

"How so?" Patrick prodded, a bit intrigued. Visitors were not necessarily uncommon due to the village's location, however, they were usually spread apart by some time.

"Three men showed up early this afternoon, men I have not seen before," Victor answered. "They spent some time in the tavern, bought some supplies, and appeared to be resting from their travels. In fact, I would not have paid them a second thought if it had not been for them commencing to ask questions around the square."

"What sort of questions?" Patrick asked, knowing that his friend would not have mentioned the men if their inquiries had not raised his concern.

"They claim that they are refugees, chased from their kingdom by war. They are asking if there have been any other people like them come through town. People who are not known in this area, people who claim to have been ousted from their homes some distance to the south. They say they are looking for their kin, as they were separated as they fled the carnage. I remembered that you were hosting such folks for a time and was on my way to visit you and see if your guests were those whom these men seek."

"Perhaps this young lady can answer that question," Patrick said, turning his attention to Marie. "What say you, Marie? Is it possible that you and your friends are the ones whom these men seek?"

"Unfortunately for them, we are not," Marie replied casually despite the knot that had formed in her stomach. "We had no other kinsmen. It must be some other people for whom they look."

"Are the men still in town?" Patrick asked.

"I believe they are," Victor replied. "Check the marketplace. They should be easy to find. After all, you know every soul in this village by nothing more than how they walk."

"Thank you, Victor. Have a good afternoon. Come by the house sometime and we shall throw down a pint or two of my special mead."

"Most certainly," Victor answered as he turned back to the village.

"Shall we go and take a look at these strangers?" Patrick asked Marie as they started back towards town.

"By all means," Marie replied, anxious to see who these men were.

Ten minutes later, Patrick and Marie stood in the shadows of one of the buildings in the town square, looking at the three men of whom Victor had spoken.

"Do you recognize them?" Marie asked Patrick as she looked the men over.

"I do not," he replied. "Do you?"

"No," Marie answered.

"There is nothing about their appearance that would indicate they are anything but who they say they are, just refugees looking for relatives," Patrick said. "Their clothes are a bit on the tattered and dirty side, which would make sense if they had just spent several weeks on the road. I am sure there were many, many people in your land whom you had never met and would not recognize."

"While that may be true, these men are not ordinary villagers out looking for their kin," Marie countered.

"Why do you say that?" Patrick inquired. "I see nothing about them that would indicate otherwise."

"They might as well be wearing armor with swords dangling from their hips," Marie answered. "Look at how they stand, how they move, how they are continually scouring their surroundings with their eyes. It is as if they are predators looking for prey, ready to pounce at a moment's notice. That is not the posture of a farmer, or a blacksmith, or a man who makes his living by fishing or building tables and chairs for your home. Those men are trained fighters."

"You can tell that just by looking at them?" Patrick asked, somewhat dubiously.

"For nearly as long as I can remember I have been surrounded by such men," Marie replied, nodding her head. "I have watched them many times, whether on the training grounds or in the courtyard bragging of their latest contests and conquests. Soldiers have a way about them, an attitude, which permeates every part of their being and shows very clearly. They never truly relax and are always aware of their surroundings. Just like these men."

"Do you believe that they, too, are looking for Andrew, just like the man who came through here before your group arrived?"

"I cannot think otherwise," Marie confirmed. "They are soldiers plain and clear, and they certainly are not men who served in my father's army. They know about the invasion of my father's kingdom, and they claim to have come from Durinburg. There is no doubt in my mind, they are most definitely looking for Andrew, if not our whole group."

Patrick did not say anything for a few moments as continued looking at the men. It was as if was trying to put together the pieces of a puzzle. He started thinking aloud.

"Three years ago, Andrew makes off in secret, afraid that he was being pursued by someone who was seeking to steal what he calls an 'inheritance,' of which he had come into possession," Patrick mused. "Andrew travels around for nearly two years and a half before stumbling upon Durinburg, where he stays for nearly six months. Your land is invaded, and you and your friends, including Andrew, flee and come here. Just days before you and your friends arrive here, a man comes through asking if any other strangers had passed through town recently. Today, these three men, claiming to be from Durinburg, arrive in town and start asking about other strangers passing through town. You have confessed to being convinced that these men are not ordinary citizens but soldiers, likely looking for you and your friends. We know that it was King Gallard and his army that invaded your land, therefore it would follow that these men are part of King Gallard's army and are here at Gallard's orders. King Gallard reigns over Nordham, which is where you are headed. You say Andrew has family in Nordham, which would make a reasonable person presume that Andrew is from Nordham. These men are not looking for all of you, they are looking for Andrew," Patrick surmised, putting the pieces together. He turned to Marie. "Why is Edwin Gallard looking for Andrew? What is this 'inheritance' that Andrew possesses that drove Gallard to mobilize his army and chase Andrew many hundreds of miles from home?"

"That would be another question to which only Andrew knows the answer," she lied, not wanting to give away any more information about them and their travels.

"Is it possible that Andrew stole something from King Gallard, something precious enough to the king that he would pursue Andrew for at least three years in order to recover it?"

"Andrew is no thief," Marie replied staunchly. "He is the most honorable man I have ever met."

"You know him so well, yet you do not know why he is being pursued," Patrick stated.

"What I do know," Marie said, "is that these men are looking for more than just one man, they are looking for several people traveling together. If they discover that you are harboring such a group, they will come to your place seeking us and I do not think that their intentions would be amicable."

"Then we must see to your safety and that of your friends," Patrick said as he gave the three men one more glance before turning away. "Come, we must hurry. It is only a matter of time before they learn that I am hosting a group of travelers and decide to pay my home a visit. You cannot be there when that happens."

Patrick and Marie made a hasty retreat, completely forgetting about why they had come to town in the first place.

Chapter 6

You do know that it will not be as simple as casually strolling up to your nephew, telling him that his father is dead, and informing him that he is the heir to a non-existent throne of a king who died a few hundred years ago," Lawrence said to Andrew as he pulled a piece of meat off the rabbit that was roasting over the campfire by which both men were seated.

"It had occurred to me," Andrew replied, staring into the fire.

"So, how do you plan to manage the matter?" Lawrence asked, placing the plain-tasting morsel into his mouth.

"That, my friend, is the question," Andrew answered.

"And it is not as if your brother's family will be able to stay in Nordham," Lawrence continued. "Not if you suspect there is even the smallest chance Gallard knows your nephew is the true Heir of DuFay."

"I do not see how he could know," Andrew said. "My adopted family had been in that land for several generations, long before Gallard came into power. If Gallard had known, he would have acted long before now. Donald and his family did not even know of their ancestry. You saw what it took for me to convince Donald of his true lineage. No, I think it greatly unlikely that Gallard knows the truth to Donald's line."

"But when you show up and tell your brother's wife and her son that he is the descendant of a great king, the bird will be out of the cage, and you will not be able to control it. Word will eventually get around, you know how difficult it is to keep a secret. That word will eventually make it back to Gallard, and you know beyond a doubt what he will do."

"He would not harm Alexander, not until he has the sword, and I vow here and now that Gallard will never touch that sword," Andrew replied firmly.

"Perhaps," Lawrence answered, "though I am not as convinced of that as you are. You know Gallard better than I do, no doubt about it, I have never met the man. However, based on your tales of him and seeing how he drove an entire army so far in pursuit of you and the sword, I doubt there is much that he would abstain from in his efforts to obtain it. If not the boy, he could threaten the boy's mother. What are you prepared to do if it comes to that?"

"I am prepared to do what I have to in order to keep it from coming to that," Andrew answered. "Come morning, we will push harder and travel faster. We will get to Nordham before Gallard's men. We will spare no time in explaining the situation to Cynthia and Alexander, and we will take them to safety."

"Considering they believe you to be dead, that should not prove the least bit difficult," Lawrence muttered.

"They are not strangers to me, nor distant kin I have not seen but for the rare festival or celebration," Andrew countered. "They are family, my family, as close to me as anybody has ever been. Cynthia trusts me beyond doubt. If I tell her that she and Alexander must leave in order to preserve their safety, even if the threat is anything but certain, she will do so. Now that Donald is gone, she has no reason to stay."

"Well then," Lawrence said, wearying of the conversation, "if that is the plan, then let us get a few hours of sleep before we must dash off and save the Heir of DuFay." He tossed a couple of large pieces of wood on the fire before lying down and pulling several thick blankets over his body. Andrew stared into the fire, watching as the flames attacked the dry wood and momentarily grew before settling down to a small blaze. He feared that Lawrence was right, that convincing his sister-in-law to suddenly abandon the only home she had ever known would prove to be no easy task. But it was something that had to be done, and done quickly, of that he was certain. Weariness overtaking him, Andrew followed Lawrence's example and stretched out for the night.

As the men slept, the flames of the campfire licked at the last of the unburned wood in the pit and cast off a faint yellowish glow that was quickly consumed by the dark of the night. The forest was silent except for the occasional tree creaking as a light gust of wind passed over the canopy. Andrew and Lawrence were curled-up under their blankets, neither wanting to lose what warmth they had by uncovering and re-starting the fire. The cold of the night was an inconvenience that both men had become resolved to, and something they would have to endure for a few more nights. Their sleep was light and not the deep, restful sleep that both men needed for their journey.

Lawrence jolted awake and sat up. He looked into the darkness of the forest and cocked his head sideways, listening for any sound that was out of place in such a serene setting. Something had caused him to awaken. He knew better than to ignore his instincts. He reached over and touched Andrew on the shoulder.

"Andrew," he whispered, giving Andrew a little nudge. Andrew was immediately awake and sat up as well.

"What is it?" he asked, his right hand grasping the sword that was always within reach.

"Something is not right," he said, looking into the dark. From several feet away they could hear their horses start moving about nervously. Annon let out a deep breath, which to Andrew was as good as any alarm.

"We are not alone," Andrew said as he tossed the blankets off his body and reached for a second, smaller sword.

"Indeed, MacLean, you are not alone," a voice called from the darkness. "You have company this evening."

"Who are you and what do you want?" Lawrence called out. "I do not appreciate such a restful sleep being disturbed."

"That is the least of your worries this evening," the voice continued.

"Come forward, and we will stoke the fire so you can shed the evening chill," Andrew said. "Perhaps my companion has left some rabbit on the spit, and you can enjoy a warm bite."

"Your hospitality is amusing," another voice called out. "Unfortunately, we have not come for your wit or that rodent you call food."

"That is too bad. My wit is legendary and the rabbit, well, though not legendary, is not bad at all. My friend here can perform wonders when it comes to roasting game."

"Speaking of legendary," the first voice returned, "if you would be so kind as to hand over the DuFay Sword, we can avoid any nastiness and let your friend return to his much-needed rest."

"I do not have the sword with me," Andrew informed him. "I may not be the wisest man on earth, but I certainly know better than to keep such a sought-after icon so close, especially when I know I am being hunted."

"A wise man would do as he is told and relinquish the sword, that is, if he values the lives of his friends," the first voice replied.

"My friends are just that, my friends. They have no involvement with the sword or my business. They are to be left alone."

"They are involved!" the second voice shouted. "They became involved when you joined with them in your flight from Durinburg."

"Give us the sword, and no harm shall come to them," the first voice said, reassuringly. "As for you, well, what harm comes to you is in your hands. King Gallard is most anxious to see you again, however, he did not specify whether he wanted to see the whole you or just your head. Should you fight us, I am fairly certain which it will be."

"Who are you?" Andrew asked, peering in the darkness at a shadow he suspected was the man. "There is a familiarity in your voice."

"As well there should be," the man answered as he stepped forward and into the faint light from the dwindling fire. "It was your betrayal of King Gallard that gave me my position."

"Devlin," Andrew said as the man's face became illuminated by the firelight.

"Who is this?" Lawrence asked as he continued to survey

their surroundings, trying to determine how many men were hiding in the darkness.

"He was second-in-command to me in Gallard's army," Andrew answered.

"And now I am leading King Gallard's army, second to Commander Walter Brewster," Devlin stated with an air of authority. "I have been tasked with tracking you down and bringing you, and the DuFay Sword, back to King Gallard. There, you will face the fate of all traitors. A well-deserved fate."

"I did not turn against King Gallard," Andrew argued, hoping to buy enough time to figure out how he and Lawrence were going to get out of such a dire situation. He knew that there were more than just two men confronting them, but how many he could not tell. "King Gallard turned against me. You know how faithful I was to him and how hard I fought for him. On the very day he drove me from the land, I led his army...no, WE led his army, to victory." Andrew paused for a moment, reflecting on that battle. "However, if I had known then the reason for the battle, as I do now, there may have been a different outcome."

"Treason is treason. Betrayal is betrayal. Gallard was your king, and your duty was to serve him, to fight the fights he told you to fight, without pause, without question. You turned your back on your duty, on your king," Devlin argued.

"There is no honor in fighting an unjust war, an unprovoked war, for a king consumed with power and prestige," Andrew replied. "There is a power higher than any worldly king that must be obeyed first and foremost. I will always subject myself to the King of the cosmos before subjecting myself to a king of the land."

"In that case, I hope this king to which you refer appreciates your loyalty and rewards you greatly when you see him, because you are about to meet him face-to-face," the second man, whom Andrew did not recognize, said as he stepped out of the darkness. As he stepped forward, so did six other men, all with swords drawn.

"Kill me and you will never find the sword," Andrew warned as he prepared to defend himself.

"If the sword is not here, with you, then it is back in Stanwyck," Devlin replied. "Rest assured, we will tear that village apart, we will tear apart the home of your host, and we will squeeze your friends until their last breath leaves their bruised and broken bodies to find the sword."

"No, you will not," Andrew staunchly replied. "Your last breath shall leave your bruised and broken body, here, tonight by this campfire. You should not have threatened my friends."

"And you should not have betrayed your king," Devlin countered as he launched his attack on Andrew.

Immediately the second man who had been speaking launched an attack against Lawrence and the other six men moved closer and looked to join the melee. To Andrew and Lawrence's advantage, the closeness of the trees inhibited the attackers from being able to engage simultaneously, but both men were continually at a two-on-one disadvantage. The fighting was fierce. Andrew parried a blow from Devlin while stepping sideways to avoid the thrust from a second attacker. Lawrence was in a similar dance, doing everything he could to avoid being struck without having the opportunity to be the aggressor. A blazingly quick swipe of Andrew's sword sliced through the mid-section of his second attacker, who dropped his sword and fell backwards, away from the fight. However, one of the erstwhile bystanders quickly took his place and brought fresh energy to the fight. Lawrence ducked from a sword that was intent on removing his head from his body and lashed out at the attacker's legs, his sword slicing through flesh and producing a scream of agony from the attacker, who fell to the ground, grasping his leg and trying to stem the flow of blood. Lawrence did not pause but turned to parry what he sure was an incoming blow from the first attacker. Unfortunately, the blow did not come from exactly where he expected but from his left side, where another enemy had suddenly appeared. Thanks to the training he had received from Andrew,

Lawrence's reflexes contorted his body to avoid the sword, but not completely. The tip of the sword sliced through the garments covering his upper body and left a four-inch gash in Lawrence's left shoulder. Lawrence ignored the pain and thrust his swords backwards, into the man's abdomen. That took three of the attackers out of the fight, but there were still five more.

Andrew knew that it was only a matter of time before he and Lawrence succumbed to exhaustion and could no longer put up any kind of defense. Devlin was every bit as skilled with the sword as Andrew and having to fight a second man at the same time put Andrew at a great disadvantage. He had just kicked the second man in the chest, sending him reeling backward, when he felt a sharp pain in his side. Even in the dimness of the fading firelight, Andrew could see a devilish grin on Devlin's face. There was a pause in the melee. The man Andrew had knocked down got up quickly, and another man soon joined the two attackers. Now it was three against Andrew and two against Lawrence. Both Andrew and Lawrence were injured. Devlin and his standing men were unscathed.

"The outcome was decided before the first blow was delivered," Devlin said matter-of-factly. "As hearty a fighter as you are, as well as your friend here, you had no chance. You forget, we had the same training as you did. I am your equal if not superior to you in fighting, and these men are highly skilled as well. Your blood testifies that the fight is over. Relinquish the sword, and your friends will be spared. Do the honorable thing."

"I have done the honorable thing," Andrew replied. "I have fought against tyranny and power-hungry men who believe they have some inherent right to rule over other people. I have fought for the people, and I will continue to fight for the people until I draw my last breath. Edwin Gallard will never possess the DuFay Sword."

"We shall see," Devlin said as he and his men poised themselves to continue the fight. Without warning, out of the darkness, an arrow whistled by Andrew and imbedded itself in the torso of one of his attackers. The man looked down at the arrow in disbelief, then fell lifeless to the ground. A second arrow, this time coming from in front of Andrew, followed in the blink of an eye and pierced one of Lawrence's attackers, who staggered backwards several steps before falling to the ground. Devlin and his two comrades stopped in their tracks, looking frantically into the night.

"Drop your weapons," a man's voice commanded. When Devlin hesitated, a third arrow darted not six inches from his right ear. "I said drop your weapons," the voice repeated. "The next arrow shall not miss." Devlin looked at his men and nodded, and all three dropped their swords. Andrew and Lawrence quickly took the men's weapons and tossed them out of reach. "Now," the voice continued, "on your bellies, your noses in the dirt." Slowly, the three men complied and soon were defenseless.

Andrew looked in the direction from which the voice had come but could not see a person. He became aware of movement to his right, a body stepping from behind a tree. Even in the dimness of the night, it only took a moment for him to recognize one of his saviors.

"Marie!" he exclaimed as the young woman stepped up to his side. "What are you doing here?"

"Saving your stubborn, egotistical hide," she replied with a grin. Out of the darkness stepped Patrick, who had been the one addressing Devlin.

"How many of you are there?" Lawrence asked, scanning the darkness.

"If you had not noticed already, I am one of a kind," she replied teasingly. "However, if you are asking how many have come to rescue the two of you, well..." She called out to the darkness, "You can come out now." A young man, who looked to be in his midtwenties, appeared from the shadows. Marie turned back to Lawrence. "You are now looking at the entire rescue party."

"Just the three of you?" Andrew asked incredulously. "What possessed you to believe that just the three of you could execute a rescue? And how did you know that we were going to be attacked? And who is this boy?"

"This boy is someone who just killed a man to save your life," the young man replied confidently. "And the name is Elijah."

"Well, there is the answer to your third question," Marie stated. "To answer your first question, we were relying on your fighting skills to take out at least half of your attackers." She looked at the dead men on the ground. "Obviously, we were a bit over-optimistic on that front. To answer your second question, three of these men came into town soon after the two of you left, asking questions about others who may have been passing through the area. They presented themselves as refugees, fleeing the war in Durinbug, looking for their kin from whom they had been separated. It only took a moment to recognize them for what they truly were, fighters and not mere travelers. And it did not take a genius to determine for whom they were really searching."

"The men came to my home, Andrew, looking for you and your friends," Patrick said, stepping into the conversation. "Thankfully, Marie and I suspected that they would, so we were able to hide her and the others before the men arrived. I spoke with them briefly, telling them that we had given a group of travelers food and rest for two days before they continued their journey, to the east. Either they did not believe me, or they were intent on heading north anyway."

"I cannot apologize enough for putting you and your family in such a position," Andrew said. "It was the one thing I feared the most and the reason I had to leave. Both times."

"I understand, Andrew, there is no need for an apology," Patrick replied. "Marie was bound and determined to catch-up to you and Lawrence and warn you of these men. There was no dissuading her."

"No, there would not be," Andrew said as he looked at Marie with a slight grin. "And she calls me stubborn."

"What now?" Patrick asked, looking at the men on the ground. "What do we do with these men?"

"I have a few ideas," Lawrence replied as he kicked his last attacker in the ribs. The man grunted, but that was the only sound he made.

"We cannot kill them," Andrew replied, looking at the men. "Nor can we tie them up and leave them here."

"We cannot let them go," Lawrence argued. "That would be the end of Stanwyck, and Gallard would know for certain that you returned to Nordham."

"We cannot take them with us," Andrew said. "I have no desire to play nursemaid to three prisoners for the next week. Even so, what could we do with them when we reach Nordham? No, the only solution is for Patrick, Elijah, and Marie to take them back to Stanwyck where they can be held until we do what we must do."

"You mean Patrick and Elijah will take them back," Marie corrected Andrew. "I will be accompanying you to Nordham."

"Marie, we have discussed this previously and the decision was made that you would stay in Stanwyck," Andrew replied.

"Lest you forget, I am stubborn," Marie retorted. "And you will not be making decisions for me again. If it were not for me," she looked at the dead men on the ground, "let us just say that events would have played out quite differently this evening and I warrant not entirely to your liking. Plus, you will need someone to tend to those wounds of yours."

"What, these scratches?" Lawrence asked as reached over his shoulder and touched the area of his wound. He pulled back his hand, the palm of which was covered with blood. "I have had worse."

Andrew knew that any continued arguing would not change the all-but-determined outcome. Marie was going with them, and that was all there was to it. Continued discussion would only create a rift between them, which Andrew did not desire.

"Patrick, these men are quite dangerous. Especially this one," Andrew said as he nudged Devlin with his foot. "Do you believe that you and the boy will be capable of escorting them back to Stanwyck?"

"The name is Elijah," the young man said through gritted teeth. "Do not refer to me as boy again."

"We brought bindings, just in case something like this happened," Patrick replied. "Elijah is a strong young man, too. I have no doubt we will be able to manage these men once we secure their hands and feet."

Andrew knelt on the ground next to Devlin.

"I know your nature is to fight," Andrew said. "It would be my first instinct as well, should I be made captive. However, as you can see, we are sparing your life and on my word no harm shall come to you and your comrades. In due time, you will be granted your freedom once again and you may go where you wish. I only ask that on your word, you do not try to escape or harm these men."

"My word?" Devlin repeated, almost with a laugh. "You want my word that I will not try to escape or harm these men? MacLean, I will try with all my might to escape. And if in doing so these men get in my way, I give you my word that harm SHALL come to them."

"Very well," Andrew said as he stood. "Patrick, Elijah, I shall leave their fate up to you. If they try to escape, do with them as you will for if they do escape, they will do with you as they will."

"Understood," Patrick answered as he retrieved some bindings from a large pouch by his side. "Gentleman, please place your hands behind your back, with your palms touching."

"And while Patrick is taking care of that business, allow me to take care of your wounds," Marie said to Lawrence and Andrew. Both men removed their tunics with no argument.

Chapter 7

W elcome to the land of Nordham," Andrew announced as the trio passed a large pillar of rock which had a crest chiseled into its ancient body. The group had continued their journey without interruption or confrontation and now, six days later, had finally reached the outskirts of the land that Andrew had called home, the only home he had ever known. It was midday, although there was no sun visible in the cloud-choked sky to gauge a more precise time.

"I do not wish to demean your homeland," Lawrence said as he took in their surroundings, "but I have to say, the landscape is every bit as cold as this bitter wind that blows over it." The landscape was a mixture of flatlands and rolling hills of black and gray volcanic rock interspersed with small areas of what could hardly be described as grass. The land was mostly void of vegetation other than what appeared to be moss growing on the rocks and every now and then, a small scrub-brush which had somehow managed to take root and survive in the piles of rocks. Trees were all but non-existent. Many of the rock outcroppings had snow drifts piled up against their windward sides, and while it was not snowing at the moment, the frigid wind and cloudy sky warned of a front moving in that would certainly bring a fresh white dusting to the land.

"Rest assured, what we see here is not indicative of the entirety of my homeland," Andrew replied, though he felt more of a stranger to this land than someone who had lived here most of his life. "If you look to the east, you will see the volcano which was responsible for creating this waste of a land a hundred years ago if not more. Once we pass through this lava field we will enter a more pleasant landscape, where there are trees and brooks and lakes and crops. Perhaps another hour of riding and we will come to my village."

"Speaking of which," Marie chimed-in, "have you determined how you plan to approach your brother's wife? Are you also not fearful of being recognized by others?"

"As for being recognized, I believe my cloak and hood should provide enough camouflage to hide my identity," Andrew replied.

"Yes, that worked SO well back in Stanwyck," Marie said sarcastically.

"As for approaching Cynthia," Andrew continued, ignoring Marie's jab, "I believe the best approach will be a direct approach."

"You have not seen her in over five years, she believes you are dead, and you think the best approach is to walk up to her and say, 'Hello, Cynthia, remember me? By the way, your husband is dead, your son is the heir to an ancient kingdom, and your very own king is intent on stealing that throne no matter the cost,'" Marie asked.

"Not in those exact words, but that is the general idea," Andrew replied.

"And if she is being watched by one or more of the men that Gallard sent, the men that were traveling ahead of us?" Lawrence asked, ever the one to be thinking strategically.

"That could pose a problem," Andrew conceded.

"Then allow me to offer a solution that will present the least of risks," Marie said. "If Gallard's men are here, the three of us riding into town together would get their attention, which we do not desire. If they are instead watching Cynthia, the three of us approaching her, or even just you yourself, may alarm them."

"What are you proposing?" Andrew asked.

"You tell me where to find Cynthia. I will ride ahead on my

own. I will contact her and very gently tell her what has happened, and that her husband sent me to find her and tell her of his fate. I will then tell her that you survived the battle so many years ago but Devlin, seeking to take your place in Gallard's army, falsely accused you of treason and brought contrived evidence against you. Your only option was to flee for your life. Your journey took you to my homeland where we met. Gallard sacked the land and during the battle, Donald was mortally wounded. You found him on the battlefield, brought him to me for medical attention, and he asked me, or rather the both of us, to travel back to Nordham to tell his family that he is dead and for you to take care of them."

"How long have you been formulating this plan of yours?" Andrew asked, surprised by the thoroughness of her plan.

"For about the past week," Marie replied. "You certainly did not seem to have a solid plan, therefore, I figured it was up to the intelligent one in the group to do so."

"Ah, and since I had not come up with a plan, you decided to do so yourself," Lawrence said smartly.

"It is a good plan," Andrew conceded. "However, if Walter is here, which I cannot be but certain that he is, he will be watching Cynthia and Alexander. If you were to approach Cynthia and he recognized you, our presence would be revealed and there would be no way we would be able to get close to Alexander."

"Perhaps I could borrow your cloak of invisibility," Marie replied sarcastically.

"A clandestine presence is our only hope of securing and protecting Alexander," Andrew continued, unphased by her comment.

"Walter has never met me," Lawrence said. "Even if he saw me, he would have no idea who I was. I could find Cynthia and deliver the message to her." He stole a glance at Marie and gave her a mischievous grin. "I would not even need your cloak of invisibility."

"He may not know who you are, but a strange man approaching Cynthia would certainly raise his suspicions," Andrew countered. "No, we cannot approach her ourselves."

"Then who?" Marie asked. "We are a bit short on choices here. Unless you have some secret method of communication with her that involves bird calls or smoke signals, I do not see how we are going to reach her."

"We have someone else contact her," Andrew replied. "I lived here for over twenty years and while I do not know every person in Nordham, there are a great many with whom I had close friendships. I will, with much discretion and caution, approach someone I know I can trust and after convincing them that I am no spirit come back to haunt them, have them pass a message to Cynthia to meet me."

"Yet if Walter is watching Cynthia, as you say," Marie countered, "he will follow her straight to you and our entire plan will be foiled. How do you plan to get around that?"

"He cannot suspect that she is doing anything out of her ordinary routine," Andrew responded. "That way he may relax his eyes for just long enough that we can meet her, and he never know. There is a shop in the village, and I was close to the family that owns it. I will sneak in and speak with them. I will have the owner's wife pay a visit to Cynthia and tell her that her husband has sent her a gift, and she needs to come and get it. Walter would never be suspicious of these women speaking, nor of Cynthia paying this store a visit. When Cynthia comes into the store she will be taken to a back room, and I will be there waiting for her."

"Did he just call himself a gift in a rather roundabout way?" Lawrence asked Marie.

"I believe he did," Marie answered. "Actually, I think it would be better if all three of us were there. I do not plan on waiting out here in the cold while you are in town carrying out your plan, and if you do not want me to accidentally be spotted by Walter roaming the town square, we should stay together."

"Does my plan otherwise meet with your approval then?" Andrew asked.

"Well," Marie replied, acting as if she were truly pondering his question, "I believe it does make sense and unless the genius of the group riding on your other side has any brighter ideas, we should go with it."

"Well, genius?" Andrew asked, looking at Lawrence.

"I have given this plan much thought and I think…," he paused for dramatic effect, "it is acceptable."

"Good. Now let me go and be resurrected," Andrew said with a smile.

Chapter 8

C ynthia MacLean was just finishing feeding her four hogs when she noticed someone approaching her home. The person was bundled against the cold and at first, she could not tell who it was or whether it was a man or woman. As the person neared, hands appeared and pulled back the hood to reveal the face of a woman who was near sixty years old.

"Miriam. What a surprise. What brings you all the way out here on such a gray day?" Cynthia asked.

"A visitor has come to my store," the older woman replied, thoughtfully, "someone who wishes to speak with you. He asked that I come and bring you back to the store."

"A visitor?" Cynthia asked. "Who is it? Why does he wish to speak with me?"

"He asked that I not reveal his identity at this time. He said that he has news of Donald and a gift and wishes to deliver them to you in person."

"Why would he not come to me himself?" Cynthia inquired, suspicion rising in her.

"He said it was best that he is not seen at this time," Miriam replied. "Cynthia, this is someone I know, someone whom I trust. It is most definitely someone with whom you need to speak. He asked that we come quickly, as the matter is urgent, and time is not a friend."

"Very well," Cynthia answered, her curiosity peaked now more than ever. "Allow me to retrieve some more weather-appropriate attire and I shall accompany you back to the village." She disappeared into her house and within a few moments came back out fully wrapped against the cold. The two women turned and commenced the 15-minute walk back into town with not another word exchanged between them.

The relative warmth of the interior of the dry-goods store was a much-welcomed greeting as Cynthia and Miriam finally arrived. There was nobody else visible in the store.

"So, where is this visitor with such an urgent message for me?" Cynthia asked, looking around.

"He is in the back room," Miriam answered and guided Cynthia through a doorway that was covered by a large blanket. There were three other people in the room. A woman and man were sitting around a small table engaged in conversation, which ceased as Cynthia entered the room. Another man was standing beyond the seated pair, his back to them, a hood drawn up over his head.

"Well, let us get on with it," Cynthia said, addressing the people at the table. "What is this news of my husband and gift that you have for me?"

The man and woman seated at the table did not speak but instead, turned and looked at the standing man. He slowly turned to face Cynthia and pulled the hood back from his head. There was not a moment of hesitation as Cynthia immediately recognized the visitor.

"Andrew!" she gasped in surprise and amazement as her hands reached up and covered her mouth. "How..." she stammered, her words sticking in her throat. "How is it that you are here? You are dead!"

"Let us say that the news of my death was quite premature," Andrew replied, a smile forming on his lips. The initial shock wore off just enough that Cynthia rushed forward and threw her arms around Andrew. Tears of joy streamed down her face. Andrew returned her embrace, but inside he dreaded what he needed to tell her that would convert the tears of joy into something much different.

"I cannot believe you are here!" Cynthia cried as she finally pulled back from Andrew. She lifted her hands to his face, cradling his cheeks in her hands. "My dear Andrew. Where have you been all these years?"

"That is a very, very long story," Andrew replied. "Unfortunately, we do not have the time at the present for the complete telling. Time is not our friend. I will tell you everything, but right now I must know, where is Alexander?"

"I sent him off earlier today to complete his chores," Cynthia replied, a little curiously. "Why do you need to see Alexander? Why the urgency?"

"We need to find him and bring him here," Andrew answered without explanation. "Where would he be right now?"

"I am not sure," Cynthia replied, now totally confused. "I sent him off to gather more wood for the stove, he was to fill the water barrel, he was to come to the village and pick-up some items from the blacksmith, just routine chores. Of course, being a young man, there is no telling what may have distracted him and where he would be at this moment. Andrew, what is going on? Miriam said that you have news from Donald. Is that true, or just a ruse to get me to come here?"

Andrew looked down at Maria and Lawrence. Marie gave him a nod of encouragement, and he knew that he could forestall the unwelcome news no longer.

"Please, Cynthia, sit down," Andrew said, guiding her to a chair beside Marie at the table. Cynthia sat down, a bad feeling forming in her stomach. Andrew sat in the last vacant chair, facing Cynthia. He reached out and took her hands into his, then looked her in the eyes. "Your husband, my brother...he is..." Andrew fought back the tears that suddenly welled-up in his eyes. "He is...dead."

"Dead?" Cynthia repeated, the emotional shift from joy to grief grabbing at her heart. "Donald is dead?"

"Aye, I am afraid so," Andrew answered as fresh tears rolled down Cynthia's face.

"You are certain of this?" she asked, although deep down she knew Andrew would not say such a thing if there was any lack of certainty.

"I was there," Andrew replied, the memory of his brother's death charging forth. "We were in battle. He..." Andrew paused, gathering himself, trying to avoid the stammer that was creeping into his voice. "He died saving my life. He died in my arms."

"Oh, Andrew," Cynthia cried, leaning forward and embracing Andrew once again, this time out of grief instead of joy. Marie and Lawrence could do nothing but look down, the emotional intensity of the moment impacting them all. Several minutes passed without a word from anybody.

"How were you and Donald together?" Cynthia asked, finally pulling away from Andrew. "He was with Gallard's army far, far away from here."

"First, we need to find Alexander, then I can tell you everything," Andrew replied. "This involves him to no small degree. Miriam," Andrew called out, and the older woman appeared from the front of the store. "I need to impose upon you once more, and I apologize for having to do so. We need to know if Alexander has visited the blacksmith yet, and we need to know if anybody, especially his friends, have seen him today. Would you be able to pay a visit to the blacksmith, and then start spreading the word amongst any of the young men you see that Alexander's mother is looking for him? Tell them you have a package that he needs to take home right away. Hopefully, he will get the word soon and come to us, instead of us having to go look for him and expose ourselves."

"Yes, of course," Miriam replied and left the building.

"Andrew, what exactly is going on here?" Cynthia asked, looking between Andrew and his companions. "Who are these people, and why are you here?"

"It all began over five years ago, when Gallard led his army into battle..." Andrew began and commenced telling her of his journey.

Chapter 9

The knock on her front door surprised Kristen MacLean. She was rarely visited, as she routinely visited her friends during her errands in the village. Perhaps it was Cynthia, she thought to herself as she laid down the quilt she had been working on and rose to open the door. She was a bit startled, and confused, at who stood in front of her.

"Mrs. MacLean, I hope I am not disturbing you or have come at an inconvenient time," Walter Brewster said with a courteous smile.

"Um, no, not at all," Kristen said as she looked past Walter at the three men who accompanied him. "To what do I owe this visit?" she asked.

"If it would not be an imposition, may I come in?" he asked. "The air is quite chilly, and I would be most inconsiderate asking you to speak with me in the cold."

"Of course, please, come in," she replied and moved aside. Walter nodded to his men, who assumed positions as if setting watch.

"May I offer you something hot to drink?" Kristen asked, a knot beginning to form in her stomach. She knew Walter's position as a special advisor to King Gallard and that he had gone to war with Gallard nearly four months earlier. It was a campaign for which Gallard had taken a majority of his army, including her son, Donald. If a high-ranking official in Gallard's administration was paying her a visit, it could only mean one thing.

"No, thank you," Walter replied. "I am sure my visit is quite the surprise, and I will not do you the discourtesy of delaying the reason for my visit. I have news of your son."

Kristen's knees began to tremble, and she sat down before she collapsed, fearing the next words from Walter's mouth. "Donald," she barely more than whispered, but loud enough for Walter to hear.

"Actually, while I do have news of Donald, I was thinking of your other son."

"Andrew?" Kristen asked, now more confused than ever. "But Andrew was killed in battle more than five years ago. You know this," she said.

"I realize how difficult this must be, considering the amount of time that has passed, but I assure you, Andrew is most certainly alive," Walter replied.

"I...I do not understand," Kristen stammered, her mind a whirlwind. "If he was not killed in battle, why did he not come home? Where has he been? Where is he? He certainly would have returned home."

"It is a sad story," Walter began to answer, "and an unfortunate one. After the battle to which you have referred, word came to King Gallard that Andrew had betrayed him and was actually a spy for the opposing army."

"That is complete nonsense!" Kristen exclaimed. "Andrew was no spy and was completely loyal to Gallard! As one of Gallard's high-ranking advisors, you knew Andrew well. You know that such an accusation could be anything but false."

"Yes, yes, we all knew Andrew's loyalty and devotion to King Gallard. He proved it over and over, many times on and off the battlefield. However, the evidence presented to King Gallard was quite incriminating and very convincing. Ordinarily, such an accusation, with the evidence presented, would warrant the immediate penalty of death. However, Gallard's affection for Andrew would not permit him to issue such a command and therefore, he banished Andrew and decreed that if Andrew were ever seen again near Nordham, he would be executed immediately, without trial, without pause."

"Then why tell everyone, why tell me, his mother, that he was dead?" Kristen asked.

"The king did not want to tarnish Andrew's name, or the MacLean family name," Walter replied. "He still maintained great affection for your family."

"And now, after all this time, you come to tell me of this?" Kristen asked. "Why now?"

"There has come to King Gallard irrefutable proof of Andrew's innocence," Walter answered. "I have a declaration signed by Gallard himself clearing Andrew of all charges and re-instating him as the commander of his army, a position in which Andrew belongs. There are rumors that Andrew has been seen around Nordham, but he will not chance revealing his presence to anyone other than his mother. I am hoping that if he does come to visit you, that you will send word to me so that I can bestow upon him this full pardon and return him to his rightful position of prominence."

Kristen looked at Walter closely. There was something about him, about his story, that she did not trust. She believed the report that Andrew was alive, but that is as far she her trust would take her. While she was considering Walter's story, there came a knock on the door and one of Walter's men entered the house. He bent down and whispered something to Walter. Walter thought for a moment and briefly stole a glance at Kristen. He then replied to his man, quietly, but not quietly enough that Kristen did not overhear his words.

"Escort him there, gently, and we will meet you." The man turned and left.

"Good news," Walter said with a menacing smile. "Andrew is in town. Shall we go meet your very-much-alive son?"

"Wait," Kristen said, "you said that you also have news of my other son, Donald."

"Oh, yes, that I do. I am afraid that news is not quite as cheerful as that of Andrew being alive. You see, Donald is, unfortunately, very much dead. Now, if you will, please dress warmly, as it is quite chilly outside."

Chapter 10

Y ou are telling me that my son, my only son, is the heir to the throne of a long-lost kingdom?" Cynthia asked Andrew as he finished telling her of the DuFay legend and his journey over the past five and a half years.

"Yes, that he is," Andrew replied.

"And King Gallard may have sent men to do him harm so that he, Gallard, might claim this long-abandoned throne for himself?"

"As ruthless and determined as Gallard is, I do not believe that he would harm Alexander physically," Andrew replied, trying to provide some degree of comfort to Cynthia, though none of this could in any way be less than emotionally traumatic. "I would think that his plan would be to remove Alexander, to spirit him away somewhere until he, Gallard, had accomplished his goals and established himself on this ancient throne. Once that has been achieved, Alexander would no longer represent a threat to him, and Gallard would release him."

"But you do not know that for sure," Cynthia replied.

"I will do everything in my power to protect Alexander," Andrew assured her. "To the very end of my life I will."

A commotion in the front of the store interrupted the conversation and the four occupants of the back room looked at each other, alarmed. Andrew nodded to Lawrence and the two of them rose from their chairs, unsheathing their swords.

"Behind us," Andrew commanded Cynthia and Marie. Cynthia immediately positioned herself behind Andrew. Marie paused for a moment, but Lawrence none-too-gently took her arm and pulled her behind him. She opened her mouth to protest when the curtain to the other room was drawn back and Walter stepped into the room. There were a few seconds of silence before Walter spoke.

"It has been quite a long time, MacLean," Walter said, his casual tone a bit disturbing to Andrew.

"Not long enough," Andrew replied coldly, his body tensing for action.

"Long enough for this scar you gave me to heal quite nicely," Walter replied. "People around here see it as a bit of a badge of honor, I must say."

"I will be more than happy to provide you with many more badges," Andrew retorted.

"Come now, let us not make this more difficult than it needs to be," Walter said. "There need not be any bloodshed today. You know why I am here. Relinquish the sword to me, and I shall be on my way back to King Gallard before nightfall. You may be on your way to wherever your heart desires, you and your friends. I am sure Lady Talbot would much enjoy an end to her long days on horseback and long, cold nights on the ground."

"What I would much enjoy..." Marie began icily but was cutoff by Andrew.

"The sword is not for Gallard," Andrew replied quickly. "He is not the Heir of DuFay, and he will never ascend to that throne."

"The Heir of DuFay is the one who possesses the DuFay Armor," Walter answered. "Gallard has the breastplate and I venture he has the shield by now as well. You will relinquish to him the sword. He is already on the trail of the remaining pieces. The moment he possesses all six, he shall become the Heir of DuFay."

"He shall never hold the DuFay Sword," Andrew replied matter-of-factly. Walter gave an exaggerated sigh.

"I must say, if you had given it up so easily, I would have been greatly disappointed," he said. "This way, it is much more enjoyable. Tell me Andrew, have you had an opportunity to visit your mother since you came home? No? Well, allow me to arrange a little reunion." He looked over his shoulder and called to the adjoining room. "Bring her in."

There was only a moment's delay before Kristen MacLean was pushed past the curtain and into the now-crowded room.

"Andrew!" she cried in disbelief when her eyes met her son's. She moved to rush over to Andrew, but Walter blocked her way.

"Now, now, let us not be hasty," Walter said as he held Kristen back.

"You monster!" Andrew cried as he took a step forward. A small dagger appeared in Walter's left hand, and he lifted it to Kristen's throat. Andrew stopped mid-step. "Release her, now!" he commanded.

"Not yet," Walter replied, the tip of the blade resting against Kristen's neck near the jugular vein.

"I swear to all that is holy, if you so much as place the tiniest of scratches on my mother, if you harm a single hair on her head…" Andrew growled.

"I know, I know, you will rip me to pieces," Walter replied dismissively. "Believe me, I do not want to harm your mother in the least of ways. She is such a precious woman. And I do not wish to get ripped to pieces. Our fates are in your hands, Andrew. The fate of every person in this room is in your hands. All you need do is relinquish the sword to me. You have my word that neither your mother nor your companions here shall suffer any harm."

Andrew knew that he had no choice. His mind was whirling, trying to find a way out of this nightmare, but there was no scenario in which lives were not lost. He looked at Marie and Lawrence. Both nodded, affirming what needed to be done. He turned back to Walter.

"Very well," he said reluctantly. "Release my mother and I shall give you the sword."

"I think I shall hold on to her until you place the sword of

DuFay in my hand," Walter countered. "You will understand if I do not trust you."

"Outside," Andrew directed. Walter paused for a moment, then nodded in agreement. He guided Kristen through the front of the store and out into the gloomy day. Andrew, Marie, Lawrence, and Cynthia followed. What they saw caught them all by surprise. There were sixteen armed men standing in front of the store, all poised as if ready to launch into battle the instant the order was given. Cynthia gasped as she saw Alexander standing in front of one of the men. She went to rush over to him but was none-too-gently restrained by the closest soldier. She tried to fight against him, but he quickly overpowered her and subdued her. Walter pulled Kristen along with him until he was standing just a few feet in front of his men. He turned and looked at Andrew.

"As you can see," Walter said, gesturing towards his men, "any resistance or lack of cooperation shall have rather dire consequences. Let us conclude our business here, MacLean, and go our separate ways. The sword if you please."

Andrew took one final look at the situation and knew that he had absolutely no alternative but to cooperate and give the sword to Walter. He also knew that there was little chance of there not being bloodshed once Walter had the sword. Though the physical wound that Andrew had given Walter so many years ago had healed, Andrew knew that the emotional scar would not heal until Walter had taken his revenge. How that revenge would play out was not yet clear.

"Miriam," Andrew called to the shop keeper, who had exited her store with everybody else. "If you would, please bring me the sword."

The older woman stepped back into her building and within sixty seconds re-appeared with a tightly wrapped bundle. She gently handed it to Andrew, who then turned and held it out to Walter.

"Unwrap it," Walter commanded. Andrew complied. He untied the two leather straps that held the protective fabrics around the sword and the sheath in which it had been placed. Then, holding the sheath in his left hand, he drew the sword from it and held it out for all to see. Gripping the sword by the blade, he walked over and presented it to Walter. Walter grabbed the hilt of the sword and lifted it from Andrew's hands. The smug expression on his face as he looked at Andrew was almost too much for Andrew to stomach. He released his grip on Andrew's mother, who took one step away from him then turned, fully intent on slapping him in defiance. Andrew quickly took hold of his mother and pulled her away from Walter, hoping to stave off the soon-to-come violence as long as he could.

"It is more magnificent than I could ever have imagined," Walter said reverently as he looked deeply at the sword, admiring the smallest of details. "This is indeed the sword of a great king. A great king who will be most grateful, and most generous, when I place it in his hands." He looked at Andrew. "Now tell me, do you not feel that a burden has been lifted from you? This thing which has driven your life for nearly six years, which drove you from your homeland, this curse to you is finally lifted. You can lead a normal life now... for the fleeting time that will be."

Walter nodded to his men. The two closest to Alexander moved quickly and bound his hands and placed a hood over his head. They mounted their horses, with Alexander lifted-up and set in front of one of the men. Cynthia screamed to her son and fought to rush over to him, but the soldier who had been restraining her tightened his grip on her.

"What are you doing!?" Andrew demanded, fighting every instinct in his body to rush Walter. "Leave the boy out of this!"

"That I cannot do, for the boy is very much a part of this," Walter replied, enjoying Andrew's anger. "Plus, I cannot disregard the orders of my king. King Gallard's orders to me were three-fold: First, obtain the sword. Second, secure the boy until Gallard has secured the DuFay throne."

"And the third order?" Andrew asked, although he knew the answer.

"And third, deliver unto you the penalty for treason. I believe you know what that penalty to be."

"Where are you taking my son?" Cynthia demanded, struggling in vain against the man who held her.

"King Gallard is quite a merciful king and not the monster that some people make him out to be. Alexander is a precious member of Gallard's kingdom, a young man whom the king admires. No harm shall come to your son. However, until King Gallard obtains the entirety of the DuFay Armor and reestablishes the great kingdom of the past, he has insisted that your son be kept close to him. Therefore, Alexander shall return with us to King Gallard."

"Rest assured, Gallard is every bit the monster that some people make him out to be," Andrew stated, "as are you. I wonder, do you have the courage to deliver my penalty in person, or will you have someone else do so in your stead?"

"It would give me immense pleasure to do so myself, however, I must not waste another moment in making my return to Gallard," Walter replied. "I shall be satisfied with the report of my men once they conclude their business here and join me on the road." Walter climbed aboard the horse that had been brought over to him. Six more of his men also climbed aboard horses, while the remaining eight began to fidget, knowing that a fight was but moments away.

"We shall meet again," Andrew said firmly, there being no doubt, no question in the statement. "When we do, there will be no power on earth that shall prevent me from delivering unto you the penalty for your wicked deeds."

"And here I thought such judgment was reserved for the Almighty alone," Walter teased as he turned his horse. "I always knew you had a high opinion of yourself, Andrew, but that is taking it a little too far." He kicked his horse in its ribs, and it took off down the road. The eight men on horseback followed him. Alexander fought and called out to his mother, but his resistance was futile. Cynthia cried out for her son. There was nothing she could do but watch him disappear down the road. The dust had not settled before Walter's men started moving in on Andrew and Lawrence. Cynthia and Kristen moved back toward the store. Marie did not join them but started looking around frantically.

"I do believe the odds are slightly against us," Andrew said as he drew his sword.

"Come now, we have faced worse," Lawrence replied as he drew his own sword. "Plus, not a one of them looks to have seen his twentyeth year."

"Yes, you are right," Andrew agreed as he took a closer look at the men in front of them. Indeed, they were all quite young, which would generally mean quite inexperienced. And perhaps impressionable. "Perhaps we can make that play into our hands." Andrew addressed the young men who were slowly advancing on him and Lawrence.

"Before we begin, I would ask one question of you," Andrew said, looking from one man to the next. "Which of you is willing to die for a king who has betrayed you?"

"You are the one who betrayed King Gallard," one of the men answered. "For that, you shall die."

"Where is your king?" Andrew pressed. "Where is his army? I will tell you. Your loving king and his entire army are over a thousand leagues from here, leaving you and the kingdom he claims to love unprotected, vulnerable to attack. He left what, maybe two-hundred armed and trained men to protect his kingdom? And if you represent the force that he left behind, well, should more than a band of vagabonds with slingshots set upon this village, it shall surely fall. Does that sound to be something a loving and loyal king would do to his own people?"

"King Gallard is a valiant and loving king," another of the men replied. "He shall return once his campaign ends."

"Gallard is not returning," Andrew countered. "We were there, we were in the battle. Your king took his entire army away from its homeland to attack a kingdom that was half the size of Nordham and posed no threat to it. What reason would a king have for doing such a thing? Power. He is seeking something that does not belong to him, to which he has no right. He may have left some low-level bureaucrat to oversee the kingdom in his name, but I tell you, Gallard is not returning. He has discarded you as though you were nothing more than an expendable, worn-out garment. He cares not what happens to you."

"Your words of poison shall accompany you to your grave," the man replied.

"Perhaps so," Andrew answered casually. "It is likely that my companion and I will meet our fate here, today, at your hands."

"Your optimism is much re-assuring," Lawrence said as his eyes examined their opponents, determining which ones would be the stronger and more of a threat.

"But I assure you, we will not be the only ones left lifeless on the ground when the melee has run its course. Most of you know who I am. You would do well to recall who helped in your training when you were but young boys, barely able to lift a sword. You know my skills with the sword exceeded those of every other man under Gallard's command. My companion here is equally skilled with the sword."

"Now, let us be honest, Andrew," Lawrence said, his grip tightening on his sword. "I believe it was well established that my skills have exceeded yours."

"Gregory," Andrew called to one of the young men to his right. "You know me. You know how many hours we trained together, and how we talked about honesty, loyalty, integrity, and faith. You know that if I have chosen to oppose Gallard it has to be for an exceptionally good and very sound reason."

"Do not listen to him," the man who had first spoken to Andrew instructed the one called Gregory. It was this one whom Andrew now took to be the leader, whether officially or unofficially, of this group. And the most dangerous. "Gregory, he is a traitor and a liar."

"You know better, Gregory," Andrew countered. "Your king has abandoned you and your home. As I repeated to you over and over during our years of training, always fight for what is honorable, and always fight against what is not. I have returned to a homeland from which I was unjustly banished, seeking only to protect my family. Your king has abandoned his homeland seeking only to increase his own glory. Which is honorable?"

"Gregory, we are your brothers," the leader said, trying to sway his comrade whose face had begun to show signs of doubt. "We cannot remember a time that we were not together, from being friends as young boys to now, trained warriors. If your loyalty does not lie with us, with your king, where does it lie? With a traitor?"

"Colin, you have known Andrew as long as I have," Gregory responded to the man. "You know that he was always honorable and trustworthy."

"What I know is that King Gallard has declared Andrew to be a traitor," Colin responded.

Gregory looked at his comrades, then looked at Andrew. A great conflict raged within him. He trusted Andrew, but he also had sworn loyalty to Gallard, and that was not something which he took lightly. He could not choose sides.

"I will not fight against you, Andrew, but I shall not fight for you, either."

"Then you are a traitor as well," Colin spat at him. "Once we have disposed of these two, you will be arrested and stand trial for treason." He looked at Andrew. "This conversation has ended. Your sentence shall be carried out. Seven against two shall see to that."

"I promise you, by the end of this fight, at least three of you will lie lifeless on the ground," Andrew responded, trying to delay the fight as long as he could and hopefully narrow the odds a bit more. "Now I ask again, which of you is willing to give his life for a lying, disloyal king?"

With a shout of rage, Colin rushed Andrew and raised his sword high above his head, seeking to quickly end Andrew's life. The young man threw a powerful sword stroke at Andrew, but Andrew easily dodged the inexperienced assault and forcefully struck the attacker on the back of the head, knocking him unconscious.

"Well, that would seem to answer your question," Lawrence

said, gazing at the still form on the ground. "Six against two. Yes, much better odds."

With additional shouts, the remaining six men launched their attacks against Andrew and Lawrence. Gregory stepped back, refusing to get involved in the battle. Both Andrew and Lawrence held their long-swords in their right hands and had drawn short-swords with their left hands. The fighting was fierce from the onset. Neither Andrew nor Lawrence was able to take any kind of offensive position and could for the most part only deflect the repeated blows. One of the attackers came too close to Lawrence, and Lawrence was able to club him on the side of the head, momentarily knocking him out of the fight. However, a second attacker was just behind the first and was able to lay his sword against Lawrence's left arm just about the elbow, parting garment and skin. Lawrence wheeled around and deflected a second blow from the same man that was coming from his opposite side and in the same motion, plunged his short sword into the man's mid-section, reducing the attackers' numbers by one. Five against two.

Andrew strained to deflect the blows that were being aimed at him from three sides. He successfully parried two of them but a third snuck through and slapped his right thigh. Thankfully, it was the flat side of the blade that had hit him, so there was no resulting injury other than what would be a dark bruise. However, he was not so fortunate when another of the rapidly coming thrusts broke his defenses and pierced his left chest by about an inch and left a three-inch wide gash. Ignoring the wound, Andrew retaliated by sweeping his long sword towards the attacker and smashing the flat end of his sword against the man's left shin. With a shout of pain, the man crumpled to the ground, holding his broken leg. Now it was four against two. Andrew began to believe that he and Lawrence might just actually survive the fight.

Just as it appeared that the odds were starting to turn, Colin regained consciousness and joined the fight. Back to five against two. He immediately set his sights on Andrew, furious that Andrew had so easily taken him out of the fight at the onset. The leader once again rushed Andrew though this time, not as haphazardly. He pulled to a stop just a few feet from Andrew and delivered the blow that had been his intention when the fight started. Andrew dodged the blow but had to back-up to do so and when he did, he tripped over the broken-legged man who was still on the ground, groaning in pain. Andrew fell, and upon instinct and reflexes alone immediately rolled to his right. He felt the air move past his ear and the grains of dirt splash against his cheek as the attacker's sword slammed into the ground. Instead of jumping to his feet, Andrew rolled back left and swung his right leg out, connecting with the back of his attacker's legs. Colin fell to the ground. Andrew spring to his feet and was about to plunge his sword into the man's chest when he was knocked to the ground from behind. His long sword was jarred from his hand. The second attacker raised his sword and started to bring it down on Andrew. Andrew lifted the short sword as protection, but he knew that it was a useless gesture. Before the attacker's sword made it half-way down in its death blow, another sword came out of nowhere and parried the stroke. His defender followed the parry with a strong kick to the attacker's groin and when the man doubled over in pain, Andrew's savior viciously kicked the man in the head, knocking him out of the fight for good. Now it was four against three. Andrew quickly grabbed his sword and leaped to his feet. He could see Lawrence still fighting two of the other men and Gregory was still standing away from the fight. His savior was facing away from him so Andrew could not tell who it was. The man took two long strides and quickly engaged one of Lawrence's attackers. Within seconds the newcomer's sword had removed yet another of Gallard's men from the fight. Three against three. Just as quickly, an arrow whistled through the air and struck yet another of the attackers in the chest. Andrew stole a glance behind him and saw Marie notching another arrow in her bow.

Colin was quickly back on his feet but did not immediately attack Andrew. Although he knew that Andrew and Lawrence were both injured and tiring, the newcomer was both fresh and exceptionally large. With five of his comrades permanently taken out of the fight, he knew that despite Andrew and Lawrence being tired and injured, there was no winning this fight.

"ENOUGH!" he called out, resigning the fight. His last standing comrade paused, fight still left in him, but slowly dropped his sword to a non-threatening position. Lawrence, breathing heavily, was slow to relax his posture. He was in fight-mode, which for him was not easily turned off. Andrew stared at the young man who was bleeding from his nose as well as from a couple of places on his torso. Andrew could not remember having successfully struck the man but then again, when the fighting begins and is as furious as it was, things can become a blur. "That is enough," he repeated, this time more calmly. Seeing that the fighting was truly over, Andrew took the time to look over at his savior...and was shocked.

"Angus?!" he exclaimed, taken completely by surprise at the man's sudden appearance. "What...How is it that you are here?"

"There will be time for stories later," Angus replied. He gestured towards King Gallard's men. "What of these men? Two of them are still capable of fighting and the third could regain consciousness at any time."

"It is not these three that worry me, but the dozens of others that could descend upon us at any moment," Andrew replied, looking around their surroundings. "Surely word of the fight has spread. We must take leave of this place before the choice to do so is no longer ours to make."

"Where to?" Angus asked. Andrew looked at Cynthia, who was standing with Miriam and his mother inside the shop's doorway.

"Alexander," Andrew replied. "Walter and his men took Alexander, and they are returning to Durinburg. Our priority must be to rescue Alexander. After that, we can take pause and think more clearly on our futures."

"Durinburg?" Angus replied in disbelief. "I lost count of the days it took to get here from there, and now you wish to turn around and go back?"

Lawrence looked at Andrew. "You know that Walter will most likely post ambushes along the road on the off chance that we actually survived this fight," he said. "And it would not be young boys we would have to fight through. While I prefer to be the optimist of the group, I have to admit I have my doubts as to our survival of such a gauntlet."

"Lawrence, my friend," Andrew said as he reached out and placed a hand on Lawrence's shoulder, a teasing smile on his face. "Have you no faith in me? Whenever have I lead you into harm's way?"

"When have you NOT?" Lawrence responded, wide-eyed. "Up until I met you, I had never faced a battalion of battle-hungry warriors, had never walked into an enemy encampment to rescue a princess and nearly lost my life in doing so, had never been forced to flee death through a dark, dank tunnel that at any time could fall upon my head, and had not faced seven-on-two odds in a fight to the death."

"Exciting, is it not?" Andrew replied with a broad smile. "You can thank me later for saving you from a life of boredom and monotony." He turned and looked at Gallard's men. "First, however, we must bind these men."

"I think not," Colin said as his third man had regained consciousness and was ready to engage if the fight continued. "You and your companion are nearly spent and despite the arrival of this other man, you truly stand no chance should the fight continue. No, it is the three of you who shall be bound."

"Think again," Marie called out from the side of the store where Cynthia, Miriam and Kristen were watching the events. She had a bow in her hand and an arrow notched, drawn back and ready to be fired. "Should you flinch in a way that seems unfriendly to me, this arrow shall be buried in your chest before you can blink. And before the brains of your companions can comprehend what has happened, one of them shall lie on the ground beside you. At that point I do believe Andrew and Lawrence, despite the weariness of their muscles, should be more than capable of disposing of the remaining man on their own. The choice is yours."

All eyes were turned on Marie. Facial expressions ranged from disbelief to amusement to surprise...and to resignation. Colin looked the situation over and fully believing that Marie was capable of doing what she had threatened, nodded to his men. They dropped their weapons.

"That was unexpected," Lawrence said as he looked at Marie who was slowly approaching them, the bow still drawn.

"We have little time," Andrew responded. "We need to get them secured and make our escape." He looked at Gallard's men. "Into the store. Miriam," he called to the storekeeper, "we will need three strands of rope for binding these men."

As the men obeyed and entered the building, Andrew's mother rushed over and embraced her son.

"Thank the Lord that you are okay," she said, burying her face into his shoulder. "I cannot believe that you are here! What happened to you? We were told that you had been killed in battle, and then Walter said that you had not been killed but had betrayed Gallard and were banished. Where have you been all these years?"

"It is a long story, Mother," Andrew replied as he watched Lawrence and Angus bind Gallard's men.

"Walter said that Donald is dead," she continued, a glimmer of hope in her eyes. "Is it possible that he was lying?" Andrew turned and looked his mother in the eyes. He could see the hope in her, which made his answer that much more difficult.

"I am afraid, in this case, he was being truthful," Andrew answered. "Donald and I were in a battle against Gallard's men. He saved my life by forfeiting his."

"How was it that you were together?" Kristen asked, confused.

"There is much I must tell you, but now is not the time," Andrew responded. "We have to leave right away if we are to rescue Alexander."

"I just got you back and now I must say goodbye?" she asked incredulously.

"For a time," Andrew replied. "Just for a time. There is much that we must do. Cynthia can explain everything to you. I promise, as the Lord allows, I shall return."

"Speaking of explaining things, would you like to explain to us how we are going to rescue Alexander?" Lawrence asked as Marie tended to his wounds. "Unless you have a small army of friends who are willing to stand by your side, I do not see how we stand a chance against Walter and his men. He will have eyes in the back of his head. There is no way we could sneak up on him."

"It is the very fact that he will be focused on what is behind him that will allow us to sneak up on him," Andrew replied. "I am counting on it." Andrew looked over at Gregory who had followed them into the building. "If you remain, your life will be forfeit, you know that," he said to the young man.

"Aye, that is for sure," Gregory responded. "But it is a choice that I made, and I shall answer for it."

"We could use your help," Andrew said. "What I said about Gallard is true. There is no honor in staying here and being executed as a traitor to a king who has betrayed his own people. You can come with us. I am not certain of where our path will ultimately take us, I can make no promises to you of our future, but at least you will have a future."

Gregory did not pause long before responding.

"I have always looked up to you as an honorable man," he replied. "I will come with you, and you will explain to me what truly happened to you and why you left King Gallard. If your story is believable and not foul in nature, I shall continue with you. Otherwise, I shall go my own way."

"Fair enough," Andrew nodded in agreement. He then turned and spoke to Colin.

"My mother and sister, Cynthia, have no part in what I do," he said sternly, his sword placed just below Colin's Adam's apple.

"They are not to be touched, harmed or dealt with unjustly in any way. Their lives shall go on as if today never happened. I am leaving Nordham now but shall return from time to time, in secret. If upon my return I hear of any mistreatment of them, I shall hold you personally responsible and your life, and that of any family you have, shall pay the price for their harm. Do you understand? They are to be left alone," Andrew said emphatically.

"I understand," Colin said in all sincerity.

Lawrence looked over to Andrew as Marie finished tending to his wounds.

"If it is not too much trouble," he said, standing-up, "would you mind explaining just how you plan to sneak-up on Walter and rescue Alexander?"

Andrew looked at Lawrence with a mischievous grin. "I know a short-cut."

Chapter 11

T ell me your idea of a short-cut is not what I am thinking it is," Lawrence asked Andrew as the group topped a knoll beyond which a vast, endless sea came into sight. Sitting on the shore was a bustling harbor town comprised of three dozen buildings. Several piers jutted out into the water at which numerous boats and watercraft of assorted sizes and designs were anchored. There was a flurry of activity around the boats as fish and various goods of trade were offloaded and loaded. Andrew smiled.

"Do not tell me that you are afraid of a little boat ride?" he teased his friend.

"If he is not, then I have no hesitation in expressing my lack of desire to set foot off dry land," Marie offered.

"You practically grew up on the shores of quite a large lake," Andrew countered. "Do you expect me to believe that you never ventured across the lake?"

"Of course I did," Marie replied. "This, though, is not a lake. This is an ocean. There is a difference."

"This is our only option if we are to have an opportunity to rescue Alexander," Andrew said. "There are no other roads that could put us ahead of Walter and as we all agreed, it is likely that he has set ambushes along the road in the event we somehow escaped our doom in Nordham."

"Only to meet it at the hands of some beast of the sea as it drags us to the icy depths," Lawrence murmured.

"I have made my share of journeys across this very sea and as you can plainly see, no beast sent me to a watery grave," Andrew responded.

"When did this happen?" Marie asked. "Are you now going to tell us that in addition to being a soldier and a farmer and a scholar, you are a master mariner as well?"

"Oh, no, not at all," Andrew replied with as humble a look as he could muster. "Master may be a bit of an overstatement."

A look of resignation crossed Lawrence's face. "I give up. Is there anything that you cannot do?"

"When I was first driven away by Gallard, I came here. I did not know where to go, and this had the appearance of a place where a man could easily disappear. An opportunity to work on one of the boats and earn a reasonable wage was presented to me and, being that room and board are not free, I accepted the offer. I stayed close to six months. During that time, I made around two dozen voyages across the sea and visited many towns, trading whatever goods could be traded. It was not an easy life, to be sure, but there was something special about it, something about being out on the water that appealed to me. The story behind the sword haunted me, though, and I knew I had to explore it. So, one day I took Annon on one of my trips and we never came back."

"How long do you expect it will take us to get ahead of Walter?" Angus asked.

"Two days with a fair wind," Andrew answered.

"Then let us pray for a fair wind," Marie said. "I do not relish being at the mercy of wind and wave longer than necessary."

The group entered the thriving town Porthmaddon. Horse-drawn carts loaded with goods passed them coming from and heading to the docks. Dozens of people walked the streets, entering and exiting the wide variety of shops that lined the way. The smell of the sea was strong, filling the nostrils of the visitors with fish and salt. To Andrew, the odor was a familiar friend from the past. To the others, it was a foul stranger, offensive and inescapable. Marie could not help but wrinkle her nose in disgust. Lawrence was little better in hiding his displeasure. Gregory did not appear to be affected by the aroma.

They approached a building that was obviously a tavern based on the sign that reached out to the street. Andrew stopped.

"I need to locate a boat that will take us to Abershire, which should easily get us ahead of Walter and his entourage," Andrew informed them. "You will be able to find food and drink in there," he said, indicating the tavern.

"The stench of this place has all but robbed me of my appetite," Marie said, her face still wrinkled in disgust.

"I will meet you here as soon as I am able to find us transportation," Andrew said as he tugged on Annon's reins. "It is likely that we will not be able to leave until morning, so ask the tavern master if he would be able to arrange accommodations for us for the evening. Lawrence, I would advise that you not over-indulge in the ale this evening. Come morning, you might regret it."

"Do you know how long it has been since I have had a good, stout ale?" Lawrence replied. "I have more than a few nights of missed pints for which I must make-up."

"Suit yourself. You cannot claim that I did not warn you." With that, Andrew continued down the crowded street. The remainder of the group dismounted their horses and after securing them to posts, entered the tavern.

To Andrew, it was as if the town was stuck in time. Every building, every sound, every smell made him feel as if he had left just a few days ago. Though he recognized none of the faces that he passed on the street, he could not suppress a nod and a smile of greeting to many of them. Memories came flowing up from the depths of his mind. That building there, where he had filled numerous carts with goods to be delivered to a town across the water. The tavern across the street where he had spent many evenings with his sea-faring companions and had participated in his share of barroom fights. The inn where he had spent most of the nights while in town, between trade voyages. The ever-present screeching of seagulls floating overhead as they scanned the ground looking for a free meal. The ever-present smell of the bounty of the sea as fishermen peddled the day's catch. He had not spent much time here, yet there was a deep-rooted feeling of belonging in this town.

He guided Annon towards the docks where half-a-dozen boats were being loaded with goods. He looked closely at the ocean vessels and the men scurrying around the decks, some laboring with loading the cargo, some directing the laborers. The boats varied in size and build with some designed for smaller inventories of cargo and shorter trips while others were larger and constructed for more lengthy voyages and more cargo. Two of the smallest boats were no greater than thirty feet in length with beams of ten to fifteen feet. They had a single mast of up to thirty feet in height and a single large square sail. One oar-style rudder protruded off the stern to guide the boats. Two of the vessels were between fifty and sixty feet in length with a beam of up to twenty feet. Both had one castle on the stern. They were fitted with a single mast and a square-rigged single sail. A single rudder mounted on the stern provided for steering. They both appeared sturdy and well capable of handling what foul weather the sea could conjure. It was another boat, however, that prompted Andrew to rein Annon to a stop.

This vessel rose above the others in size and artistry. It was easily over a hundred feet in length with a beam of thirty feet. This was a square-rigged ship with three masts, one amidst-ship, a second extending from the high stern castle, and a third smaller one on the forecastle. A spider-web of rigging stretched from the masts to the deck and rails. The mainsail, which appeared to be undergoing some repairs, had an elaborate design painted on it depicting a majestic red bird of prey in flight, with claws extended as if but moments from grasping its next meal. There were intricate carvings in the wood from bow to stern. The stern castle was dotted with several colorful stained-glass windows. From water to deck was approximately ten feet. Cargo nets that appeared ready to burst from their loads were being hoisted up off the dock and pulled onto the deck, where they were quickly emptied and returned for their next load. Andrew gazed at the mighty vessel in admiration. He spotted a tall, slender, deep-tanned man with head of wind-blown gray hair and a full gray beard standing by the stern rail, closely watching the activity on the deck. Andrew dismounted, looped Annon's reins around a post, and walked down the dock until he was standing below the man. The man on the boat paid no attention to Andrew, if he had even noticed his approach.

"It is a fine-looking vessel, that much I will admit," Andrew called up to the man, "however, word on the docks is that the captain is a drunken lunatic who could not navigate his way to a rational thought let alone a port more than two leagues away." The man on the boat turned his attention to Andrew and glared at him with menacing eyes for about five seconds before responding.

"Aye, a lunatic I may be, but doubt not my ability to navigate my way to beating senseless an impudent landlubber, drunk or sober," the man replied gruffly. "If you care to test me, by all means, the ladder to your thrashing is right there," he said, indicating a rope ladder hanging from the deck rail. Andrew looked at the old man for a moment before grabbing the ladder and as if he had climbed it a thousand times, quickly ascended to the deck. He walked over to the man who obviously was the captain of the ship.

"Your hair is a bit whiter than I remember and I do believe there are a few more wrinkles woven into your cheeks," Andrew said as he gave the appearance of examining the man.

"Your waist is a bit thicker than I remember, and I do believe I see a few strands of gray in that...what is that on your face? Do you call that a beard?" the captain responded, returning Andrew's scrutiny. The men looked at each other for a moment before breaking into wide smiles and hugging each other in greeting.

"Andrew MacLean, as I live and breathe," the captain said, releasing his grip and pulling away. "Never did I think the day would come that you would set foot on the Osprey again."

"Nor I," Andrew replied. "It pleases me to see that the sea has not swallowed the legendary Captain Sigmund Eriksson."

"Bah!" Captain Eriksson scoffed. "I am about as legendary as your ability to hold your ale which, if I am not mistaken, was always the weakest of the crew."

"You have me there," Andrew admitted. He looked at the activity on the deck. "It appears that you are preparing for another journey."

"That we are," the captain confirmed. "It takes wind in the sails to put coins in the purse." He looked at Andrew. "Tell me, my old friend, what brings you back to Porthmaddon and the Osprey?"

"If you happen to have a bottle of Kingston Spiced Rum in your cabin, I will spin you a yarn the likes of which you have never heard," Andrew replied.

"Lad, I have been a man of the sea for over forty years and have heard every tale, from the shortest to the tallest, known to man. However, as I am thirsty, I shall indulge your yarn just the same. You know the way," Captain Eriksson said, gesturing down the stairs.

Chapter 12

Two hours after having boarded the Osprey, Andrew led Annon back through the streets of Porthmaddon to the tavern where he had left his companions. He walked slowly, enjoying the memories that continually reached up from the depths of his mind. Part of him felt as though this was a place where he could live out his years in peace and tranquility. There was a calmness to the town which he enjoyed, although most small towns would seem calm to him after what he had endured during the past five and a half years. Still, the town felt familiar and inviting. That is, until an over-whelming sense of being followed shoved aside the tranquility and replaced it with caution. Andrew did not change his pace, nor did he start looking around, seeking to identify the source of this uneasiness. He continued as before, maintaining a slow walk, looking from building to building as he had been doing, smiling, and nodding greetings to people that he passed. He used his peripheral vision as much as possible to detect anything that might seem suspect, that might indicate he had a shadow within the shadows of the buildings. While he did not see anything that appeared out of the ordinary, he could not shake the feeling that he was being purposefully observed. He soon arrived at the tavern and after securing Annon, he entered the establishment.

The tavern was crowded but it only took Andrew a few seconds to locate his friends. He nudged his way through the throng of customers and sat in the lone empty chair at their table.

"Well, that did not take long," Marie said sarcastically as Andrew lowered himself into the chair.

The Heir

"Were you successful in finding us passage?" Lawrence asked.

"It took a little convincing but yes, I have made arrangements for transportation to Abershire," Andrew acknowledged.

"I do not know if I am relieved or disappointed," Lawrence said as he finished off a pint of ale. "Two hours of sitting here, contemplating two days of being holed-up in a box while bobbing up and down on the water like a piece of driftwood has done nothing positive for my resolve."

"Is it the hours or the ale?" Andrew asked with a smirk.

"Could be the ale," Lawrence replied as he signaled the bar maid for another round.

Angus looked up from his own mug of ale and addressed Andrew.

"Now that you have secured our travel arrangements, would you mind entertaining us as to your plan to rescue the boy?"

"Before we go any further with the plans, there are two matters that must be settled," Andrew replied, looking at Angus.

"Those matters being?" Angus asked.

"You and Gregory."

"Me and Gregory?" Angus repeated. Gregory sat up in his chair at the mention of his name. "How so?" Angus continued.

"To put it mildly, you were highly entrenched in King Talbot's plans to obtain the Dufay Armor and deceive the people by claiming that Talbot was the Heir of DuFay," Andrew replied. He stole a glance at Marie to gauge her sensitivity to the mention of her father's name, but her face did not give any indication of a reaction. Andrew continued.

"The good king and his purposes are no longer with us. Therefore, I must wonder as to your ultimate purpose now."

"You must wonder as to my purpose?" Angus asked incredulously, sensing that his honor was being questioned.

"What is your purpose?" Andrew asked directly, shrugging his shoulders. "I believe it to be a fair question. Your king is gone, and your kingdom is gone. Where lies your loyalty, your purpose?"

"Let me tell you about my loyalty," Angus growled, putting

forth significant effort to contain his anger. "I boarded a boat and sailed across a lake as a diversion so you and your friends could escape Gallard's onslaught. Risking great peril, I returned to the castle to see if I could determine Gallard's plans. I was close enough to him to overhear his instructions to another man to return to Nordham and kidnap the lad, to find you, to obtain the sword, and kill you and anybody with you. I road night and day to the point of exhaustion in hopes that I could forewarn you of this danger. When I finally caught up with you and your friends, you and this one over here," he nodded in Lawrence's direction, "were within minutes of having your intestines sliced out of your bodies. Without hesitation, I leaped in and to put it bluntly, saved your lives. Therefore, I believe it to be quite clear as to where my intentions lie. The one who needs to provide an explanation as to intentions and purposes is this boy over here," Angus said as he looked at Gregory. Everybody else at the table did likewise.

Gregory, who had been silent most of the journey to the town and had not been involved in much of the conversation while waiting for Andrew, answered.

"Call me boy again and we shall step outside and have more than words," Gregory said, glaring at Angus. He was not intimidated by Angus' size, or at least was putting forth a good front. "As of this moment, I am uncertain as to my intentions and purposes. It is time for me to determine the exact nature of my resolve in continuing to accompany you," he said, looking at Andrew. "You will now put forth a full explanation of your accusations against King Gallard, your disappearance so many years ago, and your intentions from this day forward. When you are finished, I shall make my decision."

"Fair enough," Andrew replied and for the second time in as many hours, recited the story of how he had been pulled into the DuFay legend, and the truth behind the legend.

Chapter 13

There was only a hint of glow over the eastern horizon as Andrew rushed around the room, waking his companions. They had all been required to sleep together in the same small room, as it had been the only one available for the night.

"We must leave now," he said as he shook each person in turn. "Get up and get your things together. We cannot waste any time."

"You will receive no argument from me," Marie said sleepily as she pushed herself up from the cot on which she had slept. "I believe someone left a fish to die on this poor excuse for a bed."

"What is the rush?" Angus asked as he quickly pulled his boots on and secured his weapons.

"Trouble. I spotted the men we fought in Nordham just down the street. There are easily twenty of them now. They must have ridden all night to get here," Andrew answered as he gathered his possessions.

"How could he have known this was our destination?" Lawrence asked. "You did not even tell us your plan until we got here."

"Colin is quite intelligent," Gregory answered. After listening to Andrew's story and getting corroboration from Marie and Lawrence, he had elected to stay with them. "He knew that Andrew's first order of business would be to rescue his nephew. They likely escaped their bindings quite quickly and rode hard to catch up to us on the main road. I presume it became evident that we were not traveling on the main road and being that the only other route was by sea, they rode all night to get here."

"It is not important how he knew we were here, what is important is that the numbers against us are too great. Surely Colin learned from our fight yesterday and would make wise use of that knowledge. We cannot fight them."

"Then how do we get away?" Lawrence asked. Though he was never one to shirk from a fight, he knew that Andrew was right.

"I have a plan," Andrew replied. "Follow me."

The group descended the stairs from the second-level room and entered the main area of the tavern. Although there were no customers present at the moment, an older man stood behind the bar, preparing for the crowd that would eventually fill the tavern.

"Do you never sleep, Oluf?" Andrew asked the old man as they stole across the room. "You were standing in that exact same spot when we retired last evening, and the hour was quite late at that."

"There is no time to sleep when you run a tavern in a town full of thirsty seamen who come and go at all hours of the day and night," the tavern owner replied. "My apologies for only being able to provide you with a single room, especially to the lady," he said. "Did you sleep well?"

"Considering that the cot smelled like last week's catch of the day was just removed from it five minutes before we entered the room…" Marie started.

"We slept well enough," Andrew interrupted, not wanting Marie to insult the generosity of the old man. "We appreciate the accommodations."

"What is this plan of yours?" Angus asked as they approached the front door. Andrew reached over and cracked-open the door. He peered down the street and saw Colin with ten other men. They were peering into windows and checking doors to see if any were unlocked. It would be only a matter of minutes before they made it to the tavern.

"I only see eleven of them. That means there are at least that many more checking the rest of the town. This is not going to be easy," Andrew replied, closing the door. "I will walk outside and let them see me. I will lead them away from the tavern, in the opposite direction of the docks. Once we are out of sight, you will grab our horses from the stable and head down to the docks and find the Osprey."

"How will we know which boat is the Osprey?" Marie asked.

"It is the largest boat in sight, you cannot miss it. If that is not enough, there will be the big O-S-P-R-E-Y painted on the stern. Ask for Captain Eriksson, he will be awake and preparing to get underway. Let him know that our departure has become a bit more urgent than it was when I spoke with him last evening and we need to set sail as quickly as possible. I will evade Colin and his men and join you."

"And if you do not show up?" Marie asked. "How long are we to wait?"

"You do not wait," Andrew replied succinctly. "If I am not there by the time the sails are set and the lines cast, you leave. You disembark in Abershire as planned and make your way to Stanwyck. If I am able, I will meet you there. If I am not able…well, Stanwyck would be a good place for you to settle anyway."

"I am coming with you," Lawrence said. "You know very well that you need someone to cover your back."

"Not this time," Andrew replied, shaking his head. "I know this town and its nooks and crannies. I can move very quickly on my own and should have no trouble eluding Colin and his men." He could tell that Lawrence was about to argue and cut him off. "There will be no discussion of it. There are at least ten more of Colin's men somewhere in town and if you run into them, you will need every sword possible to escape. This is how it must be done."

"You are a stubborn one," Marie said, concern obvious in her voice.

"Having you call me stubborn is more than a little ironic," Andrew replied, smiling at her. They locked eyes for a few seconds before Andrew continued, something unspoken passing between them.

"Get ready," he said to the group, reaching for the door handle. He cracked it open and saw Colin and his men just thirty yards down the street. "I will see you on the Osprey." With those final words, he stepped outside and closed the door behind him.

Within five seconds there was a shout from Colin as he spotted Andrew.

"MacLean!" he yelled out, not concerned about waking those who were still sleeping within hearing distance. "MacLean!"

Andrew turned towards Colin and did his best to appear startled. He immediately turned and ran up the street as if in panic. As planned, Colin and his men ran after him, leaving the street deserted.

Lawrence cracked the tavern door and seeing not a soul on the street, turned to the others.

"They are gone. The horses are in the stable behind the tavern. Quickly!" The four companions exited the tavern and ran down the alley to the stable where they hastily retrieved their horses and took off for the docks.

While Andrew was sufficiently convinced that he could elude his pursuers, he knew that they were much younger than he was and likely had much more stamina, and the longer that the chase lasted, the less his chances of successfully getting away and getting to the Osprey without being seen. He darted down one alley and then the next, zig-zagging his way through the town. He could hear Colin shouting orders to his men, splitting them up to cover more ground and cut-off Andrew's escape routes. This actually played to Andrew's favor, as he was more than confident that he could take-on and subdue one or two of his pursuers at a time. Andrew paused in a dark doorway that was partially blockaded by a stack of wooden crates. He saw the three-foot long handle of a large sledgehammer leaning up against the door and grabbed it. Within thirty seconds, two of the men chasing after him cautiously walked down the alley towards him. It was clear that they were inspecting every possible place Andrew could be hiding and it would be only a matter of seconds before they stumbled upon his actual hiding place. Their swords were drawn, which most likely gave them a false sense of security. It was the only advantage that Andrew might have, them being just the least bit less alert than they otherwise would be. Just as the first man started to poke his head around the crates, Andrew swung the hammer and slammed it into the man's chest, knocking the breath out of him. As he collapsed to the ground, Andrew pulled the hammer back and swung it at the second man. Having seen his companion go down, the man was prepared and stepped-back and the hammer missed. Almost simultaneously the man swung his sword at Andrew. Andrew's reflexes brought the handle of the hammer up to block the incoming strike. The sword slammed into the wooden handle, breaking it in two. As the man drew the sword back for another strike, Andrew did not pause but launched himself at the man and slammed him up against a wall. Before the attacker could get his balance, Andrew rammed a knee into the man's midsection, knocking the breath out of him. Andrew threw a massive uppercut to the man's jaw, snapping his head backwards and further weakening him. Without pausing, Andrew grabbed the man's head with both of his hands and slammed it into the wall, knocking the man into unconsciousness. Andrew turned his attention to the first attacker who was striving to catch his breath. The man was on his hands and knees, working his way back to his feet, but Andrew would have none of that. He sent a powerful forward kick to the side of the man's head and robbed him of his consciousness, too. Giving a final look to the men to ensure that they were out of the chase, Andrew disappeared down the alley.

Lawrence, Angus, Marie, and Gregory had been able to retrieve their horses, including Andrew's, without being seen and made their way to the docks. As they turned the corner around the last building, Lawrence, who was in the lead, held up his hand and stopped. The others nearly ran into him.

"What is it?" Angus asked, immediately behind Lawrence.

"It would appear that our escape by the sea has been anticipated," he replied. "The other half of Colin's men are stationed on the docks. We cannot get to the Osprey without being detected."

"What do we do now?" Marie asked anxiously. "We are all but trapped. We cannot go back through the town lest we run into Colin and his men."

"We could fight them," Angus said, his right hand going to the hilt of his sword. "The docks are narrow, which would help offset the advantage they have in numbers. They would not all be able to fight us at once. Plus, they are likely exhausted after riding all night. I am confident we would have no difficulty in disposing of them...permanently."

"Gregory, it is most likely that you have friends among them," Lawrence said. "Are you willing to fight your friends, even kill them, if necessary? If we engage them, there can be no hesitation on your part."

"There has to be another way," Marie said almost pleadingly.

"There is," Gregory answered. "At least, I hope there is. I can use my familiarity with them to my advantage and their disadvantage."

"How?" Angus asked. "Do you believe that simply by being one of them you will be able to talk our way past them? Surely Colin has told them of your traitorous actions. You will just as likely be skewered the moment you get within range of their swords."

"We shall see," Gregory said, moving up from the rear. He handed the reins of his horse to Angus. "If I am wrong, well, perhaps I can provide a distraction so you can otherwise escape unseen."

"Foolish boy," Angus muttered.

"I told you to not call me boy again," Gregory said, menace in his voice, "and if you did, we would have more than words to exchange. I will keep that promise. Now take the horses and hide behind that building over there. I will clear the way." With that, he headed down the long walkway to where the boats were docked.

"I have a bad feeling about this," Lawrence said as he led the others to their hiding place. "What is to keep him from trying to redeem himself by leading his friends to us?"

"Nothing," Angus replied. "Absolutely nothing."

They moved their horses to the side of the building where they would be completely out of the sight Gallard's men. Then, they moved to where they could observe what transpired on the dock. They watched Gregory as he headed down the boardwalk in what seemed to be an increasingly rushed pace.

"Why is he in such a hurry?" Marie asked.

"Perhaps he is eager to prove his loyalty to Gallard by turning on us," Angus responded, disgust riding his words. "He is showing how anxious he is to get away from us."

"I cannot believe that," Marie countered. "He is in just as much danger as we are. They must know that he refused to join the others in the fight in Nordham and that he voluntarily left with us. I cannot imagine how he plans to talk his way out of his treason."

"We shall know soon enough," Lawrence said. "He has reached them."

Lawrence, Marie, and Angus watched as Gregory approached the first of Gallard's men. They had been dispersed along the dock, in effect blocking passage to every boat, but at the sight of Gregory they gathered together. The morning light was still too weak for them to see the confrontation in detail, and they were too far away to hear what was being said. It was obvious, however, that a heated argument was in progress. Most of Gallard's men had their swords drawn and were taking offensive positions around Gregory. Gregory, in turn, was gesturing strongly, almost pleadingly, as he spoke. At one point one of the men closest to Gregory reached out to grab him by the arm but Gregory jerked his arm away and unsheathed his sword, as if preparing for a fight. Instead of attacking, though, he turned the sword around and handed it to the man and lifted his hands into the air.

"This does not look like it is going well," Lawrence said. "Whatever he is saying, it does not appear to be working in his best interest."

"Or ours," Angus added. "He is going to deliver us to them to save his own life. We need to prepare ourselves for escape."

"Not yet," Marie said as she watched the exchange on the dock. "There is still hope."

Gregory continued his pleading. At one point, he turned and pointed up the boardwalk.

"There goes your hope," Angus stated sarcastically. "He just told them where we are hiding."

"I am not so sure," Marie replied, straining to see in the dim light. "I do not think he was pointing at us."

As they watched, Gregory turned and motioned for the men to follow him. The men looked at each other, obviously unsure what to do. Gregory motioned even more urgently and finally, the men appeared to succumb to his pleadings and started to move. He ran up the boardwalk and the men followed. They reached the end of the boardwalk and Gregory turned up the street, in the opposite direction of Lawrence, Marie and Angus. The threesome looked at each other questioningly but did not hesitate as the last of Gallard's men disappeared down the street. They quickly led the horses down the dock and towards the Osprey.

While his companions were safely boarding the Osprey, Andrew continued his efforts to elude his pursuers and find a way to make it to the ship. While running down an alley between a bakery and a dry goods store, Andrew found an unlocked door for each building, directly opposite each other. He cracked open the door to the bakery, then entered the dry goods store and closed the door. He looked around for something he could use as a non-lethal weapon. His foot kicked a small two-gallon keg that was full and heavy. He picked up the keg and waited. Fifteen seconds later he could hear footsteps coming down the alley and two figures passed the tiny window near the door. They paused at the open bakery door, suspecting that Andrew had entered the building to hide. Before they could investigate, Andrew burst through his door and slammed the keg against the back of the head of the man closest to him, knocking him out. The second man, sword in hand, slashed at Andrew but Andrew easily dodged the strike. As the man tried to position himself for a second attack, Andrew rushed him and slammed him against the wall. Seemingly unphased, the man swung his sword-hand at Andrew and caught him in the side of the head. The blow was not enough to knock Andrew out, but it was enough to knock him backward and off-balance. With barely a hesitation, the man drew his sword back and rushed forward, aiming to skewer Andrew's chest. Andrew spun away and the man's momentum caused the sword to imbed itself in the wooden wall of the dry goods store. The second that the man spent trying to pull the sword out of the wall was all that Andrew needed. With all of his strength, Andrew brought down a mighty two-fisted blow to the back of the man's head. The attacker immediately went limp and fell to the ground. Before Andrew could take a breath, three of Gallard's men appeared at the end of the alley. They spotted Andrew and raced after him.

"This is NOT how I had envisioned this day starting," he said to himself as he raced to the back end of the alley and turned the corner. He was not able to stop himself as an unexpected wall appeared before him and Andrew ran into it.

"This is new," he said to himself. "The one place for someone to build a wall in the past five years." There were no doors in any of the three walls that now boxed him in. He was trapped. Thus far he had used non-lethal measures to subdue his attackers, but he knew that the time for half-measures was over. Having seen their comrades beaten, there was no doubt in Andrew's mind that the three men now closing in on him were out for blood. He drew his sword and prepared for combat.

"You have put up a good fight, MacLean, but there is nowhere else for you to run," the man in the middle said.

"Colin," Andrew replied, recognizing the voice. "I must say, I am quite impressed that you were able to track us to Porthmaddon. Unfortunately, you should have stayed in Nordham. I cannot afford the risk of you continuing to delay me in rescuing my nephew."

"That is a task I am afraid you are not going to be able to complete," Colin replied. He nodded to the man on his right who lifted a bow and notched an arrow, pulling it back and aiming it at Andrew's heart. "While I could end your life here and now, I believe the reward from Gallard for bringing you to him alive would be greater than the satisfaction of seeing that arrow protruding from your chest. Therefore, you are going to drop your sword, lay on the ground face-down, and place your hands behind your back. You will be bound hand and foot and that is how you shall remain until I place you in front of Gallard. If you fail to comply, then Rutger shall loose his arrow and your life will be ended."

While Colin was speaking, Andrew took note of a shadow moving along the top of the building behind the men. It was definitely a person, but that is all that Andrew could discern. His attention was diverted so he did not fully hear Colin's question the first time.

"I say again, MacLean, what will it be?" Colin asked, his patience running out.

Andrew slowly lowered his sword and laid it on the ground. He went to his knees as if complying with Colin's directions. Seeing Andrew unarmed and appearing to give up, Rutger released the tension on the bow. As if on cue, the shadow on the building dropped to the ground behind him. Before anybody could react, the figure swung a five-foot long bow staff and struck Rutger on the back of the head, knocking him out. In what appeared to be a well-coordinated and choreographed move that boarded on dancing, the shadowy figure twirled and slammed the wooden staff into Colin's back. Colin screamed in pain and fell to his knees, providing an excellent line of attack to his head which the shadow did not hesitate to exploit. The third man, not fully comprehending what was going on, had yet to move. The end of the staff was thrust into his solar plexus, knocking the breath out of him. As he bent over, the shadow slammed the staff into the back of his head, knocking him out. All this took place in just over five seconds. Andrew was still on his knees as his savior stepped forward. The person was wearing a hooded cloak which prevented Andrew from being able to tell anything about the one who had just saved his life. A gloved hand reached up and pulled the hood back, revealing a face Andrew did not think he would ever see again.

"I believe a word or two of gratitude is in order," a feminine voice said. The woman was about five feet, eight inches tall, lean, and obviously quite agile and powerful. Her choice of clothing did well in hiding her womanly figure. Her raven-black hair flowed down her back and her green eyes seemed to practically glow in the dim lighting.

"Victoria," Andrew said, grabbing his sword and standing. "What a surprise. I see you have learned some new skills over the past few years."

"And I see that you still like to fight against the odds," she replied.

"Old habits and all," he stated. "It is a situation I have been finding myself in all too frequently recently. While I would love to stay and catch up on the past five years, I am short on time. Therefore, I will offer my sincere gratitude for your assistance and bid you farewell."

"Well, that is certainly more than you offered the last time you left town," she retorted accusingly.

"I would that I had time to explain," Andrew replied apologetically, "but I have traveling companions with whom I must rendezvous. Let me just say that we have a very urgent task to complete and there remain nearly a dozen men seeking to stop us, and it is only a matter of time before they are successful in finding us and doing just that."

"By urgent task, you mean rescuing your nephew, correct?" she asked.

"How did you know?" Andrew responded, surprised.

"You know well how small of a town it is," she answered. "As for your companions, they are already on the Osprey and as for those other men chasing after you, they are currently on the far end of town."

"Those green eyes of yours have certainly seen a lot this morning," Andrew noted, looking at her a little suspiciously.

"That they have," she replied. "They have also seen the Osprey preparing to set sail and if you wish to not be left behind, then you best follow me." Without waiting for Andrew to respond, Victoria turned and hurried back through the alley and toward the main street. She only paused a second to ensure that none of Gallard's men were in sight and then ran down the street. Andrew, still marveling at her sudden appearance yet feeling somewhat emasculated by having been rescued by her, remained close on her heels.

As they approached the docks, Andrew could see that the Osprey was already moving. Hearing shouts behind them, Andrew turned his head and saw at least fifteen of Gallard's men giving chase. He and Victoria ran as fast as they could down the boardwalk and onto the pier to which the Osprey had been birthed. The ship was picking up speed as an early morning breeze filled her sails and there was no way she was going to be able to stop and permit proper boarding. A large cargo net fell from the side of the ship, dangling a mere two feet from the water line. Andrew could see his companions standing along the rail, yelling encouragements for him to hurry. With a final burst of speed, Andrew leaped off the dock and grasped the net. He felt Victoria do the same. As they climbed, Victoria lost her grip and nearly fell into the water where she could easily have been swept under the ship. Andrew's quick reflexes allowed him to grasp her left hand and swing her back to the net, where she reclaimed her grip with her right hand and was able to find the net with her feet. Andrew gave her a smug grin.

"That makes us even in the 'lifesaving' category today," he said as they continued the climb. It took less than a minute for them to haul themselves over the side rail and nearly collapse on the deck, both trying to catch their breath. Gallard's men could only stand at the end of the dock, watching the ship sail away.

"That was cutting it a bit too close," Lawrence said as he reached down to help Andrew to his feet. However, in doing so, he caught sight of Victoria and instead of grasping Andrew's outstretched hand, he offered his hand to her. "Allow me to provide some assistance," he said with a mischievous grin. Victoria hesitated a moment, then accepted his hand and was pulled to her feet.

"I am Lawrence Morecraft," he said, introducing himself without releasing her hand. "And who might you be?"

"That," Captain Eriksson said, walking down the steps from the stern castle, "is my daughter, Victoria. And you would do well to release her hand."

Lawrence looked at the captain and then back at Victoria, who shrugged her shoulders, and let go of her hand. "I was simply being a gentleman," he said with an innocent grin and a slight bow of his head.

"Victoria," Captain Eriksson addressed his daughter, "I did not know that you would be joining us on this voyage. If I recall correctly, and I am certain that I do, you generally prefer land under your feet and not the sea." His tone was almost one of chiding.

"I assure you it was not my intention when I awoke this morning," she replied and then nodded towards Andrew. "However, after saving James' life, I felt it less than prudent to remain in town and seeing how you were preparing to set sail, it seemed joining you was the most expedient venue for escape."

"James?" Marie asked, looking from Victoria to Andrew inquisitively. "Who is James?"

"He is standing right beside you," Victoria answered, pointing to Andrew. "James Doogan." Marie shot a questioning, almost accusing, look at Andrew.

"Uh, Victoria," Andrew said with an almost apologetic smile, "there is something I must tell you. My name is not James Doogan. It is Andrew MacLean."

Victoria looked at Andrew, confusion in her eyes, then looked at her father and then at the others. She looked back at Andrew.

"You must understand, when I was here so many years ago, there were circumstances that required me to keep my name a secret," he said in explanation. "If I had stayed longer, of course, I would have told you my real name."

"So, you lied to me," Victoria said, her confusion beginning to turn to anger. "All that time, you lied to me."

"To be fair, I lied to everybody," Andrew responded with a joking tone.

"I am not everybody!" Victoria retorted, giving in to her anger. "I cannot believe that considering all the time we spent together, you never told me your real name! You did not even bother telling me before you slipped out of town with nary of word of fair thee well!"

"Does anybody else smell the deja-vu floating along the breeze?" Lawrence asked with a big smile on his face, enjoying the discomfort that Andrew had to be feeling.

"Yes, there does seem to be a pattern forming," Marie answered. She glared at Andrew. "At least this one appears to be of an acceptable age and not so young."

"Now, that situation with Naomi was not my fault and as I told you, I did not encourage her in any way. Victoria is older, much older than Naomi," Andrew retorted. As soon as the words left his mouth, he realized how they sounded and he looked at Victoria, whose eyes were throwing darts at him.

"Wait, that did not come out as I had intended," Andrew said, trying to recover from what Victoria surely had taken as an insult. "You are not old, that is not what I meant. You see, Marie was referring to a friend of mine from a few years ago, she was just a friend, a young girl who had something of an attraction to me, and…"

"I am not interested in hearing your explanations and excuses," Victoria said dismissively, waiving him off. "You made it clear five years ago when you left town without saying goodbye that you did not consider me worthy of explanations." She turned to the captain. "Father, you know where to find me if you have need of me." With that, Victoria turned and passed through a doorway that led to the lower decks. The others were left in silence for a few moments. Captain Eriksson had a look of exasperation on his face. Lawrence could barely contain the laughter that was begging to come out. Angus' look was one of impatience. Gregory's expression was more of confusion than anything. Marie's amusement at Andrew's predicament could not be stifled.

"I like her," she finally said, breaking the silence. "I think she and I could be great friends."

"That would be SO wonderful," Andrew replied sarcastically. "We should get below decks and prepare for the voyage. I want to make sure that the horses are well secured." He walked across the deck and through a doorway, descending a set of stairs.

"Below decks it is," Lawrence said, and the rest of the group followed Andrew.

Chapter 14

A steady thirty-knot wind drove the Osprey across the rolling sea under a gray sky. Salty spray peppered the deck as the wind picked up droplets of water from the white caps that broke off the waves surrounding the ship. Deckhands scurried about the ship tending to chores as the first mate barked out orders. Andrew stood solidly facing the wind, enjoying the periodic mist that showered his face. It had not taken him long to get his sea-legs back and he could keep his balance during all but the highest of waves. Lawrence, on the other hand, was not fairing as well. He leaned over the rail for the third time in the past ten minutes, losing whatever food he had tried to eat in the past several hours.

"It is possible that I may have had a pint or two in excess last night," Lawrence managed to say as he straightened back up and gripped the rail to maintain his balance.

"Or four. Rest easy, you shall get used to the motion of the ship before you know it," Andrew replied, patting Lawrence on the back. "Plus, I doubt that there is a morsel left in your stomach to regurgitate."

"Truer words have never been spoken," Lawrence replied.

"Let us join the others below decks. The motion of the ship shall be somewhat less intense, and we should finalize our plans for when we dock," Andrew suggested. Lawrence did not hesitate to accept the offer and the two men left the wet, windy weather for the drier and warmer bowels of the boat. They joined Angus, Marie, and Gregory two decks down.

"How are the three of you faring?" Andrew asked as he and Lawrence sat at the table around which the others were gathered. Gregory appeared to not be suffering the nauseating effects of the boat's motion. Angus was putting forth a strong front, but the color of his face and general expression showed that he, too, was not enjoying the ride. Marie had her head down on the table, her forehead resting on her folded arms.

"I despise you, Andrew MacLean," Marie managed as she lifted her head a few inches. "You and your short-cut. If this was such a great idea, why did we not come to Nordham this way in the first place? We would have beaten Walter and been well gone by the time he arrived."

"Are you insane? Sail at this time of year?" Andrew answered, trying to lighten the mood a little, but was not successful. "Storms are quite common on these waters at this time of the year, and they can be most violent. There are more than a few vessels sitting on the seabed that would attest to that. The winds come out of the northwest as the seasons change and would have been against us, thereby negating any time advantage we would otherwise have enjoyed. It is only out of desperation that I have chosen this method of travel. Captain Eriksson assured me that while the voyage may not be the most comfortable, the winds and waves should not rise to the point of being great threats to us."

"How comforting," Marie said, resting her head back on her arms.

"What is your plan?" Angus asked, always looking to get down to business if not having an excuse to take his mind off the stomach-churning motion of the ship.

"Abershire is less than a day's ride from Stanwyck," Andrew answered. "When the ship docks, we shall make for Stanwyck. Being a prominent village on the main route from Nordham to Durinburg, I am confident that Walter will pause there to get supplies and rest for the night. That will give us the opportunity to ambush him and get Alexander. It should be at night when they are the least on guard."

"You do recall that he has a dozen men with him that we know of," Angus reminded Andrew. "There are just five of us. I do not like those odds."

"Six," a voice called out from behind them. Everybody turned to see Victoria. "What can I say? I have a weakness for rescuing men and boys." She approached the group. "My father explained to me in full your situation and I wish to help."

"This is not your fight," Andrew reminded her. "It could have long-lasting consequences that may not be in your favor."

"Do not try to dissuade me...what is your name again? Albert? Allen? Oh, yes, Andrew. Do not try to dissuade me, Andrew, you know it will do you no good."

"Oh, I definitely like her," Marie said. "She must come along."

"Very well," Andrew conceded, "that gives us six."

"We are still at a great disadvantage," Angus noted. "If we were able to take four or five of them out before they knew what was happening and even the numbers, based on our skills with the sword, it would put the odds in our favor."

"I would prefer that we avoid engaging in a physical altercation," Andrew said. "I do not wish to put Alexander in harm's way."

"Andrew, Walter put Alexander in harm's way the moment he kidnapped him," Lawrence said. "You have to know that based on Walter's contempt for you, there is no way he will relinquish Alexander voluntarily. Blood will be spilt, of that you can have no doubt."

"You also know that we cannot take prisoners," Angus continued.

Andrew considered the words of Lawrence and Angus and knew that they were right. Walter would never return to Gallard without Alexander, which meant that if they were successful in rescuing Alexander, Walter would simply come after them again and again until Alexander was in his possession and this time, ensure that Andrew was dead. There would be a fight to the death, it could not be avoided.

"We will need help," Andrew finally admitted. "Patrick, back in Stanwyck, helped once before, perhaps he will be willing to help again. We might be able to recruit one or two other men to help as well."

"Then what?" Angus asked. "We cannot know that Gallard's instructions to Walter were not to either bring him back alive or dispose of him altogether. No matter how many men we have, if Walter sees the fight turning against him and that defeat is certain, he could very well take Alexander's life. You know that Alexander will at least be bound, if not protected by a dedicated guard. We need to determine a way to protect Alexander or move the fight away from him."

Andrew thought for a moment, looking around the table at the others. How could they avoid Alexander being caught in the middle of the fight? His eyes fell on Gregory, and an idea formed in his mind.

"Gregory, how are your acting skills?" Andrew asked with a sly smile.

Chapter 15

S ir, there is a rider coming up behind us. He is riding hard."
Walter turned to the man making the report.

"Is he alone?" he asked.

"As far as I can determine, he is alone," the man confirmed.

"MacLean?" Walter asked.

"I cannot say for sure whether it is MacLean or not. He was too far away. He should be here in a few minutes."

"We are close enough to Stanwyck that it could be anybody," Walter said. He looked up through the tree canopy at the dimming daylight. "Tell the men to make camp, we can rest for the night and resupply in the morning. Station two men on the road to intercept the rider. If it is MacLean, bring him to me. Otherwise, let the rider go."

The guard acknowledged the order and passed the word to make camp. He then chose another guard to accompany him to confront the rider.

"Do not put hope in rescue," Walter said to Alexander who was bound and sat on a horse that was tethered to Walter's horse. "Even if Andrew somehow managed to escape my men in Nordham, as mighty a fighter as he is, it will not be possible for him to defeat all twelve of my men." Walter dismounted his horse and helped Alexander off of his. A few minutes later, the man who had originally reported the solo rider approached Walter and this time, he was not alone. Following him was a young man, slouched over, appearing exhausted and barely able to keep from falling off his horse. His mid-section was wrapped with a blood-stained bandage and a similar bandage was wrapped around his head. His clothes were filthy, but still recognizable as those belonging to one of Gallard's guards. His face, arms and legs were also partially caked with dirt. Walter approached them as their horses were brought to a stop.

"Who is this?" Walter asked, looking at the stranger. "Boy, what is your name?"

"I am Gregory Albright," the rider said, the words hardly more than a harsh whisper. "A loyal servant to King Edwin Gallard."

Walter looked at the other man questioningly. "Did we lose a man on the trail?" he asked.

"No sir," the man replied. "All of our men are accounted for. He claims that he has come straight from Nordham."

Walter looked back at Gregory suspiciously. "What is your purpose? Why are you here?"

"To warn you," Gregory answered, fighting to keep his eyes open. "I was one of the guards tasked with disposing of Andrew MacLean after you and your men left Nordham. As we commenced to engage with him and his companions, several of MacLean's old friends, traitors to King Gallard, joined with him and fought against us. We were outnumbered and it was nothing short of a slaughter. I alone survived."

"How is it that you escaped with your life while others did not?" Walter inquired accusingly.

"They must have presumed me dead," Gregory replied. "I was struck in the head and rendered unconscious. It must not have been long. When I regained my senses, MacLean and his men were standing not too far from me and my fallen comrades. I could hear them making plans to rescue the boy. They eventually moved away to gather supplies and make preparations for coming for the boy. When I was sure they were out of sight, I ran to my horse and have been riding as hard as I could short of killing my horse to catch-up to you and your men."

"Never have I known a man as resilient as Andrew MacLean,"

Walter said, exasperation in his voice. "He just will not die. How many men are with him?"

"Easily a dozen men," Gregory answered. "Perhaps more if he was able to convince others to join him. MacLean was a popular man and is very persuasive. From what I overheard of their conversation, the other men were none too happy with the kidnapping of the boy."

"They should worry less about a boy and more about being loyal to their king," Walter countered. "It will be a lesson they learn none too gently. How far behind do you estimate them to be?"

"A couple of hours, perhaps three," Gregory replied. "They were intent on riding hard and fast to catch up with you as quickly as possible. They presumed you would take rest and re-supply in Stanwyck. It is their plan to attack after dark when the men are sleeping."

Walter did not say anything for nearly half a minute as he considered Gregory's report. Finally, he looked at the guard who had led Gregory to him.

"Johansen, take the men one-half mile up the road. Create a blockade by cutting down trees and laying them across the road. Fifty feet beyond the barrier, cut two additional trees just to the point of them falling but secure them with ropes so they remain upright. Station four men on either side of the road with bows and arrows. Station two men by the ropes. You and the remaining guard will be stationed just on this side of the barrier. When MacLean and his companions stop at the barrier, have the men slice the ropes and allow the two trees to fall, boxing-in MacLean. The men along the side of the road will then let loose with a merciless barrage of arrows until they have none left. If MacLean or any of his men remain standing, then our men shall attack with their swords and finish them off. I want MacLean dead, here, tonight. I want this thorn removed from my side once and for all. I will remain here with the boy."

"Consider it done," Johansen said as he moved away to carry out the orders.

"I can fight," Gregory said as he struggled to stay on his horse. "Just tell me what to do."

"You shall stay with me and help guard the boy," Walter said. "Your wounds will all but render you useless in a fight. My men can manage MacLean. Go set up a tent for you and the boy and get a fire started. There is some food, though not much, but we will resupply in Stanwyck in the morning. Then tend to your wounds as best as you can."

"As you wish," Gregory said, slowly sliding off his horse. He staggered for a few steps, then paused to gain his balance.

"One last thing, soldier," Walter said. "If anybody other than me approaches you and has intentions of taking the boy away, no matter the reason, kill the boy. Those are the orders of King Gallard himself."

"Understood," Gregory replied as he shuffled away.

Chapter 16

T wo hours had passed since Walter gave instructions to his men to set-up the ambush for Andrew, and the last rays of the late-evening sun fought to break through the foliage of the forest. Walter sat by his fire, anxious for word of Andrew's demise while also contemplating his future. He held the DuFay Sword in his hands, looking it over and over, marveling at its beauty and detail. Walter kept imagining the look of satisfaction on Gallard's face when handed the sword and the boy. It would be a step closer to realizing his ultimate goal of ruling his own land, under Gallard of course. At least, for a while. His ambitions reached much higher than that.

"It is difficult to take your eyes off of it, no?" a voice called out from the darkness. Walter looked up, startled. He had been so enthralled with the sword and his dreams that his usually sharp senses failed to warn him of danger.

"Show yourself!" Walter commanded as he stood up, his senses now back to their normal state of attunement and telling him that a threat was present. He peered into the darkness and could barely make out a shadow as it moved from behind a large tree. As the light from his campfire revealed the individual, Walter spat out the name with disgust.

"MacLean!" he growled, anger welling up inside of him.

"The one and only," Andrew replied, then corrected himself. "Well, actually, not the one and only MacLean. I mean, there are other MacLeans, I am sure. My mother for instance, poor woman, frightened something awful by you and your men. You should not have done that to her, it was quite rude. And then, of course, my nephew, Alexander. He is most definitely a MacLean."

"Both of whom, I assure you, shall join you in death quite soon," Walter responded.

"That is quite the presumption on your part," Andrew replied, taking a guarded step closer to Walter, his hand resting on the hilt of his sword."

"No so much," Walter countered. "I have given orders tonight for the execution of your dear mother. One of my guards has already departed to carry out that order. And I have given instructions to the man guarding the boy to kill him if anybody other than me approaches them. Should you try to take the boy away, his throat will be slit before you can call out his name."

"You mean Gregory, the injured young lad who rode into your camp two or so hours ago?" Andrew asked innocently. A questioning look crossed Walter's face. "He is with us, as a matter of fact, so Alexander is quite safe. You have been so intent on the sword that you failed to notice they stole into the night some time ago, not twenty yards from where you sat. You are getting careless in your old age, Walter. And as for my mother, I assure you that all your men have been accounted for and there is nobody riding back to assassinate her. The ambush, well, it was not a bad idea in and of itself. Had we not arrived several hours before you did, it might have actually worked."

"How did you get here ahead of us?" Walter asked, confused. "You certainly did not pass us on the road and there are no other roads leading from Nordham to Stanwyck." Andrew could see that Walter was stalling, working on a plan to attack Andrew.

"No other land roads," Andrew responded. "Fortunately, I know the sea and I know others who do so much more than I. A well-rigged and handled ship can cut days off an otherwise long land trip. You can thank Gallard for that. No, wait, I am afraid you will not be able to do so. Your last words to Gallard, whatever they were, will indeed be your last words to him."

"What of my men?" Walter asked, brushing off Andrew's threat.

"Your men," Andrew said thoughtfully. "Your men have likely met their demise by now. My people ambushed them as they waited to ambush us. Ironic, is it not? And now, our game of chase shall come to an end. This business of the Heir of Dufay shall come to an end. Gallard shall waste his remaining days, however many they may be, chasing that which he will never attain, that to which he has no right. The name Dufay shall fade into history once again, as it did so long ago."

"Then let us end this game here and now," Walter said confidently as he dropped the DuFay Sword and withdrew his own from its sheath. "Your very name has become vile to me, and I shall take immense joy in ridding the earth of it."

Instead of charging violently, Walter slowly circled around his campfire and Andrew did likewise, keeping the fire between them as the two men sized each other up one last time. Their last fight, nearly six years ago, proved them to be all but equals when it came to one-on-one combat. But tonight, one of them would prove to be more than the other's equal.

Walter made the first move, leaping over the fire and throwing a downward blow towards Andrew with the intent of ending the fight before it really began. However, Andrew anticipated this move and even before Walter's feet were on the ground, Andrew had stepped forward and to the side, dodging Walter's sword and restoring a safe distance between them. Walter landed on the ground and immediately whirled to face Andrew, and only his battle-trained reflexes allowed him to move just enough to dodge the knife that Andrew had hurled at his chest.

"Enough of this," Walter growled and stepped over the campfire, ignoring the heat from the two-foot-tall flames. He sent a slashing blow towards Andrew's mid-section which Andrew parried easily. Walter quickly reversed directions and brought a blow from the opposite direction, which Andrew dodged. Andrew then stepped-forward and sent his own powerful blow towards Walter, which the large man easily deflected. Andrew continued raining blows down upon Walter, all of which were parried. Walter then returned the favor, sending multiple salvos at Andrew. Mindful of his balance and surroundings, Andrew backed-up while defending himself against the onslaught. He remembered Walter being strong, but it seemed to Andrew that Walter's strength had only grown over the years. His strength may have grown, but his strategy had not. He continued to rely on brute strength to attack Andrew instead of a calculated and orchestrated plan. Andrew patiently waited for the right moment, the very briefest of moments when Walter would raise his sword overhead for one final, battle-ending blow. And then the moment came. Andrew could see the rage in Walter's eyes as the man raised his sword high over his head and set all his weight to accompany the downward blow. Andrew did not pause. He thrust his left hand towards Walter's mid-section, a dagger with a five-inch blade magically appearing in his hand and sank the blade into Walter's gut to the hilt. At first, Walter did not appear to notice what had to be a very painful injury. He brought the sword down upon Andrew, who did all he could to brace against the blow. There was another barely perceptible change in the timing of Walter's attack, the pain from the dagger finally registering in his brain, and Andrew took advantage of it. He lunged forward, ramming his shoulder into Walter's chest, knocking him backward and off-balance. Walter took several unsteady steps back, trying to regain proper fighting balance, but Andrew did not pause. It was his turn again to rain blow after blow upon Walter. Walter continued to deflect each blow. Somewhere during the melee, he was able to grab the dagger that was in his stomach. He feigned going to the ground and when Andrew altered his attack accordingly, Walter quickly drove Andrew's own dagger into his thigh. Andrew cried out in pain and took a couple of steps backward. He quickly pulled the dagger out and threw it into the darkness. Even though Walter was bleeding heavily from his wound, Andrew felt that his own wound was the worst, as it threw off his balance.

Walter took notice of this weakness in Andrew and went on the offensive. He continually changed his angle of attack, from left to right, from high to low, which required Andrew to continually alter his balance and stance to ward off the blows. The pain in his thigh grew with each step, each movement. He had to do something different before his leg gave out on him. He had to put Walter in a defensive position. With perfect timing, as Walter drew his sword back for another massive strike, Andrew stepped forward and struck Walter as hard as he could in the midsection. This time, Walter felt the pain. Andrew punched him again, his hand covered with Walter's blood. Walter cried out but Andrew could not tell whether it was a cry of pain or a cry of frustration. With Andrew so close to him, Walter could not fully swing his sword at Andrew so instead, he slammed the hilt of his sword against Andrew's temple. The powerful blow stunned Andrew but instead of stepping backward, Andrew lunged toward Walter and wrapped his arms around the beastly man, holding on as tightly as he could and pushing Walter backward. Walter brought the hilt of the sword down on Andrew's right shoulder, narrowly missing the back of Andrew's head. Pain shot down Andrew's right arm and nearly made him drop his sword, his only defense against Walter's vicious sword strikes. Andrew's thigh protested mightily at the task that was being thrust upon it and Andrew knew that he would not be able to keep pushing Walter back. Therefore, he changed tactics. With Walter resisting being pushed back, all his strength was focused on a forward direction. Andrew suddenly stopped pushing Walter and instead, shifted his momentum and stepped backward, pulling Walter with him. After just two steps, Andrew pivoted and with a mighty heave, threw Walter to the ground. Walter's head hit a large rock, opening a large scalp wound and nearly knocking him unconscious. Andrew stomped on Walter's right wrist, cracking the bones and causing Walter to drop his sword. And just like that, the fight was over. Andrew kicked Walter's sword a safe distance away, then stood triumphantly over this foe.

"Your heart is filled with hate for me, though I have never done anything to you to deserve such hatred," Andrew said, looking down at the defeated foe. "You hate me for the sake of another man, who has deceived you beyond what you could imagine. You hate me for your own ambitions." As Andrew spoke, Marie, Lawrence and Angus stepped forward from the shadows. "I beseech you, Walter, to let go of your hate. See that I am not your enemy. See that we are equals. See that life is more than power and prestige. There was a time long ago when we were brothers in arms, when you trained me to be the fighter that I have become, and we were all but kin. Let me help you now, help you see what deception and true betrayal has hidden from you for these many years."

Walter looked up at Andrew, knowing that the fight was over. Though the fire still burned inside of him, his broken wrist, the gash in his head, and the blood pouring from his gut spoke to his fate.

"All you had to do was give Gallard the sword," Walter replied bitterly. "It was not even yours to keep. You had no more right to it than Gallard. Had you done so, you would not have been an outcast and spent the past six years of your life wandering from land to land, seeking something that truly did not concern you. You would have risen even higher in Gallard's kingdom, surely becoming part of his inner circle in due time. There would have been no end to your fortune and glory."

"A man who seeks only his fortune and glory will find nothing but death and destruction," Andrew replied. "This is a lesson that Gallard will learn in time. The sword and shield shall never be his to possess and without them, he will never be able to lay claim to the throne of DuFay."

"Though I fail today, there will be others to continue the mission. Others who seek the glory that Gallard shall bestow upon them when they present the sword and shield to him, with or without your head in accompaniment."

"Let me share with you the true way to glory, the way to ease your pain and suffering. Let me share with you the love of a Savior," Andrew all but begged.

"I have no interest in whatever it is that you wish to share with me," Walter retorted firmly. "Know this, MacLean. You will never have a moment's rest as long as you possess that sword. King Gallard will do everything in his power to obtain it, and he will not stop hounding you until he does so. And as long as I am alive, neither shall I."

Andrew looked down at Walter, pitying the man and his heart full of darkness. Walter was dying, there was no doubt about that, and there was nothing Andrew could do to save him. He had lost too much blood and there was no doubt that the injury to his skull had not fully taken effect yet. There was only one thing that he could do, one act of mercy, for his former mentor and now self-sworn enemy.

"You leave me no choice," Andrew said as he bent down and picked-up Walter's own sword. "I have offered you an olive branch, a chance at peace and life, but you have spurned it. Today you have been given a choice between life and death, and you have rejected life." Andrew straddled Walter, lifting the man's sword high in the air. "This decision of yours shall haunt you in the final moments of your life." With all his strength, Andrew brought the sword down...and buried the tip six inches into the ground not one inch from Walter's head.

"Whenever those final moments actually come upon you," Andrew said, stepping away. Marie, Lawrence, and Angus stepped closer to Andrew and looked down at Walter. Walter's face was a mixture of confusion and fear, pain and relief.

"I do not understand," Walter finally said when he realized that Andrew had not finished him off. "Why?"

"Your life is not mine to take," Andrew replied, stepping aside. "If God is merciful enough to save you from your injuries, perhaps he will be merciful enough to save you from death." Andrew then squatted down so that his mouth was but inches from Walter's ear.

"But know this, my friend. If by God's mercy you survive your injuries this night, and if you determine to continue upon the course that brought you here and seek to do harm to me, my friends, or my family, there is no power in heaven or earth that will keep me from ensuring every last drop of blood is drained from your worthless body, whether it be before or after your heart has stopped beating. If you do indeed see the next dawn, I implore you, abandon whatever arrangement Gallard has promised you and seek a life of peace, joy, and kindness elsewhere. Your life, your heart, they do not belong to Gallard. Seek to protect them with more passion than you possessed seeking to destroy me." Having said his final words to Walter, Andrew walked off into the darkness.

"Well, that was quite surprising," Angus said, looking off into the darkness where Andrew had disappeared.

"No, it was not," Marie responded, following Angus' gaze. She had always known Andrew to be an honorable and compassionate man and had greatly respected him for these qualities. But what he had just done, the compassion that he had just displayed, was beyond anything she could have ever expected. Something inside of her stirred, something that she had long fought against, but there was no fighting against it now. She walked into the darkness, following Andrew's lead.

Chapter 17

Despite the near-freezing temperature and the frosty flakes that floated on the light midday breeze, Andrew's brow glistened with perspiration as he drove an ax into the short log propped up in front of him. The log split easily, and Andrew tossed the two pieces into a pile that already contained several dozen other split logs. He had been chopping wood for the better part of an hour to help increase the stockpile of firewood that would be needed to ensure a warm home throughout the winter months. The exercise also helped him expend his pent-up energy and keep his muscles toned. He had noticed Marie as she slowly made her way to him, but he did not pause his chore. She finally stopped a few feet from him and after he had chopped up a couple more logs, she spoke.

"It appears that the wood pile has grown quite a bit in the past couple of weeks," she said.

"Aye, that it has," he replied, bringing the ax down on another log.

"It has been quite pleasant the past two weeks, not chasing anyone, not being chased by anyone, just being able to relax and recuperate from what seems like an eternity of running," she said.

"It is a rest that we all have needed for some time," Andrew agreed.

"It does seem that everybody is rested and feeling well. I am so glad that Heather was able to overcome whatever had ailed her and she is back to her normal self."

"Yes, that was good to see. She certainly was in a bad way there for a time."

"I noticed that you have not spent much, if any, time with her since our encounter with Walter," Marie noted with an inquisitive tone. When Andrew did not respond, Marie continued.

"Has something happened that has come between the two of you?" she inquired. "Not that it would be any of my business," she added quickly. Andrew took a few seconds before responding.

"No, nothing has happened," Andrew finally answered. "I believe we both came to the realization some weeks ago that whatever it is that we desire to find in a mate was not to be found in each other. Our differences present a chasm that neither of us is able to cross."

"Oh," Marie replied, "that is somewhat surprising."

"I do not see how," Andrew said as he split another log. "You two are best friends and although I may not know women all that well, I know enough to understand that there are no secrets between best friends. I am sure the two of you have discussed this topic already and she likely provided you with a similar answer as have I."

"You have me there," Marie answered with a sheepish grin.

"So, that then begs the question of why you are here and what it is that you truly want to talk about," Andrew said, setting the ax down and facing Marie.

"Can I not engage in simple, casual conversation?" she asked in reply.

"Marie Talbot, I have known you for not quite a year and although that is not an exceptionally long time, it has been long enough for me to come to the understanding that conversations with you are rarely simple and casual. Therefore, please, indulge me with what is truly on your mind. I was hoping to finish chopping this pile of wood before the end of the day."

"Very well," Marie responded, her light and playful tone taking on a more serious nature. "It has been two weeks since our encounter with Walter. We have all recovered from our running and fighting and one most miserable boat ride the likes of which I never desire to endure again for the rest of my life. We are all wondering, what is next? What is your plan?"

"My plan?" Andrew repeated questioningly. "My plan for what?"

"For what?" Marie repeated, astonished. "Your plan for the future. The DuFay legend. Our next move. Where do we go from here?"

"Oh, that plan," Andrew replied. "My future. Well, to be honest, I was giving great consideration to going back to Abershire, where we made port at the end of that boat ride that did not sit so well with you. Being back on that boat and in that sea-side town brought back some great memories and I must confess, I do love getting out on the sea from time to time. There is plenty of farmable land in the area and a man could do quite well in the trade business."

"What?" Marie asked, dumbfounded. His answer was totally unexpected to say the least. "Your plan is to go be a farmer and live by the sea?"

"After what I have been through these past six years? Aye, it sounds like heaven on earth to me," he answered.

"But… but… what about the DuFay legend? What about Gallard? What about everything you have fought for these past months if not years?"

"Number one, I have the sword and shield, so there is no concern of Gallard ever being able to claim the DuFay throne by obtaining all of the pieces of the DuFay Armor. Number two, there is no DuFay throne for Gallard or anybody else to sit on in the first place. Number three, the only living descendant of Reginald Dufay of which we know is now safe. Any day now, Lawrence and Angus will return with Alexander's mother, and they can live out their days here, even under a different name if that would make them feel safer. And number four, I have finished my quest. I have found the rightful heir of Reginald DuFay. Job done. Quest over. Time to settle down and enjoy the rest of my life."

"But what about the other pieces of the DuFay Armor?" Marie argued. "The helmet and the sash and the boots. You heard what Walter said, that Gallard was already looking for them. What happens when he finds them?"

"Nothing happens," Andrew replied. "What is he going to do with only four of the six pieces of the legendary DuFay Armor? Claim two-thirds of the DuFay throne? Besides, he could just as easily make replicas of the sword and shield even if he obtained all the other pieces. What common person would even know whether they were real or replicas? How many people even know what the original pieces look like? If Gallard were smart, he would simply make one of each, claim that he was the descendent of DuFay, and go about ruling the world. Who could contest his claim? Trying to track them down and obtain them would be a senseless waste of time and effort. More than that, we would not even know where to start the search."

"Number one, you are wrong about the replicas," Marie replied, mocking Andrew's prior response to her. "There are people who know what the originals look like and the markers that prove their authenticity. Should Gallard present anything but the originals to claim the throne, he could easily be proven to be false. Number two, you are wrong about not knowing where to start the search."

"How do you know these things?" Andrew asked suspiciously. "What have you been withholding from me?"

Marie looked away from Andrew for a moment before responding, taking in their surroundings, as if making sure nobody was within earshot. She turned her eyes back to his.

"As you are aware, my mother had knowledge of the DuFay legend. You, Donald, and I reviewed several pages of her writings where she spoke of the armor of God. It was not clear from those few pages how my mother knew of DuFay and the armor, and that had perplexed me to no small degree. I discovered many more pages from her journal after I had sent those few to Habersham to be translated. Unfortunately, with the very suspicious death of the linguist who had translated those original pages and Gallard's attack upon my father's kingdom, there was no time seek out someone else to assist in additional translations.

However, I did know that the majority of her writings were in Greek. I also knew that Joseph, our librarian, possessed several books in Greek and a reference book that would help in translating the writings. I borrowed those books, but Gallard attacked, and we had to flee before I had time to start translating the rest of my mother's writings."

"And at some point, between fleeing your homeland and now, you found the time to translate her writings," Andrew surmised.

"What do you think I did in the back of that wagon for what seemed an eternity between Durinburg and Stanwyck?" she replied. "I was not able to fully translate everything, that would take a lot more time and knowledge of the Greek language which I do not possess. However, I was able to learn a good bit about my mother's past."

"And how she came to know about the DuFay legend," Andrew stated.

"Precisely," Marie confirmed. "And, surprisingly enough, how my father came to know about it as well." She paused for a moment for effect.

"I am all ears," Andrew said, taking the bait when she did not continue.

"As best as I can determine," Marie continued, "my mother was an orphan and raised primarily in the care of a church in her homeland. While her general chores and responsibilities were focused on serving the community, she had a passion for learning and spent many hours in the church's library. She also…" Marie paused for a moment, contemplating her words, "…explored certain rooms and sections of the church that may or may not have been formally off-limits to her."

"The apple certainly did not fall far from the tree," Andrew murmured, loud enough for Marie to hear but she did not retort.

"It appears that this church either had a connection to the DuFay legend or simply an extensive collection of DuFay-related documentation that was mostly off-limits for persons other than clergy. Over her years growing-up in the care of the Church,

Mother learned more and more about Reginald DuFay and the legend of his armor."

"What about your father?" Andrew asked. "How did he learn of the legend? And do not for a moment think about telling me that he was one of the priests."

"No, he was not one of the priests," Marie replied dismissively. "I knew that my father was the son of a king from a rather distant land. He was visiting my mother's homeland as a student. They met, fell in love, and got married. That was all I knew until I read Mother's journal. She wrote about sharing her discoveries of the DuFay legend with Father. That is how he knew."

"Fascinating," Andrew stated somewhat sarcastically. "Your mother grew up in a church, explored areas off-limits to her, learned about the DuFay legend, met your father, told him about DuFay, and they got married. Your father decided somewhere along the line that he wanted to assume the role of the DuFay heir, he learned that Durinburg was where the story started all those years ago, therefore he moved into the DuFay castle and set himself up as king of the land. And now, more than twenty years later, here we are. So, how does all of this relate to the marks of authenticity on the armor and where one would start the search for them?"

"My mother read documents that described in precise detail the markings on the armor, documents that purported to be original from the blacksmith that forged the armor, to be passed down through the DuFay generations and to never leave the family's possession."

"I see," Andrew stated. "I presume that the starting point for your search would be your mother's homeland, which is...?"

"Buckington," Marie answered with a smug smile, as if revealing some great secret.

"Buckington?" Andrew asked with a questioning expression.

"Yes, you know of it?" Marie asked excitedly.

"No, I have never been there, nor can I say that I have ever heard of it before just now, yet...there is a sense of familiarity that I cannot explain."

"It is not far, perhaps two-days' ride from here," Marie said, her eagerness not hidden in her tone. "Surely that is not too far for us to spend a few days exploring."

"I was done with DuFay ten minutes ago, and I am still just as done now," Andrew said, turning and positioning another log for splitting. "No more exploring for me."

"What about Alexander and his claim to the DuFay throne?" Marie said in disbelief. "What about Gallard and his maniacal fixation on stealing that throne? Does none of this matter to you?"

"It does not," Andrew admitted. "I have said it before, there is no DuFay throne to which Alexander has any claim. That throne crumbled many, many years ago. Kings come, kings go. Kingdoms rise and kingdoms fall. It is the way of history."

"Your callousness is extremely disconcerting," Marie chastised Andrew. "I do not understand how you can be that way after all you have seen and experienced."

Andrew gazed at Marie for a moment before responding.

"I understand your obsession with the DuFay legend," he finally said, exercising great restraint in keeping any hint of condescension out of his voice. "It was obviously extremely important to your mother, so important that she hid her thoughts in language. It also had a powerful impact on your father. He saw that it was pleasing to the eye and would bring him power, and he consumed the legend as Eve consumed the apple in the Garden of Eden. I understand how you wish to finish your mother's work, and how you wish to see the legend's end fulfilled to vindicate your father's nefarious actions. But these are foolish endeavors."

"No, the foolish endeavor is trying to reason with you," Marie spat back at him. "This is your own family, and you are turning your back on them, robbing your nephew of his rightful place in history. Where is your loyalty to them and what should be theirs?"

"What you consider to be Alexander's place in history was taken from him long, long ago when Robert DuFay lost his kingdom," Andrew countered. "Whatever his place in history is now, it is not mine to give or take. That is God's job, not mine." He turned and raised his ax, readying it for another powerful log-splitting stroke. "And it would be wise to never again question my loyalty to or love for my family." He threw the ax into the piece of wood, ending the conversation.

Chapter 18

L awrence closed the door to the tavern behind him and it took a few moments for his eyes to adjust to the gloomy interior of the room. The room was filled primarily with men of the village, most sitting around tables drinking and carrying on, but there were a few women here and there other than the serving staff. The tavern, like most similar establishments, had a musky smell of smoke, spilled ale, and bodies that had gone without washing for much too long. It was something Lawrence had long grown accustomed to and it no longer bothered him. He scanned the room and his eyes fell on four familiar faces on the far side of the tavern. Lawrence pushed his way through the crowd and stopped at the table.

"Lawrence!" Andrew called out to his friend, a smile born more from intoxication than joy breaking out on his face. "Join us, my friend! There is a spare seat right here that has been waiting for you all evening. However, as you are aware, tradition dictates that the price of admission is a round of fresh ale."

"It is not ale that I have come for this evening," Lawrence replied, looking around the table and meeting the eyes of Andrew, Angus, Gregory, and Victoria. "I am looking for Marie."

"And you came here?" Andrew replied, half-laughing. "You know quite well Marie would not be caught dead in the company of the likes in here. It is a bit below her standards if you know what I mean."

Lawrence did not miss the sour tone to Andrew's voice and words but did not comment on them.

"I did not expect to find her here," Lawrence responded, "although I have looked in just about every other place in this village. Until today you could not go a day if even half a day without seeing her, but it has now been two days and I am rather concerned."

"Perhaps she just needed a little alone time," Victoria suggested. "Women can be like that when they have spent too much time in the company of the opposite gender. For example, for me, that is generally about..." she paused for a moment, feigning deep thought, "about two hours." She looked around the table, then added sarcastically, "Maybe less."

"There are two things that are troubling to me," Lawrence continued, sitting down. "None of the McKenzie family have seen her either and you know she has spent much time in that household. Add to that the fact that Walter's body does not lie where you left him, and it should concern you, too."

"You saw Walter's wounds after our fight," Andrew said, dismissively. "They were mortal wounds. He lived no more than another hour after we left and a wild animal, a wolf or even a bear I would venture, drug his body away and made a nice meal of him."

"The Andrew MacLean I know would never make such an assumption," Lawrence shot back.

"Meet the new Andrew MacLean, a man who minds his own business and has abandoned chasing legends, tales, and meaningless pieces of armor to live a normal, and simple, life," Andrew replied. "If you wish to know where Marie is, for what reason I could not imagine, then allow me to suggest that you speak with her very-best friend, Heather. I would wager that Heather knows her location this very moment."

"Then you would lose that wager," Lawrence informed him. "I spoke with Heather not an hour ago, and she confessed that she did not know where Marie might be."

"If Marie were truly wishing to be alone for self-reflection or some other reason, her best friend certainly would not reveal her whereabouts," Victoria said. "Honor among girls and all of that."

"Honor or not, if she values her friend's safety, she will tell me," Lawrence said as he rose from the table.

"How about that round?" Andrew asked, and Lawrence answered with a glare of aggravation. "Okay, later." He and the others watched Lawrence leave. "He will be back," Andrew said, looking at his companions. "That man cannot resist a good, stout ale."

True to Andrew's prediction, Lawrence returned an hour later, but it was obvious that ale was not on his mind. He approached Andrew purposefully, if not menacingly, placed both hands on the table, and bent close enough to Andrew that he could smell the ale on his breath. He glared into Andrew's eyes.

"Pay your tab."

"My friend, you are a little too close for my comfort. It would be wise of you to back-off just a wee bit and not get in my face again," Andrew replied, the smile on his face turning from one of joyfulness to one of warning. Lawrence did not move.

"Is that a threat, such as the one that you gave Marie two days ago?" Lawrence asked.

"What makes you think I threatened Marie?" Andrew asked innocently, not denying the allegation.

"I just came from speaking with Heather. She relayed to me the conversation you had with Marie two days ago and it certainly sounded as though you threatened her. Does the sentence, 'It would be wise to never again question my loyalty to or love of my family' ring a bell?"

"It was a warning, not a threat," Andrew replied. "Imagine someone accusing you of not loving your family, not loving your friends, of turning your back on them when all you have done is the exact opposite. It is an accusation that I will defend myself against most passionately. It is one way to end a friendship, although there are many other ways as well," Andrew said as he purposefully looked down at Lawrence's hands pressing against the table.

Lawrence did not move for a few seconds, looking into Andrew's eyes, considering what to do next. Finally, he relented and straightened from the table. The others at the table had been poised for a fight, but now relaxed. A waitress approached the table with four mugs of ale. She set them on the table, one in front of each sitting person. Before Andrew could reach for the mug in front of him, Lawrence grabbed it and gulped the contents, then gently set it on the table.

"Your drinking is done for the night," he said, looking at Andrew. "You and I are going on a journey. Your horse is outside, saddled, and waiting for you."

"Is that so?" Andrew asked, bemused. "And where do you think we are going?"

"Buckington," Lawrence said, "to find Marie."

Chapter 19

B uckington was no small, rural village. It was a large city, a major point of commerce in the region. A ten-foot wide, twenty-foot-tall stone rampart formed the first line of defense for the city. It was laid out in the shape of a pentagon with each side extending over one thousand feet in length. Along the rampart ran a six-foot tall parapet wall with four-foot-wide crenels spaced every ten feet to allow defenders to launch arrows or other projectiles towards the invading army, and then being able to quickly duck to the side for protection. Approximately fifty feet inside this wall was another wall, twenty-five feet tall, with towers built on each corner of the pentagon. The area between the two walls was used for keeping livestock and for small crops where they would be protected against vandals and invaders. Within the inner wall was the city, comprised of at least one hundred and twenty buildings of both stone and wood construction, some just a single story tall, others two to three stories tall. Some structures stood alone, but the majority were built side-by-side, sharing common walls. Unlike many other cities that had gradually grown from small villages which had no pre-determined plan and ended up being mazes in which a person could easily get lost, Buckington was laid out with purpose and easily navigable brick and stone streets. A twenty-foot wide, three-foot deep river ran through the middle of town, six feet below street level. There were grassy banks along the river between the water and the retaining walls that protected the city from flooding. Stone and wooden bridges stretched across the river every two hundred feet. Several thousand people meandered through the streets and buildings, the lifeblood of the city. The main gate into the city consisted of two very thick and sturdy wooden doors, each at least ten feet wide and fifteen feet tall, reinforced with iron brackets. There was also a very formidable looking iron portcullis that could be lowered in the event of a siege. Four armed and armored guards stood outside of the gate, carefully scrutinizing every person that approached the city. Each was wearing a tunic over his armor that had a large red cross printed on its front. As Andrew, Lawrence and Angus approached them, the guards took non-threatening positions to block their progress.

"Welcome to Buckington," one of the guards said as the trio reined their horses to a stop. "Our city is a very friendly one, providing much to those who come in peace." He paused for a few seconds, taking a closer look at the men in front of him. "It also offers, well, rather unpleasant repercussions for those who do not come in peace. It appears that you have been on the road for some time. What would be the purpose and planned duration of your visit?"

Though he was tired and not in the mood for what he perceived to be an interrogation and intrusion into his personal affairs, Andrew decided that the wiser course was to accommodate the guard's inquiries and present themselves to be the truly peaceful travelers that they were.

"It is true, we have been on the road for over two days now. I am sure our somewhat disheveled appearance gives honest testimony to that. We have come to Buckington in search of a friend of ours, a young lady twenty-five years of age. She disappeared from our village several days ago and we have reason to believe that Buckington was her destination. She was traveling alone and therefore we are quite concerned for her safety and well-being."

"Such a woman traveling alone is quite uncustomary, and needless to say quite dangerous," the lead guard replied. "To undertake such a journey, well, she must have had great motivation."

Understanding what the guard was implying, Andrew responded as politely and innocently as he could to allay any suspicion of their intentions.

"My companion," Andrew said, indicating Angus, "has known this young lady for over twenty years and took responsibility for her safety and well-being when her father passed away not long ago. She became quite distraught, as her mother had passed away when our friend was quite young, and our efforts to console her were not as effective as we had hoped. Her mother grew up in this town, and we believe she has come here to see if she can find people who knew her mother. If she is indeed here and we find her, and she is happy and safe, then we shall leave her to live her life as she pleases and return to our homeland. Considering how large this city is, it may take us a couple of days to complete our search."

"Very well," the guard said, seeming to be satisfied with Andrew's response. "I shall take you at your word and you shall be permitted entry. However, two things you must know: First, there are many guards stationed throughout the city to provide protection for the people and ensure that the city remains peaceful. Some are clothed in armor as we are, yet some are not and appear as nothing more than common people. Eyes shall be upon you constantly, as they are on the other people in the city, therefore consider your actions accordingly. Second, the gates are closed at sunset and will not re-open until sunrise. You must secure accommodations for the night, or you must leave the city before the gate closes. It is against the law for anybody to sleep in the streets and those that are found doing so are arrested and publicly punished the next day, then banished from the city. The punishment is both humiliating and painful. You should have no problem finding a place to lie for the night. There are several taverns that offer beds to travelers, and there are also a few inns as well. Enjoy your visit." The guards moved aside, and Andrew, Lawrence and Angus nudged their horses forward.

"I am not sure if that was a warm welcome or a cold warning," Lawrence stated as they passed by the huge wooden doors and into the vivacity of the city.

"I do not believe there is much doubt to that," Angus replied as he took a quick look behind them. "They did not question anybody who entered before us and there were a few somewhat unsavory looking characters in that crowd. It would also seem that their interest in us continues. The guard who spoke to us appears to be giving one of the other guards instructions concerning us. Either that or my paranoia at being followed and chased has yet to abate."

"It is quite evident where the power lays in this city," Andrew said.

"Meaning?" Lawrence asked.

"You saw their tunics and the red cross on them. That is a religious symbol. Those guards belong to what has at times been a rather militant sect that has its allegiance to the church and not a king. Their behavior has not always been, well, what you would call church-like to be sure."

"How do you know this?" Angus asked.

"Five years of being all but a nomad presents many experiences to a person. I have seen their handiwork in person, all in the name of the church."

"I have never seen a place like this," Lawrence said as he gazed in amazement at the stunning architecture of the buildings surrounding them. "It is as if we fell asleep and awoke fifty years later. How can man imagine and then build a city such as this?"

"It is most definitely impressive," Andrew agreed. "I have seen many cities and much in the way of advanced building, but nothing that compares to this place."

"While I certainly appreciate the spectacle that surrounds us," Angus said, "let us not forget that we must focus on finding Marie. While I have never formally been appointed as Marie's protector, what you said to the guard is all but true, Andrew. We must find her quickly and ensure her safety."

"I cannot imagine how long it will take to search the entire city for her," Lawrence said, still marveling at his surroundings. "How do you find one person among thousands?"

"We do not need to search the entire city," Andrew replied matter-of-factly. "There is only one place that Marie would be, the one and only reason that she came here. All we need to do is find the biggest building in the city, and we will find Marie."

"And what would the biggest building be?" Lawrence asked.

"The employer of those guards," Andrew replied. "The church."

"Why would she be there?" Angus asked.

"What I said to the guard at the gate was true. Marie's mother grew up in this city, but what I did not say was that she grew up in the care of the church. And it was the church that held much information concerning the Dufay legend. Marie has become obsessed with this legend and has come here to try and learn everything that her mother learned about DuFay and the history, and future, of that bloodline, which was a history closely guarded by the church."

"Apparently not that closely guarded," Lawrence countered.

"Do you remember how curious and tenacious Marie can be, how secretive and stubborn and inquisitive she can be?" Andrew asked.

"How could I forget?" Lawrence replied.

"Well, she did not get those qualities from her father," Andrew said. "Considering how important this legend is to certain people and considering the type of security that is surrounding it, I have great concern for Marie's safety if she probes too deeply and reveals what she already knows about Dufay, especially about Alexander being the true descendent of Reginald Dufay."

"Then let us not waste any time," Angus said. He stopped his horse and bent over to speak to an older woman sitting on a bench outside of a store, peeling some potatoes. "My lady, if you would be so kind, would you point us in the direction of the church?"

Without a word, the woman raised her arm and pointed across the city to several steeples that appeared to be touching the clouds.

"Our thanks," Angus said, smiling. He looked to Andrew and Lawrence. "Gentlemen, our destination."

Chapter 20

If the general architecture of the city was impressive, the craftmanship that was used in the construction of the church was hypnotically mesmerizing. One could stand and gaze at every inch of the building and never be in anything but complete awe. On each corner of the building was a steeple of incredibly ornate design that reached one hundred and fifty feet into the air, each with a wooden cross attached at the top. There were easily two dozen other, smaller but equally ornate steeples built into the structure of the building. There were multiple arches and triangular designs built onto the walls, all filled with sculptures and reliefs depicting anything and everything that could be considered religious. There were angels everywhere along with depictions of the saints of Scripture, many of which were life-size. There was a relief of David fighting Goliath and beside it, another of David fighting a lion. There was Adam and Eve in the Garden of Eden. There was Noah's ark and animals surrounding it. There were more crosses than could be counted, including many that depicted the crucifixion of Jesus and some that depicted Christ carrying his cross. There were others depicting Jesus eating with his apostles at the Last Supper. It was as if the entirety of Scripture was etched into and onto the walls of the church. There were countless stained-glass windows adorning every wall, many also depicting scenes or people out of the Bible. The framework of the windows was anything but simple, the designs containing multiple circles and arches and other geometrical shapes. Multiple roof sections on the building were layered with copper tiles, which all bore a green patina born of decades of exposure to the elements.

"There are no words," Lawrence whispered as he stood on the steps leading up to the entry doors. "How is it possible to build such a thing?"

"With enough money and imagination, what cannot be built?" Andrew replied. "The church certainly has plenty of money and the Holy Scriptures are quite inspirational. Nevertheless, I have to agree with you, it is truly beyond amazing."

After securing their steeds, the trio climbed the two-dozen, thirty-foot wide stone steps that led to the entry door for the church. The doors were no less decorated than the walls of the church, with dozens of reliefs carved directly into the woods. The handles of the doors were, not surprisingly, in the shape of crosses. Andrew grasped one of the handles and pulled. The door swung outward with little effort. He looked back at Angus and Lawrence. Angus nodded in approval, and Andrew led the way into the building.

The inside of the church was no less spectacular than the outside and if possible, it was even more impressive. Multiple stone columns held up the roof of the sanctuary, situated between row after row of wooden pews. Attached to the columns, about twenty feet off the ground, were intricately painted statues, twelve in all, which were meant to represent Christ's apostles. The walls to their right and left bore multiple tapestries of exquisite craftmanship and design, many of which included representations of the stone tablets on which the Ten Commandments were written by God himself, and other included various depictions of Jesus Christ. Along the walls were multiple ornately carved wooden tables on which stood golden candelabras. Hanging from the ceiling were three multi-tiered chandeliers, each of which easily held a hundred candles. At the far end of the room, on a four-step platform, was a wooden podium that was no less intricately carved and decorated than the rest of the sanctuary. In front of the podium was a large marble-topped alter on which set two large, gold-covered candelabras, each holding five large candles, a gold-leaf goblet, a gold-covered sword, and a large bible opened to Psalm 23. The ceiling of the sanctuary was even painted, again depicting multiple biblical scenes. Without speaking a word, Andrew, Lawrence, and Angus slowly walked up the center aisle toward the front of the sanctuary and stopped when they reached the altar. They looked at each other, not sure what to do next. Their indecision was abated when an older gentleman, who had to be at least eighty years old, wearing a white robe with a purple sash and a golden cross hanging from a chain around his neck, approached them.

"Greetings in the name of the Lord Jesus Christ," the man said, bowing his head slightly. "Welcome to Covenantal Orthodox Church of Christ. I am Reverend Antonio Vendici."

"I am Andrew MacLean, this is Lawrence Morecraft, and this is Angus Faustus," Andrew replied.

"It is a pleasure to meet you," Reverend Vendici said. "How may I be of service to you? What brings you to the Lord's house this afternoon?"

"We are looking for a friend of ours, a young woman named Marie. We were staying in a village several days from here and for some time she had quite earnestly desired to visit Buckington. She had heard of the majesty of the church here and desperately wanted to come see it for herself, as she is a woman of great faith. However, due to weather and reports of vagrants with ill-intent along the roads, we determined that it would be best to delay such a journey. Unfortunately, Marie decided to ignore such threats and set out on her own. We are, as you can understand, greatly concerned for her and wish to find her and ensure that she is safe. She would have arrived in town two days ago, three at the most. Knowing that her primary reason for coming here would be to visit the church, we thought it best to commence our search here."

"I see," Reverend Vendici replied plainly. When he did not say anything else, Andrew pressed him.

"Have you by chance seen or met her?" Andrew asked. "It is greatly disturbing to consider that she may not have made it to

Buckington. The alternative scenario is not one I wish to give thought to."

"There are a great many people who visit the Covenantal Orthodox Church of Christ on a daily basis and while I strive to personally introduce myself to each one, there are quite a few hours during the day when I am dedicated to study and prayer." While speaking, Reverend Vendici had looked at each of the men in front of him in turn, but whether it was out of politeness or curiosity was not immediately evident. However, the fact that the reverend had not given a direct answer to his question was not lost on Andrew.

"Perhaps there would be others who may have met her while you were otherwise occupied?" Andrew asked.

"Perhaps," Reverend Vendici answered, almost thoughtlessly, as he took a closer look at Andrew. His eyes, with a look that bordered on recognition, roamed across Andrew's face. He then lowered his gaze and caught the medallion that was hanging from Andrew's neck. He paused, and there was something in his expression that caused a bit of unsettlement in Andrew.

"That is a very interesting medallion you have," he said to Andrew. "May I take a closer look at it?"

Andrew took a quick glance at Angus and Lawrence. Both had questioning looks on their faces but said nothing. "You may," Andrew answered.

Reverend Vendici took a step forward, reached up, and cradled the medallion in his right hand. He bent his head forward and pulled the medallion closer to his eyes. He turned it over and looked at the back side. There was a glint in his eye and a faint smile on his lips as he gently released the medallion and looked into Andrew's eyes.

"May I inquire as to where you obtained this very beautiful medallion?" he asked as innocently as he could, although there was an underlying excitement that was not completely suppressed.

"I have had this for as long as I can remember," Andrew replied, an inquisitive look on his face.

"Perhaps handed down to you by your father?" Vendici pressed.

"Perhaps," Andrew replied, curious as to the holy man's interest in an old medallion. "I do not remember. My memory was robbed from me many years ago during..." he paused for the briefest of moments, "...as the result of an accident. I have no recollection of my childhood."

"Interesting," Reverend Vendici responded. He thought for a moment, as if to weigh a decision. "There is someone you must go speak with," he finally said as he reached up and laid a hand on Andrew's shoulder. "Someone who may be of great interest to you."

"I do not know who could be of great interest to me in this city other than my friend, Marie," Andrew replied. "Which brings us back to the question of another clergyman or someone else having seen or met Marie."

"I shall inquire," Reverend Vendici replied. "It will take some time, though. We have many clergymen here. While I do so, you need to visit this man. His name is Hewlitt Knox. He is a carpenter and operates a shop several blocks down the street. He should be there now. I believe the two of you may have quite an interesting conversation."

"What kind of interesting conversation could I have with a carpenter whom I have never met?" Andrew asked. "Shall he educate me on the best kind of tree to be used for making a wooden cross?" he asked sarcastically.

"Educating you is something I am sure he will do," Vendici said, "although I doubt it will have anything to do with wood. Just go speak with the man. When you return, I shall have the answer concerning your friend."

Andrew looked at the man for several seconds without re-sponding. He felt that he was being pulled into some nature of a game and it was a feeling that did not sit well with him. He had sworn that he was done with mysteries, legends, and games. Apparently, not quite yet.

"Very well," he conceded. "I shall visit this Hewlitt Knox and allow him to educate me on whatever it is that you believe will be of great interest to me. When we return, which I expect to be within the hour, I fully expect to hear encouraging news regarding my friend."

"Agreed," Reverend Vendici replied and with a polite bow of the head, turned and left.

"Now what was that all about?" Angus asked as the three men turned and walked out of the church. "That man of the cloth was not being straightforward with us. He refused to answer your questions about Marie directly and instead, danced around them. He knows something about her, that I can assure you. I do not trust that man, whether he be a priest or pauper."

"I have no idea what his objective is," Andrew replied, "and I do not care for secrecy and schemes. I shall visit this Hewlitt Knox, whoever he is, to satisfy the reverend. Then, we shall return to this house of mystery and demand he tell us what he knows about Marie. I am in agreement with you, Angus, he has knowledge of her. One way or another, he will share that knowledge with us, that I promise you."

"Do you wish us to go with you to visit this carpenter?" Lawrence asked.

"That will not be necessary," Andrew replied. "I think it best that the two of you secure accommodations for the evening and a place to board our horses. We passed three taverns that advertise accommodations being available. The Rose and Crown, the Red Lion, and the Fox and Hound. Once we have a place to settle for the evening, have yourselves a hot meal and a pint or two of ale. I will find you after I visit Mr. Knox and the three of us shall return to the church and have another, hopefully cordial, conversation with Reverend Vendici."

"That is an excellent plan!" Lawrence exclaimed with exaggerated enthusiasm. "I have not had a pint of ale since..." he paused for a dramatic effect, "Oh yes, since I drank yours back in Stanwyck!"

"I shall be expecting recompense," Andrew said as he gathered Annon and walked down the street in the direction indicated by Reverend Vendici.

"He has such grand expectations," Lawrence said, shaking his head, as they watched Andrew walk away. "Let us get that ale. The Fox and Hound sounds like our kind of place."

Chapter 21

T he sign over the door was simple: *Carpenter*. However, not lost in its simplicity was the quality of craftmanship as the letters, engraved into a single plank of rectangular wood, were perfect in their creation and spacing. Andrew opened the door and a bell sounded somewhere in a back room of the shop. Looking up, Andrew saw a string attached to the top of the door. Obviously, at the other end of the string was a bell, purposed to notify the shopkeeper that a customer had entered the store. Andrew closed the door and waited several seconds, then called out.

"Hello?" he called out, loudly enough that anybody in the shop should have been able to hear him.

"A moment, please," a masculine voice called from a back room.

Andrew looked around. There were numerous tables and chairs scattered around the large room along with cabinets and chests and other pieces of furniture. Other than the chairs that had been crafted to be sold in sets, no two pieces of furniture looked alike. It was obvious that the carpenter had a great imagination and was highly skilled. The room smelled of sawdust, paint and stain but was kept clean. The owner plainly took immense pride in his trade. After sixty seconds of waiting, an older man, appearing to be in his late sixties, emerged from what Andrew presumed was the main workshop. His movements were not slow, but that he suffered from some aches and pains was obvious. He walked with a slight limp and was bent forward a bit, the price extracted by his trade after several decades of bending over.

"How may I help you?" he asked as he stopped a couple of steps from Andrew.

"I am looking for Hewlitt Knox. Would that be you?" Andrew asked in reply.

"Aye, that would be me. How may I help you?" he asked again.

"I am not sure," Andrew replied. "I was, shall we say, encouraged by Reverend Vendici to come and speak with you. It seems he believes there is a conversation that we should have, though concerning what he was not compelled to say."

"Reverend Vendici, you say?" Hewlitt replied. "He indeed can be a very secretive man. What is your name?"

"Andrew MacLean," Andrew answered.

"Well, Andrew MacLean, you must have said or done something that prompted Reverend Vendici to send you my way. Let us start with what took you to Reverend Vendici in the first place."

"I came to town with two friends seeking another friend whom we believe arrived in town two, possibly three, days ago. It was our belief that she would have visited the church upon or very soon after her arrival, therefore our first point of investigation was the church. We are concerned for her safety, as she was traveling alone."

"I would not have any knowledge of a particular person arriving in Buckington, so I cannot imagine your friend being the reason for Antonio to send you to me," Hewlitt replied. "What else?"

"He took great interest in my medallion," Andrew said as he reached up and grasped the medallion and presented it to Hewlitt. "It was actually after looking at this that he said I should pay you a visit. He said that you could be a person of great interest to me, but that is all he would say."

Hewlitt moved forward so he could better see Andrew's medallion. His hand began trembling slightly as he examined it. He looked up at Andrew with great expectation in his eyes.

"Where did you get this medallion?" he asked.

"The Reverend Vendici asked me the same thing," Andrew replied. "I will tell you what I told him. I do not know where, when or how this medallion came to me. I have had it ever since I can remember, although I have no memory of my childhood prior to the age of eight or thereabouts." Andrew looked at Hewlitt a moment before continuing, considering how much he wanted to reveal about himself and his past. His instincts prompted him to continue. "I was told that my family had been traveling, though to where nobody knew, and we were attacked by a pack of wolves. As a wolf leapt for me, it was shot and killed by a man who had been passing through the area. It was pure luck that he was there, and I was not ravaged by the wolf. The man told me that the wolf crashed into me, and I was knocked back against a tree, hitting my head and causing me to lose consciousness. When I awoke, I was in the man's house and had no memory of the incident or anything prior to the incident. He described what had happened and that my father, mother, and sister had all been killed. I alone survived. He adopted me and raised me as his own son."

"Andrew, forgive me, I do not doubt your story or that you are telling me all that you remember, but this is important," Hewlitt said as Andrew finished speaking. "Please take another look at this medallion and try to recall when you first saw it. Think back to your first memories after waking up in the man's house. Was it something of his own that he gave you, or was it something that you already possessed?"

Andrew, sensing that there was something especially important about this medallion, resisted his first impulse to tell the man to go back to pounding wood and instead, closed his eyes and concentrated on events from what felt a lifetime ago. He remembered opening his eyes and being in a strange place. He remembered the MacLeans tending to him. He remembered seeing his sister as the sheet had been pulled from her face. He remembered being terrified at not knowing his name, at not recognizing his sister, at not remembering his mother and father. He remembered his adopted mother wiping his forehead with a cool, damp cloth. He then remembered something else.

"My father, the man who saved and adopted me, showed me the medallion and asked if I recognized it. He said it was found around my father's neck," Andrew answered. "I did not recognize it, but I kept it. It felt...important."

"That it is," Hewlitt replied. He reached under his shirt and pulled out a medallion that was a perfect copy of the one Andrew had.

"They are the same," Andrew said questioningly as he looked at Hewlitt's medallion. "Exactly the same." He looked at Hewlitt. "How can that be?"

"It is a very special family heirloom," Hewlitt replied, a smile breaking out on his face. "Come, sit down." He led Andrew to one of the tables in the showroom and the men sat facing each other.

"There is a very special, let us call it an inheritance, which is passed down from generation to generation in my family," Hewlitt explained. "It goes to the oldest son in each generation when they reach a certain age, but in certain circumstances, if the oldest son for some reason does not bear his own son, the inheritance passes to the brother next to him in age. That is the way it has been for hundreds of years. Being the oldest son in my family, I was the rightful recipient of the inheritance. It should have been passed down to my son, my only child, but he died of disease at a youthful age. Unfortunately, I contracted the same disease after he died, and the prognosis was eventual death. I sent an urgent message to my younger brother, my only brother, to come to me as quickly as possible in order that I could pass the inheritance on to him. He never arrived. I never knew what happened to him and his family. My disease, by some miracle, receded and I have continued to live all these years."

Andrew looked intently at Hewlitt, thoughts swirling through his mind like a swarm of bees around their nest. He knew what Hewlitt was insinuating. He just could not believe it.

"Andrew, that was more than twenty-three years ago," Hewlitt continued. "This medallion," he said, presenting the one around his neck to Andrew, "is given to the men in my family, in my bloodline going back hundreds of years, when they reach ten years of age. The one you have belonged to my brother, your father. When he was killed, it was rightfully, though unwittingly, passed on to you. Andrew, I am your uncle."

Andrew looked at Hewlitt, his eyes wide open in astonishment. He replayed Hewlitt's words over and over, one moment not believing them but the next, knowing without a doubt that they were true.

"Your real name is Robert Knox. Your father's name was Douglas and your mother's name was Melanie. Your sister's name was Stephanie. You lived in a village called Rosterdam, about a six-week journey from here. Your family was coming here. It has taken twenty-three years, but you have finally arrived." Tears began streaming down Hewlitt's checks. "You have finally arrived."

"Stephanie," Andrew repeated as though in a trance. "Stephanie," he said again as he pictured her pale, lifeless face lying on a cot in a strange home. Then she was not lifeless, she was running beside him in a field of flowers. She was throwing snowballs at him outside of a cabin in the woods. She was pushing him into a puddle of mud and laughing at him as stood up, his face completely brown. She was standing between him and an older boy who had been bullying him, holding a short, thick stick, threatening to smash the boy's face in if he ever laid a hand on her brother again. "Stephanie," Andrew whispered as tears began falling down his own cheeks. He looked up at Hewlitt. "I remember," he said quietly. "I remember everything. Stephanie. Mom and dad. The long ride in the wagon. The early snowstorms and harsh winter that made us take shelter with an older couple. The spring and our picnic." His expression slowly turned from joy to apprehension. "The wolves," he said quietly. "We ran. Mom and dad stayed behind to fight them off. I ran as fast as I could, faster than Stephanie. I did not look back, I just kept running. Then I was alone. Then there was the wolf." He closed his eyes, not wanting to remember, knowing that his amnesia had in part been a gift. "I should have stayed with her," Andrew said. "I should not have left her alone. We could have fought them off."

"No," Hewlitt said quickly and firmly. "What happened was not under your control, and you could not have changed the outcome. Even if you had stayed with your sister, the two of you were too young to fend off such vicious beasts. No, Robert, what happened was meant to happen, was destined to happen, no matter how terrible it was. It was established by God before he created the heavens and the earth. You must recognize and accept that, or you will carry an unnecessary burden of guilt for the rest of your life. You did what was planned for you to do. God spared your life and sent you on a journey. You must continue on that journey until its fulfillment."

"Journey?" Andrew asked, looking his uncle in the eyes. "What journey?"

"Your inheritance," Hewlitt replied.

Andrew reached up and grasped the medallion resting on his chest. "But I have the inheritance. I have the medallion."

"Oh, my apologies for not being clear," Hewlitt said. "The medallion is not the inheritance of which I speak."

"Then what is?" Andrew asked, his curiosity peaked.

"Have you ever heard the name, DuFay?" Hewlitt asked, a twinkle in his eye.

Chapter 22

H ave I heard of the name 'DuFay'?" Andrew repeated the question, taken aback at the very mention of the name. "That name has haunted me for what has been just shy of six years now. It drove me out of my homeland and set me on a nomadic pilgrimage that continues this day. It has cost many good people their lives, not the least of which was my brother. Yes, I have heard of DuFay, and the day shall never come soon enough that I am rid of the curse it has placed on me."

"Curse?" Hewlitt repeated. "My boy, it is anything but a curse. It once was a great name, known and respected in all the lands. It was a name to be proud of. It shall be once again. Robert, that is your inheritance. We are of the DuFay line, we are the descendants of Reginald DuFay. You are the last of the DuFay line."

Andrew stared silently at his uncle, the revelation of who he truly was stunning him into silence. He did not want to believe it. He did not want to believe that the past six years of his life had been wasted searching for the Heir of Dufay when he himself was that heir. He looked at the medallion in his hand, the markings on it still a mystery to him. He pulled up the sleeve on his right arm and revealed the scar that was placed on it by his adopted father twenty-three years earlier, an emblem that had meant no more to him than that he was part of the MacLean family. Hewlitt's eyes widened when he saw the brand.

"Where did you get that?" he asked in astonishment.

"It was after my family had been killed and I had been taken in by the MacLeans," Andrew replied. "My father gave it to me on the night in which he found me, saying it was a tradition for the males in the MacLean family to receive it. It was on that night that he gave me my name, Andrew MacLean."

"That name no longer has any meaning for you, as you now know your real name. You are Robert Knox, the descendent of Reginald DuFay," Hewlitt replied.

"No meaning for me?" Andrew asked with some offense. "That name means everything to me! It is the name given to me by a family that saved me, loved me, and took me in as part of their family. It is the name by which I am known to my friends and family. I shall not simply toss it aside because it is not my birth name. I was Robert Knox for the first eight years of my life, and I have been Andrew MacLean for the past twenty-three years of my life. Andrew MacLean is who I am, and who I shall be for the remainder of my life."

Sensing that he was pressing Andrew too much and knowing that this revelation was more than a little shock to Andrew, Hewlitt elected to stay silent and let Andrew continue to digest what he had just learned. After a few minutes, Andrew spoke again.

"The medallions," he said, looking down at his again. "What is carved into them?"

"'Put on the whole armor of God, that you may stand against the assaults of the devil,'" Hewlitt answered. Andrew closed his eyes and shook his head.

"Never more than now have I regretted finding that sword. It has been nothing more than a poisonous pestilence to me these past six years."

"Sword?" Hewlitt asked, his voice laced with eager anticipation. "What sword? Tell me of this sword and what you know of Dufay."

Andrew proceeded to recount his life since the day he had obtained the sword. He left out no detail and continued his story until the moment had had entered the carpenter's shop. Hewlitt listened intently, only stopping Andrew a few times to clarify certain information and events. Finally, after over an hour of talking, Andrew finished his tale and leaned back in his chair, mentally and emotionally exhausted.

"You have had an amazing journey indeed," Hewlitt said as Andrew's story whirled in his mind. He was beyond excitement as the implications of what Andrew said sank in. "You have the sword and shield of DuFay, two of the six pieces. Gallard has the breastplate. Amazing."

"There remain the other three," Andrew replied. "For all we know, they have been well lost in time, never to be seen again. We may be of the DuFay line, and I may be the last in that royal line and a very reluctant heir to some non-existent throne, but it is for naught without the helmet, belt, and boots. Although you have made a compelling argument, what I have seen and experienced during the past six years of my life casts much doubt on anybody being able to prove exactly who the true descendant of Reginal DuFay is and if there is even any importance in making that determination. I am no king and have no desire to be one. I am Andrew MacLean, and shall live out my remaining years as such, leaving DuFay to history."

"I understand your doubts, resistance and desire to absolve yourself of any responsibility in this matter, however, that is not so easily done. There is more at stake here than your desires. If you would indulge me for a bit longer, let us return to Reverend Vendici. There is so much more to this history that he can reveal to you. After speaking with him, your future shall be your decision."

"Very well," Andrew replied, "we shall go speak with him. He is expecting my return anyway." The men arose and left the shop.

Chapter 23

H ewlitt and Andrew sat on one of the pews near the front of the church while they waited for Reverend Vendici to be summoned. They sat in silence, Andrew still reeling from the revelation of who he really was, and Hewlitt overjoyed at Andrew's sudden and unexpected appearance. Hewlitt had been convinced that the DuFay line would die the day that he took his last breath, but now there was hope, and he had not dared hope for a long time. After ten minutes of waiting, Reverend Vendici walked through a door that led to one of the many hallways in the building and approached the seated men. He first looked at Andrew, then looked at Hewlitt. He spoke to Hewlitt.

"Is it him?" Vendici asked.

"Yes, reverend, it is him. Without a doubt. This is my brother's son, lost for twenty-three years but now found. He has knowledge of the DuFay legend and the DuFay Armor. He is the last remaining descendant of Reginald DuFay, other than me, although that shall change shortly enough."

"What do you mean by that?" Andrew asked, looking inquisitively at his uncle. "What shall change shortly?"

"The sickness that I had many years ago, the one that miraculously dissipated when your family failed to reach Buckington, has just as mysteriously returned," Hewlitt replied. "I can feel it in my body, in my bones. It has been growing steadily for the past several weeks. There is no treatment for it. I firmly believe that the Lord spared my life when you and your family were hindered from coming here, but now that you have arrived, he has placed this ailment upon me and this time there shall be no reprieve. As long as I am alive, or until I relinquish that birthright, I am the Heir of DuFay. But I cannot lead, and I cannot rule, it is not in me to do so. Therefore, I must leave in order that you may assume the role of the Heir of DuFay."

"As I told you earlier, that is a role which I have no desire to fulfill," Andrew reminded him.

"It is your destiny, Andrew," Reverend Vendici said soothingly. "I understand your hesitancy. It is a great responsibility that is being thrust upon you."

"How can you be so certain that our family is the rightful line of descendants to Robert DuFay?" Andrew asked challengingly. "Is it because of this?" he asked, pulling up his sleeve and revealing the emblem emblazed on his arm so long ago. "Do you believe us to be the true heirs simply because we have been branded? My adopted father had this symbol seared into his skin, as did his son and his son's son. How can you be sure that they were not of DuFay lineage? King Richard Talbot, whose daughter I have come here seeking, also had the same mark on his arm. How do you know that he was not the Heir of DuFay?"

"Ah, Richard Talbot," Reverend Vendici said as he momentarily looked into the distance. "That is not a name I have heard in quite some time. He most definitely is not the heir, that I can promise you most confidently."

"You knew him?" Andrew asked, surprised.

"Yes, I knew him," the minister answered. "He came here to study when he was a young man. It was here that he met a young woman by the name of Theresa McMaster, who was an orphan and a charge of this church at the time. It was here that they fell in love and were married. Theresa was a very inquisitive child and young woman, and over time she became aware of, and greatly intrigued by, the history of the DuFay line. Much of her research and investigation was, shall we say, not precisely authorized. But we granted her some leniency. I am convinced that it was through her that Richard learned of the DuFay legend and the armor. It was what drove him to Durinburg to seek whatever information he could find on DuFay, since Durinburg is where the DuFay line reigned. It is remarkable how similar Marie is to her mother. It is no wonder that she has finally found her way here."

"She is here?" Andrew said, sitting more upright. "Where is she?" he demanded. "I will speak with her."

"Worry not, she is safe," Reverend Vendici said, raising his hand in a calming manner. "She arrived two days ago and told us who she was and why she was here, to learn more about her mother who passed away when Marie was but a young girl. In fact, she is staying in her mother's old room. Her mother was quite the writer, so Marie has busied herself reading some of her mother's writings."

"What about the MacLean family?" Andrew asked, reverting to the main topic of conversation now that he knew Marie was safe. "How can you be certain they are not descendants of DuFay and heirs to the throne? They possessed this very same brand on their forearms."

"Oh, they are definitely descendants of DuFay, make no mistake in that matter," Reverend Vendici replied, taking both Andrew and Hewlitt by surprise. "However, they are of the line of the younger brother and never merged into the line of inheritance."

"I have never heard of this," Hewlitt said, somewhat offended. "Who was this younger brother? How can you be certain that the MacLeans are not of the royal line?"

"Allow me to sit down," Reverend Vendici said, lowering himself onto the pew beside Andrew. "It would be best that I start from the beginning, for Andrew's sake. Most of this you will know, Hewlitt, but some you may not know. Andrew, I do not know the extent of your knowledge regarding the DuFay legend, so please forgive me if what I say is already known to you. Reginald DuFay was the original king for whom the armor was made. The people of his land loved him without reservation. The six pieces of armor were physical representations of the Armor of God as described in the Holy Scriptures, and they were intended to be symbols of what made a man a great king. Other kings in surrounding lands respected him. While it was never documented as being official, Reginald was seen as the wisest of the kings and often, the other kings would come to him for counsel. If there was ever any disharmony between kingdoms, the disputing sovereigns would come to him to negotiate peace. In that time, such a thing was virtually unheard of. He died three hundred and fifty-five years ago. Upon his death a rumor was started that his spirit became embodied in the six pieces of armor, and as long as his descendants possessed the armor, his spirit would always be present and there would be peace and prosperity. It was a superstitious time to be sure.

"Unfortunately, over several generations, the sons of DuFay became more and more complacent in their positions and became less and less 'kingly' if you will, and much more wicked. The kingdom and surrounding lands suffered without the leadership that had made DuFay a great name. Kings began to fight each other, striving to de-throne their adversaries and take over their lands. It was a time of great tribulation. During the time of Robert DuFay, two hundred years ago, the kingdom fell under siege. Robert had two sons, Thomas the older and Kenneth the younger. In order to protect his lineage and the armor, with the hopes that Thomas would someday return, defeat the invaders, and re-establish the DuFay line to the throne, Robert secretly sent them away with his priest, whose name was Matthew Knox. The six pieces of armor were given to the king's most trusted and strongest Custodes, or Guardians, who were to take separate routes and rendezvous with the priest and king's sons at a later date. Thomas and Kenneth took the priest's last name, Knox, to protect their identity until such a time as one of them was able to retake the throne. Matthew Knox brought the boys here, which was the rendezvous point, and founded this church. Unfortunately, none of the pieces of armor made it this far and vanished, with no evidence as to their locations. For several years, Knox and the young men waited for the armor to show, but it never did. Kenneth's resentment at not being in line for the throne grew stronger and stronger, and he became extremely impatient and restless. He demanded that Thomas form an army and take back their homeland, but Thomas refused, saying it was not time and that they needed the armor. Kenneth finally decided to strike out and seek his own fortune. He left Buckington and changed his last name to MacLean. He must have made a copy of the DuFay seal to brand himself and the firstborn down through his generations on the off chance that the armor was one day brought together and he could claim the throne. Thomas stayed in Buckington, as did his posterity, and worked as a commoner. Now you know where the names 'Knox' and 'MacLean' came from."

"What of the armor?" Hewlitt asked.

"Yes, the armor," Reverend Vendici said. "Over the years there were many rumors of individual pieces of the armor appearing here and there. The Church sent agents to investigate each report and, if possible, procure the armor and bring it back here for safe-keeping until all six pieces were acquired and the Heir of DuFay could be proclaimed king. The Church was close in completing that task. At one point four of the six pieces had been found and were being held in a secret location less than two days from here. They were nearly lost when the stronghold was attacked, but the Custodes defeated the invaders. Those four pieces were then brought here, to this church, and held in secrecy. The possible locations of the other two were being investigated. Unfortunately, there was a setback. There was another young man who came to Buckington, the third son of a royal family in a neighboring country, not long after Talbot and his new wife departed. He came here to study and, through deception and intrusion upon areas otherwise off-limits to non-clergy, he learned of the DuFay legend. He was quickly and firmly expelled from the church, but he vowed that he would return one day and all knowledge about DuFay would be his. He was bitter at being so low in the royal line and therefore was determined to hijack the DuFay throne by any means possible. True to his word, ten years later he returned with a significant armed contingency and broke into the church. He ransacked the place, but the clergymen and the workers were able to hide three of the four pieces of armor. He was only able to find the breastplate, which he took, along with various documents and historical items."

"When did this happen?" Andrew asked, more of a demand than a question.

"Oh, perhaps thirty-five years ago," Vendici replied.

"Do you recall this man's name?" Andrew continued, although he was certain of the answer.

"Gallard," Reverend Vendici answered. "His name was Edwin Gallard."

"So that is how he acquired it," Andrew said under his breath, but the reverend had good ears.

"You know Edwin Gallard and the location of the breastplate?" Reverend Vendici asked, excitement riding his voice.

"I know him well," Andrew said bitterly. "I lived in his land for twenty-three years and was part of his army. Our parting was not pleasant. I believe I caught a partial glimpse of the breastplate on one occasion, but you can be assured that it remains close to him."

"What of the other three pieces of armor that the church had?" Hewlitt asked.

"The helmet, belt and boots were taken to separate locations under great secrecy and are held there to this day, greatly reducing the possibility of them being stolen as the breastplate was," Reverend Vendici answered. "As for the sword and the shield, they have not been in the Church's possession since Robert DuFay sent them their separate ways. We were close to obtaining the sword a few years back, but our courier, who had located the sword, was caught-up in a vicious battle. His life was taken from him, and the sword once again disappeared. There have been whispers that it has been seen within the past six or seven months, somewhere south of here, and our agents continue working to fulfill their charge to find it. As for the shield, we had reliable information that it had found its way back home, to Durinburg, but we were never able to verify the accuracy of that information. Now that Gallard has seized that kingdom, it will be more difficult to infiltrate his land and continue our search without raising suspicion."

"You know of that invasion?" Andrew inquired, surprised.

"Of course," Reverend Vendici replied. "There is not much that goes on in these lands of which we are not aware, especially if it has anything to do with the DuFay history. We have many operatives constantly on the move, their eyes and ears focused on anything potentially related to DuFay. Truthfully, it may be advantageous to us if Gallard was successful in finding the shield. At least we would know where the shield and breastplate were and could formulate a plan to acquire them. That would leave only the sword for us to locate and be able to crown the Heir of Dufay."

"Reverend," Hewlitt said with a smile on his face, "we do not need to be concerned of Gallard finding the shield or even the sword." Andrew shot his uncle a warning glare, but it was missed by the older man. "Andrew has them!"

"You have the DuFay Sword and Shield?" Reverend Vendici asked Andrew excitedly, his eyes wide open. "You have them in your possession?"

Andrew had not wanted to let Reverend Vendici know that he possessed the two pieces of armor, not yet. He felt once again that his life was spinning out of control and headed in a direction in which he had no desire to go. He needed time to reflect on all that had been told to him this evening. Learning that you were the descendant of an ancient king and expected to re-stablish his lineage on a long-lost throne was no trivial matter to consider. The last thing that he had wanted was more questions from Reverend Vendici, and more pressure to pursue that throne.

"I know where they are," Andrew said slowly. "I do not have

them with me on this journey. But they are well-hidden, and their safety is not a concern."

"You must bring them here," Reverend Vendici told Andrew firmly. "They belong here, under the guard of the Church. We shall then take every action necessary to obtain the breastplate from Gallard. We shall retrieve the helmet, belt, and boots from their guarded locations and once we have the breastplate, reunite the full DuFay Armor and crown the Heir of DuFay as king. Crown you as king, Andrew."

"How do you plan to obtain the breastplate from Gallard?" Andrew asked skeptically. "It is surrounded by an army of nearly five thousand men and many weeks from here."

"Gallard shall return home at some point. He will not abandon his land. I surmise that he will leave a contingency in Durinburg and once he succeeds in being crowned as the Heir of DuFay, he will return there to rule while leaving someone to govern Nordham in his absence. His army will be fewer in number as he returns home. We have a fighting force in Buckington of one thousand, and there are fifteen hundred more closeby that can be mobilized on short notice. With a well-conceived plan and execution, this should be enough to defeat Gallard and obtain the breastplate."

"Gallard's army numbers over four thousand," Andrew said. "Your two thousand, five hundred men will be no match for him."

"These men have been chosen and trained for one purpose, and that is to protect the DuFay Armor," the reverend responded. "Each one is worth at least two of any other fighters."

"Turning back to my earlier question, how do you know for certain that my uncle and I are the last in the line of DuFay and that we are the rightful heirs?" Andrew asked, not wanting to argue the point of troop numbers. "Even if this is the truth, why is it so important that the Heir of DuFay sit on a throne once again? What would make me, or any other descendant of Reginald DuFay, any better of a ruler than those who, today, sit on thrones across other lands?"

"To answer your second question, you have seen the types of men who sit on thrones in these days. Gallard and Talbot are perfect examples of men who have been motivated by greed and pride and have ruled their kingdoms accordingly. Surely at your age you have seen other sovereigns who have ruled with heavy hands, suppressing their peoples, robbing from their peoples, implementing a system of justice that is anything but just. You have seen many examples of lands in chaos and turmoil because they are governed by nothing more than self-proclaimed nobles who care nothing for the people or the land, they care only for their own enrichment. It is vital that a righteous, just, and wise king sits on the throne, one who exercises his power in accordance with the laws and statutes of the Almighty and is able to bring order to the chaos. This is what Robert DuFay finally realized the day that his kingdom was laid siege to. He had turned away from the faith of his fathers, a faith that had resulted in great prosperity for all the peoples, and it cost him not just his throne, but his life along with the lives of many of the people who had depended on him for protection. Tell me, Andrew, would you not be a better ruler than those men?" Andrew did not respond. Reverend Vendici continued.

"To answer your first question regarding our confidence in the lineage of Reginald DuFay, Matthew Knox meticulously committed to writing his history with Robert DuFay and all of the days afterward until his own death. We know a great deal about Robert's sons, Thomas and Kenneth, thanks to Matthew. When Kenneth left, one of the church's clerics went with him to keep tabs on him and document his life. Over the years, others within the clergy continued to document the searches for the DuFay Armor as well as the DuFay lineage. Hewlitt's name was the last to be documented in the DuFay ancestry, and now your name will be entered in the records following his."

"Surely there are many, many men who are righteous and wise and would make for ideal leaders," Andrew said, circling back to his first question which he did not feel the minister had answered fully. "Why is the name 'DuFay' so vital to your plan? If your history is accurate, it died two hundred years ago. What meaning does it have today?"

"My son, the 'DuFay' name has not disappeared from history at all," Reverend Vendici replied. "It is known across many lands, though it is often kept silent. When Robert DuFay's kingdom was attacked, many of his people were able to escape and were spread out in all directions. Robert DuFay promised them that an heir of his would one day possess the six pieces of armor and would re-take the throne that he was about to lose and would usher in an age of peace, prosperity, and righteousness. The people are, to this day, looking for the promised heir to the DuFay kingdom. They will not be satisfied with anybody else. That is why it must be the rightful heir. That is why it must be you, Andrew. You were born into a family of great faith, and you were taught the Word of God. Your uncle has testified to as much. I can sense that you are a man of faith, a righteous man, a humble man, and the fact that you do not desire the power, prestige, and wealth that accompanies royalty proves that you are worthy of the position."

"You know me not, Reverend," Andrew said challengingly. "Simply because I presumably am the posterity of some ancient potentate does not immediately qualify me to have a crown thrown upon my head and a scepter thrust into my hand. I am a stranger to you. You do not know whether I am a man of righteousness or a man of wickedness, a man of God or a man of Lucifer. You do not know whether I inspire men or dishearten men. Why would you, with such eagerness and ignorance, place a crown upon my head?"

"How long have you been in possession of the sword and the shield?" the pastor asked in response. Andrew considered his response for a moment, then answered.

"I acquired the sword over five years ago. The shield, much more recently."

"Why have you kept the sword for all these years?" Reverend Vendici asked. "There is no weapon like it and its value is beyond imagination. You could have demanded a great price for it and have lived a life of extreme luxury, with little to want for throughout the remainder of your life."

Andrew did not answer but stayed still, his eyes defiantly focused on the clergyman.

"Let me tell you that which you know but refuse to acknowledge," Reverend Vendici continued. "You knew of the importance of the sword. I do not know when you first learned of the DuFay legend, but you believed in it and could not bring yourself to relinquish the sword for any price. For that same reason, however it came to you, the shield remains in your possession. You feel attached to them. The thought of selling or otherwise parting with them was not an idea you have ever entertained. However, that is exactly what a man of great worldliness, a man of great selfishness and materialism, would have done. That is not you, Andrew MacLean. You are a man of honor, a man of honesty, a man whose destiny has come to light and is ready to be fulfilled."

Andrew leaned forward, toward Reverend Vendici, a motion intended to stress the words that he was about to speak.

"Let me tell you what kind of man I am," Andrew said with a calm, soft tone that left no doubt as to the resoluteness of his words. "I am a man who is tired. I am a man whose family, and history, were ripped away from him twenty-three years ago. I am a man whose life was thrown into complete chaos six years ago, losing yet another family and history. I am a man who is exhausted with his life being ripped away from him and being told who he is and who he is not. I am a man who does not desire power or praise. I am a man who desires only to live a peaceful life for the remainder of his years and to leave politics to others more suited for the profession. Now, if you please, I would speak with my friend, Marie."

Reverend Vendici replied just as calmly and softly as Andrew had spoken to him.

"My son, I understand that your life has not been what you had envisioned it to be. Very few lives live up to how they were envisioned. Our paths are not ours to determine, they are predetermined by the Almighty and we can but walk that path faithfully, wherever it leads us, always seeking to glorify our Father in heaven. Hopefully, very soon, you will accept your destiny, if not for the power and praise, for the glory it will bring God.

"It is late, and Marie will have retired for the evening. Her continuous research into her mother's life here has been exhausting, and I would not wish to disturb her. Come back in the morning and you shall see her."

Andrew glared at the reverend, his patience having run its length, and was prepared to insist none too gently that he go wake Marie and bring her to him. Hewlitt, seeing the resolve in Andrew's face, laid a hand on Andrew's shoulder.

"Andrew, I believe it would be wise to follow Reverend Vendici's recommendation. You have had quite an exhausting and revelational day. It would be best for you to come with me, have a solid meal, and retire for the evening. The morning shall come soon enough, and you will have a clear mind. If what you told me about Marie is true, you will need a clear mind when you speak to her tomorrow. Her safety within these walls is of no doubt."

Andrew did not take his eyes off Vendici but responded to his uncle.

"Very well. We shall return in the morning, my two companions and I, and we will speak with Marie. As for your hospitable offer, uncle, it is much appreciated but I shall have to decline. I must go meet with my friends. They are by now growing anxious that I have not rejoined them, and there is much that we must discuss before the morn. Reverend Vendici, thank you for your time. I look forward to seeing you again in the morning."

"It has been my pleasure," the minister replied sincerely.

With that, Andrew and Hewlitt stood and made their way down the long aisle and out of the house of worship.

Chapter 24

F inally!" Lawrence called out as Andrew approached the table at which he and Angus were enjoying their libations. Two empty platters with remnants of their dinner sat on the table. "We were just in the process of dispatching a search party to determine your whereabouts."

"I can see that," Andrew replied, looking down at the platters and empty mugs. He sat down, his body language indicating great fatigue. "Be careful of that which you seek, for what you find may not be pleasing to you."

"I take it that your conversation with Hewlitt did not go well?" Angus asked.

"Did he hurt your feelings?" Lawrence asked, sitting up, feigning fervor. "Do you wish us to pay him a visit? To teach him a lesson?"

Andrew looked at Lawrence and rolled his weary eyes.

"Of course not," he replied. "Besides, Hewlitt is well over sixty years old, and you are no match for him."

"Probably not," Lawrence said, "You must keep in mind who trained me. That would be..." he looked at Andrew and Angus in turn, "the two of you, I believe."

"Tell us of your conversation," Angus continued, ignoring Lawrence's jab. "It has been nearly two hours since we left you. Two strangers do not casually converse about the weather or debate the better pastry for two hours."

Andrew looked at his two friends, not exactly sure how to proceed with the conversation and relay to them everything that he had just learned. The closeness of their relationships demanded honesty and full disclosure. They had come with him this far. They had a right to know everything. He looked around to see if any of the other patrons were paying them any particular attention, but it appeared that the three of them were of no interest to those closest to them. Andrew leaned forward and kept his voice low in an effort to prevent their conversation from being overheard. He nevertheless chose his words carefully.

"It has come to my attention, with much certainty, that Alexander is not the individual that we believe him to be," Andrew started.

"You mean he is not the— " Lawrence began, his voice louder than what was comfortable for Andrew. Andrew interrupted him.

"What I mean is exactly that," Andrew said cutting him off. "And we must keep our voices a bit more subdued. These are words that we do not wish other ears to hear."

"He is not the person for whom you have been searching all these years?" Lawrence asked, catching Andrew's intimation.

"He is not," Andrew confirmed.

"So, you will continue your search," Lawrence said more than asked.

"There is no need," Andrew answered, still unsure how to reveal to them what he had just learned.

"I am confused," Angus said. "If Alexander is not this person, and if finding this person has been your life for well over the past five years, why would you not continue your search?"

"I do not need to continue my search, because I have learned with unequivocal certainty who this person is," Andrew replied.

"So?" Lawrence asked. "Who is it?"

Andrew looked at them somewhat sheepishly and shrugged his shoulders, discreetly pointing at himself with his index fingers.

"YOU?!" Lawrence cried out, forgetting the secretive nature of their conversation. "Do you mean that you have been searching for yourself all these years?"

"Lower your voice!" Andrew commanded, looking around to see if anybody's curiosity had been stoked by Lawrence's outburst.

"How can this be?" Angus asked quietly. "How can you be certain?"

"Hewlitt Knox is my uncle on my father's side," Andrew replied. He again looked around to make sure nobody was listening. "This medallion around my neck? It is a family heirloom. Hewlitt has one identical to it."

"That does not prove that you are...this person," Lawrence said.

"Not in and of itself," Andrew answered. "But it does prove that I am related to Hewlitt. Remember how I told you of the day that I became Andrew MacLean and part of Gallard's kingdom? How my family, which had been on a journey, was attacked by wolves, and I alone escaped with my life? We were coming here. Hewlitt had summoned my father in order to pass along this birth-right, for he was stricken with an ailment and his survival was in question. Hewlitt was my father's older brother, and they had no other brothers, nobody else to whom this legacy could be passed. With the death of my father, I naturally come next in succession once my uncle passes. And according to him, that shall be quite soon. He shall officially relinquish his rights and pass them on to yours truly."

"How does your uncle know of this lineage and that he is part of it?" Angus asked.

"Reverend Vendici," Andrew replied. "It is a long story, but the church evidently has the entire history of this matter in its possession and has carefully documented the line of descendancy. After meeting my uncle and hearing his profession, we paid Reverend Vendici another visit. There is no disputing what appear to be the facts. Reluctantly, I am the one."

Lawrence broke out laughing, leaning back in his chair.

"Forgive me, my friend, but the irony is more than a little humorous after all that you have been through."

"There is nothing about this that I find humorous," Andrew replied rebukingly. "Over five years of my life were wasted roaming from land to land, a nomad, a loner, no family, no friends, just a horse and an impossible quest. I have been chased relentlessly.

I have been in more fights than I can count at this point. I have lost a brother. You lost a close friend. An entire kingdom was laid siege to and lost because of me and my quest. I find no humor in any of that."

"Forgive me, my friend," Lawrence said sullenly, his disposition dampened by Andrew's response. "I failed to count your cost in all of this, and that cost has been great. That being said, you have an opportunity for it all to not have been for naught. You have an opportunity to make the reward exceedingly worthy of the cost."

Andrew sighed and looked into the distance. The reality of his life was slowly penetrating his persistent obstinacy. Could he ever truly escape DuFay? That name, that legend, had chased him for nearly six years now and there was no reason that it would stop doing so. He knew that he would be hounded, if not literally then internally, for the rest of his life by denying what appeared to be his destiny.

There was a sudden and very noticeable drop in the volume of the erstwhile boisterous tavern. The three men looked up and around the room to see what had subdued the mood. They only needed to follow the eyes of the other patrons. Four men had just entered the tavern, each wearing a white robe that had a red cross stitched to it over the chest. They each also had a sword attached to a thick belt around their midsection. They proceeded to sweep the room with their emotionless eyes until they saw Andrew, Angus, and Lawrence. Slowly, they made their way to the trio.

"Lovely, just what we needed this evening," Lawrence said as it became evident that the four men were approaching them. "This town needs a new welcoming committee."

"What could they possibly want with us?" Angus asked as he altered his position in his seat in the event he needed to move suddenly. "We have not had time to offend anyone or break any laws."

"The evening is young," Lawrence replied, he too adjusting his posture and ensuring he had quick access to his sword.

"I have a feeling I know what has prompted their presence," Andrew said as he remained motionless and turned his eyes back to his companions. As the newcomers reached their table, they glared at four men at neighboring tables. Without a word needing to be said, the four men quickly gave up their seats and the robed men sat down. One of them pulled his seat closer to Andrew, a bit too close for Andrew's comfort.

"Gentleman, would you join us for a pint?" Andrew asked, looking at the man who was sitting closest to him. The man ignored Andrew's question and spoke.

"I am Sir Reynald Vicenza, Commander of the Armorum Custodes. You are Andrew MacLean, yes?"

"That I am," Andrew replied unintimidated. "And these are my friends, Lawrence Morecraft and Angus Faustus." Reynald did not bother looking at the other two men. "Armorum Custodes. Armor Guardians. That is an interesting occupation."

"As I said, I am Commander of the Armorum Custodes," Vicenza continued, not commenting on Andrew's statement. "It is our responsibility to protect the church and those within it, along with keeping the general peace in Buckington. We take great interest in the arrival of visitors to our town, especially those who appear to take great interest in our place of worship." Neither Andrew, Angus, nor Lawrence replied, so Vicenza continued.

"You had quite a lengthy conversation with Reverend Vendici this evening, did you not?" he asked, peering at Andrew.

"I do not see how that would be any of your business," Andrew replied.

"You must understand, anything that involves Reverend Vendici or the Covenantal Orthodox Church of Christ IS my business," Reynaldo answered. "You should consider us an extension of the church. Now, if you please, what was the nature of the conversation you had with Reverend Vendici?"

"The nature of the conversation is none of your business," Andrew replied firmly. "It was a private conversation."

Reynald leaned forward, his elbows on his knees, his palms pressed together and his fingertips on his lips, as if in deep thought. "Perhaps we are asking the wrong person. Might it be better if we speak with your uncle?"

"Enough of whatever game you are playing," Andrew said. "We are exhausted and in no mood for such banter. What do you want?"

"I—" Reynald started, then corrected himself, indicating his companions, "—we, want you to do that which Reverend Vendici has asked you to do."

"It appears that my conversation with him was not as secretive as I presumed it to be," Andrew stated. "No matter. What I choose to do, or choose not to do, is again none of your business. My companions and I are here only for this evening. In the morning we shall tend to an appointment, and I expect shortly thereafter to leave Buckington, never to return."

"Ah, yes, your appointment," Reynald said. "You have demanded to speak with your lady friend, Marie. I certainly can understand your desire to see her. She is quite an intelligent and impressive young woman. And very pretty to say the least." Upon the mention of Marie's name, Lawrence and Angus tensed, suddenly taking more interest in the conversation. The veiled threat was obvious.

"Marie is here of her own volition and has no part in the matters that pertain to me," Andrew responded firmly.

"Of course not," Reynald said, then cocked his head to the side slightly as if in thought. "Well, she does not have to. That shall be up to you."

"Let me be very clear in what I say," Lawrence said, jumping into the conversation, glaring at Reynald. "Marie is like a sister to me. If there is even the slightest threat to her, let alone the least bit of harm come to her, there is no power in heaven or on earth that will restrain my vengeance. Those red crosses on your chest? They are meaningless to me, and they will in no way protect you. In fact, they make an ideal target. Angus, would you not agree that those crosses bear a great resemblance to the

189

targets we used in the bow shooting portion of the Skills Contest? If I am not mistaken, you and Andrew hold the records for high scores in that part of the competition."

"Aye, now that you mention it, there is quite the resemblance," Angus agreed.

"I believe that makes clear our stance with our friend and her involvement in all of this," Andrew said to Reynald.

"Very much so," Reynald replied, though not showing any signs of being intimidated. "Again, her potential involvement is up to you, Andrew. After you speak with her in the morning, you shall go and retrieve the sword and the shield and bring them back to Reverend Vendici. You will have seven days to do so. If you fail to return by next Sunday evening with both pieces of armor, your female friend and your uncle shall suffer very unpleasant consequences. Once you tell Reverend Vendici that you agree to relinquish the armor to him, he will be overcome with excitement and will dispatch members of the Armorum Custodes to retrieve the three pieces that the Church possesses, the locations of which are known only to him. Once the five pieces are brought together, you and your three friends will be free to go wherever you like, as long as it is far from Buckington."

"There are two problems I foresee," Andrew said. "First, the breastplate. Having the other five pieces of armor will do you no good without the breastplate. I presume your intention is to acquire all six pieces of armor."

Reynald smirked. "We know who has the breastplate and there is already a plan in place to obtain it."

"Second," Andrew said, his mind partially on Reynald's revelation that they were already planning to get the breastplate from Gallard, "the armor will do you no good without the Heir of DuFay to be seated on the throne. Again, I presume the throne is your objective."

"The Heir of DuFay," Reynald repeated, that obnoxious smirk on his face returning. "The Heir of DuFay is whoever we say it is. The Church will always grant its full support to the man who is placed on the throne to provide sage guidance and ensure that he makes the wisest decisions that are in the best interest of the people and the land. Reverend Vendici is blind in his dedication to this legend, to this 'heir.' He shall be shown the light."

"Who are you people?" Lawrence asked, looking inquisitively at Reynald and his companions.

"As I said before, we are the protectors of the Church," Reynald replied, smiling. "We shall leave you gentlemen for the evening and look forward to your return in seven days." He and his three companions rose from their seats and left the tavern. Within a few minutes, the boisterous atmosphere returned. It was obvious what the people thought of the Armor Guardians.

"What do we do?" Lawrence asked, looking at Andrew and Angus. "His threat against Marie is not something that I will abide. We must get to the church immediately and insist that she come with us."

"It goes without saying that Reynald will be expecting us to do just that and will have a horde of his minions in the waiting," Andrew answered Lawrence. "No, we must leave Marie where she is for the night and trust that Reverend Vendici will ensure her safety."

"Then what is our course of action?" Angus inquired. "Surely we are not going to relinquish the sword and the shield."

"It would be the easiest thing to do," Andrew said. "Give them what they want and go on our merry way, forever relieved of this burden."

"You cannot be serious," Angus said. "If you truly are the rightful heir to the DuFay throne, there is no way that you will be allowed to live. It does not appear that Reynald knows or suspects your true identity but the moment he becomes aware that you are the heir to DuFay, your life is forfeit. You heard Reynald. They can install anybody they desire on the throne once they have all six pieces of the armor. Instead of having a monarchy, where a king rules, it will be a theocracy where priests and bishops rule and they will do nothing but enrich themselves under the guise of faith-based decrees. They will force people to confess whatever faith they hold themselves and for those who do not confess, there will be great punishment and persecution.

"First, though, they will have to dispose of anybody who knows the truth. That would be you, me, Lawrence, your uncle and possibly Reverend Vendici. The only thing that will save Marie, for now at least, is that she does not know the truth."

"Do not worry, I have no intention of surrendering the sword and the shield, at least not to Reynald," Andrew replied. "I must go speak with my uncle and Reverend Vendici. Reynald believes that he has the upper hand. Perhaps he does for the moment. But we shall turn the situation around." He looked at their empty mugs. "Have another pint or two, I shall return soon." Andrew stood up and walked out of the tavern.

"Another pint or two it is," Lawrence said, signaling to the server.

Chapter 25

I t looks as though we have a welcoming committee," Lawrence noted as he, Andrew and Angus climbed the steps to the entrance to the Covenantal Orthodox Church of Christ. The sun had climbed above the horizon and was about an hour into its journey across the cloudless sky but had yet to warm up the invigorating morning air. The temperature held around 40 degrees. Reynald Vicenza and four of the Armor Guardians stood at the door to the church, in essence blocking it. Andrew was not surprised. He did not feel like dealing with Reynald this morning, but obviously it was not going to be a choice. Reynald spoke as the trio reached the top of the steps and approached the door.

"Good morning," he said with a smug grin on his face.

"Good morning," Andrew replied less than sincerely. "What brings you and your four minions out on such a brisk morn?"

"We wanted to confirm your course of action before you speak with your friend," Reynald replied. "You WILL be leaving this morning to fetch the sword and the shield, correct? Last evening you had quite the uncooperative disposition and it is particularly important for us to know that after a good night's sleep, you have decided to be more acceptable to our proposal."

"You have not left me with much of an alternative," Andrew replied. "Either I deliver the sword and shield to you, or you impose harm upon my friend and my uncle. Their lives are much more valuable to me than those two pieces of armor, of which I am more convinced now than ever before are nothing but flamboyant relics from a long-lost age. You can have your legend, you can have your armor, you can have your throne, I care not. I will be far away from this land and whatever perverted plan you may be conjuring for its future. So, the answer is yes, I will be leaving this morning to retrieve the sword and shield and bring them here. No more than seven days hence."

"Very good," Reynald said condescendingly. "It pleases me that your senses have overcome your impulses. There is one additional issue we must agree on, and that is the content of your conversation with the young lady."

"I do not see how that is any of your concern," Lawrence all but growled, his patience with Reynald at the point of dissipating entirely. Reynald briefly glanced at Lawrence but did not respond to him. He turned his eyes back to Andrew.

"I remain uncertain as to her true motivation for coming here. She has professed to Reverend Vendici that she has come to learn about her deceased mother's childhood and life at the church, of which she has truly little knowledge. While that may be true, my eyes and ears in the church would indicate that she possibly seeks knowledge of some other history. It would be best if you did not reveal anything to her about our conversations, about the DuFay legend, or that you have agreed to relinquish the sword and shield, if she is even aware of their existence. You will simply tell her that you were concerned about her disappearance and that you and your friends have come here to ensure that she is safe. You will not invite her to leave with you. Do you understand?"

Andrew struggled against the fury that had built up within him, every fiber of his being desiring nothing more than to permanently remove that air of smugness from Reynald. Before Reynald knew what was happening, Andrew could plunge the dagger hanging two inches from his right hand into the man's chest. Before the action could fully register with the other four men, Andrew's sword could find its way into the next closest man's torso. Within a fraction of a second after seeing Andrew's attack, Lawrence and Angus would both dispatch with two of the other Custodes. The fourth Guardian would freeze, not knowing what to do, leaving his fate to whichever attacker moved the quickest. Probably Lawrence, Andrew thought, he had phenomenal reflexes and quickness. It would all be over within five seconds. All it would take was the initial move...

"I understand," Andrew responded calmly.

"Finally," Reynald said, holding up a hand as Andrew took a step toward the door, "these four Custodes shall accompany you along your journey. To ensure your safety and that of the sword and shield. There are many people in the world with bad intentions, it would grieve me greatly if you should meet any of them on the road and they bring harm upon you and are able to recover the sword and shield."

"That is not going to happen," Andrew said firmly. "I have no trust in you and therefore no trust in your cohorts. I shall not risk a sword in my back or a dagger across my throat while I sleep."

"I am afraid that it is not a negotiable point," Reynald said, his erstwhile faux-friendly expression taking a darker turn. Andrew was not intimidated.

"Do not mistake my cooperation for weakness or ignorance," Andrew said, stepping closer to Reynald and his voice taking on a threatening tone. "Your four colleagues can have their blood spilt on the road or on these holy steps, and you along with them. It matters not to me." Angus and Lawrence tensed, their muscles ready to move in the blink of an eye. They held, waiting to see what Andrew did next. "We will now go inside and speak with Marie, under the conditions just established. Then we shall leave Buckington, retrieve the sword and shield, and bring them back here. We shall do so within the seven-day period you have established. You will not touch or speak with Marie while we are away. You will not speak with or touch Hewlitt. If you decide to send any of your men to spy on us, they will meet their end.

These points are non-negotiable. Now, move aside. We are wasting daylight."

Vicenza's face had become red with anger, and he was visibly trembling. Nobody had ever threatened him or spoken to him in such a disrespectful manner. He was Commander of the Armorum Custodes, a man of position and power. He was subordinate only to the ordained officers of the Church and in some instances, not even then. In his mind, he and his men could easily dispatch of the three men standing in front of them and nobody would question their motives. However, that would mean the sword and shield would be all but lost. Perhaps not, though. It was possible that Marie knew something about them after all but if not, she could at least enlighten him as to where she and her friends had come from, and he could start a new search there. With the right persuasion, she would tell him everything she knew. He forcibly calmed the rage within him and was able to respond to Andrew.

"Very well," he replied between gritted teeth. "You shall not have an escort. But I warn you, Andrew MacLean, that if the sword and shield are not here in seven days, your friend's stay shall take a sudden and very unpleasant turn." Reluctantly, Reynald stepped aside, and Andrew, Lawrence and Angus entered the church.

They could see Marie sitting in the front pew on the right side of the aisle. She did not turn and look as the front door closed behind them. They walked up the aisle in silence and as they reached the first pew, Marie spoke.

"I was a bit surprised to say the least when Reverend Vendici informed me that three of my friends had come to confirm my well-being," she said, not looking up initially. She then turned and looked at the men. "I see Lawrence and Angus. Where is my third friend?"

"We were extremely concerned when you disappeared without telling anyone," Lawrence said, sitting on the pew beside Marie and ignoring her jab at Andrew. "Considering everything we have gone through in the past few months you can surely understand our apprehension."

"Such a long trip, on your own, was not exactly advisable," Angus said. "One of us would have been more than willing to accompany you."

"No, Angus, one of you was anything other than willing to accompany me," she said, her eyes shooting darts at Andrew.

"Marie," Andrew said, "When we last spoke, I was very tired, both physically and emotionally. As you can imagine, the past six years have taken quite a toll on me in many ways which has resulted in me reacting based more on emotion than reason. I seek your pardon."

"This is a remarkably interesting town," Lawrence said, "and there is much that can be learned here." He reached over and grasped her hand, not in a reassuring gesture, but one that indicated she needed to listen to more than just the words that were coming out of their mouths. His eyes conveyed the same message. "We understand that your mother was an incredibly wise and learned woman, and there is much that you can learn about her, her past, and what her interests were. You may be surprised at what you can learn here, as we have been during our short visit."

"I have re-considered our last conversation, which was quite inharmonious, and I believe that I was in the wrong," Andrew said. "There is no need for us to continue with the discussion," he added as Marie looked as though she was going to speak. "It would be best that we do not speak of it again, as it was a private matter, and the ears of others need not be privy to it." As he said this, Lawrence squeezed her hand to emphasize Andrew's point. "Lawrence and I have an errand to run and shall be back in no more than a week. Angus has taken a liking to this town and shall remain here. He shall give you someone to speak with other than these wise, but somewhat tedious, men of the cloth. And I am sure that the Armor Guardians are less than congenial and not willing to engage in, nor worthy of, conversation." Again, Lawrence squeezed her hand.

"I understand," Marie said as she nodded her head once. "Andrew, I forgive you for your callousness and apathy. I appreciate the three of you having such great concern for me and coming all this way to ensure my well-being. I assure you that I am quite well and safe here." Surprisingly, she felt Lawrence squeeze her hand firmly twice, a gesture meant to negate what she had just said. She got the message. "I shall keep to myself and continue reading my mother's writings. She had quite a fascinating childhood and learned much while she was here. Angus, I look forward to us spending some time together while Andrew and Lawrence are away on their errand."

Marie stood and in turn, gave each man a gentle hug. She then exited the room via a doorway off to one side of the sanctuary. Andrew looked around the spacious sanctuary, expecting to see at least one of the Armor Guardians monitoring their conversation, but he saw no other soul. Nevertheless, he was certain that their engagement with Marie had not gone without observation. With one final glance at the doorway through which Marie had disappeared, Andrew led his two friends back down the aisle and they exited the building. Reynald and his four comrades were nowhere to be seen.

"It appears that our welcoming committee has moved on to their other chores for the day," Lawrence noted, looking around.

"No doubt making arrangements for our shadows as we head back to Stanwyck," Andrew replied. "It must be a splinter in Reynald's thumb for him to not know where we are going."

"I shall retrieve our horses and meet you in front of the tavern," Lawrence said as he turned and walked toward the stables.

"It is a bold plan," Angus commented as Lawrence disappeared into the throng of the early morning marketers. "How much confidence do you truly bear to its success?"

"As with many plans, they can be obsolete the moment they are made," Andrew replied. "What we can have confidence in is that there will be obstacles and unforeseen challenges, and we shall have to think quickly and adapt. What we can have confidence in is our resolve, and that one way or another, we will be successful." He looked around the bustling town. "Just keep a close eye on Marie. As you know, she is a very inquisitive, stubborn, and persistent woman. She knows we are up to something, and it must be agonizing to her to not be involved, to not know what is going on. She will press you for information, but you must remain taciturn to our plan. She will know everything soon enough. Now, before we leave town, I must pay the seamstress a visit and speak with my uncle once more." With that, Andrew left Angus standing on the church steps and vanished into the crowd.

Chapter 26

Reverend Vendici was deep into a daily devotional in his private study when there was a knock on the door. He was slightly irritated at having his dedicated, and well-known, private study time interrupted, but he also knew that his counsel was often needed at the most inopportune times, so he called out, "You may enter." He turned in his chair and was slightly surprised to see the commander of the Armorum Custodes approaching him.

"Sir Reynald," the minister said in greeting, "what a pleasant surprise. What may I do for you this morning?"

"I have some exciting news," Reynald said rather casually. "I have exceptionally reliable information on where the sword and shield are located. I have dispatched my men to acquire them."

"Yes, that is very exciting," Reverend Vendici agreed, somewhat bothered by Reynald's overly calm demeanor. "Where are they? How long until we have them?"

"They are but a few days away, and as luck would have it, they are together," Reynald answered. "We should have them in no more than a week."

"That is very good news," Reverend Vendici replied. "That shall place us two steps closer to fulfilling our mission. We would then only have the breastplate to obtain and to locate the Heir of DuFay. We know that Gallard has the breastplate and where he is thanks to recent reports. Now that we will have the other five pieces of armor, we should look to getting the breastplate. Do you have a plan for doing so?"

"I am working on it," Reynald replied. "I have received word that Gallard is leading his army back home. There are a few places that would serve well for an ambush."

"Excellent," the reverend said. "Please keep me abreast of your progress. In the meantime, I shall continue our efforts to locate the heir. I believe we are close to identifying him."

"Perhaps you should send for the helmet, belt and boots to be brought here, for the sake of time and for safekeeping," Reynald continued. "It would undermine our mission and set us back many years if any of them were to be stolen or otherwise lost."

"I do not see that happening," Reverend Vendici replied, getting a sense of where Reynald was going. "They are safe where they are. Only I know of the locations of all three. Bringing them here would be premature and present an unnecessary risk of being lost during transit."

"I can see how you would be concerned," Reynald said. "However, with a large enough contingency of my men accompanying each piece of armor, the chances of them being stolen or lost would be infinitesimal."

"That may be true, but I still believe the risk to be unnecessary until we have the sword, shield, breastplate and heir in our hands," Reverend Vendici said, hoping to end the conversation. Reynald was not finished.

"Reverend, let me be forthright," Reynald said. "There can be no more delays in bringing order and uniformity to the land. The world continues to grow increasingly wicked, of this you are quite aware. It cannot afford more years of chaos until such time as this 'Heir of DuFay' is located if he even exists. For all we know, there is no heir and the line died out long, long ago. We must take action. It is the will of God that there be peace and harmony amongst men, and it is the Church's duty to ensure that this happens for we have seen that left to themselves, man only increases in wickedness. I will have the sword and shield here in a week. You will send for the helmet, belt, and boots. Within two weeks we shall have acquired the breastplate and have it within these walls. Then we shall crown the Heir of DuFay, or whomever we say is the heir, and seat the new king. We can then establish the leadership and oversight that is much needed, along with uniformity in faith and worship."

"As I said before, I believe we are close to identifying the true Heir of DuFay," Reverend Vendici replied. "I will not send for the armor until that person is brought before me. I greatly admire your dedication to our mission and desire to see it fulfilled, but we must ensure that it is accomplished properly, and that means putting the right man on the throne."

"The right man is who we say it is," Reynald argued. "Are we not in the position to determine who that person is? Are we not the best people to determine who that person is instead of crowning a stranger with no certainty of his ability to govern in accordance with the will of the Almighty? Our responsibility is to the people, to the land, not to one individual man. You WILL send for the armor, and you will do so immediately."

"You are Commander of the Armorum Custodes, and you report to the Church," Reverend Vendici responded firmly. "The Church does not take orders from the Armorum Custodes."

"It does now," Reynald replied matter-of-factly. "Our duty is to protect the Church, and the Church's duty is to minister to the people. The Church is failing on that responsibility, therefore, the Armorum Custodes must do what is necessary to ensure that the people are ministered to properly."

"What will you do if I do not send for the armor?" Reverend Vendici asked.

"This is an old building," Reynald said. "It would be a pity if a fire should break out."

"You would do not such thing!" the reverend cried in astonishment. "That would be a crime against the Church and punishable by death!"

"Accidents happen," Reynald continued unabashed, looking around the study. "Perhaps someone is studying in one of the libraries and accidentally knocks over a candle. Perhaps one of the many transcribers becomes weary and has the same accident.

It is cold this time of year and there are many fireplaces in the church. It would not be unthinkable that a hot coal escapes a fireplace and lands on a rug or tapestry." He turned and glared at Reverend Vendici. "As I said, you will send for the helmet, belt and boots immediately. When they arrive, you will relinquish them to me for protection. I will also maintain possession of the sword and shield, for safekeeping. Then when we have the breastplate from Gallard, you will crown the Heir of DuFay. Do you understand?"

"I understand that you are a wicked man and leave me with no options," Reverend Vendici replied bitterly. "I shall send for the armor. They should arrive back here within the week. May God have mercy upon you, Reynald, for I see you traveling down a path towards destruction."

"He has," Reynald replied with a smile. "He has." With that, he exited the holy man's study.

After a moment of contemplation, Reverend Vendici took a piece of paper and wrote two sentences on it. He then called one of his aides into his study.

"Get this to Hewlitt Knox as quickly as possible," the reverend instructed. Without question, the young man took the note and left the study.

Chapter 27

It was late in the afternoon, just an hour before sunset, as Andrew and Lawrence finally arrived in Stanwyck. There was not a lot of activity, as most people had completed their daily business and were back home for their evening meal. They did not meet anybody on the road as they passed the outer perimeter of the village.

"It feels as though we have stepped back in time," Lawrence said as they rode by the outer buildings of Stanwyck and headed toward the village square. "After having spent but a day in Buckington, Stanwyck feels quite modest to say the least."

"I cannot argue," Andrew agreed. He took a casual glance over his shoulder. "How many men would you say have followed us from Buckington?"

"Perhaps half a dozen," Lawrence replied. "Their attempts at stealth have failed quite impressively. Even dressed as ordinary travelers their coordinated movements and posture give them away."

"I would not put it beyond Vicenza to have sent two groups after us," Andrew countered. "The one behind us was meant to be seen, while the other escapes our attention by hiding in the shadows."

"Stanwyck is small, it would be difficult for them to remain in the shadows if that were the case. I believe the group on the road is the only one Vicenza sent," Lawrence replied. "They will maintain their distance until we retrieve the sword and shield and begin our return journey, at which time they will ambush us and rob us not only of the weapons, but our lives as well."

"These men will have been trained much more robustly and thoroughly than anyone we have fought previously," Andrew noted. "In truth, I have my doubts as to our survival should it come to combat."

"Then let us hope it does not come to that," Lawrence responded.

"If our plan is successful, we should have no worries," Andrew said. "See if you can find Victoria and Gregory. Let us meet at the tavern in an hour. I must pay the blacksmith a visit, then we shall discuss the next steps in our plan."

"Considering the threats we may soon face, I trust you will be stocking up on weaponry," Lawrence said as he turned his horse to his right and commenced his search for their two friends.

"At least two pieces," Andrew replied, watching Lawrence ride away. He turned and headed down the street toward the opposite end of the village where the blacksmith's shop was located. It only took him a few minutes to reach the shop and he was relieved to see that the blacksmith was still there, but it was obvious that he was about to cease work for the day.

"You will have to come back in the morrow," the blacksmith called out as Andrew approached the outdoor work area where the blacksmith was busy collecting various tools and taking them into the more secure shop. "My work is done for the day, and I have a hot meal waiting for me at home to which I am much looking forward."

"I understand," Andrew replied, stopping and dismounting Annon. "My day has been long and I, too, look forward to ending it with a plate of fresh food and a pint or two of ale. I pray that you would indulge me for just a few minutes as you finish securing your shop."

The blacksmith stopped what he was doing and turned to look at Andrew. "Make it quick," he said, standing up to his full height. As would be expected, the blacksmith was a large man, standing six feet, six inches tall with very wide shoulders, with arms and a chest that were built-up from years of handling heavy iron and steel. Andrew could imagine what a vice-like grip the man had to have. It almost appeared that the man was puffing-out his chest to intimidate Andrew into keeping the conversation short, but Andrew could see that the man's torso was immense, and he did not need to do anything to appear more daunting.

"I am in need of a sword and a shield," Andrew said plainly.

"Come back in the morn and you can have your pick," the blacksmith replied, motioning to a wall inside his shop that was lined with swords and shields.

"That I can do, but would you mind if I take a very quick look at what you have?" Andrew asked. The blacksmith appeared to be agitated and reluctant to oblige Andrew, but he gave in. "You have until I finish bringing these tools into the shop, which will be less than a minute."

Andrew quickly walked into the shop and looked at the weaponry. There were a dozen swords hanging from brackets on the wall and half that many shields propped up against the wall. No two were alike and they all reflected very skilled craftmanship.

"Your work is most excellent," Andrew said as the blacksmith stood in the doorway, obviously anxious for Andrew to leave.

"Come back in the morning when the light is better and you can inspect them more closely," the blacksmith said, ignoring the compliment. "We can negotiate the price then."

"I am not interested in any of these," Andrew said as he finished looking over the inventory and turned to the blacksmith. "They are all very finely made and show great skill. However, I wish to commission two, shall we say, unique, pieces of armor."

"Stranger, I am tired, and I am very hungry," the blacksmith said. "Come back in the morning and we can discuss your needs. I will let you know that I have many custom orders waiting to be filled, not to mention the daily needs that come to me. It would be several weeks before I could commence work on a sword and shield for you. If you are in immediate need, I recommend you choose from my inventory."

"That I cannot do," Andrew replied and walked over to one of the several tables in the shop. He retrieved a medium-sized satchel from his belt and, after glancing around the shop and through the doorway by which the blacksmith stood, satisfied that there were no eyes to see their business, emptied the contents on the table. The black-smith's eyes widened as he saw numerous small jewels fall onto the table along with a bar of solid gold.

"You see, the sword and shield that I need are very, very special, and I venture unlike anything you have ever crafted," Andrew said. "I have no doubt that your skills and talents are up to the task. However, I am in a bit of a rush, and I cannot wait several weeks for them to be completed. In fact, I only have two days before I must leave town to deliver them to a special person for a highly formal special coronation. I need to know if you will be able to help me." Andrew went on to explain to the blacksmith exactly what he needed. The blacksmith took a few minutes to glance around his shop at some of his finished pieces and some that were in various stages of completion. He then looked at the colorful pile on his table. It was not a difficult decision.

"Aye, I can help you," he answered. "It would not be possible to begin from nothing and fabricate what you need in such an abbreviated period of time, however, I do have several projects in various stages of fabrication, and I can easily adapt them to meet your needs. The day after tomorrow, in the evening, they shall be ready."

"I shall meet you then," Andrew said as he walked out of the shop.

As he walked to the tavern, Andrew could not shake the feeling that he was being watched. He looked around carefully but did not see anybody or anything that should raise such a feeling within him. The few people that were milling about appeared to be just ordinary village folk who did not give him a second glance. Nevertheless, the feeling persisted. He was about to attribute the paranoia to fatigue and hunger when a deep voice called out to him, a voice that he knew all too well. A voice that he thought he would never hear again.

"Andrew MacLean," the voice simply stated. Andrew turned to face the direction from which the voice had come. To his surprise, Walter materialized from the shadows. He was not alone. Ten other men, armed and ready for a fight, followed him. Colin was amongst them, his expression throwing darts of vengeance at Andrew.

"Your escape in Porthmaddon shall not be repeated here, MacLean," Colin said with an evil grin. "You have no friends to save you. You are alone."

"I would say that I am surprised but somehow, I am not," Andrew said as he surveyed the situation. He looked at Walter. "I take it that my exhortation to you regarding your choices in life fell on deaf ears?"

"I have been given a commission which I fully intend on fulfilling as long as there is breath in my body," Walter replied firmly. "As you have not wavered in yours, I shall not waver in mine."

"About that," Andrew started to reply but was cut-off by Walter.

"The sword," Walter said plainly. "I will have the sword now. Surrender it to me and no harm shall come to your friends. Yes, we know of the family with whom you have been staying. Refuse, and we will make you watch as we snatch the lives out of them, one by one, slowly and painfully, until you give me the sword."

Andrew recognized the direness of the situation. He could not take-on and defeat ten men in a fight. Without Lawrence at least at his side, he had no chance. Even with Lawrence fighting with him, there would still be no chance of survival. He was dissecting the scene, scrutinizing the men around him, trying to determine if there was a weak link that he could possibly fight through and get away, when another voice called out from behind Walter's men.

"MacLean, do you have an issue with these men?" Andrew re-cognized the man speaking as one of the Armor Guardians that had followed him and Lawrence from Buckington. Andrew could see the other five spreading out, preparing for what was likely to turn into a violent engagement with Walter and his men. He never thought he would be happy to see the Armor Guardians, but at that moment, he saw his salvation.

"As it so happens, I do," Andrew replied.

"What do they want?" the man asked.

"Surprisingly enough, the same thing that you want," Andrew answered.

"Gentlemen," the Armor Guardian called out to Walter and his comrades. "I am Sir Francis Cardona, Captain of the Armorum Custodes, serving the Covenantal Orthodox Church of Christ in Buckington. This man is on Church business. You will leave him to carry out his affairs."

"I have heard of the Armorum Custodes," Walter said, not intimidated. "Men who believe that a robe with a cross on it makes them holy and righteous, better than those around them. I despise your sanctimonious sect. This man has something that belongs to King Edwin Gallard, ruler of Nordham, something he stole nearly six years ago. King Gallard has tasked me to retrieve it and I fully intend on completing that task."

"We cannot allow that to happen," Captain Cardona replied, ignoring Walter's insult. "We were dispatched as his guardians to ensure that his venture is successful and that he returns to the Church that which belongs to the Church. And we shall do just that by every means necessary." Sir Cardona let his ordinary-looking cloak fall from his shoulders to reveal a tunic with the Armorum Custodes symbol on the torso. His companions did likewise. They drew their swords and prepared for a fight.

"You are defeated before you fight," Walter said, trying to intimidate the Armor Guardians. "You are outnumbered, and I dare say, out-killed by my men. You should leave and save your lives."

"That one," Andrew said to Sir Cardona, pointing to Walter, "is Edwin Gallard's military advisor and commander of the royal army. He has intimate knowledge of the DuFay breastplate, knowledge which I am certain would aid in your efforts to obtain it. It would be my recommendation to spare his life in order that your commander has the opportunity to acquire that knowledge, by whatever means he deems appropriate."

"We shall take that into consideration," Sir Cardona said less than convincingly.

"So be it," Walter said. "Men, attack!"

Nine of the ten men that had been focused on Andrew quickly drew their swords, turned and rushed the Armor Guardians. The Guardians reacted instantaneously and engaged Walter's men. One of Gallard's men instead rushed Andrew. Andrew saw the look of hate and revenge in Colin's eyes as the young man raised his sword, preparing to attack Andrew. Walter called out to Colin for him to stop, but Colin did not listen. Although he knew that both groups wanted him alive, Andrew could see that Colin's damaged ego had overtaken his self-control. He quickly drew his sword and took a defensive posture, successfully parrying Colin's first strike. Andrew knew that Colin was beyond listening to Walter and beyond self-control. That was all the advantage that Andrew needed. As Colin turned for a second blow, not fully on balance, Andrew rushed in and body-slammed Colin, knocking him backward several feet. Just as Colin got his balance and appeared poised to rush Andrew again, a sword was thrust through his torso from behind. A look of pain and surprise crossed Colin's face as he fell to the ground.

Andrew looked around and not seeing another immediate threat, checked to make sure that Walter was still there. Due to his broken right hand and not fully healed stomach injury, Walter was not participating in the fight but remained in place, confident that his men would be victorious. First there was one, then two of Walter's men on the ground with fatal injuries, then two of the Armor Guardians were down as well. It was seven of

Gallard's men against four Guardians. The furious fighting continued and by now, a dozen or so townsfolk had gathered, at a respectable distance, to see what was causing the resounding racket. Two more of Walter's men fell, creating a five-on-four fight. Another Guardian fell. Five against three. Andrew started to fear that Walter's men might defeat the Guardians, which he could not allow to happen. He quickly joined the melee and engaged the closest of Walter's men. Not expecting the attack, the man fell quickly. Four of Gallard's men against three Armor Guardians, plus Andrew. Andrew wasted no time in attacking the next man. In mere moments, the odds evened out with three of Gallard's men against the remaining three Custodes. Concluding that the Armor Guardians could take care of the last of Walter's men, Andrew turned his attention to Walter. He was just in time to see the man turn and try to make his escape. Andrew bolted from the field of battle and chased after Walter. Knowing the village layout and where Walter was likely headed, Andrew ran down a side alley to cut-off Walter. Stepping from the alley into a main thoroughfare, Andrew nearly knocked Walter over.

"That is quite far enough," Andrew said, the tip of his sword mere inches from Walter's gut.

"You should have killed me when you had the opportunity," Walter growled, knowing that he would not be able to put up much of a fight due to the injuries Andrew had imparted upon him just a couple of weeks earlier.

"Others have thought the same and there are times that I have questioned my decision to spare your life," Andrew replied. "As fate would have it, doing so has proven rather beneficial to me. Thanks to you and your men, I am rid of those who, I believe, were sent to ultimately kill me."

"The one guardian, the captain, said they were sent to protect you," Walter said, a confused look on his face. "He said you were on a mission for the Church. Why would you believe they were going to kill you?"

Andrew considered carefully what to say. Knowing that Walter was going to be interrogated by the commander of the Armorum Custodes, Andrew did not want to say anything to Walter that might jeopardize his plans. An idea came to him, a way to use Walter to his benefit.

"It is quite the long story," Andrew answered, "so I will spare you the intimate details. My search for the Heir of DuFay led me to Buckington. There is a church in Buckington that has traced the lineage of Robert DuFay, the last DuFay to sit on the throne, and they have finally located the true heir to Reginald DuFay. However, a rather radical sect of the church wants to place their preferred person on the DuFay throne instead of the rightful heir. I was sent here to retrieve the DuFay sword and shield, lest one of my closest friend's life be forfeited. All they need to do now is bring the DuFay Armor together and coronate their chosen one as king. They are at this moment retrieving the helmet, belt, and boots from secret locations and after I give them the sword and shield, they shall have five of the six pieces. They say that they have a plan to obtain the breastplate from Gallard and complete the collection. I had reason to believe that once I relinquished the sword and shield, I would be killed to protect the secrecy of their treachery."

"You have the shield?" Walter asked, surprised.

"I do," Andrew confirmed, giving no additional details.

"Edwin will never relinquish the breastplate," Walter said. "He is obsessed with it and being crowned the Heir of DuFay. He will storm whatever village, town, or city he must in order to get the remaining pieces. This Buckington you mentioned sounds like an ideal place to visit next. The DuFay Armor is as good as in his hands."

"That will never happen," Andrew replied matter-of-factly. "The armor is being taken to—" Andrew paused, appearing to catch himself before saying something he did not want to say "—well, let us just say a very secure and old stronghold that has not been used in some time. There it will be safe until the breastplate is obtained and the heir can be crowned king. No army has ever been able to defeat this citadel, and no army will ever be able to do so."

"You underestimate the resolve of Edwin Gallard," Walter stated. "You are doing him a favor by bringing the other five pieces to one location. It will not take us long to determine where this 'old stronghold' is and once we do, Gallard shall descend upon it like a furious tempest. No man shall be left standing. Gallard shall have the DuFay Armor and shall be crowned as the Heir of DuFay."

"Considering how Gallard and his men are five weeks away at the minimum, I do not see that as a threat," Andrew responded.

"Are they?" Walter said, a wry smile on his face. "Are you certain of that?"

"Are they not?" Andrew asked.

"I cannot say where Gallard is this very moment," Walter replied, "but it was never his intention to permanently stay in Durinburg. We only went there because you and the sword were there, and we knew that there was a good chance the shield was there. As the sword and shield are no longer there, Gallard has no reason to remain. He may be five weeks away, he may be five days away," Walter said slyly, "you have no way of knowing."

"Why would he come here?" Andrew asked, confused. "He has no idea that I am here, nor that the sword and shield are here."

"Do you believe that those men lying on the ground were the only ones who were with me?" Walter asked in response. "How do you suppose I survived our fight? I have men everywhere, MacLean. Do you not think it possible that I sent men back to Gallard two weeks ago to inform him of your presence here? Or that I sent word to Nordham to have a company of men dispatched to Stanwyck? You know nothing, MacLean."

"What I do know is that it is very unlikely that you shall ever see Gallard again," Andrew said as two Armor Guardians approached them.

"MacLean," Captain Cardona called out.

"Take this man back to Reynald, I am certain much information can be drawn from him," Andrew answered.

"The sword and the shield," Cardona continued. "Give them to us."

"It has been a long day, and the sword and the shield are not readily accessible," Andrew replied. "I gave them to a friend for safekeeping and that friend is not here, therefore I do not know their exact location. He shall return the day after tomorrow. I will get them then and present them to you to take back to Buckington with your prisoner."

"That was not the agreement," Cardona said, sensing something was amiss. "Commander Vicenza was quite emphatic that you bring them back personally."

"And I was quite emphatic with your commander that he not send Armorum Custodes to follow us," Andrew countered. "It was fortunate for us both that we did not follow-through with our promise to dispose of anyone sent after us."

"You are placing the life of your female friend in Buckington in peril," Captain Cardona replied. "If the sword and the shield are not in the hands of the Church by sundown five days from now, it shall not go well with her."

"They shall be in your possession two evenings from now," Andrew replied, "then it will be up to you to get them to Buckington. My friend's life and health shall not be in jeopardy."

Cardona considered his limited options. Two of his men had been killed. Two others were gravely wounded during the fighting and their survival was in question. He had an obligation to do whatever he could to save their lives. He could not return to Buckington without the sword and shield. Then there was Walter, Gallard's man. Cardona did not know what information the man might be able to provide that would aid their efforts to obtain the breast-plate, but any information would be helpful. He did not know if Andrew was lying about not knowing exactly where the sword and shield were located, although his gut instincts told him that Andrew was not being truthful. If he had more men, he might be able to press the issue with Andrew and determine whether or not he was telling the truth. But as it stood, that would not be an option. Finally, he responded.

"I do not believe you, MacLean," Cardona said, eyeing Andrew with great distrust. "I have no doubt that you know where the sword and shield are and could retrieve them this moment if you so desired. However, with two of my men dead and two others with grievous wounds, and now this prisoner to account for, it seems my options are limited. We shall see to the care of our comrades and to the burial of the two who whose lives were sacrificed in the name of the Church." The guardian gave Andrew a warning glare. "We shall keep an eye on you, MacLean. Do not attempt to leave the village. Two days from now, I fully expect the sword and shield to be delivered to me. If they are not..."

"I know," Andrew interrupted, finishing the thought, "my friend's life shall be in peril."

With that, the two custodes led Walter away and back to the scene of the fight. Andrew followed, though a bit more carefully to ensure that there were no threats lurking in the shadows. A large crowd had gathered, including Lawrence, Victoria, and Gregory. Andrew approached his friends.

"It would appear that our tagtails found a bit of trouble," Lawrence said, then he saw Walter having his hands tied by one of the custodes. "Ah, that would make sense then. I suppose this had something to do with you?"

"Something," Andrew acknowledged.

"Who are the men with the red crosses on their shirts?" Victoria asked.

"Armorum Custodes, or Armor Guardians, from Buckington, sent to follow us and procure the DuFay sword and shield," Andrew answered. "Most likely after relieving Lawrence and me of our lives."

"How do they know that you have the sword and shield?" Gregory asked.

"It is a long story," Andrew replied. "Lawrence and I need something to eat. Let us go to the tavern and we will fill you in on everything that has happened."

The foursome left the battle scene and walked across the village to the tavern. It was bustling as usual, but they were able to find an unoccupied table and sat. After ordering food and drink, Andrew proceeded to recite to Victoria and Gregory all that had happened over the past two days. He avoided saying the name "DuFay" and spoke as softly as he could to keep potential eavesdroppers from hearing his words. They sat in silence as Andrew spoke, listening intently to every word, digesting the ramifications. When he finished speaking, Victoria finally spoke.

"So, you are the heir?" she asked, then said as a statement, "You are the heir."

"I am," Andrew confirmed with a wry smile. "Whether I like it or not, and I assure you it is 'not,' I am the heir."

"What are you going to do?" Victoria continued. "You have stated in no uncertain terms that you have no desire to be crowned as the Heir of DuFay and king."

"That is true, but I may have to acquiesce in order to avoid Vicenza from implementing his plan for a Church-run government and establishing what amounts to a theocracy, which is what he is planning," Andrew answered.

"Even if you should change your mind, you would have to have all six pieces of the armor in your possession. You said that the Church has three of the pieces. You have two and Gallard has the last. You could at most possess only five of the six pieces, with the breastplate remaining with Gallard," Victoria stated. "How could you get the breastplate from Gallard?"

"I am working on it," Andrew said, though his tone lacked confidence. "As fate would have it, Gallard and his army are returning home. Reverend Vendici sent my uncle a note which was passed on to me just prior to leaving Buckington. Brewster all but confirmed the information. Their journey will take them past Stanwyck. Vicenza will undoubtedly execute an ambush in an attempt to get the breastplate."

"Does he have a fighting force large enough to accomplish that?" Gregory asked.

"I am not sure," Andrew admitted. "Reverend Vendici previously informed me that there are approximately one thousand Armorum Custodes here in Buckington and another one thousand, five hundred that are spread out within a day or two of Buckington and can be called to arms on short notice."

"Two thousand, five hundred," Gregory said thoughtfully. "You know that Gallard's army numbers just under twice that many."

"That is Vicenza's problem," Andrew replied.

"All that aside," Gregory continued, "I feel as though I am missing something. You are here to get the sword and shield and give them to Vicenza. If you do not, Marie's life may be in danger. If you do, then how would you get them back?"

"The DuFay sword and shield shall not be relinquished to the Armorum Custodes, I can assure you of that," Andrew replied. "They cannot possess any of the pieces of the DuFay Armor."

"What about the three pieces that the Church already has?" Gregory asked. "Cannot Vicenza, if he is as determined as you say he is, get his hands on them?"

"Oh, he is about to get his hands on the helmet, belt and boots, for sure," Andrew answered surprisingly, "but they are not what he is expecting."

"How so?" Gregory asked.

"We have a plan. He will not lay his hands on the real armor."

"That is all well and good, but what about the sword and the shield?" Victoria asked.

"I am having artificial ones created to send back with the Armor Guardians," Andrew replied.

"What happens when Vicenza discovers they are fakes?" Victoria asked. "You have to assume that he will. He will be furious. What will happen to Marie?"

"And that brings us to the next part of my plan," Andrew said with a smile. "I need you and Lawrence to get to Buckington as quickly as you can."

"I just got here!" Lawrence cried out, throwing his hands into the air.

"I am sorry, my friend," Andrew said with a shrug of his shoulders. "The appearance of Walter has forced a modification to our plan. If more of Gallard's men arrive, and after speaking with Walter I am convinced they will, I may need Gregory to intervene, if possible. I would feel more confident in Marie's safety as well if you were in Buckington along with Angus."

"My boy," Lawrence said, placing a hand of comfort on Gregory's shoulder, "I shall leave this man of mayhem in your care. And believe me, what you have experienced so far is nothing compared to what he is capable of. Getting his companions into harm's way is his favorite past-time."

"If it is a rescue mission you have in mind, did you not say that Vicenza will have Marie under watch and therefore rescuing her would be all but impossible?" Victoria asked. "And what chance would the two of us, three if you include Angus, have against the Armorum Custodes?"

"None," Andrew admitted. "But the beauty of my plan is that you should not have to confront them. Well, maybe a couple at the most."

"That is reassuring," Victoria said sarcastically.

"You have not heard the plan," Andrew said as he proceeded to tell them the scheme that he had concocted.

Chapter 28

It was late afternoon as Andrew approached an old, abandoned farmhouse about a half-mile from the outskirts of Stanwyck. Two days had passed since his arrival back in Stanwyck, and the deadline for presenting the sword and shield to Captain Cardona was upon him. He tied Annon's reins to a not-too-sturdy hitching post outside of the house and after a quick glance to ensure he had not been followed, Andrew entered the house. It took a moment for his eyes to fully adjust to the dimmer interior of the house. There was no furniture in the house other than an old table that looked as if it would collapse at any moment. At first, Andrew believed that he was alone, but a movement in the dark corner to his right told him otherwise. His hand went to his sword out of habit, but he quickly recognized the blacksmith as the large man stepped forward, and Andrew relaxed. Without a word, the black-smith hefted a large canvass bag onto the table which creaked in protest of the weight. He opened the bag and pulled out the freshly completed sword and shield that Andrew had commissioned, both separately wrapped in canvass of their own. He unwrapped the sword and shield. Even in the dimness of the house, the two pieces of armament glinted brightly. Andrew reached out and picked up the sword.

"Magnificent work," he said, turning the weapon over in his hands. The sword's blade was like a mirror, having been buffed to perfection. Numerous colorful gemstones had been imbedded in the blade, an impressive achievement. The large two-handed hilt had been gilded and had also been buffed to a mirror-like finish. Like the blade, numerous gemstones had been imbedded in it. Distinct designs, which appeared to be words from a foreign language, had been carved into the blade near the hilt. It was unlike any sword Andrew had ever seen, save one. "It could easily pass for the real one."

"The real one?" the blacksmith asked, confused. "What do you mean the real one?"

"Nothing," Andrew replied, scolding himself internally for the slip of the tongue. He laid the sword back on the table and picked up the shield. It, too, had a great glint to it despite the lack of a light source in the house. The entire shield's surface had been gilded and buffed, and like the sword, numerous gemstones had been imbedded into it. Also like the sword's blade, there were markings that appeared to be words from another language carved into it. It was truly a work of craftmanship that surpassed words.

"The quality of your work is beyond accolades," Andrew said as he re-wrapped the two pieces of armor and returned them to the bag. "You are not a blacksmith, you are an artisan."

"The words that you had me engrave on them," the blacksmith said, "what language is it and what do they mean?"

"They are from a language that is more than two thousand years old," Andrew replied, not wanting to be specific. "It is from a land far from this place. As for their meaning, they are simply expressions of admiration and encouragement for the intended recipient, a long-time friend of mine. I must leave this very evening for the long journey to deliver them to him."

"The gemstones," the blacksmith continued. "They are not exactly what I was expecting them to be. They are a bit inconsistent with the gold gilding and the nature of the gifts, are they not?"

"There is a long story behind that," Andrew replied, eager to end the conversation and deliver the armor to the Armor Guardians. He reached into his tunic and pulled out a small leather bag that was heavy with coins. "I believe this should be more than sufficient to reflect the quality of your work and the short timeframe," he said as he handed the bag to the blacksmith. "Of course, any gold that was left over from the gilding is yours to keep."

"Of course," the blacksmith replied, although he had held no intention of returning any of it to Andrew. "I assume our business is complete?"

"That it is," Andrew confirmed. "Oh, one more thing. I would appreciate it if our business were to remain our business, at least for the next few days."

"Your business is your business," the blacksmith replied. "While I suspect that there is more to this sword and shield than being simple gifts to an old friend, it is none of my affair and my customers always have my confidence. I have much work to do. Good day." Payment in hand, the blacksmith left the farmhouse. Andrew heard him walk to the back of the house, mount a horse, and ride back toward town. He waited a few minutes, then stepped to the doorway and while remaining in the shadows, looked outside as far as he could to see if there was anybody else in the area. Satisfied that he was not being spied upon, Andrew strapped the bag to Annon's back, hoisted himself into the saddle, and headed to his meeting with Cardona.

It was a short ten-minute ride into town. Andrew headed to the jail where he had arranged to meet the Armor Guardians since that was where they were spending most of their time, keeping watch over Walter. He entered the building with the canvas bag thrown over his shoulder. Captain Cardona and his comrade were seated at a table with the town's constable. Walter was laying on the extremely uncomfortable cot in the only cell in the small building, one arm thrown over his eyes. Cardona looked at Andrew and the bag over his shoulder, then spoke to the constable.

"If you do not mind, Edward, we have business with his man that is of a rather sensitive nature," he said. "When completed,

Jeff Boles

we will depart with our prisoner and travel back to Buckington. A few minutes of privacy would be greatly appreciated."

The constable glared at Cardona, his disdain for being instructed to leave his own building not the least bit veiled. However, it was apparent that during the past two days Cardona had established a position of authority, or at least intimidation, over the constable and without a word, the man arose and left the building. Satisfied that he was out of earshot, Cardona turned his attention to Andrew.

"You have the sword and shield?" he asked.

Wordlessly, Andrew set the bag on the table and stepped back. Cardona paused for a moment, looking from the bag to Andrew, then back to the bag before reaching out and opening it. He first pulled out the shield. Carefully, he unwrapped it. Under the glow from the lantern on the table, the shield's beauty was fully revealed. Cardona slowly and gently ran his hand over the piece of armor, his admiration and reverence for it reflected in his eyes. There was the bare hint of a smile on his lips, unavoidable under the circumstances. He then retrieved the sword and even before it was fully unwrapped, Cardona could not suppress his complete awe. His eyes widened in rapturous admiration and his mouth hung open. He turned the weapon over in his hands, inspecting every inch of it. Andrew held his breath, fearful that somehow Cardona would discover that they were forgeries. However, the blacksmith's work was impeccable, and Cardona was none the wiser. He gently wrapped the pieces of armor with their individual protective cloths and returned them to the large canvass bag. He nodded to his partner, who stood and walked over to Walter's cell and opened it. Walter had sat-up while Cardona was inspecting the armor, and his expression was a mixture of admiration and determination. The guardian took leather bindings and tightly secured Walter's hands.

"I must confess that I was extremely doubtful you would actually relinquish these," Cardona said to Andrew as he stood and grasped the end of the bag.

222

"That was the deal," Andrew replied, a slight hint of defeat in his voice. "The armor for my friend's safety. Her life is more important than two pieces of armor no matter how beautiful they are."

"Then you do not fully understand the value of what is in this bag," Cardona replied almost condescendingly. "They are worth more than a thousand lives."

"You have what you came for," Andrew retorted. He looked at Walter. "And more. I am certain that the information you will be able to pull from this man will have immense value as well."

"We shall see," Cardona replied. He walked out of the jail and to three horses that were tethered near the side of the building. He tied the bag to the saddle of one horse, which his partner mounted. Cardona helped Walter onto a second horse, then mounted the third.

"It is most fortunate for you how this has turned out," Cardona spoke down to Andrew. "Commander Vicenza had a different plan. Had this man and his friends not intervened…, well, I shall leave it to your imagination." With those final comments, Cardona turned his horse and headed toward Buckington. When they were out of sight, Andrew reached over to untie Annon's reins. Gregory appeared from the side of the building where he had been spying on the conversation since Andrew had entered the building.

"I do not believe that he is going to care much for how events unfold for him and his friend." Gregory said. "I do not envision anybody showing up to intervene on his behalf."

"If I have learned one thing during my many years, especially the past six, it is that the only thing predictable about life is its unpredictability," Andrew replied. "No matter what your plans and expectations are, you must presume that unforeseen barriers will arise that will require you to alter your plan, and you must be ready to do so." Andrew looked up and down the street casually. He always had the feeling that he was being watched. He feared it would be a feeling that pestered him the rest of his life. He turned back to Gregory. "How was your scouting excursion?"

"It was very productive," Gregory answered. "A small company of Gallard's men, I would estimate fifty, are heading this way. They should arrive in a few hours. You were right."

"Any sign of Gallard and his army?" Andrew inquired.

"Not directly," Gregory answered, "but as you know, Gallard always sent a small company ahead of his army to scout for provisions and places to encamp. They ordinarily ride one to two days ahead of the main body and send reports back."

"Any reason to believe that the men you saw were anything other than such a scouting party?"

Gregory shook his head. "No. We can be sure that Gallard is but a few days away at most. I could go out again, skirt around the scouting party, and confirm in person."

"No, I need you here to meet those men when they arrive," Andrew said. "When they arrive, you will go out to meet them and tell them that you were with Walter, who was on a secret mission for the king. You do not know what that mission was, but it entailed something of grand value. You were away from the group securing provisions when they were attacked by the Armorum Custodes. You arrived in time to see Walter taken into custody and the rest of his men lying on the ground, dead. You suspect that they are taking him to Buckington where the Armorum Custodes are stationed, and that they left only a few hours ago."

"When I tell them that, they will undoubtedly chase after the two guardians and Walter in order to rescue him," Gregory surmised. "After all that he has done to you, your new plan is to allow him to be rescued instead of interrogated by Vicenza, which I believe we all know would be excruciatingly unpleasant?" he asked incredulously.

"My motivation is not compassion," Andrew replied. "We need Gallard to lead his army to an old Armor Guardian stronghold called Dover Castle, in Pembrookshire, a two-day ride northeast of here and a day from Buckington. I told Walter that there is an old stronghold where the DuFay Armor was being taken and held until the breastplate was retrieved, and then the heir to DuFay would be crowned, but I did not give its name. I have no doubt that one way or another, Walter will be successful in divulging from Cardona or his fellow guardian the location of this stronghold. Once he is rescued, he will send a messenger back to Gallard to inform him that the DuFay Armor, including the sword and shield, are being held there. He will then head to Dover Castle as quickly as he can. Gallard will push his army to its limits to get there as quickly as possible. When they arrive, they will be exhausted. With the Armorum Custodes behind us, we will stand a good chance of defeating Gallard."

"What about those unforeseen barriers you mentioned just a few minutes ago?" Gregory asked, a bit sarcastically, but it was a valid question.

"If one should present itself, we will just have to adjust," Andrew answered. "I need to speak with Patrick McKenzie. Let us head to his farm. We should be able to get something to eat as well and return before Gallard's men arrive."

Two hours later, just as dusk was setting in, fifty of Gallard's men arrived in town. The leader of the company started giving directions to several of the men and they began spreading out. Andrew and Gregory stepped out of the tavern where they had been waiting and into the shadows.

"Are you ready?" Andrew asked the young man. "I hope your acting skills remain sharp, as your life just might depend on them."

"Thank you for your confidence and re-assurance," Gregory replied sarcastically. He adjusted the blood-stained tunic he had confiscated from one of the men who had been killed during the fight with the Armorum Custodes. Around his head he tied a strip of cloth that had a small blood stain on it as well. After taking a deep breath he rushed forward, half-stumbling, to the man who had been issuing orders. Andrew watched Gregory gesture excitedly as he reported to the officer the story of what had happened, their fight with the Armorum Custodes, and that

Walter had been kidnapped. At first the officer did not appear entirely convinced of Gregory's story and looked around the area suspiciously. He then looked more closely at Gregory's clothing and the bandage on his head. Although Andrew could not hear the conversation, it was apparent that something seemed out of place to the officer. He pointed to the bandage wrapped around Gregory's head in a questioning manner. Gregory appeared to ignore the question and to plead with the officer, pointing to the road that led out of town and to Buckington. Just as it seemed that Gregory's story was falling apart, Patrick McKenzie, who had been standing in a small group of townspeople watching the episode, broke from the crowd and approached the two men. He spoke to the officer while gesturing towards Gregory and nodding his head, then pointed to the same road Gregory had previously indicated to the officer. After a few minutes of contemplation and discussion with his junior officers, the lead officer called his men together. Two of them quickly turned their horses and headed back down the road from which they had arrived. The other forty-eight men headed in the other direction, towards Buckington. When they were out of sight, Andrew stepped from the shadows and joined Patrick and Gregory.

"That was a bit tense for a moment there," he said to Gregory, who was removing his bandage and tunic.

"The officer was not exactly the trusting type," Gregory replied. "I had never met him previously. He was rather dubious as to my claims of being one of Gallard's men under Walter. He was about to insist on seeing the nature of my injuries, which would have not gone well for me."

"That is why I had Patrick come along to provide corroboration for your story," Andrew said. He looked at Patrick. "Thank you for your help."

"It was nothing," Patrick answered. "I do not care for Gallard and how he pillaged our land the last time he came through our village. If I can assist in bringing detriment upon him, it is my pleasure to do so."

"Were you able to make mention of Walter's mission and him saying it should be completed within a couple of days?" Andrew asked Gregory.

"Aye, that I did," Gregory replied. "The only problem I see is that Gallard will be leading his men to Buckington and not Dover Castle," Gregory said.

"When Walter is rescued, he will without a doubt send word back to Gallard that he needs to direct his army to the old guardian fortification," Andrew replied. "If your estimation is accurate regarding the scouting party being two days ahead of the main body of the army, Gallard should arrive here sometime the day after tomorrow. Once the messengers reach him and tell him about Walter's abduction and that he believed to be near the completion of his mission, which was to obtain the sword and the shield, Gallard will push his pace. Today is Thursday. I expect Gallard's army to get here by Saturday afternoon, the evening at the latest. Sunday morning, they will depart for Dover Castle. He will drive them feverishly and they will arrive sometime Monday afternoon at the earliest."

"And then?" Patrick asked.

"Utter chaos," Andrew replied simply.

Chapter 29

It was well after dark Thursday evening when Lawrence and Victoria arrived in Buckington. There was still a significant amount of activity in the city, which was not surprising due to its size and number of inhabitants and visitors. They immediately headed for Hewlitt Knox's shop. A lantern's light showed through the lone window along the front of the shop. Lawrence rapped on the door and within a few seconds, as if he were standing by the door waiting for a knock, Hewlitt opened it. He quickly ushered the visitors in and after a brief look up and down the street, shut the door.

"I cannot express how happy I am to see you," Hewlitt said, firmly grasping Lawrence's shoulder. "It may just be paranoia enhanced by old age, but I would swear that everywhere I go I have Armor Guardians following me."

"How is Marie?" Lawrence asked. "Have you spoken with her?"

"Not directly," Hewlitt replied. "I felt it would not be prudent to do so, lest Reynald get word of it and suspicions arise. But I have spoken with Reverend Vendici, and he says that she is doing well, although she is understandably quite curious as to what is going on."

"Has he revealed any of our plan to her?" Lawrence asked, a bit concerned.

"Not that he has relayed to me," Hewlitt replied. "But he says that she is very intuitive, and she knows something ominous is on the horizon. She feels that there are eyes on her any time she steps outside of the church. Actually, she feels the same even when she does not step outside of the church."

"I am sure that Vicenza is having her watched day and night," Lawrence replied, "which could make the next phase of our plan a bit challenging. Speaking of which, please forgive my rudeness. Hewlitt Knox, I would like to introduce to you Victoria Eriksson."

"It is a pleasure to meet you, Victoria," Hewlitt said, reaching his hand out to Victoria. Without hesitation and with a cordial smile, Victoria took his hand.

"It is a pleasure to meet you as well," she replied.

"I trust you have been fully briefed on this part of the plan and what you will need to do, and the potential danger associated with it?" Hewlitt asked.

"That I have," Victoria confirmed. "However, danger and unfavorable odds are not strangers to me. I am confident in our success."

"While I do not doubt your abilities, the danger you may face will easily surpass anything you have experienced before, of that you can be confident," Hewlitt warned. "However, Andrew expressed great confidence in you as a fighter and admiration of you as a person, therefore I have no doubt that you will indeed be successful." Victoria could not suppress a sheepish smile.

"We must move quickly," Lawrence interjected. "The sword and shield could arrive as early as tomorrow afternoon, depending on how quickly Vicenza's men travel with Walter. I suspect it will be closer to tomorrow evening. According to Andrew, though, Walter was very obscure regarding whether or not he had additional men around Stanwyck. If he did, it is possible that they would be able to chase-down Vicenza's men and seize the sword and shield, in which case they would never arrive here. Vicenza would believe that Andrew betrayed their agreement, and his anger would fall on Marie. What of the other three pieces of armor, the helmet, belt and boots?" Lawrence asked. "When will they arrive?"

"Tomorrow night," Hewlitt replied. "Well, the replicas at least."

"We need to complete the exchange this evening. The darkness outside is our most important ally right now," Lawrence said.

"She will be followed," Hewlitt stated. "You know this."

"Her instructions will need to incorporate guidance on how to elude such shadows," Lawrence replied. "Andrew told you what to write. I will follow her to ensure she is successful in losing whatever tails she may have. Victoria, after we leave, you will circle back and enter the building from the rear. If there are indeed eyes focused on Hewlitt, they will need to see us both leave, otherwise suspicions may arise."

"Understood," Victoria confirmed.

"Are you ready to pay Reverend Vendici a visit?" Lawrence asked Hewlitt.

"I will wait several minutes after the two of you leave, then I will leave," Hewlitt said.

"Good," Lawrence said. "Ladies first," he said to Victoria, motioning to the front door. Without another word, they left the shop.

Hewlitt waited ten minutes before dimming the lantern and exiting his shop. He locked the door and headed down the street toward the church. As always, he felt like he was being watched but could not determine whether there truly was someone watching and following him or if it was just nerves. It was a short five-minute walk to the church. Not surprisingly, there were several townspeople sitting in the pews, spread out, meditating, and praying. Hewlitt was familiar with all of them but said nothing and continued to the pulpit area. There was a young man sitting near the pulpit, one of the associate ministers of the church, his presence intended for anybody who needed counseling. Hewlitt spoke with him, and the young man nodded, getting up and leaving the sanctuary. In a few minutes he returned with Reverend Vendici. The two men sat on the front pew.

"It is good to see you, Hewlitt," Reverend Vendici said.

"And you," Hewlitt replied.

"I trust things are going well?" Reverend Vendici asked.

"That they are," Hewlitt responded. "Business is better than it has been in a while. It is difficult for these old bones to keep up with the demands being placed on them. I have had many customers this week. They are all asking for special orders."

"I imagine it can be rather stressful," Reverend Vendici stated understandingly.

"In fact, I had two customers come in this evening with a special order. They need it completed as soon as possible," Hewlitt continued.

"I see," Reverend Vendici replied, nodding.

"How are your students?" Hewlitt asked. "I trust their studies are going well."

"You know how young people can be," Reverend Vendici replied. "Restless and anxious. It can be difficult keeping them focused, especially the ones who want to question everything. As you said, it is difficult for these old bones to keep up with the demands being placed on them."

Hewlitt chuckled. "Well, I can think of no other person who can keep them in line and provide them with clear instruction as well as you can. I will let you get back to your obligations, I know you have much to do. I simply felt the need to see a friendly face."

"As always, it is my pleasure to sit and speak with you," Reverend Vendici answered with a smile. "Have a restful evening."

"And you," Hewlitt replied. He laid a hand of friendship on Reverend Vendici's shoulder, then stood and walked out of the building. Reverend Vendici waited a few moments, then arose and left the sanctuary. Even if they had been watching, nobody would have been able to see the man of God pocket the small, folded piece of paper.

Chapter 30

The pain from the wounds that Andrew had inflicted upon him three weeks prior continued to grow the longer Walter was forced to ride. While the wounds were healing, the seriousness of their nature would require many more days for complete recovery and in the meantime, the pain was something he would have to endure. It did not help that his captors had set a quick pace. Although he was a highly skilled horseman and knew how to minimize the jolting from the horse's gait, several hours of riding were taking their toll. He was exhausted, and there was no indication that they would be slowing down any time soon. He knew that to make mention of his physical condition would be a waste of breath. So far, they had traveled in near silence. Walter decided to change that.

"Buckington," he said, breaking the silence. "That is where we are headed, yes?" When neither of the other two men responded, Walter continued. "I remember Buckington. I have been there three times in my life. It is quite an impressive city. My first visit was when I was a young child, perhaps five or six years old. My father had business there and took our entire family along. What a grand time that was. From a child's perspective, Buckington was a world of its own. When I was sixteen, I returned with a friend of mine to take advantage of the advanced educational system. We also took advantage of the diverse social and entertainment venues, if you know what I mean. From the perspective of a young man, Buckington was a world of opportunity. Unfortunately, our curiosity and ambitions got the better of us and we were required to leave. In retrospect…"

"Brewster, your reminiscence is of no interest to us," Captain Cardona said over his shoulder. They were riding in single file with Cardona leading the way. Walter was in the middle and the other Armor Guardian, who was carrying the sword and shield, brought up the rear. "To us, silence is the preferred riding partner."

"My last visit came just a couple of years after my second visit," Walter continued, ignoring Cardona. "My best friend and I just could not forget about the opportunities that were presented to us in Buckington. Our visit was quite short that time, but profitable. Very profitable. You could say that it was that visit which, through no original intention of mine, is leading me back there for a fourth time. That is, assuming we make it there."

"What is that supposed to mean?" Cardona asked. "Do you believe that you, a man who is still healing from nearly fatal wounds, have the ability to overcome us and escape? Perhaps we should tighten your bindings and double them to ensure our safety."

"I remember hearing stories of the Armorum Custodes when I was there as a young man," Walter continued. "The requirements to join the ranks were formidable. I once heard that only one man in fifty who sought to join was able to pass the tests and be accepted. Yes, strength and dedication were of utmost importance. Loyalty was the greatest requirement, though. Extreme loyalty, if not fanaticism."

"You will derive no pleasant memories from your next visit, I can assure you of that," Cardona warned.

"As I was saying, I remember hearing many stories of the Armorum Custodes," Walter said. "One of the stories was from many years past. It involved a battle, over what I do not recall, that took place at some kind of stronghold or citadel not so far from here. It was a grand battle according to the story, where the Armorum Custodes fought gallantly and overcame great odds to achieve victory. It was said that the Lord himself came down and fought alongside them, such was his affection for those men. It has always bothered me that I cannot recall the name of that place."

"Dover Castle, in Pembrookshire," Cardona replied. "Five hundred Armorum Custodes defeated a barbarian hoard that outnumbered them three to one."

"What was the reason for the battle?" Walter asked.

"It matters not," Cardona answered. "Battles are fought for many reasons. Now, I wish to ride in silence. There will be no additional conversation."

"I was simply trying to help pass the time since it appears we have much of it on our hands," Walter said. "There is something else about which I have always been greatly curious when it comes to the Armorum Custodes. Are the stories about the bath houses true?"

"I warn you," Cardona said, turning in his saddle, "if you do not cease speaking, I shall with much satisfaction gag you. And then..." He stopped mid-sentence. Something in the distance caught his eye. He stopped his horse and held up his hand. Walter's horse, which was tethered to Cardona's, stopped automatically and the other armor guardian stopped his horse. While it was several hours past dusk and darkness covered the land, the light of a full moon shone brightly and what clouds floated across the sky were thin and sparse. Cardona kept his eyes on the road and turned his head slightly, intently listening to the sounds of the night. Above the ordinary sounds of the nocturnal life that surrounded them, Cardona could distinguish a low rumble. To his trained ear, it was the sound of a multitude of horses at full gallop. He turned his eyes to Walter, who was smiling. To Walter, it was the sound of salvation.

"Gallard's?" Cardona asked, although he knew the answer. There would be no other reason for a large contingency of riders to be galloping at full speed at that time of night.

"I suspect so," Walter replied.

"How did they know?"

"Does it matter?" Walter answered. "What you need to be asking instead is how much you value your life. All you need to do is give me the sword and the shield. That is all we want. The two of you may continue to Buckington, unharmed. You do not need to lose your life tonight."

Cardona considered the circumstances. He did not believe that he would be permitted to continue to Buckington unharmed. He also knew that returning to Buckington without the sword and shield would end his tenure in the Armorum Custodes, and he would live out his life labeled a failure. Trying to outrun the pursuers was also not an option. He knew that Walter was already in great pain and an extended gallop at full speed would not be possible for him. He could leave Walter behind and make for Buckington with his fellow Guardian but with Gallard's men closing in on them so quickly, there was no guarantee that they could make it. The only thing of which he was certain was that the sword and shield had to get to Buckington, at any cost. Even if it meant his life.

"Peter," the captain said to his fellow Guardian. "I charge you with the honorable task of ensuring that the sword and the shield get to Commander Vicenza. Do not travel along the main road. Are you familiar with the woodland trail?"

"Aye," Peter responded. "I have traversed it many times."

"Then take it," Cardona instructed him. "Push your horse to its limit. Only rest when absolutely necessary and even then, make it brief. The woodland trail will get you to Buckington more quickly than the main road. Tell the Commander to ready the Armorum Custodes. An attack may be imminent."

"And you?" Peter asked.

"Tell him that it has been my pleasure and honor to serve under his command for all these years. Now ride!"

Peter, knowing the urgency of the matter, did not pause and dug his boots into the horse's ribs. The well-trained horse bolted forward at full speed and quickly disappeared into the darkness.

"An interesting choice," Walter said. "You are sacrificing your life needlessly. You could have left me here and ridden off with him."

"Our horses are wearing down, and I doubt we could get

much farther at a full gallop," Cardona replied. "While it is likely that the horses of those who pursue us are just as worn and would not be able to intercept us, it is not a wager I care to make. My primary mission is to get the sword and shield to Buckington, at any cost. While you are not part of that mission, I cannot ignore the depth of your knowledge about Gallard and the breastplate and the value of that knowledge to the Church. If I can get you to Buckington, the gratitude of the Church will be immense. Now, if I were you, I would hold on tightly. If you should choose to 'accidentally' fall off your horse, if the fall does not kill you, my sword will."

Cardona ensured that the tether leading to Walter's horse was secure, then with a shout dug his heels into his horse's sides. The stallions leaped forward and soon were at a full gallop. With his hands bound so tightly, and his right hand being broken, it was difficult for Walter to grasp the saddle horn with enough firmness to maintain his balance. He pressed his knees against the horse's sides as hard as he could, which helped him stay seated. There were several times he was all but certain he was going to fall, but his well-developed horsemanship skills kept him in the saddle.

After ten minutes, the horses began to slow down. Cardona had hoped that the beasts would last another couple of miles until they could reach the path that led to the woodland trail, which at night would be impossible to find for someone who was not familiar with it, but he knew that the steeds were spent. He could not afford the assumption that it was the same situation with their pursuers. He had to get off the road. He reined his horse to a stop. He quickly dismounted and with a dagger, severed the tether leading to Walter's horse.

"Dismount," Cardona ordered Walter, who obeyed without comment. Cardona could hear the distant pounding of hooves. They sounded the same distance away as before, which was a small relief to the Armor Guardian. He knew Gallard's men would be upon them in a few minutes. He pulled his sword from its sheath and smacked the hind quarters of the two horses with the flat of the blade. The horses immediately took off, heading towards Buckington. Cardona wasted no time.

"Into the woods," he commanded, using his sword to point to the forest off to the right. "If you make a sound, if you shout out as they go by, it will be the last utterance you ever make. Now move!"

Walter did as he was told. His legs were exhausted from the breakneck-paced ride, and he was not sure how far he could walk. He knew that eventually, Gallard's men would find the two riderless horses and would turn around and start scouring the road and woods for any indication of where he and Cardona had traversed. With there being a significant amount of undergrowth in the woods, they would certainly leave an easily visible trail. It was inevitable that Gallard's men would eventually catch-up to them.

The two men had pushed their way into the woods for about forty yards when their chasers approached the point where Cardona had abandoned the horses. He commanded Walter to stop and hide behind a tree while Cardona did the same. It would have been impossible for the riders to see them that far into the woods, at night, and at a full gallop on horses, but hiding was instinctive. Their pursuers passed quickly and gave no indication of slowing down. As the hoofbeats faded into the night, Cardona instructed Walter to continue, and the two men moved on.

For the next thirty minutes, which felt twice that to Walter, they forged through the forest. Walter continually made every effort to break whatever branches he could off the trees and bushes they brushed by without giving the appearance of leaving a trail. He shuffled his feet as often as he could, hoping to scrape up moss or overturn rocks that would help those who were surely tracking them by now. He knew that every scouting party sent out by Gallard, for whatever reason, included at least one master tracker. Walter had no doubt that their trail would be visible to such a person. His primary concern was what Cardona would do once Gallard's men caught-up to them. Knowing that he would likely be killed, Cardona would surely slide his dagger across Walter's throat or thrust his sword through his torso. If the pursuers got close enough without being detected, it was possible that one of them would be able to dispose of Cardona with an arrow before he had a chance to slay Walter. His fate was in his own hands, Walter decided.

Over the next twenty yards, Walter stumbled twice, both times managing to maintain his balance. He struggled another ten yards before stumbling again but this time, he crumpled to the ground. With earnest effort he stood but did not move.

"Keep going," Cardona instructed.

"My legs are exhausted," Walter replied. "Without full use of my hands and arms to maintain my balance while riding, I was forced to use my legs much more than usual. There is little if any strength left in them. They need rest."

"They will get plenty of rest when we reach Buckington," Cardona replied without sympathy. "Unfortunately, without our horses, we have an exceptionally long walk ahead of us. With your friends surely tracking us by now, we do not have the luxury of rest stops. Now move."

Walter complied without additional complaint and out of sheer willpower, continued walking. It was only five minutes later when the sound of rushing water reached their ears. The forest thinned slightly, and a small river came into view. The waterway was only about twenty feet wide and did not appear very deep, less than two feet at the most. Numerous rocks and boulders were visible as the flow raced over and around them. The current was not impassible but would present a mild challenge. Cardona stood at the edge of the water, looking up and down the river. They did not have time for him to find a more easily navigable path across the watery obstacle. They would have to cross where they were. Thankfully, the bank was not high, and they could easily step into the water. Avoiding the invisible underwater trip hazards would not be as easy.

"We will cross here," Cardona informed Walter.

"Surely there has to be another place to cross, where the current is slower and there are fewer hazards?"

"There is a footbridge along the woodland trail but being so far away, it is not an option for us," Cardona replied. "We do not have time to seek another crossing point. We cross here and now."

"At least untie my hands," Walter said, lifting his bound hands to Cardona. "With the weakened condition of my legs, maintaining my balance will be all but impossible if I am not able to use my arms."

"Your hands will remain tethered," Cardona replied firmly. "I recommend that you step with great caution. I am confident that a man of your caliber can make the crossing."

Knowing that additional argument would be of no use, Walter turned and waded into the water. The first few steps were actually comforting to his sore feet as the cool water soaked through his boots. The riverbed felt smooth, and the water was less than a foot deep. That quickly changed. Within another three steps, the water was nearly up to his knees and the rocks became larger and more slippery. With every slip of the foot came the potential for a painful fall. Walter was nearly half-way across when the inevitable reared its ugly head. His boot slipped across a slimy rock, right where the water current was the fastest, and he toppled into the water. Thankfully, he was able to avoid the largest of the rocks and the water softened his fall. When he appeared to have trouble getting back on his feet, Cardona stepped forward and grasped Walter by the arm. It was the opportunity for which Walter had been waiting. With unbelievable quickness, he twisted around and swiped at Cardona's legs with his right leg. Caught off-guard and struggling to maintain his balance in the current while helping Walter up, Cardona did not stand a chance. His legs buckled and his feet slipped out from under him, and he crashed into the river. He was not as fortunate as Walter had been and while instinctively trying to break his fall, his right hand smashed into a large rock and fractured. Ignoring the pain, Cardona quickly found his footing and was in the process of standing when Walter struck him in the temple with a large rock. Cardona immediately went limp and fell face-first into the water again. For some reason, Walter was struck with an uncustomary moment of compassion and quickly reached down and pulled Cardona's head up out of the water. With significant effort, despite his bound hands, he was able to pull the unconscious man onto dry land. After catching his breath, Walter retrieved a dagger from Cardona's belt and was able to slice the leather tether that bound his hands together. Using the remnants, he was able to return the favor to Cardona and bound the man's hands. He removed Cardona's boots and lacings, the latter being used to bind his feet. Confident that even if he gained consciousness Cardona would not be able to move, Walter leaned against a tree and closed his eyes, waiting for his rescuers.

Chapter 31

M arie read the note that Reverend Vendici gave to her for the third time. Had it not come directly from his hand she would have had great doubt regarding its veracity. The note instructed her to, as discreetly as possible, leave the church via a seldom-used side door and to wear a black, hooded robe with the hood pulled over her head. She was then to walk to the baker's store, spend a few minutes looking around, then leave through the back door but only after changing into a lighter color hooded robe, which would be left in the back room of the bakery for her. Next, she would walk to the seamstress' shop and follow a similar routine, this time changing robes and wearing a dark red one. After leaving through the back door, she was to go to the carpenter's shop where Hewlitt Knox would be waiting for her and would explain what she needed to do next. The note's message was adamant that she burn it prior to leaving her room. She could only surmise that whatever was happening, those who were orchestrating the chain of events were wary of eyes in the shadows and did not want her to be followed. She donned the black robe as instructed and held the note over the flame of the candle on her desk. Once lit, she dropped it into a metal pan where it burned completely. With a deep breath to relax her apprehension, Marie slowly opened the door to her room and peeked up and down the passageway. Satisfied that nobody was watching her, she quietly closed the door and proceeded to the exit.

The bakery was several buildings away from the church, so it was only a short walk for Marie. She entered the shop behind two other women. She followed the note's instructions and walked to the back of the shop where, as promised, there was a hay-colored robe sitting on a table by the door. She changed robes and left through the back door. The seamstress' shop was next, two blocks from where the bakery was located. Once again, Marie followed the note's instructions. As she walked towards the carpenter's shop, she looked up and down the street which was lined with torches on tall posts. She did not see anybody who appeared to be watching her. She reached the shop and with only a brief hesitation, she opened the door and entered.

At first the shop appeared to be empty. There was a lone oil lamp on a table in the middle of the room. Marie looked around, not knowing what to do or what was going to happen. After about ten seconds, Hewlitt appeared from a back room.

"Ah, Lady Marie, it is you. Welcome to my shop," Hewlitt said with a friendly smile. "You made it without incident I trust?"

"Other than having to change outerwear twice and exiting buildings via their back entrances, it was no more eventful than any other time walking the streets," Marie replied matter-of-factly. "Why the secrecy? What is going on?"

"As we have had very little personal contact and you know very little about me, I believe it would be best to have someone you know and trust explain the situation," Hewlitt replied. A door in the back of the shop opened and closed. "There he is," Hewlitt said, looking to the back of the shop. "Let us go in back."

Curiosity coursing through her, Marie followed Hewlitt. The back room was full of tools and half-completed projects. Marie looked around and spotted three people standing off to the side, where they could not possibly be seen by someone peering into the window from the street. It only took her a moment in the low light to recognize Lawrence, Angus and Victoria.

"I have to say, for someone whose task it was to stay incognito, you are not very skilled at being elusive," Lawrence said in greeting. "I had to distract two men who had followed you from the church."

"They are...?" Marie asked, afraid of Lawrence's answer.

"They are resting nicely, though when they awake, they will certainly have painful headaches," Lawrence replied.

"Then I shall have to work on my sneaking around skills," Marie replied, smiling. "I never saw you."

"Exactly," Lawrence replied. "I suppose I could give you some pointers."

"I would be more than happy to help train you in that area," Victoria said from beside Lawrence. "Let us just say that there are more challenges for a woman to remain unseen than a man, and there are things required that a man simply cannot teach to a woman."

"Were you the one who wrote the note Reverend Vendici gave to me?" Marie asked Lawrence.

"No, that was Andrew," Lawrence replied.

"Is he here?"

"No, he remains in Stanwyck for the time being," Lawrence answered.

"Then it is up to you to explain to me what is going on and why the great secrecy of my visit here this evening," Marie said.

"That is going to take a little time," Lawrence said. "The condensed version of the story is that we fear your well-being to be in danger from the Armorum Custodes. As you will soon understand, it was important for us to get you out of the church and out from under their eyes as quickly as possible. However, if they discover that you are gone too soon, it may negatively impact our plan, therefore we cannot simply take you away from here."

"Then speak quickly so I may return and not have their suspicions raised," Maire said.

"You are not going back," Lawrence said. "Well, you ARE going back, but it is not YOU who will be going back."

"I believe you have been hit in the head one time too many," Marie said with a confused look on her face. "You are not making any sense."

"I am going to take your place," Victoria answered for Lawrence. "We will exchange outer garments. I will return to the church in your stead. If there are spying eyes other than those which Lawrence disposed of, they will believe me to be you and be none the wiser. I shall remain in your room until the time arises that I must leave."

"And when will that be?" Marie asked.

"When this Reynald Vicenza character or others from the Armorum Custodes come to take you away," Victoria replied.

"Why would they do that?" Marie asked.

"I will explain everything once Victoria leaves," Lawrence said, a sense of urgency riding his voice. "Give Victoria your cloak so she may return to the church. We cannot afford the Armor Guardians to get anxious for not knowing where you are."

With a bit of an annoyed look but not another word, Marie removed her outer garment and gave it to Victoria. Victoria quickly donned it, pulled the hood over her head, and turned to Lawrence.

"Well?" she asked him.

"You should be fine," Lawrence replied. "The two of you are awfully close to the same height and with the hood over your head, nobody will be able to see your face in the dark as you go back to the church. Your body types are similar. You are leaner than Marie, but the cloak will conceal the difference."

"I beg your pardon?" Marie said indignantly, her hands on her hips. "Are you insinuating that I am paunchy?"

"No," Lawrence responded, a confused look on his face. "I...I was just saying…"

"I KNOW what you were saying," Marie said, glaring at Lawrence.

"I believe it is time for me to leave," Victoria said, stifling a smile of amusement. She could tell that Marie was having a little fun at Lawrence's expense, which was understandable under the circumstances.

"Reverend Vendici will meet you at the same door by which Marie left the church," Hewlitt said. "He will guide you through the church and to Marie's room and provide whatever assistance you need while you are there."

"Remember, you do not need to be clandestine when returning to the church," Lawrence reminded her. "It would be better if you were out in the open and can be seen, if there indeed are Armor Guardians out looking for Marie. Just keep your head down so your face is not readily visible."

"Do we have an idea of how long this will take?" Victoria asked as she made her way to the front door of the shop.

"Reverend Vendici said that the armor should be arriving tomorrow afternoon or evening, and the sword and shield, if all has gone according to plan, should arrive either tomorrow evening or Saturday morning," Hewlitt answered. "Once Vicenza determines that they are frauds, he will come for Marie. That could be tomorrow evening or Saturday. If possible, once the sword and shield are delivered and assuming that Vicenza does not immediately identify them as fakes, the reverend will come for you and escort you from the building. That way, you would not have to face Vicenza or any of the Armor Guardians."

"I would expect him to come alone and, having the element of surprise and considering your fighting skills, you should have no problem incapacitating him long enough to get away," Lawrence added.

"And if he does not come alone?" Victoria asked apprehensively.

"From what Andrew has said of you I am sure you would be able to exercise those eminent feminine charms of yours to effect escape," Lawrence answered teasingly. Seeing the irritant and impatient look on Victoria's face, Lawrence continued. "However, should all else fail, there will be friends close-by to ensure your safety."

"You must work on your encouragement skills," Victoria said as she turned and left the shop. Marie immediately turned to Lawrence.

"Now, you will explain to me what is going on," she said firmly. "Why would you suspect harm to come my way? And why has Andrew stayed in Stanwyck?"

"Sir Reynald Vicenza, Commander of the Armorum Custodes, has developed a rather fanatical position on the role of the church when it comes to local governing," Lawrence started as he led Marie, Angus, and Hewlitt to the back of the shop and sat at a table. "In short, he believes that the Church should govern indirectly through whoever sits on the throne. Whether it be a king or queen, that person would answer to the Church and govern accordingly. He wishes to establish whomever he desires as the Heir of DuFay and place the crown on that person's head, presumably a person who is easily controllable."

"But even if that were possible, he could not do it without the DuFay Armor," Marie said.

"He believes that he can acquire all six pieces in a very short period of time," Lawrence continued. "Under a threat to Reverend Vendici and his church, Vicenza has demanded that Vendici bring the three pieces of armor that the Church possesses to Buckington. Via his spies, Vicenza learned that Andrew has the sword and shield, and under the threat of doing harm to you, he demanded that Andrew bring both pieces of armor to him. He is under the belief that by the day after tomorrow, Sunday, at the latest, he will have those five pieces of the DuFay Armor in his possession. He claims to have a plan to get the breastplate from Gallard. Once he has all six pieces, he will force the Church to declare the person of his choosing as the Heir of DuFay and to crown that person. From that point forward, Vicenza will be the person who, in reality, governs the kingdom and from there, he will use every means possible to expand his ideology to all realms and peoples. Vicenza is a man of anger, a man of violence. This cannot be permitted to happen."

"So, Andrew is bringing the sword and shield here?" Marie asked. "I cannot envision him giving them up so easily."

"He is not giving them up," Lawrence answered. "He is sending replicas instead via two of Vicenza's men who followed us to Stanwyck."

"And when he realizes that they are frauds..." Marie started.

"He will come for you," Angus said, joining the conversation.

"That is why it was important for us to get you out of the church and take you somewhere safe. I doubt there would limits as to what methods he would implement to gather what information he could from you regarding your knowledge of Andrew and the DuFay Armor."

"But when he finds Victoria instead of me..." Marie said, her thought unfinished.

"Victoria can take care of herself," Lawrence said. "Reverend Vendici will have men loyal to him and the Church nearby in the event the situation sours."

"And Andrew?" Marie asked.

"Andrew stayed in Stanwyck to help ensure that events progress in accordance with our plan," Lawrence answered. He looked a little hesitant, then continued. "He also stayed to protect the Heir of DuFay."

"Alexander?" Marie asked. "Is there a threat to him that has arisen?"

"Actually, there has been a bit of a twist to the lineage of DuFay, and Alexander is not the heir," Angus answered.

"Then who is it?" Marie asked. "If not Alexander, then who?"

"The Heir of DuFay is Andrew," Lawrence replied with a sheepish smile.

"Andrew?" Marie repeated, astonished. "How is that possible?"

"Technically, I am the Heir of DuFay as it stands today," Hewlitt said, jumping into the conversation. "Andrew is my nephew, my only living relative, the son of my younger brother. As I have no sons, when Andrew's father was killed, Andrew became next in line after me. However, my health is failing, and I cannot sit on the throne as the descendent of Reginald DuFay. When my spirit passes into Glory, Andrew will inherit that right. If by God's grace my life is extended longer than I expect and the time comes for the Heir of DuFay to be crowned, I will officially relinquish my right and it shall pass to Andrew."

"This is unbelievable!" Marie exclaimed as she broke out into laughter. "Andrew MacLean, the Heir of DuFay! Nobody could want that responsibility less than he does. He has wasted nearly six years of his life looking for the Heir of DuFay when that person was right under his nose, and I mean that literally. What outrageous irony! I cannot wait to speak to him again."

"I am sure he will enjoy that conversation," Lawrence said, knowing that Marie was already thinking of ways to tease Andrew about this turn of events.

"What now?" Marie asked. "Where do we go?"

"We have to get you and Hewlitt as far from Buckington as quickly as possible," Angus responded. "The threat is not just against you alone, but against Hewlitt as well. Once Vicenza realizes that you are gone, he will target Hewlitt."

"I will not be going anywhere," Hewlitt replied firmly. "I am too old and too ill to travel."

"Reynald will likely come for you," Lawrence informed him. "He will try to find leverage to use against Andrew and force him to relinquish the sword and the shield. You will be all that he could possibly use."

"I understand," Hewlitt responded. "I do not fear Reynald. I can seek refuge with Reverend Vendici if I feel it necessary. And, while I may be too old and too ill to travel, I shall never be too old and ill to fight. My life will come to an end soon one way or another. Truthfully, I would rather it be in combat than lying on my bed wasting away in pain and misery."

"Where do we go?" Marie asked.

"There is a safehouse in town, known only to Reverend Vendici and the most senior of clergymen," Hewlitt answered. "You will stay there until Vicenza and his cohorts leave town."

"Vicenza will scour the city for Marie once he discovers the pieces of armor are fakes and Marie has disappeared," Lawrence warned.

"And we are certain that he will know they are fakes?" Marie asked.

"We cannot know for certain," Hewlitt answered her. "We have to presume that he will be able to determine if they are true or false, one way or another, whether it be right away or after some time. He has never seen the sword and shield in person, that much we know, but he may know of ways to authenticate them."

"It is late," Angus said. "Where is this safehouse?"

"I will take you," Hewlitt replied. "It is not far. We shall leave via the back door." With no other questions being offered, Hewlitt doused the lantern, and the foursome left the shop.

Chapter 32

S ir, they have arrived."

Commander Reynald Vicenza looked up from the documents he had been studying in his private quarters. He had given instructions to his men that he was to be notified the moment the legendary helmet, belt and boots were delivered. Without verbally responding, Vicenza rose from his desk and followed his subordinate. After a quick one-minute walk, the two men entered a room where Reverend Vendici and several other clergymen stood around a long table. It was Friday evening and five days since Reynald had demanded that Reverend Vendici send for the three pieces of armor, and he had been anxiously awaiting the moment they arrived. Slowly, almost reverently, the commander of the Armorum Custodes approached the table.

A large sheepskin had been laid on the table and on it were three of the most magnificent pieces of armor that Reynald had ever seen. Several candles and lanterns were set on the table and the warm yellow light they emitted caused the golden relics to all but glow. The helmet was worthy of the grandest of kings. There seemed to be no end to the precious jewels embedded in the gold. There were also many intricate, decorative designs expertly carved into the headpiece. On the inside of the helmet, he saw the famous words, written in ancient Greek. He then turned his eyes to the belt. It was a long strand of gold-covered leather approximately four inches wide, stretching close to forty-two inches from buckle to tip. Like the crown, it was highly decorated with impressions carved into it and dozens of jewels embedded into the leather. The buckle had to be solid gold. Just as with the helmet, there was writing carved into the leather in the same language. He then gazed at the boots. They were also made of leather but like the belt, covered in gold leaf. They were decorated very similarly to the belt, with dozens of precious gems and decorative impressions, along with words in the same language as the other two pieces.

"I do not know what I had imagined, but these are more beautiful than anything I could have ever imagined," Vicenza said in complete awe and admiration. "They are truly fit for a king of kings."

"There is only one King of kings," Reverend Vendici replied in an all-but scolding tone. "You must never forget that."

"Of course," Reynald responded automatically, without thought, as he continued to gaze at the treasures on the table. He reached out toward the helmet, intending on picking it up to examine it more closely, but Reverend Vendici's stern voice broke Reynald's near trance-like state.

"Do no touch that!" the reverend called out as he stepped forward and knocked the commander's hand aside. "Aside from the clergy charged with its protection, no man other than Reginald DuFay's heir may lay a hand on the armor." Commander Vicenza glared at the reverend, shocked and angered that the holy man would strike him in any fashion, especially in front of his own men. It was humiliating.

"How dare you strike me," he growled, his hand going to the hilt of his sword. "I am Sir Reynald Vicenza, Commander of the Armorum Custodes, charged with the protection of the Church and the DuFay Armor until the day they are returned to the crowned descendent of Reginald DuFay. I have every right to handle and inspect the armor at my whim."

"You forget your place," the reverend responded, not intimidated. "You answer to the Covenantal Orthodox Church of Christ through the senior clergy, which is me. It was I who recommended you to the elders for promotion to Commander of the Armorum Custodes and persuaded them to approve you. If you are discontent with your position and the limitations of your office, you have three options. First, you learn to be content with the authority and responsibilities which have been entrusted to you and were clearly explained to you upon your promotion. Second, you have the right to resign your commission. Third, we can call a special synod to evaluate your fitness to faithfully fulfill your responsibilities and determine if another change needs to be made. The choice is yours."

Vicenza's rage covered his face, his eyes wide and overflowing with indignation. His hand twitched as it touched the hilt of his sword. He had a dozen junior officers and at least a hundred men who were dedicated to his vision of the future Church and the roll of the Armorum Custodes in it. They would support any decision of his, any action of his, even unto death, with one possible exception: The murder of a man of God. He could not take that chance. He would have to be patient. He had a plan and once that plan came to fruition, he would answer to no man. Slowly he let his hand fall back by his side and he forced himself to relax. He took several deep breaths.

"Do not forget what I told you five days ago," Vicenza finally said, referring to his threat of destruction of the church. "It would be a sad day indeed, especially if certain people were unfortunate enough to be in the wrong place at the wrong time." Without waiting for a response, he boldly strode out of the room and returned to his private quarters.

It was a few hours later when there was another knock on his door and, still fuming from the rebuke by Reverend Vendici, Vicenza sharply called out.

"Enter!"

Two of his closest officers entered his office, followed by a third man who was obviously exhausted and barely able to stand. He held a large burlap sack in his arms that contained something large.

"Sir, this is Private Peter Leandry. He was on the mission with Captain Cardona," one of the officers said. "He claims to carry that which you sent Cardona to retrieve."

"Close the door," Vicenza commanded, and the second officer complied. "Where is Captain Cardona?" he asked the guardian holding the sack.

"We were forced to separate," Private Leandry responded. "Captain Cardona and I were on our way back with a prisoner when a large group of riders moving quickly appeared in the distance behind us. Suspecting that our prisoner was a comrade of theirs and they were intent on setting him free, and murdering us, Captain Cardona ordered me to ride ahead and ensure that the sword and shield were delivered to you, as per your command. I do not know whether the captain was captured or was able to elude the pursuers."

"Prisoner?" Commander Vicenza asked. "What prisoner? MacLean?"

"No sir," Leandry replied. "It is my understanding that he is the commander of Edwin Gallard's army. His name is Walter Brewster. He and a group of men tried to force MacLean to relinquish the sword and shield to them. Captain Cardona intervened, and there was a fight. We killed all of his men but spared Brewster because of his intimacy with Gallard and potential knowledge of the breastplate. We were bringing him to you for interrogation. Two of our own men were lost and two others suffered injuries that were of such a nature that it was impossible for them to return with us."

"And what of MacLean?" Vicenza continued. "Is he still alive?"

"Yes, sir," Leandry replied. "He delivered the sword and shield to us in the middle of the town. There was no opportunity to dispose of him. We knew that he had friends close-by as well. Since there were only two of us capable of engaging in a fight, we felt it best to leave him be. We did not wish to endanger the completion of our mission."

"Bring the sack to me," Commander Vicenza ordered, and Private Leandry complied without pause and set the sack on the table. "You are exhausted and undoubtedly famished. You are dismissed to take care of your needs. You are not to breathe a word of your mission to a single soul, do you understand? This mission never happened."

"I understand," Private Leandry replied. "One more thing, Commander," he said as if an afterthought. "Captain Cardona told me to tell you to prepare the Custodes, that an attack may be imminent."

"That will be all, private," Vicenza said and with a nod, the young man quickly left the room.

Commander Vicenza looked at the burlap bag on the table with great satisfaction. He now had leverage and could hold it against the reverend. He would get the other three pieces by whatever means necessary and once he had the breastplate, his plan would be perfected. He eagerly untied the cord that held the bag closed and first retrieved the sword. Then he retrieved the shield and set them on the table, side-by-side. His eyes gleamed with excitement and visions of his future as he took in the beauty of the weapons. So grand. So unequaled. He imagined all six pieces of the armor finally brought together after so long of a time having passed since they were last together, and his resolve to steal the breast-plate from Gallard as quickly as possible grew in intensity. It would not be long now. He picked up the sword and ran his hand over it, letting out a low chuckle of victory. He did not need anybody's permission to touch the armor of DuFay, regardless of what that old reverend said. The history he held in his hand was intoxicating. He laid the sword back down and turned his eyes to the shield. As with the sword, he ran his hand over it, closing his eyes as if to intensify his sense of touch. It was much smaller than he had expected, only about half the diameter of a normal shield, but considering that it was made from gold, it was not surprising. His hand glided over the shield, feeling every precious stone embedded in its surface, knowing that what he was touching was priceless. He suddenly stopped his hand and moved it back an inch, a slight frown forming on his lips. Something was wrong. He opened his eyes and looked where his fingers were on the shield and could see that there was an empty cavity where a gemstone should have been imbedded. He reached inside the burlap sack and felt around until his fingers touched the dislodged gem. He pulled the gem out and returned it to its place on the shield. However, something still did not feel right. It was the stone. Vicenza picked it from its place on the shield and held it in his hand. He then held it as close as he could to one of the candles on the desk without burning his fingers and looked as deeply as he could into the gem. He turned his attention back to the shield and upon a closer inspection, he found several other gems that were loose and easily removed from the shield. He then spotted what appeared to be a grayish streak on the shield. He scratched at it with his fingernail and gold flakes dislodged from the shield. This was wrong. If the shield were solid gold, there could be no scratches. He continued scratching and more gold came loose. Vicenza looked back at the gemstones he had pulled from the shield. He took a diamond a little more than one-quarter of an inch wide and set it on the table. He picked up one of the candle holders, which was made of bronze, and smashed it into the diamond. The gemstone shattered. He did the same with the other loose stones. They all shattered. He looked back at the shield. Realization struck him harshly. He grabbed his own sword and slammed it into the shield. A huge scratch in the shield was left by his blade. More gemstones popped-off. Vicenza raised his sword and with a powerful swing struck the golden sword on the table and was met with the same result. His fury could not be contained.

"MacLean!" he shouted as he swept the valueless weapons off the table. He smashed his sword onto the table as if trying to demolish the table itself. His two fellow Custodes stood still and silent, not knowing what else to do. After about fifteen seconds, he turned to the two men, seething.

"Get the woman and Reverend Vendici and escort them to the chamber where the DuFay Armor is being kept." The two men acknowledged the order and left the room. Vicenza returned the fake sword and shield to the bag, then he, too, left the room with the bag in-hand.

Chapter 33

V ictoria looked up from the documents she had been reading when a loud knock sounded at the room's door. Her heart skipped a beat in anticipation of who was on the other side of the door. She hoped that it was Reverend Vendici or one of the other clergymen coming to escort her safely through the church. The voice that came through the door squelched those hopes and kicked off an adrenaline rush.

"Lady Talbot, Commander Reynald Vicenza has requested your presence at a meeting with Reverend Vendici. Please come with us."

At least it was not Vicenza himself, Victoria thought, which ever so slightly relieved her apprehension at what was to come next.

"One moment, please," Victoria called out. She quickly strapped on her leather belt which held several daggers and a twenty-four-inch-long oak baton that was an inch and a half in diameter. She also sheathed a short sword. Next, she donned a thick cow-hide vest which had a place near her lower back for two more daggers. She pulled on her boots and laced them tightly. Finally came the long, hooded robe which she had worn the night before when she started her impersonation of Marie. She pulled the hood over her head and took a deep breath. The voice had said 'us.' She had no way of knowing if there were just two Custodes or several. She was confident that she could manage two of them caught off-guard but any more than that and her chances of escape were greatly diminished. She hoped that Hewlitt had been right when he said there would be friends close-by in the event things got beyond her control. She walked over to the door and, keeping her head down to avoid being recognized as an imposter, she opened it. To her relief, there were only two Custodes.

"Our apologies for the late-evening disturbance," one of the Custodes said, the same one who had called out to her through the door. "A matter has arisen. We have been ordered to escort you and Reverend Vendici to a meeting in hopes the two of you may assist us in its resolution."

Victoria simply nodded, indicating her understanding. The second Guardian led the way down the corridor and the first Guardian walked behind Victoria. She knew that at some point she would have to execute her escape, well before this meeting with Vicenza. The hallway was not very well lit, which would help conceal her movements as she prepared for her attack. She was about to strike when two more men appeared in the hallway, walking towards them. It appeared that one was a wearing a robe, similar to that which the clergy wore, and another was wearing an Armor Guardian robe. He was quite a large man, and Victoria questioned her ability to overcome him physically. She also questioned whether or not she could engage in a physical altercation with a man of the cloth. It would be his decision, she thought to herself. But first things first.

Having grasped the end of the wooden baton at her hip, concealed by her robe, Victoria whirled and within the blink of an eye, struck the Guardian behind her in the temple. The stunned Guardian fell to the ground, although he was not rendered completely unconscious. Hearing the whack of the baton against the Guardian's head, the lead Guardian turned to see what was happening. His reflexes were not good enough to dodge the incoming blow as Victoria, gripping the baton with both hands, drove the end of it into his solar plexus. The Guardian doubled over, his breath knocked out of him. Without wasting a second, Victoria raised the baton and clubbed him on the back of his head, robbing him of his consciousness. She felt a strong hand grip her left ankle. The first Guardian was struggling to rise from the floor. Victoria smashed the club into the man's hand, and he immediately released his grip. He was on his knees, but that is as far as he got. She lashed out with her right foot and kicked him in the temple. This time, he fell limp and did not move. Victoria whirled around, anticipating an assault from the Armor Guardian that had been coming down the hall toward them. The baton remained firmly in her right hand and a long dagger had appeared in her left.

"This is how you great a friend?" a familiar voice called out. It was the man wearing the Armor Guardian robe.

"Angus?" Victoria responded, surprised to see him. "Your timing is terrible," she said as she returned the weapons to their places on the belt.

"By the looks of those two Armor Guardians, it does not appear that you needed much assistance," Angus replied.

"Thankfully, there were only two of them," she said. "The outcome may have been different otherwise."

"We need to get out of here," Angus said. "Vicenza has discovered that the sword and shield are fakes, and he is a bit irate to say the least. He is calling the Armorum Custodes to station. In a few minutes, it will be all but impossible to pass through these halls to freedom. This is Luther Muire, he is an associate pastor studying under Reverend Vendici. He will lead us to safety."

"Follow me," the young man directed as he turned and walked back down the hall. Without hesitation or question, Victoria and Angus followed him. After about thirty yards, they heard the heavy footsteps of several people approaching. There was a door on the right side of the hallway and without hesitation, Luther opened it and ushed the other two through the doorway. He closed the door softly and within ten seconds, the footsteps passed by the door and faded. Just as carefully as he had closed the door, Luther opened it and peered up and down the empty corridor. He motioned for Angus and Victoria to follow him. They came to an intersection with corridors leading to the left and to the right. After carefully peering around the corner to ensure nobody was approaching, Luther headed down the left corridor. About thirty steps ahead they came to a balcony that was open to a large room. They would be in plain sight if they continued. The clergyman stopped while still out of sight and cautiously looked out over the balcony. There were twenty Armor Guardians assembled, getting orders from one of their superiors. Luther held up his hand to Angus and Victoria so they would not move. After a few seconds, the Armor Guardians dispersed, and the room was left empty.

"I cannot say that this was unexpected," Luther whispered to the others. "Vicenza is undoubtedly sealing the church to prevent anybody from entering or exiting. It is the start of his coup."

"Where does that leave us?" Angus asked.

"There are many places to enter and leave the church, and not all of them are used on a regular basis," Luther responded. "Some of them do not even have doors." He looked at Victoria. "I presume that you have no problem getting a little wet?"

"That depends on what you mean by 'a little'," Victoria responded.

"Follow me," he said without elaborating. They continued down the hallway until they came to a set of stairs to their left leading downward. Luther led the way down the fifteen steps, pausing at the bottom. Seeing and hearing nobody, he headed down the corridor to their right, and then down another set of steps. By now, they could hear voices and footsteps echoing all around them. It was only a matter of time before they were discovered.

"It is not far now," Luther said as if sensing Angus and Victoria's tension. He knew that if he were caught trying to lead them to safety, his life could also be in peril. He had to be cautious but not leisurely. They came to another intersection and Luther headed to the right without pausing to ensure that the way was clear. He nearly ran into the first of five Armor Guardians standing in the passageway. Angus and Victoria nearly bumped into Luther due to his sudden and unexpected stopping.

"What is this?" the Guardian asked Luther, eyeing Angus and Victoria. "Where are you going?"

"I am taking these two to Commander Vicenza, as he has ordered," Luther replied somewhat nervously.

"You are either lost or lying, as the commander is the other way," the Guardian responded as he reached for his sword. "I am certain that you know these walls and corridors well enough to not be lost, therefore you must be lying. Is it not a sin to bear false witness, preacher?"

"I think that in certain circumstances— " Luther began but was cut-off by Angus who stepped in front of him and none-too-gently pushed him backwards. Victoria stepped forward also.

"I am sure there are many sins of which you yourself are guilty," Angus said, taking a fighting stance, "as well as your commander. Are you aware of what he is planning, that he is intending to all but take-over the Church and turn it into a militarized institution?"

"I do not care what his intentions may or may not be," the Guardian answered. "He is my commander, and I obey his orders. His orders are to bring this girl to him, and I shall fulfill that order. I do not know who you are, but being that you are protecting her, I am sure you will be of interest to him as well."

"Protecting me?" Victoria asked, chuckling. "What gives you the impression that it is he who is protecting me and not the other way around?"

"Drop your weapons," the Guardian commanded almost dismissively. "Let us do this the peaceful way."

"Luther," Angus said, readying himself for the fight. "You will want to take several steps back at least." He unsheathed a short sword and an axe, his long sword being all but useless in the narrow, six-foot wide corridor. Victoria unsheathed her short sword and baton.

"You do not want to do this," the Guardian warned as he and his fellow Custodes unsheathed similar weapons.

"You are right, I do not want to do this," Angus agreed. "But you are leaving me with no choice." Before Angus could act, and while the Guardian's attention was on him, Victoria darted forward and with such grace that it appeared to be one motion, knocked the Guardian's sword out of his hand with her own sword and swung her baton at his head. The Guardian, though caught by surprise, was able to lift his left arm to block the blow. He reacted quickly and punched Victoria in the chest, knocking her backwards and nearly leaving her breathless. As he bent to pick up his sword, Angus kicked him in the head, knocking the Guardian unconscious. Immediately the next two Guardians jumped forward and engaged Angus. The close quarters made any kind of fighting challenging. Angus struggled to defend himself against the two men, using his sword and axe to parry blow after blow. He was not able to launch his own offensive. He felt a sharp pain in his right shoulder as the sword tip from one of the Guardians pierced his defenses. Angus felt the movement of air beside his right ear as Victoria launched a dagger at the Guardian who had just poked Angus. The blade sank deep into the man's sternum and pierced his heart, killing him almost instantly. The Guardian that Angus had kicked unconscious had come-to and tried to rejoin the melee, however, he was still off-balance, and Angus disposed of him with a single thrust of his sword. No sooner had the man fallen than Angus felt a sharp pain in his right side and looking down, he saw a six-inch shaft protruding from his torso.

"Enough!" one of the Guardians called out as he pointed a small, compact crossbow at Angus. A second Guardian also lifted a crossbow and pointed it at Victoria. "Lay down your weapons!" Angus and Victoria looked at each other. At their hesitation, the first Guardian continued, glaring at Angus. "While the girl's life is to be preserved, yours is of no matter. If you do not lay down your weapons, the next arrows will be through your heart and through her leg."

Reluctantly, injured and bleeding, Angus laid down his sword and axe. Victoria dropped her sword and the dagger she was prepared to throw.

"Now, you will—" the Guardian started but he was not able to finish his sentence due to the violent blow to the back of his head. The second Guardian armed with a crossbow also crumpled to the ground, having received a similar strike. The last remaining Guardian held his hands high in the air as the tip of a sword was pressed into the back of his neck. Due to the low light level in the hallway, neither Angus nor Victoria was able to identify their saviors.

"Well, Victoria, I believe that shall just about make us even from when you assisted me in Porthmaddon."

"Andrew?" she asked in complete surprise. "What are you doing here? How did you know we were here?"

"Of course I knew you were going to be here, it was my plan after all," Andrew replied with a tone bordering on arrogance. "Gregory and I felt that you might need some additional muscle should your escape become muddled and by all accounts, we were right." Gregory was busy gagging and binding the hands and feet of the Guardian that had not been knocked unconscious.

"Not bad for a boy, eh old man?" Gregory asked Angus with a smile. He then moved over to the two unconscious men and bound their hands and feet.

"Yes, you have the most excellent of skills when it comes to tying-up subdued foes," Angus replied. He reached down to the arrow shaft that was stuck in his side. Thanks to his thick clothing it had not pierced deeply into his body. He looked at Gregory and with a smug grin and not a sound, he pulled the blood-covered arrow free.

"Do you need that tended to, or can you wait until we reach safety?" Andrew asked.

"It can wait," Angus said.

"Good," Andrew replied. "Luther, lead on." The young clergyman, who had been keeping a safe distance from the fighting, stepped forward. He carefully made his way around the bound men and without a word, continued down the hall.

After a few more minutes of walking, the group came to a chamber that was fifty feet in diameter. In the middle of the chamber was a pool of water which was fed from a trench leading out and away from the church. The water in the trench was no more than two feet deep.

"This is an old water source that was used by the church long ago," Luther explained. "It is fed by a large pond perhaps a hundred yards from the back wall of the church. Once outside of the building, the trench is surrounded by trees on either side which creates a canopy. Although the trees have shed their leaves, you should be able to pass unnoticed. Once you reach the pond, you will be able to continue to safety. God be with you."

"Thank you, Luther," Andrew said. "I know it was a significant risk for you to participate in this escape. Reverend Vendici's trust and faith in you was well-placed. Will you be under threat if you return?"

"I will be okay," the young man answered, "although I shall not return by the way which we just came."

"You will meet us at the rendezvous point once Vicenza and his men leave town?" Andrew asked.

"Yes," Luther confirmed. "I suspect that he and his men will depart in the morning, although there is no way of knowing how many of the Armorum Custodes he will take or what instructions he will give to those he leaves behind."

"We will have to be prepared to alter our plan accordingly," Andrew said. "We will see you soon." Luther nodded and without another word, left the chamber.

"Now what?" Victoria asked.

"Now, we get wet," Andrew replied as he stepped into the water.

Chapter 34

R everend Vendici entered the chamber where the DuFay Armor were being kept, politely pushed along by the two Custodes Sir Reynald Vicenza had dispatched to bring him and Marie to the room. Vicenza was standing behind the table on which the helmet, belt and boots were laid out and had set the bag containing the sword and the shield on the table as well. There was nobody else in the room. The commander of the Armorum Custodes looked up at the trio, an accusatory look forming on his face and in his voice.

"I cannot for the life of me comprehend how two Armorum Custodes, having received years of intensive training in hand-to-hand combat, were bested by a girl who has spent her life doing little more than reading books and being waited on hand-and-foot," he said, looking at his men. "Please explain this to me and why I should not deliver most dreadful discipline upon you?"

"Sir," one of the Custodes responded, "it is to our shame that we allowed ourselves to be overpowered. However, the girl we retrieved from her quarters was not some weak, powerless, princess. Admittedly, believing her to not be a threat, our guard was down. But she was armed, and she was quick and decisive in her attack. This woman has had training and is no stranger to combat."

Sir Vicenza glared at the Custodes as his mind considered the report. Something was amiss, and he would find out what it was. "You are dismissed," he said in a dismissive tone, and the two Custodes bowed their heads in acknowledgment and left the room, closing the door behind them.

"I find that recount to be interesting and disturbing," Vicenza said to Reverend Vendici. "What are your thoughts?"

"My thoughts are that when cornered and feeling threatened, people find a strength in them they never knew they possessed and are capable of remarkable things," the reverend replied.

"Such as a weak, young woman who has been pampered all her life attacking and knocking the sense out of two well-trained, highly experienced men of combat?" Vicenza replied.

"I would not eliminate it from the realm of possibility," Reverend Vendici responded. "As your man admitted, their guard was down, which in anybody's mind would raise question as to the quality and effectiveness of their training."

"It is not their training that is in question here," Vicenza replied, "but it is your sincerity." He reached into the bag and retrieved the sword and shield. "Your instructions to MacLean, to which he agreed, were to deliver the sword and shield of DuFay to you. I had a conversation with MacLean and informed him that if he failed to comply with your instructions, there would be unpleasant consequences as they pertain to his female friend. Lest he have no true friendship with that girl and cares not for the safety and well-being of others in general, I cannot imagine why he would not comply and potentially allow harm to befall her."

"It would appear that he did indeed provide you with the sword and shield," the reverend countered.

"He indeed gave us a sword and a shield, but these are not the sword and shield of the DuFay Armor," Vicenza said, his voice beginning to take a menacing tone. He picked up the damaged shield and showed it to the reverend. "Unless I have a grave misunderstanding of history, the DuFay Shield was made of solid gold with dozens of precious stones embedded in it. This shield is nothing more than thin, useless steel covered in a light layer of gold leaf. The precious gemstones? Nothing more than colored, worthless glass. The same can be said of the sword. As you can see," he continued, lifting the sword for the reverend to view, "this by far is anything BUT a sword fit for a king."

"That is very true," Reverend Vendici responded.

"What do you know of this fakery?" Vicenza demanded.

"You would have to present such questions to Andrew MacLean," the reverend answered. "He was the one who gave the sword and shield to your men."

"When I find him, I will take immense pleasure in wringing the answers from him," Vicenza replied. "I have been inspecting these other pieces of the DuFay Armor, and I use that description lightly, for I feel that these most likely are hoaxes as well." He lightly ran his hands over each of the three items. "What do you say, Reverend?" he asked.

"What would move you to such a suspicion?" Reverend Vendici replied innocently.

"I know you and MacLean spoke on at least one occasion before he left town," Vicenza answered. "I also recall you do not share my vision of the future of the Church and the kingdom. I suspect the two of you concocted a ruse regarding the armor and are determined that the five true pieces of the DuFay Armor you possess remain far from here, at least until you locate the Heir of DuFay." The Reverend did not reply, therefore Vicenza continued. "Let me put that theory to test."

The Armorum Custodes commander unsheathed his sword and moved so that he was standing across from the crown, his eyes continually on the clergyman. Reverend Vendici's expression did not change. Vicenza hoisted his sword high above his head, gripping it with both hands. Still, Vendici remained silent and expressionless. Without uttering a sound, Vicenza brought his sword down with great force and slammed it into the table, inches from the crown. He glared at the reverend.

"You did not try to stop me," he said, "just as I suspected. These are not part of the true DuFay Armor. If they were, you would not stand there and allow me to destroy them. Where are the real pieces?"

"They are far from your hands," Reverend Vendici replied staunchly.

"You will tell me where they are, or I shall with much joy follow-through on my promise to you regarding this building," Vicenza responded menacingly. "It will burn to the ground along with everything in it, and if there are certain people within the building and they perish from the flames, well, tragedies happen. Now speak, lest my ignited anger ignites torches." Reverend Vendici knew that Commander Vicenza would do exactly as he threatened, and the veiled threat was directed at him personally. He had no choice in the matter. His face dropped into a defeated expression and his shoulders slumped.

"Dover Castle," Reverend Vendici answered reluctantly.

"Dover Castle has been abandoned for many decades," Vicenza countered. "Surely they have not remained hidden away within those walls for all these years."

"They were being kept in separate locations known only to myself, and upon my death their locations would be passed on to my successor as the leader of this church and protector of the DuFay heritage," the reverend replied. "We have a safeguard protocol in place that would protect the armor in an event such as this, where the Protector was compromised and forced to send for them. Using certain code words, the letters to the stewards of the armor would warn them of the hostile circumstances. The stewards would deliver the replicas to those sent to retrieve them, then under great secrecy take the true armor to predetermined locations until the danger passed."

"And Dover Castle is that predetermined location," Vicenza surmised.

"No, Dover Castle was never one of those locations," Reverend Vendici countered.

"Then why have the pieces delivered there?" Vicenza asked, confused.

"Because we know who the Heir of DuFay is, and the plan was to keep them close until the breastplate could be obtained from Gallard and the heir crowned as king," the reverend answered.

"You know who the Heir of DuFay is?" Vicenza asked, seeming astonished.

"We learned his identity in just the past week."

"Who is this heir?" Vicenza demanded.

"You will understand my reluctancy in divulging his name," Reverend Vendici replied.

"Reverend, you need to understand my sincerity in this matter," Vicenza responded firmly. "I shall tolerate no more lies, no more deceit, no more half-truths. You will answer my questions fully and truthfully lest the fire that is my resolve be stoked into a raging inferno that destroys you and everything you love. Now, answer me: Who is the Heir of DuFay?"

"It is the man who at this moment is delivering the sword and shield of DuFay to Dover Castle, the same man who delivered the replicas to your own men," Reverend Vendici replied.

"Andrew MacLean?" Vicenza asked, stunned. "Andrew MacLean is the Heir of DuFay?"

"Aye, that he is," the reverend confirmed. "It is indisputable."

"Unbelievable," Vicenza said. "If only things had gone according to my plan…" His voice trailed off as he considered what might have been. But as the commander of the Armorum Custodes, he knew that plans often went awry and new plans had to be formed. And it was not always an inconvenient thing. The path in front of him was clear.

"Are all of the pieces there, right now?" he asked.

"It is not likely," the reverend replied. "The instructions to the custodians were to rendezvous three days from now. Depending on the length of their journeys and the speed at which they travel, it is difficult to say exactly when they will arrive."

"Guards!" Vicenza called to the men standing outside the room. The door opened immediately and the same two Custodes who had accompanied Reverend Vendici to the chamber entered.

"Reverend Vendici is to be placed under arrest for blasphemy and scheming against the Church. Take him to the brig. He will be held there until a formal hearing can be arranged. He is to have no visitors. Find Captain Donaldson and tell him to report to me in the tactical room at once."

"What are you going to do?" Reverend Vendici asked as the two Custodes approached him.

"I am going to Dover Castle and take custody of the DuFay Armor," Commander Vicenza answered. "The Heir of DuFay shall meet his end, I shall obtain the breastplate from Gallard, and the Church will return to the role for which it was created."

"And the hearing at which I shall most definitively squash whatever false charges you choose to bring against me?" the reverend asked.

Sir Reynald Vicenza, Commander of the Armorum Custodes, leaned forward and sent a chill down Reverend Vendici's spine as he spoke softly enough so only the reverend could hear his words.

"What hearing?" he asked with a vindictive smile.

Chapter 35

W alter Brewster looked past the tree line at Dover Castle. The forest gave him and his men cover as they scouted the area to determine if there was anybody in the castle. There was a four-hundred-yard clearing between the castle and the edge of the forest, although due to limited activity in the area for many years, there was significant vegetation growth between the castle and the trees. Still, the castle was visible and there was no sign of activity. This was not the type of castle that was built as a home for royalty. This structure was built for one purpose, and that being security. The curtain wall was constructed as with most castles and rose thirty feet off the ground, looking as sturdy as the day it was originally laid. There was one difference, though, a unique feature of this castle. The front wall was concave. This provided defenders with the ability to fire arrows at intruders from multiple angles as the door came under siege and enemy combatants were more concentrated. Crenellations dotted the top of the wall, providing archers with cover between launching volleys of arrows. There were four watchtowers constructed, one at each corner of the wall, extending another twenty feet into the air, which would have given the men on watch an unimpeded view of the grounds all the way to the tree line and several miles beyond. There were two rows of arrow slits in the curtain wall, one row ten feet off the ground and the other twenty feet off the ground, with twenty feet between each window. The layout of the arrow slits enabled defenders to fire upon attackers from two different elevations and thereby two different angles. There were no tall towers or structures visible behind the wall. The entrance to the stronghold was open and was not as large as one would expect for a castle. From this distance it appeared only slightly larger than the size needed to allow the passage of one man and horse at a time. All in all, it was a very boring, non-impressive structure.

One of Walter's men, who had been dispatched to ride the perimeter of the forest line, returned to Walter's side.

"Sir," the scout said, "There is no other road or path leading to the castle than the one we are on. There are no visible tracks or evidence of anybody passing this way in recent days. I saw no activity outside of the castle. All signs indicate that the castle remains abandoned and empty."

"It appears that we have arrived before the DuFay Armor has arrived," Walter replied. "That is good. It will give us time to inspect the castle and determine if it has any weaknesses and start formulating a plan of attack once Gallard and his army arrives." Walter addressed the men behind him. "Follow me and stay in single file. Post a guard a mile down the road. If anybody is seen approaching, he is to provide us with a warning. Send another rider back to Stanwyck and ensure that Gallard knows the way here." With that said, Walter nudged his horse in its ribs and the stallion continued down the path.

"Tell me about this citadel, Cardona," Walter addressed the Armor Guardian riding by his side.

"There is not much that I can tell you other than what I told you previously," Captain Cardona replied. "I have never been here. To my knowledge, it was abandoned nearly a hundred years ago and left to vagrants and the land to reclaim."

"Yes, the great Armorum Custodes victory over the barbarian horde," Walter said. "I asked you what prompted the battle and you refused to answer the question."

"Why is that important to you?" Cardona countered. "That battle took place over a hundred years ago and has no bearing on anything today."

"I love history," Walter replied. "Something as grand as five hundred Armorum Custodes defeating three times their number, or was it five, now that is history worth knowing. So, I ask again, over what did they battle?"

Cardona looked intently at Walter for a moment, wondering why this seemed to be important to the man. Although he was a captive, his life spared for some reason which he could not fathom, Cardona was still an Armor Guardian and did not want to give his captor any more information than necessary, no matter how trivial it seemed.

"It is my understanding that the barbarians felt this was sacred land and it was wrongfully taken from them and occupied by foreigners, therefore they fought to reclaim it."

"While that may hold some truth, though very little in my estimation, there must be more to the story," Walter replied. "Strongholds such as this are built for a reason, which is either to protect a territory, a town, or protect something of value. Buckington is too far away from this stronghold for it to have provided any kind of protection for the town. I would venture that it was constructed to protect something of value, something of excellent value. As a captain in the Armorum Custodes, surely you know much more about the history of this place than you are willing to confess. You need to do better than a story of a fight over sacred land. After all, I did save your life," Walter added somewhat sarcastically.

"Truthfully, I know very little more than what I have told you," Cardona replied. "There were rumors that the stronghold was originally built to protect something of immense value, and it was this that the barbarians were truly after. However, after the Armorum Custodes defeated the barbarians, whatever was being protected was taken away and eventually, Dover Castle was completely abandoned."

"Now THAT has a stronger ring of truth to it," Walter said, mostly satisfied with Cardona's answer.

The group stopped as it arrived at the castle. A trench twenty-feet wide and five-feet deep had been dug along the base of the wall. A water-filled moat at one time, it was now mostly dry and choked with overgrowth from years of not being maintained. Sharp wooden spikes could still be seen sticking out of the ground, which would not have been seen when the moat was full of water. A wooden bridge stretched across the trench from the only door visible in the castle's walls, left in that position when the last person exited the facility many years ago. The men dismounted their horses and leaving the animals, cautiously walked across the ancient bridge and passed through the gatehouse. The opening was only six feet wide, just wide enough for a small cart to be pulled through. It was high enough that a rider on a horse could pass through without fear of striking the head jamb, but not much higher. A single large door, now lying on the ground, would have closed the entrance. A wooden portcullis was in the raised position, as if its sharp points were ready to dive downward and impale intruders at any moment. There were multiple arrow slits in the side walls. Due to the close quarters, it was likely that these openings would have been used for jabbing pikes at intruders rather than firing arrows. There was a second portcullis ten feet into the entranceway. The ceiling in the gatehouse tunnel contained several murder holes through which defenders could drop boiling water, boiling oil, and even shoot arrows at intruders. Walter led the group through the now-innocuous opening and into the castle's interior grounds.

There was one large structure in the middle of the complex, two-stories tall, and multiple smaller structures built adjacent to the outer wall. Wooden stairs had been constructed every fifty feet to give access to wooden platforms built into the wall where archers would have been stationed during battle. In some places the platforms and stairs had collapsed. In other places, they looked as if they could fall if even the smallest of birds was to land on them. None of the structures had roofs, their wooden supports having crashed down decades earlier. As with the exterior grounds, the courtyard had become overgrown with weeds and small trees. A stone well was located in the middle of the courtyard. Walter called to one of his men.

"Walk the perimeter of the wall and see if there are breaches, weak points, or other means of entering or exiting the castle," he instructed. "Also look for signs of recent activity. Just because it appears abandoned does not mean that it has not been occupied recently."

"Sir," the man acknowledged and hurried away. Walter turned to a second man standing close-by.

"Newton, we will make camp in the woods on the far side of the castle and hold there until Gallard and his army arrive. I suspect they should arrive the day after tomorrow. No fires. We must remain unseen. Leave as little trail as possible. See to it."

"Yes, sir," Newton replied and left to carry out his orders.

Walter spent the next hour working his way around the buildings, leaving no corner unseen. It had not been built for comfort or royalty but for one purpose alone, and that was to house and protect the DuFay Armor. There was enough room to house and feed up to three hundred men at one time. The small structures along the wall were obviously stables for horses and livestock. There was also a shack that must have been used by a blacksmith based on the large firepit contained within it. Several other, smaller structures had to have been dedicated to food storage. Walter expected to find remnants of defensive weaponry, such as catapults or ballistas, but found none.

"I must say, I am very disappointed," Walter said, turning to Cardona who was still by his side. "This is by far the least impressive castle or citadel or whatever you wish to call it that I have ever seen, and I have seen quite a few. I can only wonder what it was in this place that represented such grand value that it was worthy of a battle that became a legend. Being a captain in the Armorum Custodes, surely you have some knowledge of what it was."

"I am sorry to disappoint you, but I have told you all that I can," Cardona replied, lying. Of course he knew that the citadel was originally constructed to protect the DuFay Armor many, many years ago, and that the barbarian horde was anything but that. It had been an invasion by a desperate despot who was looking to steal the DuFay Armor and crown himself as the Heir of DuFay. Once the protectors of the DuFay Armor realized that its location was known, the pieces were separated and sent to different towns, never to be in the same place at one time until the true heir was located. But he was not going to give Brewster the satisfaction of that knowledge.

"Let me tell you what I think," Walter said, not buying Cardona's profession of ignorance. "I think the Armorum Custodes were protecting a legend, a legacy, which could change the face of the lands for generations.

"What is your interest in this place?" Cardona asked, tired of the conversation and Brewster's arrogance. "Why have you come here?"

"To repeat history," Walter said determinedly, "but this time, the result will be quite different."

Chapter 36

L uther Muire walked quickly down the stone corridor, more out of nervousness than eagerness. When he had decided to join the ministry of the Church and study to become a preacher and teacher of the Word of God, he never envisioned that times such as this, or a day such as this, was possible. Just a few days ago his routine included studying, teaching, leading prayer meetings, and ministering to those in the community who were in need. Now it seemed that his routine had been expanded to include rescuing strangers and friends, tasks that placed his very life in peril. But the Church was under attack, and he was a soldier of God, a servant of the Almighty. He would do whatever was needed to defend the Bride of Christ and those within it.

He slowed his pace and calmed his breathing as he approached the cell where Reverend Vendici was being held captive. Outside of the cell door stood a single guard, which was a relief to Luther. Any ensuing violence would be extremely limited and the danger to life minimized. The last thing he wanted was for another life to be snuffed out within the walls of church. The House of the Lord was no place for such mayhem. It was a place of peace and serenity, a place of worship and learning. Violence seemed blasphemous to the purpose of the building. Yet, what happened next would be out of his control. He prayed silently for the Lord's hand in what would transpire and that there would be no violence. The guard looked up as Luther approached.

"I wish to speak with Reverend Vendici," Luther informed the guard.

"Per Commander Vicenza's orders, Reverend Vendici is permitted no visitors," the guard replied.

"This is important church business," Luther continued. "Reverend Vendici is still the senior pastor of this church, and his responsibilities were not abated with his unjust incarceration. I must see him."

"I do not care what business may require his attention," the guard responded, agitation riding his voice. "There are other clergymen, yourself included I would presume, who can handle whatever it is that the good reverend would otherwise tend to. You will not speak with him. Now go about your business elsewhere."

Instead of leaving, Luther casually took a step down the corridor past the guard so that the guard was facing away from the direction in which Luther had approached. He reached into a pocket of his tunic and retrieved a folded piece of paper.

"Will you at least see that he gets this letter?" Luther asked, handing the paper to the guard. After a moment of reflective hesitation, the guard took the letter and began to open it.

"That is not for your eyes!" Luther said sternly, his voice rising.

"Nothing gets passed through this doorway that I have not thoroughly inspected," the guard countered. "I will determine if its contents warrant being given to the reverend."

"That is private!" Luther continued, his voice growing in volume and anger. "How dare you violate the privacy between a man of God and one of his sheep? This is outrageous!" Luther moved as if to take a step toward the guard and the guard immediately reacted.

"You will leave now, or I shall throw you in a cell of your own!" the guard warned, his hand going to the hilt of his sword. "As for this letter, I promise you Reverend Vendici will never see it!"

"You should not make promises that you cannot keep," a voice whispered into the guard's ear. The guard attempted to pull his sword, but a powerful hand reached out and grasped the guard's wrist, preventing the sword from leaving its sheath. Having been focused on the young clergyman, the guard had not detected anyone approaching from the other direction. "Release your grip," the voice commanded. Feeling a sharp point in his ribs, the guard reluctantly obeyed. His sword was removed and handed to young Luther.

"You see, young Luther, no blood, just as I promised," Andrew said with a smile as he stepped from behind the guard. Gregory, Angus and Lawrence followed.

"By the grace of the Lord," Luther said, his pulse starting to slow a bit. "This is not exactly the kind of ministry I signed-up for."

"You are in the business of saving people, no?" Lawrence asked, delivering a less than gentle pat on the clergyman's back. "Well, you have saved several people in these past two days. I would say you are fulfilling your calling quite well."

"The key?" Andrew asked, looking at the guard. Reluctantly, the man retrieved the key from his tunic and handed it to Andrew.

"Thank you," Andrew said as he inserted the key in the door's lock and turned it. He then pulled the door open. Reverend Vendici stood in the doorway, as if he had just been preparing to open the door himself.

"Reverend?" Andrew said, his hand motioning towards the corridor. Reverend Vendici wasted no time in exiting his cold, dank cell.

"I do not know why we still have these repulsive rooms," the reverend said as he looked over his rescuers. "They do not belong in the house of the Lord. Relics of the past. I shall have these doors removed and never again shall a person be subject to imprisonment within these walls." He looked at the guard. "Well, with one exception," he added. He turned his attention to Andrew. "Vicenza?"

"He left this morning with what looked to be about one hundred of the Armorum Custodes," Andrew replied. "I suspect that he will arrive at Dover Castle tomorrow."

"And Gallard?" the reverend asked.

"He should arrive in Stanwyck with his army this evening," Gregory replied. "He will let his men rest for the evening, re-supply as much as he can, and leave for Dover Castle tomorrow morning. He should arrive there sometime Monday."

"Re-supply?" Lawrence said questioningly. "It will be more like pillaging than re-supplying. That town does not have enough food to feed an entire army. It is winter. They will not be able to grow more food for several months. They will starve."

"It is not my intention to sound cold or cruel, but the prospect of starvation could be a great motivator," Andrew replied. "The people of that town are still harboring grudges against Gallard for when he came through on his way to Durinburg and confiscated much of their food and many of their livestock. Those who were hesitant to join us will do so with much eagerness after Gallard leaves them with such a bleak future."

"The people of Buckington are generous, and there is an abundance of food and livestock here," Reverend Vendici said. "I am certain there will be no hesitation in them sharing what the Lord has provided them. The people of Stanwyck shall not go hungry."

"What now?" Luther asked.

"We shall rendezvous in my private study in one hour and discuss the next phase of our plan," the reverend replied. "Luther, do you know who the senior Armorum Custodes officer is while Vicenza is away?"

"That would be Captain MacCallum," Luther replied.

"Ah, that is good," Reverend Vendici said, nodding his head in approval. "Alistair has never truly approved of Reynald's philosophies or methods. This is greatly to our benefit. If you would, please locate him and escort him to my study to meet with us. If he questions my freedom, simply tell him that while I am no Paul, an angel of the Lord opened the cell door and set me free," he said with a smile. "And send for the members of the church's council. Have them informed that there is an emergency, and we must meet immediately."

Luther nodded and quickly walked up the corridor.

"Let us leave this dank dungeon," the reverend said to the others. "I am eager to wash the stench of this place from my bones. As for this young man," he said, looking at the guard, "place him in the cell for now. We shall send someone for him later." Without further conversation, the group departed.

An hour later, Andrew, Gregory, Angus and Lawrence arrived at Reverend Vendici's study. The door was open, so they walked in. The reverend, Luther, and a man they assumed was Captain MacCallum were already present. Andrew closed the door behind them.

"Since time is of the essence, I will keep the introductions short. Gentlemen, this is Captain Alistair MacCallum of the Armorum Custodes. He is the senior officer in charge of the Guardians, with Vicenza and his other officers away. I have explained to him, though in much brevity, the circumstances in which we find ourselves. Captain MacCallum, this is Lawrence Morecraft, Angus Faustus, Gregory McPherson, and Andrew MacLean."

"MacLean," Captain MacCallum said, looking at Andrew. "So, this is him? This is the Heir of DuFay?"

"That he is," Reverend Vendici confirmed.

"It is indisputable?" the captain asked, still looking at Andrew.

"That it is," the reverend replied. Captain MacCallum continued to look at Andrew as he weighed the revelation in his mind and what his next words and actions should be. Finally, he turned his eyes back to Reverend Vendici.

"Very well," he said. "What is it that you desire of me and be quick about it. I am disobeying the orders of my commander by not immediately placing you back in custody. I have also been charged with calling the remaining Armorum Custodes to station in preparation for a potential attack."

"Your commander," the reverend said reflectively. "Your commander, with whom you have had not a few disagreements, yes?"

"That is not relevant," the captain replied. "He is my superior, and his orders are to be obeyed."

"Captain MacCallum, you are quite aware that Commander Vicenza is anything but a moral man, and many of his orders and actions at least have the appearance of bordering on the edge of immorality," Reverend Vendici responded. "As I have explained to you, and what comes as no surprise I am certain, Vicenza is intent on acquiring all of the pieces of the DuFay Armor and having crowned as the Heir of DuFay whomever he desires. Through this person, Vicenza will establish a church-state and in essence, rule from the shadows. This cannot be allowed to happen. You know Vicenza. You know his eccentricities and his charismatic nature when it comes to worship, if you could even call what he would do worship. His actions would bring corruption and rot to the Bride of Christ."

"What would you have me do?" the captain asked. "He is my superior officer, and I will not lead a coup against him nor participate in one. He was promoted to his position by vote of the Council, and only the Council can remove him from his position."

"What if I told you that the Council has already voted to remove Vicenza from the position of Commander of the Armorum Custodes?" Reverend Vendici responded.

"I would say that such action is long overdue," Captain MacCallum replied.

"And what if I told you that the Council unanimously voted approval of his replacement?"

"I would say that for a man to receive such a vote of confidence would be an honor beyond words," the captain replied. "Hopefully, the Council exercised more wisdom in this choice than its last one."

"I assure you, it did, Commander MacCallum," Reverend Vendici replied, the faintest of a smile forming on his lips. "That is, assuming you accept the Council's vote and are willing to take on the responsibilities of the position. I assure you, the next few days are going to be nothing like you have ever seen or imagined. You are the man for the job, Alistair. Your commitment is to the Church and the Lord, not to man and his ambitions. What say you?"

Alistair MacCallum stood in stunned silence, trying to comprehend what he had just been told. Sir Reynald Vicenza had been his commanding officer for the past ten years. Despite their conflicts, he still respected Vicenza's position and would never do anything to rebel against that authority. However, if what the reverend had just said was true, Reynald Vicenza was no longer Commander of the Armorum Custodes and therefore he would not be contesting Vicenza's authority. He knew Vicenza would fight this decision and would never accept it, whether a member of the Armorum Custodes or not. Commander was not a position that he had aspired to, but Alistair knew the choice that he had to make.

"With all humility, I accept the vote of the Council and the position of Commander of the Armorum Custodes," he said, slightly bowing his head.

"Excellent," Reverend Vendici said, a satisfied smile now on his face. "Unfortunately, there is no time for the pomp of a formal ceremony, but I assure you, once our task is completed, we shall adhere to custom. We have already sent word to the remaining Armor Guardians that Sir Reynaldo Vicenza has been removed as Commander of the Armorum Custodes due to actions detrimental to the Church and the Gospel of Christ, and that you are his replacement."

"You knew I would accept?" Commander MacCallum asked, puzzled.

"Of course," the reverend replied. "I know you quite well, Alistair. I knew you would feel a slight conflict at first but in the end, would know what you had to do."

"What is next?" the newly promoted man asked.

"Andrew?" Reverend Vendici said, looking at Andrew.

"Walter Brewster and his small contingency of 50 men will have arrived at Dover Castle by now," Andrew replied. "Finding the place abandoned, he will assume that the messengers with the DuFay Armor simply have not arrived. He will make camp in hiding and wait for Gallard and his army to arrive. Tomorrow, likely mid-morning or early afternoon, depending on how quickly they ride, Vicenza and his men will arrive. Finding the castle deserted, they will also assume they have arrived before the DuFay Armor. Having no reason to avoid detection, as they are the guardians of the church and the DuFay Armor, they will make camp within the castle itself to wait for the armor's arrival."

"If he finds the place deserted, will Vicenza not simply assume that Reverend Vendici was lying to him and make a hasty return to Buckington?" Commander MacCallum asked.

"He does not know where the armor has been kept all these years or how long it would take for the custodians of the armor to make the journey to Dover Castle," Reverend Vendici replied. "I told him that it was likely the pieces would not arrive until Monday, two days from now. That should keep him in place long enough."

"Long enough for what?" Commander MacCallum asked.

"For Gallard and his army to arrive," Andrew answered. "If we are correct, Gallard will leave Stanwyck and march to Dover Castle in the morning. It will take them less than two full days to make the trek, thereby placing their arrival sometime late Monday afternoon or evening. Brewster and his men will rendezvous with Gallard. With Vicenza and his men inside the castle, Brewster and Gallard will assume that the DuFay Armor is there as well, being protected by the Armorum Custodes. They may attempt negotiations, but if so, it will be brief. Gallard will then launch an attack."

"They will not be able to penetrate those walls," MacCallum said matter-of-factly. "They will only be sacrificing their own men. Even with just one hundred Armorum Custodes with him, Vicenza could hold out indefinitely. At least, that is, until they ran out of supplies."

"They will not have much with them in the way of supplies," Andrew replied. "They would not have planned on an extended stay, perhaps a few days at most. But it does not matter to us. He could stay contained for eternity for all we care. What matters to us is Gallard's attention being focused on Dover Castle and how many of his men are lost in his attack on the castle."

"So, we have Vicenza and his one hundred Custodes holed-up in Dover Castle, and we have Gallard and his army attacking the castle," Commander MacCallum said. "What does that accomplish?"

"Gallard's full attention will be on attacking the castle and he will spare no sweat in doing so. His men will be weary from weeks of marching and the siege upon the castle. While there will not be any hand-to-hand combat, Vicenza will still have his men rein a barrage of arrows at Gallard's men. While I do not suspect that Gallard's army will experience a significant casualty rate, every man that is taken from the field helps dwindle Gallard's army so that when we attack, we have a better chance of defeating him and taking the DuFay Breastplate," Andrew replied.

"Attack?" MacCallum asked in disbelief. "With what? You would need a massive army of your own and unless there are significant details of which I have not been made aware, that is something you are sorely lacking."

"No, we do not have a massive army," Andrew conceded. "However, we do not need one. Gallard's men will be weary from such a long journey and their assault on the castle. I suspect they will spend the first few days building catapults and siege towers before commencing their attack. We will launch our attack after they launch theirs, as their full attention will be on the castle. Patrick McKenzie, a friend of mine and an influential man in Stanwyck, is recruiting a fighting force. They will leave Stanwyck Tuesday morning and rendezvous with us at Sedgwick Henge on Thursday, which is close to an hour's ride from Dover Castle. Once we get confirmation that Gallard's assault has commenced, we will launch our own onslaught."

"What is the size of Gallard's army?" Captain MacCallum asked.

"Gregory?" Andrew said, turning to the young man.

"When he left Nordham and headed to Durinburg, he had five thousand men with him," Gregory answered.

"Angus, how many of Gallard's men would you estimate were eliminated during his onslaught at Durinburg? Nearly three hundred attacked us after we emerged from the escape tunnel. We left none alive." Andrew asked.

"I would estimate we eliminated another five hundred during the battle," Angus replied.

"That still leaves us gravely outnumbered," Captain MacCallum said. "How many men do you believe your friend will be able to enlist in this ill-fated endeavor?" MacCallum asked. "Fifty? One hundred? Are there that many able-bodied men in Stanwyck willing to leave their families and fight an army of over four thousand?"

"After Gallard rapes their village of the food for which they toiled tirelessly this season and confiscates many of their livestock, there will not be a single man unwilling to stand up and fight for justice, if not revenge," Andrew replied. "Patrick assured me he could gather several hundred men at least."

"Several hundred men against four thousand," MacCallum scoffed. "A suicide mission if there ever was one."

"Reverend?" Andrew said, turning to the clergyman.

"As you know," Reverend Vendici said to Commander MacCallum, "there remains a force of at least nine hundred Armorum Custodes here in Buckington. We also have another one thousand, five hundred men in inactive reserves. Men that you were already preparing to call to report for duty. Messengers have been sent to call those men to arms and to rendezvous with us at Sedgwick Henge no later than Thursday, along with McPherson's contingency. That should give us well over twenty-five hundred swords."

"Will the Armorum Custodes be required to fight against Vicenza and the men with him?" MacCallum asked. "While these men are trained to follow orders and are loyal to a fault, I venture there would be much hesitation in fighting their brothers."

"There would be no reason for them to engage in combat with their fellow Custodes," Andrew replied. "Once our mission against Gallard is complete, the fighting will be over. Vicenza and his men are not the enemy. We will have all six pieces of the DuFay Armor and Reynald Vicenza will be a disgraced man, no longer a member of the Armorum Custodes. His ultimate fate will be up to Reverend Vendici and the church's Council."

"I will need the details of your plan of attack," Commander MacCallum said to Andrew. "The numbers will still be against us and with no disrespect to your friend and those he enlists in this potentially perilous endeavor, they are not an organized, experienced military unit. We will have to plan accordingly."

"I agree," Andrew said, and he went on to explain their plan for attacking Gallard and obtaining the DuFay Breastplate.

Chapter 37

S ir Reynald Vicenza led the group of one hundred Armorum Custodes along the only road that provided access to Dover Castle. They had traveled through the frosty night under a cloudless, star-filled sky and it was late Sunday morning as they neared their destination. Vicenza held his hand up to bring the small army to a stop as one of his scouts returned from his reconnaissance mission.

"Somewhere between thirty and fifty men on horseback passed through here no more than two days ago," the man reported.

"The Armor Custodians?" a senior officer riding alongside Vicenza, Captain Christian Bellows, asked his commanding officer.

"Perhaps," Vicenza replied, "although I doubt there would be such a large complement, as it could possibly bring attention to them which they would want to avoid. Reverend Vendici told me MacLean was taking the sword and shield to the castle. The tracks could be those of him and his companions." He looked at the scout. "Continue."

"They went to Dover Castle," the scout said, "but the place is empty. It appears that several men entered the castle's grounds and walked about, as if searching the castle, but they did not stay. There is no sign of encampment within the walls recently."

"Did the reverend lie to you?" Captain Bellows asked Vicenza.

"I would not hold him above misleading us in a situation such as this, but he knows quite well what I will do if he has lied to us," Commander Vicenza replied. "It is possible MacLean has been here, hidden the armor, and for whatever reason left."

"They could not have returned along this road, or we would have seen them," Bellows said.

"I did see tracks leading away from the castle, in the opposite direction of the road," the scout continued. "I did not follow them."

"Curious," Bellows said thoughtfully.

"Curious indeed," Vicenza replied. "If not MacLean, then perhaps a scouting party for the couriers to ensure the castle has not become inhabited after all these years."

"If that were the case, would they not leave several men there to secure it until the armor arrives?" Bellows asked.

"That they would," Vicenza answered. "I believe we can disregard the idea of it being a scouting party for the armor-bearers. Were there any wagon tracks?"

"No, sir, just horse tracks," the scout replied.

"Thirty to fifty people on horseback with no wagons for supplies or carrying personal belongings," Vicenza said thoughtfully. "We can also dismiss a group of common folk traveling through the area. Follow the tracks and see where they lead," Vicenza instructed the scout. With a nod of acknowledgment, the scout turned his horse and rode away.

Vicenza motioned to his followers and the army resumed its journey. In another fifteen minutes they cleared the tree line and Dover Castle came into view. It took several more minutes to cover the additional four hundred yards through the overgrowth to the castle's gate. After a few minutes of contemplation, he turned to Captain Bellows.

"Set the Armorum Custodes standards high on the towers to ensure they are plainly visible. When the armor bearers arrive, we want to ensure they know it is the Armorum Custodes that occupy Dover Castle. Station a two-man watch on the road five miles out. I want forewarning of anybody who approaches."

"Do you expect trouble?" Bellows asked.

"Always," Vicenza replied. "I presume the horse tracks we have seen do not belong to a group of vagabonds or people looking for a new home, but to Walter Brewster and his men. Private Leandry said that it was a large group of riders that approached him and Captain Cardona on their way back to Buckington with Brewster in custody. Being that Brewster is King Edwin Gallard's top man, it would be no surprise that a rescue mission was put into play."

"That would be reasonable," Bellows agreed. "Yet what would prompt Brewster to lead his men to Dover Castle?"

"He would have no reason to come here unless he was under the impression that the DuFay Armor was here, or would be here soon," Vicenza replied.

"But how could he know?" Bellows asked. "You yourself did not know until two days ago, and the only other people who knew were Reverend Vendici, who informed you, and the custodians of the armor who were told, in great secrecy, to bring the armor here."

"MacLean knew," Vendici said. "Why else would he have replaced the true sword and shield with cheap replicas and place the life of his lady friend in danger? And even then, it was not his lady friend but another stand-in, a replica if you will. Captain Cardona instructed Private Leandry to warn us of a possible attack. I had assumed that he meant an attack on Buckington, which is why I only brought one hundred men with us and left orders with Captain MacCallum to call the remaining Custodes to station in preparation for an attack. Private Leandry also mentioned that Brewster seemed overly curious about Dover Castle. Somehow, Brewster has deduced that the DuFay Armor is coming to Dover Castle. Surely he has sent word to King Gallard, who will turn his army and come here instead of continuing to Nordham."

"If the armor couriers do not arrive before Gallard does, they will immediately turn away the moment they discover his army and we will lose the armor," Bellows noted. "We will not know where it will be taken."

"Vendici will know," Vicenza replied. "He will tell us, lest he lose his precious church if not more."

"How will we know if this happens, if the couriers turn back?" Bellows asked. "We could be stuck here for who knows how many days or weeks while the armor is spirited away."

"Our scouts," Vicenza replied. "We will have one party remain unseen off the road. Once Gallard's army passes them, if he indeed comes this way, they will be instructed to remain in place and intercept anybody else who travels along the road. If the couriers, then the Custodes will escort them to Buckington and keep them in custody. They will ignite a large bon-fire as a signal to us that the couriers have been apprehended and are safe, at which time we will make our escape."

"What do we do in the meantime?" Captain Bellows asked.

"Prepare for a fight," Commander Vicenza answered. "The men shall all camp within the castle's walls. The vegetation between the castle and the forest will help slow down whatever attack is thrown at us. Have the men gather wood for fires and for making arrows and spears. Search the fields for rocks that can be used for the murder holes should the gate be breached. If none are found, see if there are walls that can be broken down and the blocks used as such. See if several ballistas can be put together and set on the towers to give us a longer firing range. Repair and reinforce the gate. Send out hunting parties to gather whatever game they can, as we may be forced to hold out for many days, and we only have limited supplies. There is a well in the castle, see if there is water in it and if it is drinkable. If not, there is a stream just within the tree line on the east side of the castle. Assign men to gather as much water as possible. Dispatch two riders back to Buckington with word to call to arms the Armorum Custodes reserves and the Guards we left in Buckington. Have them get here as quickly as possible with as many supplies as possible. There is a hidden tunnel on the north side of the castle designed for bringing in supplies and allowing people to come and go under secrecy in the event the castle was attacked. Have the tunnel inspected and ensure that it is cleared. It will serve as our escape route. I expect Gallard and his army to arrive within the next two days if they are indeed coming, well before our men will be able to make the journey from Buckington. If they can catch Gallard by surprise with an attack on his flank, we may stand a chance at defeating him. Send word to the senior officers to meet me inside the castle immediately. We have much to discuss. Now see to it."

"Yes, sir," Bellows replied and left Vicenza's side.

Walter Brewster sat on the makeshift stand that had been constructed in one of the trees near the edge of the forest to provide a better vantage point for spying on the castle and the road leading to it. He watched until the end of the conversation between the two men at the head of the company of Armorum Custodes. A lone rider was making his way around the castle's wall and looked to be following a trail. Brewster knew the trail which the man was following. He quickly climbed down from the stand and jumped on his horse and headed back to his camp. When he got there, he paid a visit to his prisoner, Captain Cardona.

"Well, Captain, it would appear that some of your friends have arrived at Dover Castle," he said. "A hundred at least, I would estimate. I would presume that the DuFay Armor is with them."

"The DuFay Armor?" Cardona asked, genuinely baffled. "Why would the DuFay Armor be here?"

"Come now, Captain, there is no need for you to continue to profess ignorance," Brewster responded.

"I truly do not know why the DuFay Armor would be brought here," Cardona replied sincerely. "To my knowledge all pieces were being returned to Buckington. It would make no sense for them to be brought here."

"I have it on good authority that the pieces of armor other than the breastplate are being brought here, supposedly under great secrecy, until the breastplate is obtained, then they will be taken to Buckington," Brewster said. "MacLean and his fellow conspirators are fools. They are all but handing the DuFay throne to King Edwin Gallard. Gallard and his army should be here sometime tomorrow afternoon, the evening at the latest. He will tear down these walls and take the DuFay Armor and fulfill a life-long quest." As he finished speaking, one of his men approached them.

"Sir, a rider is approaching from the castle. It appears that he is following our trail."

"Yes, I suspect he is," Brewster responded.

"How do you want us to handle him?"

"Bring him to me," Brewster instructed the man. "I am sure Captain Cardona would appreciate a little friendly company as he watches the decimation of his fellow Armorum Custodes."

Chapter 38

King Edwin Gallard was exhausted. The past several months had taken an enormous toll on him and his army, having marched nearly two thousand miles and engaged in a major battle. His relentless quest for the DuFay Armor and throne had pushed him and his men to the point of breaking and he knew all too well that another major conflict, if drawn out, could be the end of him. Week upon week of marching along with supplies that were barely enough to keep up with the most basic of needs had given birth to much discontent among the ranks. Gallard was more than aware that whispers of insurrection had been filtering throughout the army, and his power was on the verge of foundering. But he could not abandon his purpose, his pursuit, his obsession that began so many years ago. He was close, so close, and with a little luck and a little more blood and sweat, he would attain his goal. A voice called out to him, and Gallard opened his eyes, not even aware that he had closed them and was drifting off.

"My lord," the voice called again, not having gotten a response from the king the first time.

"What is it?" Gallard responded, fully alert.

"We are approaching Dover Castle," the scout responded. "There is no sign of activity outside of the castle's walls, although there are many tracks along the road leading toward the castle. There are standards flying on the towers, therefore we know the castle is occupied, but we have no way of knowing by how many people. The grounds outside of the castle stretch approximately four hundred yards from the castle's walls to the forest surrounding the castle. The area had been cleared at one time but has become choked with vegetation and small trees. The castle has only one small visible entrance. I estimate the walls to be thirty feet tall."

"Any sign of Brewster and his men?" Gallard asked.

"Not yet, sire."

Gallard turned to the man next to him, Donovan McMaster, his Chief of Staff, who was one of the only three men in Gallard's kingdom who knew of the DuFay Armor and the true purpose of Gallard's quest.

"Donovan, get men busy clearing the field and set-up camp," the king instructed. "We only have a few more hours of daylight left. I want the castle surrounded. Put the carpenters to work building belfries and catapults. They have three days. Tomorrow, we will attempt to negotiate the surrender of those inside the castle. If they refuse, then we shall attack Thursday. That gives our men two full days of rest. I want them well-rested before we lay siege. See to it."

"Yes, my lord," Donovan said, then rode ahead to carry-out the king's orders. As he disappeared from sight, another rider approached the king. It was Gallard's chief military advisor and commander of his army, Walter Brewster.

"Building belfries would be a waste of time, my lord," Walter said in quite a cool tone as he stopped his horse by Gallard's side. He still remembered quite vividly the king's threat against him in their last conversation, that if Walter did not have the sword or Andrew MacLean's head in his possession the next time they met his life would be forfeited. He honestly did not know whether Gallard would follow through with his promise or if the passage of time had softened him.

"Brewster," King Gallard said simply in return, which did not ease Walter's anxiety. "And why is that?"

"There is an old moat surrounding the castle. A tower could not be moved close enough to the wall. Also, there are additional ditches dug in the field one hundred and one hundred fifty yards out from the castle. If towers are constructed along the forest line, closest to the supply of building materials, we could not move them to the castle."

"Could we not bridge the ditches?" Gallard responded.

"We could," Brewster replied. "It would just take time."

"I have a force of four thousand men behind me," the king said. "That is more than enough to either build bridges across the ditches or fill them in with enough dirt and debris to provide passage for the towers in very little time." With Brewster not replying, the king continued. "I take it you have neither the sword nor MacLean's head to offer me."

"No, my lord," Walter replied, convinced that the king was now going to have him executed. "I had the sword in my possession just a few weeks ago along with the boy, however, we were ambushed on the way to deliver them to you, and both were taken from us."

"Ambushed by who?" Gallard asked.

"MacLean and his companions," Walter replied. "I caught up with him in Nordham. I took the boy and the sword and left him in the hands of an execution squad. He somehow escaped and was able to circle around and set up an ambush in front of us before we reached Stanwyck. One of our own men, Gregory McPherson, has turned against us and joined MacLean. It was likely by his assistance that MacLean still lives. I fought three of them but was not able to overcome the unfavorable odds and was severely wounded, coming within mere breaths of my life ending. Several of my men found me and saved my life." Walter could not admit to Gallard that Andrew had bested him in a fight, yet again, and therefore lied.

"I see," Gallard replied. "Had you taken his head with your own sword when you had the opportunity in Nordham, we would not be in this predicament, is that not correct?"

"You are correct," Walter replied, knowing that he had made an unwise decision back in Nordham. "You would have the sword and the shield along with the Heir of DuFay."

"MacLean has the shield?" Gallard asked, surprised.

"Yes, my lord," Walter replied. "By his own admission. We nearly had him again back in Stanwyck, and could have had both the sword and shield, yet once again he received assistance, this time from a company of Armorum Custodes from Buckington. MacLean was delivering the sword and shield to them, as he was told by the Church that it had identified the DuFay heir. All eight of my men were slain. My injuries prevented me from being an effective a fighter and despite my best efforts, I was subdued and taken prisoner."

"And where are they now, the sword, shield and MacLean?" Gallard asked.

"As for MacLean, I know not," Walter answered. "We were in Stanwyck the last time I saw him. I suspect he may have headed to Buckington. Regarding the sword and shield, that is why I sent word for you to bring the army to Dover Castle."

"You know for a fact that the DuFay Armor is within those walls?" the king asked.

"MacLean said the armor was being taken to an old stronghold for safe keeping until the breastplate was obtained, then it would be taken to Buckington where the Heir of DuFay would be crowned. As we were making our way to Buckington, before your scouting party came to my aid, one of my captors, Captain Cardona, confirmed that Dover Castle is an old, but abandoned, Armor Guardian stronghold. The only one within a week's ride at least. When we arrived two days ago the castle was empty but yesterday, at least one hundred Armor Guardians arrived and are at this moment holed-up in the castle. There would be no reason for them to be there unless they had the DuFay Armor and were guarding it. The Armor Guardians who had me in custody also had the sword and the shield and were taking them to Buckington. While I was able to capture the one, Captain Cardona, the second one was able to get away with the armor."

"Why, then, am I about to lay siege to an old castle instead of Buckington?" Gallard asked, exasperated.

"Because the DuFay Armor is not in Buckington," Walter replied. "It was all being brought to Dover Castle, the sword and shield from Buckington and the other three pieces from undisclosed locations. Your best opportunity to acquire the five pieces you do not have is here and now."

"What of the man you captured, Captain Cardona? What does he know of Dover Castle and the plans for the DuFay Armor?" Gallard asked.

"He claims to have no knowledge of the plans for the DuFay Armor, other than the pieces being taken to Buckington. He may not even be aware that the plan was to transport the sword and shield to Dover Castle once they arrived in Buckington. His only order was to retrieve the sword and shield from MacLean and take them to Buckington."

"I pray that you are right, Brewster," Gallard said in a warning tone. "It has been an extremely long and costly journey. Not only did we lose a host of men in Durinburg, but we also lost many on the road due to illness and exhaustion. My plan was to rest and replenish in Stanwyck so the men would have the energy to continue to Nordham. Now, I can only give them two full days of rest before having to call them to action again. Our only saving grace is that they are not facing another army but stone walls, the likes of which we have conquered before. Have you been able to determine if the castle has any weaknesses?"

"There are no physical weaknesses we have been able to identify," Walter replied. "There are only two true weaknesses: Lack of supplies and lack of manpower. The Armor Guardians did not bring a significant amount of food and water with them. They sent men out to capture game for eating, and from what we could see, they were able to kill enough to last a week at most. There is a well on the castle's grounds, so they may have water. We could wait them out. Once they run out of food, they will have no choice but to either surrender or die of starvation."

"It is the Armorum Custodes," Gallard said. "They will not surrender. I remember hearing that they were several thousand in number. If there is only a hundred within those walls, where are the rest?"

"That I do not know," Walter admitted. "I presume in Buckington."

"That is disconcerting," the king said. "I do not like un-knowns. Send men to Buckington to determine where the rest of the Armorum Custodes are right now. We cannot wait for those inside the castle and risk the rest of the Guardians pouring upon us. Tomorrow, we will attempt to negotiate with those inside Dover Castle. I fully expect them to reject all terms of surrender. Therefore, two days later, we shall attack. With only one hundred men to defend the castle, we should over-run it very quickly. Bring this Cardona to me. I wish to speak with him. Perhaps he has knowledge that a more intense interrogation can wring from him."

"As you wish," Walter said and with great relief, rode away from his king.

Chapter 39

Sir, riders are approaching. They are displaying a white flag."
Commander Reynald Vicenza looked up from the meager breakfast he had been trying to enjoy, considering the limited food they had brought with them. The arrival of the large army prior to the arrival of the armor-bearing couriers had been a great spoiler of his plan to obtain the DuFay Armor. His only hope was that his scouts would intercept the couriers on the road to Dover Castle and escort them back to Buckington. Now, his primary focus was on how to escape Gallard's army.

"Find Captain Bellows and send him to me," Vicenza ordered.

"Yes, sir," the messenger said as he bowed his head and left the room. Less than two minutes later, Captain Christian Bellows entered the small room where Commander Vicenza was finishing his breakfast.

"Yes, sir?" Captain Bellows said as he entered the room.

"We have messengers approaching, undoubtedly to offer terms for our surrender," Vicenza said. "Either Reverend Vendici lied to us about the DuFay Armor being brought here, or those bringing the armor were delayed or have been traveling very slowly. In either case, we can be assured that Dover Castle shall not see the DuFay Armor. With limited rations, we will not be able to survive more than a few days before the men begin to get hungry and mutinous murmurings spring up among the ranks. We are outnumbered four-to-one at least and there is no fighting our way out of this predicament.

"We cannot send a messenger back to Buckington and have the Armorum Custodes sent to our aid. He would undoubtedly be captured. We cannot be certain that our scouts on the road were successful in returning to Buckington, either. We must assume that we are on our own. Did you inspect the tunnel?"

"Yes, sir, I did," Bellows answered. "There is approximately two feet of water covering the floor. Fifty feet in, the ceiling has collapsed. I have men working to clear it, but at this time there is no telling how much of the cave has collapsed and if there are other barriers further in. I would venture that based on the type of earth in this area, which is exceptionally soft, we could expect that the cave will be impassible."

"Double the men you have working to clear it," Vicenza ordered. "Tell them their lives are dependent on clearing the tunnel and providing us with an escape from what otherwise will either be death by starvation or death by the sword. See to it."

"Yes, sir," Captain Bellows answered and left the room. Vicenza sat in silence for a moment, gathering his thoughts and considering his options, then stood and headed for the front gate. It took him all of sixty seconds to make the trek.

"How many are there?" Vicenza asked the guards at the gate.

"Only two, sir," one of the guards responded.

"Open the gates," Vicenza ordered, and the guards complied. There were three different gates that protected the passage into and out of the castle. The outer wooden gate, which had fallen from its frame years ago, had been re-hung and reinforced. As it opened, Commander Vicenza stepped through and came face-to-face with King Edwin Gallard and Commander Walter Brewster.

"I am King Edwin Gallard of Nordham," the king introduced himself, "and this is Walter Brewster, commander of my army."

"I am Sir Reynald Vicenza, Commander of the Armorum Custodes of Buckington," Vicenza replied. "You are quite far from your homeland, King Edwin Gallard. I can only presume that the posturing of your men is an indication of your intension of an incursion."

"You and your Custodes are at least a day's ride from your own home," Gallard responded. "One would have to wonder what has brought one hundred Armorum Custodes this far from home."

"It is not your business what the Armorum Custodes do," Vicenza countered. "However, to placate your curiosity, the Armorum Custodes have an annual gathering at Dover Castle in commemoration of the great victory the Custodes achieved over marauding invaders many years ago at this very location. Though outnumbered at least five to one, the Custodes had little difficulty repelling the invasion and slaughtering their enemy."

"I read of that event back in my youth, when I was studying in Buckington," Gallard responded, not the least bit intimidated. "It was a magnificent display of strength, though it be against an untrained and unsophisticated horde of filthy barbarians. Truth be told, it sounded more like a horde of women and children, the men were so weak. Truly an event the Armorum Custodes should hold in great esteem."

"Why are you here?" Vicenza asked, getting to the point.

"You know why we are here," Gallard responded pointedly. "We know what the Armorum Custodes protect within these walls. For the past forty years I have been seeking the DuFay Armor, and today I have found it. I will have the armor."

"Your informants have led you down the wrong path," Vicenza replied. "There is no armor within these walls other than what these Custodes have as their personal armor. The DuFay Armor is many miles from here, in locations known only to the esteemed Reverend Antonio Vendici of the Covenantal Orthodox Church of Christ."

"I know that the armor was ordered to be brought here," Gallard responded. "That is why you and your band of Custodes are here. You are protecting the armor while you scheme to steal the breastplate from me, which I assure you is an impossible endeavor."

"I assure you, great king, that the DuFay Armor is not within these walls," Vicenza replied. "You and your Commander are welcome to enter and scour every inch of Dover Castle."

"If it is your expectation that the Armor Guardians army will come to your rescue, I must advise you that your messenger did not make it to deliver the message," Walter said. "We captured him just a few miles down the road. You are on your own."

"Sir Reynald Vicenza, Commander of the Armorum Custodes, I implore you to relinquish the DuFay Armor and save the lives of your men and yourself," Gallard said. "As you can see, there are nearly four thousand men surrounding Dover Castle. You have no means of escape. You have limited supplies which I suspect will last only a few days. There is no scenario by which you and your men leave this place with the DuFay Armor."

"Of course not," Vicenza replied, then stressed, "because the armor is not here! You believe we have limited supplies? Such an assumption is not a sound military strategy. How long will your men be able to assault this citadel before they begin to starve and rebel against you? You cannot send men to Buckington for supplies, lest they be captured by the Armorum Custodes. These walls are tall and thick. You will not be able to get past them and any attempt to approach will result in a hail of spears and arrows that will blot out the sun. Are you men able to walk through fire? They would have to after we rain Greek Fire on the battlefield. The Armorum Custodes are trained well beyond anything your men have experienced. They have successfully defended this stronghold before. They will do so again."

"What of Buckington?" Gallard responded. "Will they be just as successful in defending their home? Once we leave this place with your corpses rotting and left to the vultures and rats, we will descend upon Buckington like a tumultuous tempest that no eye has ever seen. The Armorum Custodes will be destroyed in its entirety and then we will decide how much of the town to leave standing. If you relinquish the armor, you have my word that you and your men will be permitted to leave this place with their lives, and Buckington will remain unscathed. Relinquish it not, and all that I have said will be done."

"Your majesty, even if the DuFay Armor was within these walls, the order of the Armorum Custodes was created to protect the armor until the heir to Reginald DuFay was identified and could retake the throne that was lost so many years ago. Therefore, it would be impossible for us to surrender the armor, for we would be surrendering our pride, heritage, and dignity. Your siege against Dover Castle may ultimately be successful, yet it will be futile, for the DuFay Armor is not within these walls."

"Very well," Gallard replied, still not believing Vicenza. "Truly I expected no other outcome of this conversation. It is a shame that so many brave, loyal men will die on these grounds for the sake of a few pieces of ancient armor."

"I could not agree more," Vicenza said, then turned and ordered the gates closed.

"You are certain the armor is inside?" Gallard said as he and Brewster turned and headed back to their camp. "We interrogated Captain Cardona quite intensely and he continued to profess no knowledge of the DuFay Armor being brought here. We also interrogated the scout that you captured but the result was the same."

"As I told you before, my lord, I had reliable information that the DuFay Armor was being brought here for safekeeping," Brewster replied. "Vicenza's story of commemorating some ancient Armorum Custodes battle holds no truth. There is no reason for them to be here other than to protect the DuFay Armor. We shall break through their defenses within days and the armor will be ours. If by some chance Vicenza has been honest and the armor is not here, I shall personally ride to Buckington and using any and every means necessary, wring the information from this Reverend Vendici. We will have the armor."

"What is your battle plan?" the king asked. "We cannot afford another Kirkshire. Taking two months to breach these walls only to find no armor within could be the end of our quest. We have pushed our men to their limits and this last expedition has cost us dearly, both in terms of lives and finances."

"There are no indications of weakness in the curtain wall, and there is only one door for entering and exiting," Brewster replied. "There is no outside water source that could provide a point of entry that could be exploited. There are no long-range weapons within the castle. While the Armor Guardians may have bows that could reach up to three hundred yards, they would not be highly effective at that range. With limited ammunition, they would conserve what they have and only use it for closer encounters. We need to make them use as many of their arrows as we can and dwindle their supply, if not deplete it completely. As is the usual case, the front gate is the most vulnerable part of the castle and where we should focus our attack, but not the only point of attack. The vegetation that we have removed to make camp is a tool that we can effectively utilize. We shall pile the cut vegetation and additional branches and limbs from the forest along the base of the wall and ignite it. The smoke will at least serve as a partial barrier to the line of sight of the Guardians and interfere with their ability to accurately fire upon our men.

"Under cover of wood shielding, we will construct a battering ram on the road leading to the castle's entrance. After weakening the door and portcullis with fire, we will move in with the battering ram and smash our way into the castle. There are two doors and two portcullises, therefore this action will have to be completed four times. I do not believe that they have enough materials to sufficiently reinforce the doors.

"Also, to help divert the Guardian's resources, we shall construct wooden ladders and set them against the side and rear walls. There is little chance that we will actually use them to try and gain access, but the Guardians will not know that. They will have to assign men to protect against intrusion."

"What of catapults?" Gallard asked.

"It would take too much time to construct catapults that would be of sufficient size to have a significant impact," Brewster replied. "Also, we would be lacking in ammunition. There are few rocks of significant size in the fields surrounding the castle or in the woods. We do not have any materials to create incendiary bombs."

"We could send men to Buckington to acquire the necessary compounds," Gallard suggested.

"That we could," Brewster replied. "My concern would be curious eyes. If the Armorum Custodes are not aware of our presence here, a report of unknown men buying incendiary materials could raise concerns. We certainly do not want to do anything that may give rise to suspicions and an investigation. Also, there is nothing but grass behind those walls to burn. It would be wasted effort."

"What of the belfries?" Gallard asked.

"It is going to take more than a few days to build them of sufficient size to access the top of the wall," Brewster said. "I do not believe the belfries to be a weapon we can effectively utilize without a commitment of being here for a week or more."

"I want every weapon we can possibly muster put in force against that castle," Gallard countered. "The more we throw at it, the quicker it will fall. With the manpower that we have, there is no excuse for not being able to construct at least two belfries quickly. See to the preparations," Gallard ordered. "We shall launch our attack the morning after tomorrow. I want this to be over quickly. Push the men. Within a few days, Dover Castle shall be ours and we will scour every inch of that fortress. If the armor is not there, I will give you leave to pay the reverend a visit. Let us hope you have more success with that commission than your last one."

"As you wish," Brewster acknowledged and left to carry out his orders.

Chapter 40

Nobody knew when Sedgwick Henge had been constructed and what its purpose had been. There were no signs of settlements, either temporary or long-term, in or around the earthwork. The henge was a circular earthen embankment five feet tall with a diameter of three hundred feet. On the inside of the bank was a ditch five feet deep. Within the circle were fifteen piles of large boulders that had no apparent pattern or obvious use. It was truly a mystery of the ancient world.

Andrew MacLean stood alone, deep in thought, as he gazed over the ruin. He could not help but wonder who built the henge and why. It could serve no military purpose and without signs of settlement, it could not have been home to a family or community. Perhaps it had been constructed as a place of worship or for some other sacred purpose. For all he knew, he could be walking over a grave with every step he took. If that were the case, what were the people like who now laid under his feet? Were they a peaceful people, a royal people, a religious people? There was no way of knowing. The sun was four hours into its daily trek and the sky was dotted with bright white clouds. A cool breeze put the tall grass and other vegetation in motion. Andrew pulled his overcoat together to resist the chill. He knew that this moment of peace would soon end, and he would be forced into battle yet one more time. One more time, he thought. Please, Lord, just one more time. He heard his name called out and turned to see Captain MacCallum approaching him.

"Andrew," Captain MacCallum called out. "The reserves of the Armorum Custodes have arrived. True to Reverend Vendici's word, there are fifteen hundred of them. Counting those we brought with us from Buckington, that gives us just under two thousand five hundred Custodes. Your friend, McKenzie, has brought three hundred men with him, for what they are worth. Very few, if any, have true battle experience. They will be more of a hindrance than a help when the fighting begins."

"Do not underestimate the potential of those who have been wronged," Andrew replied. "Those men will be fighting for their families and their ability to survive the remainder of the winter months. They know that if they are victorious, they will be able to return much of that which was stolen from them by Gallard."

"I do not doubt their resolve, but their skill with the sword and ability to take another man's life is another matter."

"Then we must give them what training we can in the time that we have," Andrew responded. "Split the men into groups of fifty. For each group, assign one of your most skilled Custodes as their trainer. Assign additional Custodes to pose as opponents to McKenzie's men. Spend the day instructing the men and sharpening their skills with the sword. Teach them how to focus in battle and not get distracted by the chaos that will surround them. Remind them that these men stole from them and put at risk the lives of their families and if they are not defeated, they will pillage Stanwyck yet again when the army passes by on its way back to Nordham. Teach them that they are fighting for the future of their families and their town. Every opponent that is removed from the battlefield is one less threat to their future. They cannot hesitate, they must fight with determination and resolve. By this time tomorrow, their test will come. They must be prepared."

"It sounds as though you have seen many battles and have trained many men," MacCallum stated.

"Aye, that I have," Andrew replied reflectively. "That I have."

"Then we shall train these men and prepare them as best we can for what they will face," Captain MacCallum said.

"When you have arranged for the training, let us meet one more time in my tent to finalize our plan of attack," Andrew said. "I will gather the others."

"Give me an hour," MacCallum said, then turned to carry out his assignment. Andrew stood in silence for a minute longer, then turned to find his friends.

True to his word, an hour later Captain MacCallum entered Andrew's tent. Already present were Angus, Lawrence, Gregory, Patrick McKenzie, and Luther.

"Our scout has informed me that Gallard has commenced his siege on Dover Castle as of this morning," Andrew reported. "We will continue to get reports as the day progresses. We estimate he has at least four thousand men, possibly more. With only one hundred Custodes at his disposal and limited supplies and ammunition, I do not how long Vicenza will be able to withstand the siege. Gallard has constructed several catapults, but their impact should be limited due to the height and strength of Dover Castle's walls."

"Did you really just say that?" Lawrence asked. "Catapults? Impact?"

"He is also having at least two belfries constructed in an attempt to reach the castle's walls, but they are several days from being completed," Andrew continued, ignoring Lawrence. "Captain MacCallum, to your knowledge, are there any weaknesses in the castle that could be exploited by Gallard and his men?"

"None," MacCallum answered. "Well, with one possible exception. There was a tunnel leading away from the castle which was designed to be used for ingress and egress should the castle come under attack. Reinforcements and supplies would funnel through the tunnel."

"Did you really just say 'funnel through the tunnel'?" Lawrence asked, this time laughing aloud. Captain MacCallum looked at him, not amused.

"Should we assume that Gallard will stumble upon this..." Andrew paused for a second, considered his choice of words, then stole a glance at Lawrence, "...way of entering and leaving the castle, thereby ending this battle quickly?"

"While not impossible, it is unlikely," Captain MacCallum answered. "There are two points of tunnel access outside of the castle. One is in the forest and extremely well hidden. You could walk within two steps of it and not know that it was there. The other is between the castle and the forest, an emergency exit should there be a collapse, inside what had served as a food storage shelter."

"What would prevent Gallard and his men from discovering the emergency exit?" Andrew asked.

"The shelter is long gone, only a few foundation stones remain to testify it ever existed," Captain MacCallum answered. "The entrance is covered by slabs of stone which by now are covered by dirt and grass. There is nothing there that would give evidence of its existence. The question is whether or not the tunnel is still traversable. Without use or maintenance for many decades, I suspect it is in a state of great disrepair and cave-ins are likely to have happened. If it were passable, I promise you Vicenza would have used it for escape already. If he and his men are still defending Dover Castle, that is why."

"What of the ability of the Custodes to defend the castle?" Andrew asked. "How long do you believe they can do so? Is there a chance that, since they are not protecting the DuFay Armor and have no reason to fight, they will surrender to Gallard?"

"They should be able to repel the invasion for as long as their supplies last," MacCallum answered. "They did not take much with them, therefore, I would estimate they could fight effectively for no more than four or five days. Will Vicenza surrender the castle to Gallard? I would venture no, he would not. It is unlikely that Gallard would allow the Custodes to return to Buckington and Vicenza would assume the same. Gallard would know that eventually, he would have to fight them again and it would be best to dispose of them at Dover Castle and reduce what resistance he may face in the future. Vicenza will do everything possible to escape through the tunnel, regardless of how much digging is necessary, before surrendering."

"In that case, we can have a high level of confidence that Gallard and his army will still be engaged with Vicenza and his men come tomorrow," Andrew stated. "We will leave late tomorrow afternoon, two hours before sunset. It should take us an hour or so to get to Dover Castle. Our objective is the DuFay Breastplate, which we can be assured is being held and protected in Gallard's personal tent. Once our attack begins, Gallard will undoubtedly muster as many men as he can around his tent to protect himself and the breastplate, which will make it extremely difficult to get to. Though weakened by their long journey, they still outnumber us, so we cannot rely solely on our ability to defeat his army spread-out over such a large battlefield. We must rely on deception and misdirection. Alistair, what is the terrain like around Dover Castle?" Andrew asked.

"Dover Castle sits in a flat circular clearing that extends nearly four hundred yards from the castle's wall to the tree line. There are no streams or bodies of water within the clearing, although considering how many years have passed since the stronghold was abandoned and all care ceased, it is possible that small ponds may have formed in various areas. There were two trenches dug in the clearing circling the castle, the first one-hundred yards out and the second an additional one-hundred-fifty yards out. These were to prevent, or at least make extremely difficult, the use of towers to gain access over the walls. Whatever growth there was in the clearing has certainly been removed or greatly reduced by Gallard to eliminate obstacles for his men."

"Gallard has his army spread out around the castle," Lawrence chimed in. "It is completely surrounded. Where do we start?"

"We start by letting Gallard know that we are coming," Andrew said with a smile.

"What about stealth? What about sneaking up on him?" Angus asked in disbelief. "You want to warn him that he is about to be attacked?"

"In a manner," Andrew said, then went on to explain his battle plan.

"It is a bold plan, that much is for certain," Angus commented after Andrew finished. "Somewhat unorthodox to say the least."

"We prefer bold and unorthodox," Lawrence said. "It staves off boredom."

"What of Vicenza?" Captain MacCallum asked. "He will believe that the Armorum Custodes have come to rescue him and that he is still in command, if he survives the battle."

"That is one of the reasons that Luther is here," Andrew replied. "He is the representative of the Covenantal Orthodox Church of Christ and has the written orders that relieve Vicenza from his duties and promote you to the position of commander. He will be taken into custody and returned to the Church to face the consequences of his treachery."

"It sounds like you have missions for all your male companions," a feminine voice said from the entrance to Andrew's tent. "What of us women?"

All heads turned to see who was speaking. Victoria and Marie stood in the entrance, hands on their hips, intent looks on their faces.

"What are YOU doing here?" Andrew said to Marie with a bit of rebuke in his voice. "You were to remain in Buckington and help safeguard Reverend Vendici and the DuFay Armor."

"Yes, well, I decided that the Armor Guardians that were left there can do a much better job of that than I can," Marie replied boldly.

"It is extremely dangerous for you here, Marie," Angus chastised her. "You should return to Buckington immediately."

"I will not," Marie replied firmly. "I…" she started, then glanced at Victoria, "…we, have proven many times that we can fight, Victoria more than myself. I have been training with her for several days as well. You know first-hand my skills with the bow, and my skills with the sword have been honed to a fine edge. I dare say our effectiveness will be much greater than that of the farmers and shop keepers that Patrick has gathered, no offense," she added, looking at Patrick.

Andrew walked over to Marie and placed his hands on her shoulders.

"That is exactly why we need you in Buckington, to use your skills to protect Reverend Vendici and the armor," he said encouragingly. "We did not ask you to stay there because you are weak and not able to fight, quite the opposite. You have been more passionate about the DuFay Armor than I ever have been, and I am even Reginald DuFay's heir! You are strong, Marie Talbot, and the most intelligent and driven woman that I have ever known."

"You mean stubborn, do you not?" Lawrence threw in.

"You are not helping," Andrew said, stealing a side glance at his friend. He looked back at Marie. "Who better to protect the DuFay Armor? I dare say, Reverend Vendici is probably the only person who is more impassioned about the armor than you are. You have seen through her journals how zealous your mother was of the DuFay legend and the armor and were it not for those journals, we would not be here right now. It is as if you are continuing, and finishing, her work. Protecting that armor is a responsibility that I would not entrust but to those closest to me. You have been the closest to me in this quest. There is no person I could have more confidence in than you."

Marie looked deeply at Andrew, unsure how to respond. She had no idea that he thought of her in such a way, that he trusted her more than Lawrence or anybody else he knew, especially after their last conversation before she stole off to Buckington on her own. She looked at Lawrence and Angus, both giving her slight nods of approval. She looked at Victoria, who had become a close friend in the past several days.

"It would be my honor to be by your side in this task," Victoria said sincerely.

"I do not know what to say," Marie finally spoke, looking at Andrew. "I had no idea—"

"Just say that you will do this for me, for us, for the DuFay family," Andrew said, interrupting her. "We are so close to the end."

"Then yes, I will protect the DuFay Armor, with my life if it comes to that," Marie replied. "It will be my honor."

"We will not let it come to that," Andrew said reassuringly. "If we are not successful in obtaining the breastplate, if by God's providence I do not survive this battle, then you are to see that the DuFay Armor is destroyed."

"Destroyed?" Marie gasped. "Why?"

"This armor, this legend, has cost many lives over the years," Andrew replied. "It no longer represents what it was created to represent, the true armor of God: The belt of truth, the breastplate of righteousness, the gospel of peace, the shield of faith, the helmet of salvation and the sword of the Spirit. Man's greed and lust for domination has turned the armor into a means for stealing that which does not belong to him: Power. Forgetting what the armor stood for and not living according to its principles is what caused Robert DuFay to lose the armor, and his life, so many years ago. If we are not successful in our endeavor, then we must ensure that no more lives are lost by others trying to succeed where we fail. If the armor is destroyed, then what we have been through will never happen again."

"Then you better succeed, Andrew McLean," Marie said. "I expect to see you in Buckington in no more than four days, with the breastplate." She looked deeply into his eyes once again, not wanting to leave, but knowing that she had to. With a final glance at Lawrence and Angus, the two people she had become closest to over the past year outside of Andrew, Marie turned and left the tent.

"Watch over her," Andrew said to Victoria. With a nod, Victoria turned and walked away.

"Well, that is a first," Lawrence said as watched Victoria leave the tent.

"What is a first?" Andrew asked, turning back to the others.

"I have never known Marie to back down once her mind has been made-up," Lawrence said. "She never backed down to her father, that is for sure."

"As I said, she is an intelligent woman," Andrew replied. "She knows that protecting the armor is vital at this stage."

"Perhaps, but I believe it is something else," Lawrence said with a grin.

"Let us get back to our planning," Andrew said, ignoring Lawrence's inference.

Chapter 41

Dover Castle appeared to be caught in the middle of a raging inferno as flames reached up the castle's walls on all sides and smoke raced high into the sky. The fires had been started the day before and Gallard's men continued to fuel the fires by gathering whatever dead material they could find in the forest as well as cutting down smaller trees. Under cover of arrow shields, they continually tossed the fuel onto the fires. From within the castle, the Armorum Custodes attempted to keep the assailants away from the walls by launching multiple volleys of arrows, but the shields used by the invaders all but eliminated any effectiveness the arrows might otherwise achieve. If there had been more men inside the castle, they might have been able to douse most of the fires by forming lines to carry buckets of water from the well to the tops of the walls and dropping the water. However, with the limited number of men and virtually no buckets on hand, this defensive measure was not available to them on a large scale. They were only able to transport and drop a small amount of water through the murders holes in the gatehouse to try and prevent the doors and portcullises from burning, but even that was having an extremely limited impact.

"Status report," Commander Vicenza snapped to Captain Bellows who had just entered what was serving as Vicenza's war room.

"The enemy has succeeded in battering down the first gatehouse door and portcullis," Bellow replied. "The second portcullis is burning as we speak."

"Then throw more water on it!" Vicenza ordered.

"Sir, we are doing what we can with the limited materials we have on-hand," Bellows responded. "There was virtually nothing left in this place when it was abandoned and what may have been here has been pilfered. As you know, we were not anticipating having to defend the castle when we left Buckington and therefore did not bring any weapons or tools accordingly."

"Continue," Vicenza said, not responding to Bellows' comments.

"The enemy is in the process of constructing two belfries. It looks as if they will be completed and ready to move into place if not tomorrow, the day after. The enemy has built makeshift bridges over the trenches and moat."

"How did we permit them to build bridges?" Vicenza demanded. "Do we not have bows and arrows? Did we not construct ballistas to fire upon the enemy?"

"Yes sir, we do, and we did," Bellows replied. "We have been successful in taking down several dozen of the enemy at least, perhaps a hundred of them. You must remember, we have limited ammunition. We can slow their progress but not eliminate it."

"What else?" Vicenza asked. "What about the tunnel?"

"We have been successful in clearing a long stretch of the tunnel," Bellows answered. "However, there appears to be a complete collapse of the tunnel two hundred yards out. We have no materials for shoring the ceiling. Many of the men are all but exhausted from digging."

"They are Armorum Custodes, they will dig until they drop, if necessary," Vicenza countered.

"We did reach the emergency exit point, approximately one hundred and fifty yards into the tunnel," Bellows said. "It may be possible to escape via that route, however, it lays in the middle of the field and is surrounded by Gallard's men. Even if we were able to dislodge and move the covering slabs, we would find ourselves in the middle of enemy forces.

"The enemy has also constructed two enormous ladders, which they appear poised to set against the northern and eastern walls," Bellows continued.

"Focus our men on those walls," Vicenza directed. "Pull them from tunnel duty. If the enemy is successful in getting over the walls, we are defeated."

"What is the status of our ammunition?" Vicenza asked.

"We are down to about thirty percent of what we had initially," Bellows reported. "I expect we will deplete most, if not all, of that as we defend against the ladders and continue to defend the gatehouse. By this time tomorrow, we will likely be reduced to hand-to-hand combat."

"That is the strength of the Armorum Custodes," Vicenza said, almost reverently.

"Perhaps so," Captain Bellows replied, "but we both know that one hundred swords are no match for four thousand."

"You may carry out your orders," Vicenza said. "You are dismissed."

"Yes, sir," Captain Bellows said and left the room.

"How much longer?" King Edwin Gallard asked his military commander as they looked across the battlefield at Dover Castle. The sun had dropped below the tree line and daylight was fading quickly.

"Perhaps tomorrow," Walter Brewster replied. "We are half-way through the gatehouse. The ladders are in position at the bases of the northern and eastern walls. The fires along the northern and eastern walls have burnt down to the point we can set the ladders and send men up. We have noticed a drop in both the frequency and number of arrows from within the castle, which would indicate they are low on ammunition. Our first wave over the walls will be by our most trained and skilled swordsmen. Once we get over the walls, the fight will be all but over."

"Good," Gallard said. "I want this wrapped-up by tomorrow evening, whatever it takes."

Before Brewster could say anything else, one of the king's messengers rushed up, out of breath.

"My lord!" he said, panting.

"What is it?" Gallard asked.

"There is a force approaching from the south, along the road!" the scout said.

"How many men?" Brewster asked.

"I could not tell," the scout replied. "It looked like several divisions at least. They were flying the same banner as that which stands over the castle."

"The Armorum Custodes," Gallard said. "So, they are coming after all, as I had suspected they would." He turned to Brewster. "What does their force number?"

"Our best information indicates two thousand, five hundred, assuming they have recalled their reserves and are at full strength," Brewster replied.

"We have to presume that they have done just that and are here to keep us from getting the armor," Gallard replied. "This is confirmation that the DuFay Armor is indeed inside Dover Castle. Halt the siege and pull every man south to confront the Custodes and protect the breastplate. Our greater numbers should ensure us victory. Once we have obliterated them, we will make a final surge against the castle and claim the DuFay Armor, and the crown. See to it."

"Yes, my lord," Brewster said and rushed off to carry out the king's orders.

"Commander, you need to see this. The enemy's forces are withdrawing."

Commander Vicenza looked up at the report from Captain Bellows. Without a word, Vicenza followed his captain to the tower on the southeast corner of the building. Gallard's forces appeared to be retreating towards the king's tent. The northern sector of the battlefield was abandoned as the men rushed southward. The east and west sectors showed the same movement.

"What is happening?" Vicenza asked Bellows. "What are they doing?"

"It appears that they are preparing to defend against a southernly attack," Bellows responded, watching the movement of the troops. "See how they are forming lines?"

"It can only mean that our brothers have come to our rescue," Vicenza said. "I knew they would not abandon us. They must have learned that Gallard was heading to Dover Castle and knowing we were here, called together the reserves and are now launching an offensive."

"With their attention to the south, perhaps we could leave unnoticed through the gatehouse and work our way to the north, then circle back and join our brothers," Bellows suggested.

"The battering ram is blocking the exit, and the portcullis is still on fire," Vicenza said. "See if the portcullis can be raised and the fire extinguished. If so, we can push the battering ram out of the way and make our escape."

Captain Bellows was turning to instruct his men on what they were going to do when something to the north caught his eye.

"What is that?" he asked nobody in particular as he saw movement along the tree line.

"Where?" Vicenza asked, turning to see what had captured Bellows' attention.

"There, along the tree line," Bellows pointed. "It looks like... there are troops coming out of the forest."

"Custodes?" Vicenza asked.

"I cannot tell from this distance and the darkness, yet who else could it be?" Bellows replied. "They are moving south. It appears to be a large division of archers leading the way. And look! Horses pulling catapults! It must be the Custodes! They are moving-in to launch an attack! But I do not see any infantry. That is odd."

"Why would Gallard pull his men south if the attack was coming from the north?" Vicenza asked.

"Because an attack IS coming from the south, or so he believes," Bellows replied. "I would venture that the southern attack is a decoy, and the main attack is coming from the north.

With his attention diverted southernly, Gallard will not immediately notice the movement to the north."

As they were speaking, one of the Custodes ran along the rampart from the northeastern tower and stopped when he reached the two men.

"Sir, it appears that some of the troops moving in from the north are working to raise the ladder that the enemy has left at the base of the wall."

"Spread the word, get all of our men to the northern wall, now!" Vicenza said without pause. "Go!" The man turned and ran down the tower's steps. Vicenza could hear him yelling to his fellow Custodes.

"This should make our escape a bit easier to say the least," Bellows said as he and Vicenza headed along the rampart to the northern wall.

By the time the commander and captain had reached the northern wall, the ladder had been set and the Custodes were quickly taking advantage of their route of salvation. Within a few minutes, ninety-eight of the men were safely on the ground. Captain Bellows nodded to his commander and took his turn. Vicenza took a moment to gaze across the battlefield. He saw the advancing force stop one hundred and fifty yards from Gallard's army on both the east and west sides of the battlefield and commence its attack. The archers proceeded to launch volley after volley of arrows into the midst of the opposing forces. Within sixty seconds they had launched a dozen volleys. The bowmen stepped back, and the catapults began launching their deadly missiles, a mixture of incendiary bombs and caltrops, iron weapons made up of two or more sharp nails or spines arranged in such a manner that one of them always points upward from a stable base. The explosions by the incendiary bombs were not large, but they were effective in causing multiple injuries and throwing fear into their targets. Vicenza had seen enough. He quickly climbed down the ladder to join his men. As he reached the ground, the saving forces began to retreat to the north.

"Who is commanding the Custodes?" he asked the closest officer.

"Commander MacCallum," the officer answered as they rushed to the forest.

"Commander?" Vicenza asked, taken aback. "You mean captain."

"No, sir. He has been promoted to commander."

"We shall see about that," Vicenza said.

As they reached twenty yards into the tree line, the entire detachment came to a halt. The archers dropped their bows and picked up swords and spears that had been left in predetermined locations.

"What are you doing?" Vicenza asked the officer who remained close to him. "We must continue our retreat and get to Buckington as quickly as possible."

"That is not the plan, sir," the officer replied.

"I am Commander Sir Reynald Vicenza of the Armorum Custodes, and I am giving the order to return to Buckington!" he shouted.

"No, sir, you are not," the officer replied, "and we are staying here."

Vicenza could only stare at the man in disbelief.

"The attacking force is retreating," Walter Brewster informed King Gallard.

"Retreating? Why would they be retreating?" Gallard asked.

"My assumption is that their goal was to rescue the men who were trapped inside the castle," Brewster replied. "Along with the DuFay Armor."

"What about the army that was approaching from the south?" Gallard asked.

"There is no sign of them," Brewster replied. "They had to be a diversion, meant to pose as a threat to your majesty in order to draw our troops from the northern sector."

"We cannot allow them to get away," Gallard said. "We must pursue and destroy them."

"That may not be the wisest strategy, your majesty," Brewster replied. "We need to regroup and make a plan for attacking Buckington, for that is certainly where they are taking the armor."

"No, we end this tonight," Gallard said. "The armor cannot be allowed to disappear yet again."

"My lord, look at your army. We have suffered at least three hundred fatalities and twice that in casualties, if not more," Brewster replied.

"We know that the Armorum Custodes force is divided," Gallard replied. "Send at least one-half of the remaining men who can lift a sword after the retreating Custodes. Chase them down and destroy them. The remaining troops will stay here and protect the breastplate."

"I cannot strongly enough express my disapproval of this plan," Brewster said, inching as close to insubordination as he could without crossing the line. "We should not divide our army. We should stay together and protect the breastplate as we make plans for our next move."

"No!" Gallard shouted. "I have given the order. Now carry it out!"

Brewster knew that the king was acting on sheer emotion now, consumed by his desire to obtain the DuFay Armor, and was not giving full consideration to his strategy. They did not know how many men had been in the detachment that had attacked them, nor did they know how many men had been in the southern detachment that served as a diversion or where those men were at that very moment. There were too many unknowns to divide their army and lessen the protection surrounding the breastplate. If they lost the breastplate, their quest was over. It was a quest that Walter Brewster had grown extremely weary of and for the first time since Edwin Gallard had begun his scheme when they were but young men, Walter questioned his resolve to continue alongside Gallard in what was appearing to be madness. Edwin Gallard was not the same man he had grown up with.

"Captain Harper," Brewster called out to the officer standing just outside of Gallard's tent. "Take two divisions and pursue the retreating enemy. None are to be left alive. It is suspected they have taken items of terrific value from the castle, an incredibly special set of armor, which belongs to King Gallard. Find that armor. Now go!"

Without a word, Captain Harper nodded and carried out his orders.

Chapter 42

hat is the plan?" Vicenza asked the officer beside him, Captain Franklin Rowe. "Why did Gallard draw his men to the south?"

"We sent a division of infantry, comprised mostly of civilians from Stanwyck, to be seen approaching along the road from the south," Captain Rowe answered. "We knew Gallard would suspect that the Armorum Custodes were coming to protect the DuFay Armor, which he believed to be in Dover Castle, and then attack him and steal the DuFay Breastplate. Gallard would automatically rally his troops around himself and the breastplate to protect against the southern attack. With their attention to the south, we would be able to advance and launch an aerial attack before they could ready a defense. At the same time, we could rescue you and your men."

"And now?" Vicenza asked.

"Now, there will unfold one of two scenarios," Rowe replied. "The first scenario, the one our battle plan is contingent upon, is that Gallard send troops for a counterattack. The initial attack force we used numbered three hundred men. We have three times that number in the woods, armed with pikes, bows and swords. As soon as the enemy approaches the woods, our archers will release a volley of arrows, then we shall rush forward and dispatch of those still able to fight."

"Gallard would send that many, if not more," Vicenza noted. "If he believes that we have the DuFay Armor, he will stop at nothing to obtain it."

"To help improve the odds in our favor, we dropped hundreds of caltrops during our retreat," Rowe said. "They will be virtually invisible in the dark. Every advancing soldier that steps on one will end up with a hole in his foot and be rendered useless. We estimate half of them, at most, will make it across the battlefield. We will be able to take out the others quickly."

"And if Gallard does not mount a retaliation attack?" Vicenza asked.

"In that event we will make our way through the forest, around the battlefield, and join the southern detachment in their assault on Gallard," Rowe answered. "It is the same movement whether Gallard counterattacks us or not."

Cries of pain came from the battlefield as Gallard's men rushed across the land and impaled their feet on the caltrops. There was a stirring amongst the trees as the Custodes readied themselves for combat.

"It seems the question of retaliation has been answered," Rowe said. "Prepare yourself."

Within sixty seconds, Gallard's forces, significantly reduced in number as they crossed the battlefield, approached the tree line at a running pace. If there had been two thousand soldiers dispatched by Gallard originally, true to Rowe's estimate, only one-half had made it across the battlefield. They were merely twenty yards out when Rowe gave the command.

"Now!" Captain Rowe shouted, and the archers released their arrows. Several dozen of the enemy fell in their tracks, but the headrush continued. Immediately, the Armor Guardians rushed out of the woods and confronted the enemy.

The leading line of Gallard's men were still working around their fallen comrades and not prepared for the onslaught by the Custodes. More cries of pain echoed across the battlefield as men were impaled by pikes brandished by the Custodes. Dropping the pikes, the Custodes unsheathed their swords and continue the assault on Gallard's men. Vicenza quickly joined the melee, disposing of one, then a second, then a third assailant. He was knocked to the ground but quickly rebounded and countered an attack. The Armorum Custodes fought as their legendary brothers had, not giving ground, always pushing forward, always disciplined and purposeful in their methods. To his surprise, Vicenza heard multiple explosions and flashes of light from the middle of Gallard's men. The battle continued for an hour, but Gallard's men were no match for the highly trained, well-rested and well-fed Armorum Custodes. Gradually, the force that Gallard had sent north was whittled down from nearly two thousand to a few hundred, and then a few dozen. Finally, none were left. The battlefield fell silent. There were no celebrations. Such displays were not the way of the Custodes. Vicenza found Captain Rowe, bloodied and filthy, but alive and surveying the field.

"A decidedly overwhelming victory, one that the Armorum Custodes can be proud of," Vicenza said.

"The battle has been won, but the war continues," Captain Rowe replied. "We cannot rest. We must leave our dead and wounded as they lay and rendezvous with Commander MacCallum and MacLean. They will need our swords for the next phase of the plan."

"MacLean?" Vicenza repeated. "What does MacLean have to do with any of this?"

"Everything," Captain Rowe replied. "This entire battle plan was his idea."

"What do you see?" King Gallard asked his military advisor, who was standing on a makeshift platform, looking to the north, past Dover Castle. The last of the day's light was spent, and the distance was too far to make out any details. But by the glow left by the incendiary grenades the Custodes had used, the king's military advisor was able to see enough.

"A slaughter," Brewster replied. "An absolute slaughter. I would be surprised if a single one of our men has survived. The attack was reckless and rushed. Captain Harper did not have time to properly prepare."

"You should have led the attack yourself!" Gallard retorted. "At least there would have been a higher probability of victory."

"No, my lord, it was best that I stay here," Brewster replied. "You need me to find a way to get you out of this debacle."

"A debacle you created by insisting I divert my army," Gallard countered. "We have lost nearly half of our men with nothing to show for it. The armor, if it were ever here to begin with, is long gone."

"Then we will be fighting for our survival," Brewster said, and walked away.

Chapter 43

It was two hours after the battle had ended when Captain Rowe and Reynald Vicenza entered the tent where Andrew and Commander Alistair MacCallum were going over their battle plan and preparing for the next phase. Both looked up as the newcomers entered.

"Captain Rowe, I am very happy to see you survived the engagement," Commander MacCallum said. "Status report, please."

"The operation proceeded precisely as planned," Captain Rowe replied. "I estimate we eliminated nearly two thousand of their forces, either through injury or death, and we were successful in rescuing our fellow Custodes who were trapped in the castle."

"Our losses?" MacCallum asked.

"Seventy-five," Rowe reported solemnly.

"I regret every death suffered within the Armorum Custodes, but to have taken out so many of the enemy and suffered such a small rate of attrition, it was a great victory," MacCallum replied.

"We still have wounded men at the battle site," Rowe stated. "They will need medical attention as quickly as possible."

"I will see to it," MacCallum replied. "Go, see that you and your men get rest this evening. The next phase of our plan commences in the morning."

"I was under the impression that the assault was to continue this evening," Rowe said, a bit perplexed. "We could have stayed with our injured men and provided them with what comfort and attention they needed."

"The plan has changed," MacCallum said, glancing at Andrew.

"Very well," Captain Rowe said. "I shall see to the rest and comfort of my men." He gave a nod of respect and left the tent. No sooner had he departed than Vicenza spoke.

"The good captain informed me that you have been promoted to commander and have been directing the Armorum Custodes," Vicenza said to MacCallum. "It is truly an honor, and I offer my congratulations."

"Thank you," MacCallum returned.

"However, as I am Commander of the Armorum Custodes and have been for the past ten years, and as so its highest-ranking officer, I shall now relieve you of these responsibilities you have taken on in my absence and shall take command of the battle plan."

"With all due respect, Reynald, that is not going to happen," Commander MacCallum replied.

"I will have the respect that is due me," Vicenza growled. "You will address me as 'Commander' or 'Sir.'"

"With all due respect," MacCallum replied, "you no longer have claim to either. The Church has not only removed you from the position of Commander of the Armorum Custodes, but it has also excommunicated you from the Custodes and stripped you of your title."

"You are lying," Vicenza accused. "Long have you opposed me at every opportunity, disrespecting me and my position, desiring nothing more than our positions be reversed. Your jealousy and resentment of me are well known throughout the Custodes. Your personal ambitions and agendas shall not be a stain upon the reputation of the Armorum Custodes. I shall see to it that you suffer the consequences of your attempted usurpation."

"Ironically, that is exactly why these actions have been taken against you," Luther Muire said, stepping forward from where he had been seated in a front corner of the tent, unseen by Vicenza. "As a result of actions against the Church and its mission, including the false imprisonment of its Senior Pastor, the esteemed Reverend Antonio Vendici, in order to pursue a personal agenda of power and authority, in direct opposition to the teachings of Scripture and the Lord Jesus Christ himself, Head of the Church, to whom all glory be given, the Council of Covenantal Orthodox Church of Christ has voted unanimously to remove you from the position of Commander of the Armorum Custodes, strip you of your knighthood, and cause you to appear before the Council to answer for your actions and to suffer such punishment as the Council deems proper."

"This is outrageous," Vicenza said, the reality of the young pastor's words sinking in. "I have done nothing but seek the glory and empowerment of the Church for the good of all."

"And you shall have an opportunity to present a defense of the charges that have been leveled against you," Luther said, then added, "unlike your plan for Reverend Vendici." He then turned and pulled aside the tent flap and addressed two Custodes standing outside. "Gentlemen, per order of the Council of Covenantal Orthodox Church of Christ, Reynald Vicenza is to be taken into custody and returned to Buckington, where he shall stand trial for his actions." The two guards entered the tent and glared at Vicenza. With a final look around the tent, the disgraced man stepped forward and left with the guards.

"Now that we have addressed that unpleasantness," MacCallum said, turning to Andrew, "what is our next move? Why have you decided to postpone the attack until tomorrow?"

"Fighting in darkness is an unnecessary hazard for all," Andrew replied. "We have for all intents and purposes reduced the size of the battlefield in half which means all combatants would be fighting in much closer quarters than normal. In darkness, there is a greater opportunity for mistakes to be made and our men to accidentally kill each other. We have two small companies out this evening setting-up barricades along the eastern and western sections of the battlefield to ensure that Gallard's men have no means of escape to the north and continue to be hemmed-in. We also know that there are hazards on the battlefield that we put there ourselves, and we do not want our own men getting injured. We need to send a recovery party to the north where the injured Custodes are and bring them back to camp and see that their wounds are tended to properly. Some of them may still be able to fight, or at least sit on their horses and give the appearance of being battle-ready. If we must fight, it is vital that we have every sword that is available."

"What do you mean, 'If we must fight?'" MacCallum asked. "I thought the plan was to decimate Gallard's army and ensure that he never poses a threat to the DuFay Armor again."

"I would accomplish the latter without requiring the former, if I can," Andrew replied. "Gallard's men are exhausted, and they just suffered a tremendous loss. Their motivation has fallen with every one of their comrades that lies on the battlefield. They are hungry, and they have been away from home for what, three months now? They want nothing more than to return home to their families where they can return to their normal lives."

"That may be so," MacCallum said, "but do you believe they would disobey their king, revolt against their king, and potentially have their families and homes taken from them?"

"If we can present such a show of force that they are wholly demoralized and are convinced there is no road to victory, yes, I believe they would. What are they fighting for?" Andrew asked. "Are they fighting to defend their homes? No, that much is clear to every man in Gallard's army. You can rest assured they do not know the real reason Gallard has taken them so far from home for so long and what could be worth the deaths of two thousand of their brothers in arms. They have no motivation to continue fighting."

"But we do not have a force large enough to instill such fear," MacCallum argued.

"I believe we do," Andrew replied. "We line the battlefield with every Armorum Custodes who can sit on a horse, in full battle gear, brandishing their lances. We set among them our bowmen and infantry which will carry pikes. Behind our troops, we create massive bonfires which, though not having any effectiveness in actual battle, will present quite an intimidating vision. They will remember the carnage we wrecked upon them this evening and they will be shaking in their boots."

"Do you believe Gallard to be one to stand down?" MacCallum asked. "From how you have described him, he does not sound as though he is the type of man who will simply give-up on this legend, on obtaining the DuFay Armor."

"When he realizes that the DuFay Armor is forever out of his reach and that the true heir of Robert DuFay has been identified and will be crowned king with or without the breastplate, it is my hope that he abandons his quest and retreat home."

"I do not know the man, yet my instincts tell me he has invested too many years and too many lives in this quest," MacCallum replied. "He will not relent. However, the decision is yours. Tell me what you plan to do."

With a smile, Andrew once again explained his plan for stopping Gallard and putting an end to the life of chaos created by the DuFay Armor.

Chapter 44

W alter Brewster stood in silence, gazing at the imposing horde that lined the battlefield less than two hundred yards from his troops. The enemy had lined-up in the early hours of the morning as dawn broke but had not moved over the next fifteen as Brewster called his men to arms. Smoke from what had to be massive bonfires filled the air behind the enemy line and flames could be seen reaching into the sky. He could see the condensation coming from the mouths of the men and horses that faced his army due to the chilly morning air. An occasional snowflake fluttered through his line of vision, but the temperature was the least of his concerns. His men were nervous and continually looked to each other for reassurance but found none. They were still feeling the impact of the prior night's defeat and the vision before them was ominous. Had he not been a veteran of multiple battles and the military advisor to his king, Brewster conceded that he might have been intimidated as well. But he was not. His mind was fully in war-mode, trying to determine the best way to attack the opposition and defend his king. He knew his options were limited and he could not depend on his exhausted and demoralized troops to be one-hundred percent effective.

King Gallard exited his tent in full battle gear. Brewster did not know whether the king dressed that way based on intention or show. It did not matter. The king walked over to his military advisor.

"Report," he commanded.

"The enemy began forming nearly twenty minutes ago," Brewster replied. "They have not moved since first appearing. There have been no attempts at communication. I immediately called our troops to arms. I estimate their force to number over two thousand. After last evening's losses, we are down to the same number if not fewer. The majority of their force is heavy cavalry, intermixed with bowmen and infantry. As we experienced last evening, they have multiple catapults which I am certain sit behind their troops, out of sight. For now."

"We have infantry, bowmen and cavalry as well," Gallard said with a haughty tone.

"Our cavalry is inferior to theirs in number and armor," Brewster countered. "I estimate we have the same numbers in bowmen. Regarding the infantry, again, the numbers are close to identical, however, our men are exhausted and weak."

"You sound like a man who has lost his confidence," Gallard said.

"I am a man who sees beyond numbers," Brewster replied. "Whether we like it or not, those men on the other side of the battlefield are, for the most part, trained and conditioned well above and beyond our men. They have not been on the road for three months and they have not had their food rationed every day. If we do engage in battle, I am not optimistic as to how long our men could fight effectively."

"Would you rather retreat, in shame?" the king asked.

"My lord, retreat is not an option," Brewster replied. "We have a report that the road has been blocked by more than a dozen large trees. If the enemy pursued us, our situation would be more dire than it is here."

"What, pray tell, is your recommendation, Military Advisor?"

"My recommendation, your majesty, is that we entertain what appears to be an offer of negotiations," Brewster said, seeing three men on horseback displaying a flag of truce about one hundred yards from the front of Dover Castle.

"My horse," Gallard simply said, and one of his aides rushed to bring the stallion forward.

Within ten minutes, Gallard and Brewster had covered the three hundred yards between the king's tent and the three men, who had not moved since taking position. Stopping about ten yards from the opposing men, Gallard recognized one of the men and spat his name with the utmost animosity.

"MacLean!" the king said, his disdain for Andrew on full exhibit.

"Your Majesty," Andrew politely returned. "It has been some time since our last encounter. You look well. Stressed, but otherwise, well."

"In truth I had hoped to see you again someday, though under much different circumstances," the king replied. "Instead of you being on a horse, I had envisioned your head in a basket."

"I have to say, I am, once again, happy to have disappointed you," Andrew replied.

"Perhaps if my military advisor had been a bit more competent, I would have gotten my wish and not be standing in front of you at this moment."

"If your military advisor had been more competent, or less gullible, you most certainly would not be standing here," Andrew replied. "I do not believe you are familiar with my friends," he said. "This is Commander Alistair MacCallum of the Armorum Custodes, and this is my friend, Lawrence Morecraft. Unfortunately, he does not have an official title or position."

"How about 'Captain of Getting Your Bum Out of Trouble?'" Lawrence offered.

"The Dufay Armor," Brewster stated, ignoring Lawrence. "It was never here."

"I would not say never," Andrew replied, "but it has been quite a long time. I believe nearly one hundred years."

"Where is it?" Gallard asked. "Buckington, I would presume."

"In quite the safe place, which shall remain unknown to you for now," Andrew answered. "I am certain you can understand our disinclination to reveal its location."

"You have presented a flag of truce," Gallard stated, knowing it would be useless to press Andrew on the location of the DuFay Armor. "I presume you wish to discuss terms."

"As you can see, the Armorum Custodes, along with several hundred men from Stanwyck whose crops and livestock you pillaged, twice, present quite an opposing force," Andrew started.

"As you well know, Gallard's army is a well-trained military force in its own regard," Brewster countered.

"I also know that your army is exhausted and afraid," Andrew replied. "Three months on the trail have stolen their energy and I would venture their resolve as well. Being this close to home, I am certain many would rather lay down their arms and return to their families than risk death for whatever excuse you have given them for such a long campaign."

"Their resolve has not waivered," Gallard replied, "nor has mine."

"Your self-serving quest is over," Andrew stated plainly. "The DuFay Armor, for what it is worth, is far from you and you will never possess it. The Heir of DuFay has been identified by the custodians of the DuFay Armor, the Covenantal Orthodox Church of Christ, with whom I believe you are quite familiar. You have lost over half of your army since you departed for Durinburg three months ago and the men that remain are spent. I propose that you lay down your arms, you relinquish the DuFay Breastplate, and you relinquish the crown that you do not deserve. Those of your men who need medical attention will receive it, and all your men will all be provided with enough supplies to see them home. Do this, and we all walk away from this battlefield with our lives."

"You lie," Gallard said. "The line of DuFay died out long ago. There is no heir. I am as much the Heir of DuFay as you are."

"It is rather ironic that you put it that way," Lawrence said.

"How so?" Gallard asked, confused.

"Because the Heir of DuFay is sitting on his horse, directly in front of you," Lawrence replied with a smug smile.

"Rubbish!" the king cried. "MacLean is nothing more than an orphan from a poor family from some distant land. There is no royal blood coursing through his veins."

"It is true," Commander MacCallum confirmed. "The Covenantal Orthodox Church of Christ has traced the lineage of Robert DuFay since the day he lost his kingdom and the armor. There is no ambiguity, no uncertainty. I presume that is not something you discovered during your studies at the church, or during your subsequent raid of the church."

King Edwin Gallard considered his circumstances. He knew that he was defeated, of that there was no doubt. His men, in their condition, could not present a significant challenge to the Armorum Custodes. If he continued to fight it would be out of pure ego and pride, and only result in the slaughter of his men. His quest was over. His hatred for Andrew only intensified.

"I will not give up my crown," he finally said through gritted teeth.

"That is non-negotiable," Andrew replied. "Nordham was my home for more than half of my life. The people deserve leadership that is honorable and trustworthy, leadership that can bring greater prosperity to the land. You are none of that. You do not deserve to wear that crown."

"Who do you believe you are to make such a demand?" Gallard growled. "Heir or no heir, you have no authority to demand that I abdicate my crown. I am king of Nordham by blood and hereditary right and shall remain so until the day I die."

"A man being handed a crown simply due to his family name does not make that man worthy to wear the crown," Andrew countered.

"You have no idea what I had to do to get this crown!" Gallard retorted defensively. "I was the runt of the litter, third in line to the crown, having virtually no chance of ever becoming king. I was relentlessly teased by my older brothers and routinely omitted from official functions and conversations. To them, I was nothing more than a little boy who existed solely for their ridicule and amusement. I studied and I learned, becoming more suitable to wear a crown than any of them. Yet I was still held in low esteem. So, I waited. My father died and the crown passed to my older brother. Both of my brothers were arrogant and obnoxious, having only pleasure and entertainment on their minds, neither fit nor worthy to sit on the throne. The people suffered. Something had to be done to protect the people and the kingdom. I did what nobody else would do, such was my love for my people, and the crown passed to me. Do not tell me I am not worthy of this crown. I earned it, and I shall not relinquish it!"

"I told you," Commander MacCallum said to Andrew. Andrew looked at the commander and took his eyes off the two men in front of him. It nearly cost him his life. Gallard looked at Brewster and gave him an almost imperceptible nod. In the blink of an eye, Brewster threw aside the heavy outer garment he had been wearing and hoisted a miniature crossbow. Just as he was ready to pull its trigger and launch a very lethal looking arrow at Andrew, Lawrence pulled the reins on his horse and jumped in front of Andrew. The arrow struck Lawrence in his torso, knocking him off his horse. Both Andrew and MacCallum's horses were startled by the sudden movement, which likely saved Andrew's life as Gallard, like Brewster, retrieved a hidden miniature crossbow and pulled the trigger. The arrow narrowly missed Andrew and struck Commander MacCallum in the upper right chest, knocking him off his horse. Both he and Lawrence lay on the ground, unmoving. Andrew had no way of knowing the severity of their injuries but assumed the worst.

"Coward!" Andrew shouted, drawing his sword. "How dare you disrespect a flag of truce! Your lack of honor only proves that you do not deserve that crown!"

Before Andrew had finished admonishing Gallard, a shout went up from the Armorum Custodes. The archers let loose a barrage of arrows and before they had found their targets, the heavy cavalry charged, followed by the infantry.

"I shall defend my crown to the death!" Gallard shouted in reply. "And today, the line of Reginald DuFay ends!"

Sword drawn, Walter Brewster kicked his horse in its ribs and the beast lunged forward. Andrew did the same. Both men took massive swipes at the other but neither blow caught flesh, only the opponent's metal. They turned to make another pass. Before he could charge, Andrew's horse let out a tremendous cry of pain and reared backwards. Unprepared, Andrew was thrown to the crown. Annon limped away several steps and as he did so, Andrew could see the arrow protruding from the horse's chest. He looked at Gallard, who still brandished the crossbow he had just fired at the stallion. A fury arose in Andrew, a fury that he had felt only once before, when his brother Donald was struck down in what now seemed an eternity ago. He started to charge the king, every muscle in his body prepared to cut Gallard down, but Brewster was already on a full gallop towards Andrew, and he was forced to go on the defensive. In the last split-second, just as Brewster was pulling his sword back for a life-ending strike, Andrew dropped to the ground and swept his sword at the legs of the running beast. With a scream of pain, the horse's left front leg buckled, and it tumbled to the ground, throwing Brewster ten feet through the air. Seeing the king's military advisor lying on the ground, stunned, Andrew turned his attention back to Gallard. The king had just finished loading another arrow into his crossbow and aimed it at Andrew. Out of pure reflex, not even planning the movement, Andrew dove to his right and rolled several feet. The arrow narrowly missed him, imbedding itself in the ground a foot from Andrew's head. A quick look at Brewster told Andrew that the man was still trying to clear his head from the violent fall and was not an immediate threat. Andrew turned back to Gallard.

"Dismount!" Andrew commanded, pointing his sword at the disgraced king. "Look at your men! Even now they are being destroyed because of your ego. Dismount and surrender, the Armorum Custodes will withdraw, and I will not cut you down for such a cowardly attack on my horse."

"I will not," Gallard replied defiantly. "I will have your head this day, if not by military commander's sword, then by my own."

"So be it," Andrew replied. As he rushed the king, out of the very corner of his eye, he saw Brewster leap forward. Years of training and experience moved his body without him thinking and he was able to parry the deadly sword strike. Pivoting, Andrew slashed at Brewster who successfully defended against the blow. Brewster lunged at Andrew, who took a step back and parried the strike, then riposted with his own strike. Brewster successfully parried Andrew's attack. The two men continued to exchange blows, none of which struck flesh. Andrew could tell that Brewster was favoring his right arm and attacking primarily from his left side, undoubtedly due to his hand not having healed enough to hold the sword. Andrew feinted to his right, causing Brewster to pull his sword back to try and parry the incoming strike. Instead of thrusting, Andrew disengaged and pivoted, sending a wide-arcing slash at Brewster's right side. Brewster tried to dodge the strike, but his balance was slightly off, and he was not able to move as quickly as he needed to. Andrew's sword sliced across Brewster's hip. To his credit, Brewster did not cry out in pain, but he did take several steps back. Blood ran down his leg from the inch-deep gash, but the injured man ignored it and tightened his grip on his sword. Andrew circled Brewster and moved to where his opponent was between him and Gallard.

"Your life does not have to end here," Andrew called to Walter. "The last time we fought, I offered you mercy, but I also offered you a warning. I am willing to offer mercy again if you lay down your arms."

"And suffer the humiliation of defeat?" Brewster retorted. "I think not."

"There is no humiliation to be suffered," Andrew responded. "For how many years have you sought and fought for the DuFay Armor, all the while not understanding its true meaning? As Scripture says, 'Finally, be strong in the Lord and in His mighty power. Put on the full armor of God, so that you can take your stand against the devil's schemes. For our struggle is not against flesh and blood, but against the rulers, against the authorities, against the powers of this dark world and against the spiritual forces of evil in the heavenly realms. Therefore, put on the full armor of God, so that when the day of evil comes, you may be able to stand your ground, and after you have done everything, to stand. Stand firm then, with the belt of truth buckled around your waist, with the breastplate of righteousness in place, and with your feet fitted with the readiness that comes from the gospel of peace. In addition to all this, take up the shield of faith, with which you can extinguish all the flaming arrows of the evil one. Take the helmet of salvation and the sword of the Spirit, which is the word of God.' The quest for the DuFay Armor has been grounded in lies, not truth. There has been nothing righteous about it, nothing peaceful about it, nothing that is of true faith. It does not lead to salvation and has been in complete contradiction to the Word of God. Edwin Gallard was your friend at one time, your best friend, but look where his lies have led you. Laying down your sword is not defeat, it is victory: Victory over hatred; victory over jealously; victory over greed; victory over slavery. Lay down your earthly armor and put on the full armor of God. Look around you. Gallard offers you death. The Lord offers you life and friendship."

Walter Brewster, trusted and loyal friend and advisor to King Edwin Gallard, paused in his attack. For the first time since joining Gallard on the quest for the DuFay Armor, there arose within him a great conflict. He looked around the battlefield and back to his own men who were slowly being destroyed by the Custodes. Andrew was right. All that Edwin Gallard had ever truly offered him was death. While it was true that Gallard had

Jeff Boles

offered him a land of his own to rule, albeit under Gallard's authority, the path had been full of death. Walter recalled every one of the battles he had fought with Gallard and the countless lives he had ended with his own sword, all for the allurement of power. Gallard had long ago become consumed by his lust for power which had transformed into a man without mercy, without compassion. Walter knew that the same had happened to him, and he suddenly loathed himself. He saw the wickedness in his heart and his deeds. It was as if he had been blinded in his youth and his sight was mercifully restored. He looked at Andrew and dropped his sword.

"I choose life," Walter said and while it was not a smile that crossed his face, it was a look of a peace which he had never known.

"And you shall receive the death due a traitor," King Gallard said as he aimed his crossbow at Walter and shot him in the back. The arrow penetrated deeply and pierced Walter's heart. A look of surprise swept across Walter's face. He took a few unsteady steps towards Andrew, then collapsed to his knees.

"Forgive me," Walter said with his last breath as he crumpled to the ground.

"Murderer!" Andrew cried out, glaring at Gallard. "You monster!"

"And now, so ends the lineage of Reginald DuFay." Gallard said contemptuously as he aimed the re-loaded crossbow at Andrew. Before Andrew could move, an arrow whistled through the air and embedded itself in the middle of Gallard's chest. The king looked down at the arrow in disbelief. He turned his eyes to Andrew and tried to say something, but his voice failed him. His strength leaving him, the king struggled to remain upright in his saddle, but it was a losing fight. As he began to lose his grip, Andrew rushed over and caught Gallard and eased him to the ground. In less than fifteen seconds his last breath left his body, and just as the man fell into Andrew's arms, so fell the reign of King Edwin Gallard.

Andrew turned to see where the arrow had come from.

"I believe my title is well-earned," Lawrence said as he lowered the crossbow that Walter had used but lost when he was thrown from his horse.

"It took you long enough," Andrew replied, trying to hide the elation that his best friend was alive. "It would appear you need more training."

"Apparently so," Lawrence replied with a smile.

"MacCallum?" Andrew asked.

"Unconscious, but breathing," Lawrence answered.

Andrew looked around for Annon and spotted his long-time friend and companion lying on the ground, thirty feet away.

"Signal the Custodes to cease the attack," Andrew instructed Lawrence, almost absent-mindedly. "Gallard's men are free to return home. See that the wounded receive medical attention. I will be along shortly."

"Understood," Lawrence said solemnly and, after retrieving his own horse, headed for the battling armies.

Andrew slowly walked over to Annon, a fog of disbelief shrouding the reality of the scene. His stallion was still breathing, but each breath gave testimony to a great struggle for life, a struggle that was in vain. The volume of blood that had poured from his wound spoke to the fatal nature of the injury. Andrew sank to his knees where Annon could see him. The horse lifted his head slightly, but the loss of blood had greatly weakened him and despite how hard he struggled, he could not hold his head up. Andrew stroked Annon's forehead gently.

"You have fought valiantly, my friend," Andrew said, tears streaming down his cheeks. "You have been a great warrior, far beyond comparison, never failing a task set before you. When I had nobody else, when my own country turned against me, your companionship kept me alive, always moving me forward. You have been as good a friend as any man could ask for. A death in battle is an honorable death, even for a horse. I shall miss you terribly. Sleep, my friend, sleep."

With a final snort, the mighty stallion breathed his last.

Chapter 45

T hroughout its two-hundred-year existence, the Covenantal
Orthodox Church of Christ had never seen a crowd as large
as the one that filled it on this historical day. Every pew was
packed, and the walls of the sanctuary were lined with people
standing for this momentous occasion. The steps leading up to the
church's doors were spilling over and a tremendous multitude of
people filled the streets around the holy building. There was a
powerful air of reverence that consumed the entire city of
Buckington, and all daily routines had ceased. The population of
the city had doubled, as people from surrounding lands came to
celebrate this legendary moment, a moment many had thought to
have faded with time but was now being fulfilled. The sun
gleamed brilliantly in the cloudless, deep azure sky as if it knew
the auspicious nature of what was about to happen.

Reverend Antonio Vendici stood at the podium in front of the
great mass before him. He was clothed in a magnificent cassock
made of deep burgundy jacquard with two black velvet front
panels and a gold embroidered cross on both sides of the chest.
The wrist-length cuffs were embroidered with gold thread as
were the buttonholes running the front length of the robe and
the hem of the garment. Eight clergymen were seated fifteen feet
behind him, four to his left and four to his right, representing the
full session of the church. They wore robes of similar design to
Reverend Vendici's, although instead of burgundy with black
velvet panels, they were off-white with pure-white panels. On a
table in front of the podium were displayed the six pieces of the

DuFay Armor, each laid on a plush pillow of purple velvet with gold-thread trim. The rays of light shining through the multitude of stained-glass windows, along with the glow from hundreds of candles in the chandeliers and sconces around the sanctuary, gave the armor a radiant splendor. Ten feet to the right of the armor sat Andrew MacLean in a chair fit for a king. The oak chair was six feet, six inches tall. The seat and back were covered with a deep blue jacquard fabric and the intricately carved wooden frame was decorated with patterns of birds, foliage, and animals on a gilded background. Four gilt lions served as the feet of the chair. Andrew was adorned in a deep, ruby red coronation mantle, highlighted by gold trim, which extended to just a few inches above his ankles. He nervously surveyed the grand room in front of him, all his life wanting nothing but to avoid being the focal point of attention. In a few minutes, thousands of eyes would be focused upon him. Reverend Vendici gazed around the buzzing room and within moments, the church was entombed in silence. He gave one last look down at the podium, as if checking his notes, but he needed no notes. He had prepared for this day throughout his forty-year tenure as the senior pastor of the Covenantal Orthodox Church of Christ. Notes were not needed.

"Three hundred and fifty years ago, a righteous and wise king ruled. He loved the Almighty, and he loved his people. He ruled with compassion and generosity, he ruled with mercy and love. He knew that his position was given to him as a gift from God, and he earnestly sought to fulfill his responsibilities for the glory of God. He knew that it was not the armor of man that stood as a barrier to wickedness, but the armor of God and he never let his people forgot this. The Lord blessed him, and his kingdom, tremendously. There was peace as had never been known and has not been known since. The land produced in abundance and was truly a land flowing with milk and honey. The people rejoiced in the blessings given to them by God, and they loved their king. To show their love, the people of the kingdom gave of their wealth and commissioned their most skilled craftsmen to create for their king gifts in the form of the armor of God: The belt of truth; the breastplate of righteousness; the shoes of the gospel; the shield of faith; the helmet of salvation; the sword of the Spirit. This armor was kept in the church, where all could see it every worship service and be reminded that every day, they needed to put on the full armor of God. As the apostle Paul wrote, in Ephesians: "Finally, be strong in the Lord and in the strength of His might. Put on the full armor of God, so that you will be able to stand firm against the schemes of the devil. For our struggle is not against flesh and blood, but against the rulers, against the powers, against the world forces of this darkness, against the spiritual forces of wickedness in the heavenly places. Therefore, take-up the full armor of God, so that you will be able to resist in the evil day, and having done everything, to stand firm. Stand firm therefore, having girded your loins with truth, and having put on the breastplate of righteousness, and having shod your feet with the preparation of the gospel of peace; in addition to all, taking up the shield of faith with which you will be able to extinguish all the flaming arrows of the evil one. And take the helmet of salvation, and the sword of the Spirit, which is the word of God.

"'Gird your loins with the truth.' The truths of Scripture, which set us free from the lies of Satan. 'Put on the breastplate of righteousness.' The breastplate protects the heart from the arrows of Satan. As Scripture says, 'Keep your heart with all diligence, for from it spring the issues of life.' It is not our righteousness that protects us, for we have none in and of ourselves. It is the righteousness of Christ. 'Shod your feet with the preparation of the gospel of peace.' The path to heaven is narrow, and Satan works to place obstacles on the path and lead us off the path. We must be able to march wherever God leads us in this spiritual war and walk over the obstacles Satan places in front of us, so we can spread the Gospel to the world. 'Take the shield of faith with which you will be able to quench all the fiery darts of the wicked one.' Satan throws at us darts of temptation, darts of doubt. Faith is not our ourselves but is a gift from God, which shields us against Satan's fiery darts. 'Take the helmet of salvation.' The helmet protects our head, where our thoughts and knowledge lie. A strong helmet is a strong knowledge of our salvation that protects us from doubts and deceptions. 'The sword of the Spirit, which is the Word of God.' The Word of God is sharper than any two-edged sword. It is a weapon that is used in defense against the lies of Satan, and it is a weapon that is used to attack Satan and destroy his lies, thereby furthering the kingdom of God.

"The man who puts on the full armor of God is a strong man. The man who takes off the full armor of God is a weak man. King Reginald DuFay was a strong man who encased himself in the armor of God every day of his reign. However, his sons and his son's sons did not. Piece by piece they took off the armor of God and became vulnerable to Satan's attacks. In the days of Robert DuFay, great-great grandson of Reginald DuFay, the armor of God had been forgotten, and the people lived for their own pleasure. God brought judgment upon them and took the throne from Robert of DuFay and the line of DuFay. But where there is judgment, there is also mercy. On the last day of his reign, and the last day of his life, Robert DuFay repented of his sins and apostasy. In secret, he sent his sons and the armor far away, with encouragement to be faithful to God and someday return and retake the throne. The legend of the DuFay Armor was born, testifying that when the armor was reunited with the heir of Robert DuFay, the spirit of Reginald DuFay would be resurrected and fill the heir, who would again put on the full armor of God and reign in righteousness. Yet God's judgment was not complete. The armor was lost, and the DuFay throne has remained vacant for two hundred years. The Covenantal Orthodox Church of Christ was founded by Matthew Knox, Robert DuFay's priest, who led his sons through their escape. For two hundred years, the Covenantal Orthodox Church of

Christ has chronicled the descendants of Robert DuFay and searched for the armor, longing for the day on which the two would be reunited and the crown, and throne, returned to the line of DuFay. Today is that day.

"Andrew MacLean, son of Robert DuFay, son of Reginald DuFay, arise and step forward," Reverend Vendici directed Andrew. With but a moment of hesitation, Andrew stood and walked over to the table on which the DuFay Armor was displayed. Reverend Vendici, carrying a small book, stepped around the podium and down three steps to Andrew's level.

"Andrew, what to you is a journey that commenced six years ago is a journey that our Heavenly Father foreordained before the beginning of time," the reverend said. "Every hardship you endured, every stumbling block, was put in place to lead you to where you stand now. When you first learned of your identity and your heritage, you wanted nothing to do with it. You were adamant that you did not want this honor, this responsibility, and that I did not know what kind of man you really were. Over the past few weeks, I have seen the kind of man that you are, and there is no doubt in my mind that you are a man after Reginald DuFay's heart. More importantly, though, is that God knows your heart, and he has given you a heart for him." Reverend Vendici reached over to the table and picked-up the crown.

"Kneel, Andrew MacLean," he instructed. Andrew complied.

"Two hundred years ago, Robert DuFay, King of Durinburg, charged his priest, Matthew Knox, with the task of placing this crown on the head of his heir and re-establishing the reign of the DuFays when the proper time had come. That task has fallen to the highest-ranking clergyman of the Covenantal Orthodox Church of Christ throughout the years. As the senior pastor of this assembly, that task has fallen upon my shoulders, and I am honored that this day I am able to fulfill this task.

"Hewlitt Knox, older brother of your deceased father, heir to Reginald DuFay's kingdom, has relinquished all rights and responsibilities as the descendent of Reginald DuFay. Those rights and responsibilities now fall upon you, the last in the DuFay lineage. I charge you, Robert Knox, now known as Andrew MacLean, to take upon you this crown and wear it to the glory of God, putting on the full armor of God, so you may stand firm against the schemes of the devil. Be strong in the Lord and in the strength of his might. Rule with wisdom, justice, and righteousness. Maintain the laws of God and the true profession of the Gospel. Serve the Lord your God only. Do you accept these responsibilities and swear before the Lord to carry them out faithfully and to the best of your ability?"

"I do," Andrew replied.

With the utmost reverence, Reverend Vendici placed the magnificent crown on Andrew. He then took a small bottle of aromatic oil and sprinkled several drops onto Andrew's head.

"I therefore anoint you, Andrew MacLean, as King of Durinburg, heir to the throne once sat upon by Reginald DuFay. May the Lord bless you and keep you, may the Lord make his face shine upon you. May He use you mightily in the building of His kingdom on earth and cause many nations to turn to him and be blessed. Stand, King Andrew MacLean."

As Andrew stood, a deafening shout erupted in the immense sanctuary as every seated person stood.

"Long live the king! Long live the king! Long live the king!"

Andrew gazed around the room, the surreal nature of the atmosphere making him wonder if what was happening was real or a dream. His eyes fell on the first pew, twenty feet from him. Marie, Lawrence, Angus, Victoria, and Gregory looked back at him with such respect and admiration that he had never known. Tears of joy ran down Marie's cheeks and Andrew could have sworn that Lawrence's eyes were moist as well. Six years ago, when he had started on his quest to find the Heir of DuFay, Andrew could never have envisioned that his journey would lead him to this place and time. He knew that had he suspected such a destination lay ahead of him, he would have chosen another path. Yet he also knew that the will of God could not be thwarted, and whatever path he may have chosen would have led to the same destination.

"Your majesty," Reverend Vendici said as the noise from the crowd abated. "When Robert DuFay sent his sons away, moments before his sacrificial death, he gave his eldest, Thomas, a book. He charged his son to read the book every day and to take to heart its instructions and exhortations. That book was the Book of Psalms and Proverbs. I give to you the Book of Psalms and Proverbs and as King DuFay did with his son, I charge you to read this book every day, to learn from it, and to use the wisdom and discernment contained in these pages to live your life and rule your kingdom." Andrew reached out and took the offering.

"I give my word that I shall do so," Andrew replied. "For God's glory."

Chapter 46

T he city-wide celebration that followed the coronation ceremony was unlike anything Buckington had ever seen. The streets were filled with jesters, minstrels, acrobats, jugglers, and dancing. Stages had been set up for plays and performances. In front of the church, there was a stage on which replicas of the armor of God were set and pastors from the church preached messages on the meaning and importance of the armor of God. There were archery contests and sword-fighting exhibitions as well as hand-to-hand combat demonstrations. Food stalls were set up on every street corner offering the best of local delicacies as well as exotic foods that many people had never tasted. It was an endless buffet of meats, cheeses, stews, breads, and pastries. When the daylight faded, torches on high poles lining the streets were ignited and the festivities lasted well into the night. It was truly a celebration fit for a king.

The newly crowned monarch sat at the head of a grand banquet table as the remnants of a great feast were removed by young boys and girls who were either students attending the church's school or volunteers from the community. Lawrence, Marie and Angus sat to his right. Reverend Vendici, Hewlitt, Victoria, and Gregory sat to his left.

"Now THAT was a meal worthy of lore," Lawrence said, leaning back in his chair. "I do not believe I will need to eat again for a week."

"As soon as the sun rises you will be searching for breakfast," Marie taunted him, "although it may do you good to miss a meal or two."

"I cannot argue either point," Lawrence said, grinning and patting his stomach.

"Was the food to your liking, Your Majesty?" Marie asked Andrew, giving him a teasing smile.

"Please, you do not need to call me that," Andrew replied, waving his hand. "I am not that pretentious. You may address me as 'Your Highness,' or 'Your Lordship,' or 'Your Excellency.'"

"After all of your professions of not wanting power or a position of prestige, and how much you despised kings and rulers, look where you ended up," Marie said, shaking her head. "It always struck me that you protested just a bit too much whenever it was suggested that you take a position of leadership."

"I assure you, it still does not sit well with me," Andrew replied. "I feel anything but regal. Those who sit on thrones have been groomed to do so from childhood. They have been trained and instructed in the ways of royalty and governing. I have been trained in the ways of combat and weaponry. While those skills have their uses, even for a king, there is much that I lack."

"You have proven that you are a man who can inspire and lead," Reverend Vendici responded. "You have also shown in words and deeds that you are a man who humbles himself before the Almighty. Humility is one of the most significant attributes of a successful leader. You must recognize your limitations and surround yourself with advisors, people who offer credible professions of faith, who have strengths where you have weaknesses, and who can offer wise and wholesome counsel."

"And I thought finding the Heir of DuFay was difficult," Andrew replied, clearly in jest.

"He was under your nose the entire time," Marie countered. "If you keep your nose out of the air, you just might be able to see better."

"Now that the pomp and circumstance are over, what are your plans?" Angus asked.

"We will see to the return of Edwin Gallard's body to his home, where he shall receive a king's burial alongside his father and brothers," Andrew answered.

"He is not worthy of being buried with his father and brothers," Lawrence said bitterly. "It would be an insult to those who sat on the throne before him."

"That is not for us to decide," Andrew replied. "He was a king, he was my king, for over half of my life. If it were not for him and his generosity towards my family, I cannot imagine what would have happened to me. Though I am convinced that his soul shall endure everlasting torment in the abyss, his body shall receive a proper burial."

"After that?" Angus asked.

"Durinburg," Andrew answered.

"Durinburg," Lawrence repeated. "You do recall that little invasion and the people being scattered to the four winds, including four of us who are sitting at this table."

"I have been proclaimed King of Durinburg," Andrew replied. "Not King of Buckington or King of Nordham or of any other country or city. If I do not return, what has this been all about? So many lives have been lost on account of this crown. Shall those deaths be in vain?"

"They have not been in vain," Marie replied. "Those deaths have ensured that a wicked man did not seize power he had no right to. We cannot begin to estimate the lives that would have been lost as Gallard ravaged city after city, country after country, seeking to enhance his domain. I loved my father, but he became corrupt and sought the same thing Gallard did. Now that the armor has come together and the Heir of DuFay has been crowned, the world does not have to worry about another Edwin Gallard or Richard Talbot."

"The world will always have to worry about such men," Reverend Vendici countered. "Satan will always have his servants seeking to devour those they can, which is why it is vital that righteous men stand firm for the Lord and seek opportunities to be in positions of power and influence. Word is spreading that the Heir of DuFay has been crowned and Durinburg once again has a king. Those who fled during Gallard's invasion will return home. Many others will migrate there if for no other reason than the promises of a legend. It is vital that the king be there to rebuild the country and re-establish the influence Reginald DuFay once had."

Lawrence sighed. "And I was so looking forward to establishing a reputation in all of Buckington's pubs." He looked at Reverend Vendici. "I mean, a good reputation, that of a man of self-control and moderation," he added.

"None of you are under any obligation to return to Durinburg with me," Andrew stated, looking around the table. "Marie, I realize that the circumstances under which you were forced to leave your home may have created memories you care not to revisit by returning. Gregory, with Gallard gone, there would be no danger in you returning to your home and no reason for you to embark on such a long journey to a foreign land. You proved yourself to be an invaluable part of our team, and for that we will be eternally thankful. Victoria, you also have no reason to leave your home. I do not know if we would be here, now, under these circumstances if you had not joined us. Angus, you were one of Talbot's most trusted advisors if not his most trusted advisor. Like Marie, you may have unfavorable memories of Durinburg and desire to leave those memories in the past and start a new life here or in Stanwyck, or perhaps even in Nordham. And Lawrence, well, Durinburg has only one tavern. You may get bored."

"As has been firmly established in recent days, you need someone close-by to get you out of the difficult situations you tend to get yourself into," Lawrence replied. "I could not in good conscience allow you to venture off on your own. You will need a dependable chief advisor."

"You will need to rebuild an army," Angus said. "Having come to know you as I have, if it would be pleasing to you, I would be honored to assist you in that undertaking. I know of no other way of life for me, and I have much to atone for."

Victoria looked at Andrew. "I have to confess, life in Porthmaddon had become exceptionally stale until you showed up again. Being that I have never had the desire to follow my father's path to the sea, there are no shackles to restrain me from pursuing a different path." She cast a sideways look at Lawrence with a hint of a flirtatious smile. "Life in Durinburg could be decidedly interesting." Lawrence smiled back at her.

"While it is true that Gallard and Brewster are gone, there may remain those who are knowledgeable of my defection and my return to Nordham may not be welcome," Gregory said. "I believe Buckington to be a city in which there is great opportunity."

"Do you have any carpentry skills?" Hewlitt asked. "My days are few, and I have no sons to inherit my shop. Once I become incapable of working, I will be forced to close the shop and sell it. Furniture building is a solid trade and there is much demand for it. I could provide you with instruction. You would have good and profitable work for the remainder of your life."

"I appreciate the offer," Gregory answered. "We can discuss your proposal later."

Everybody at the table looked at Marie who had yet to provide Andrew with an answer. She returned their looks with an expression of 'Is the answer not obvious?'

"You once tried to leave your friends behind and venture off on a long journey by yourself," she said, looking at Andrew. "It was made abundantly clear that your friends would not allow such a thing to happen. Durinburg, despite what happened, is the only home that I can remember. It is without question that I will return. Besides all that, you will need someone to catalogue the antiques and treasures we discovered in the lower level of the castle. The history of the DuFays that has long been hidden in the shadows shall be brought to light."

"What about the others?" Lawrence asked. "Heather, Steven, Mrs. Bergman, your mother, Ian, Alexander and his mother."

"The decision to return to Durinburg with us, or stay where they are, is theirs and theirs alone," Andrew replied. "The Bergmans have become entrenched in the lives they have built in Stanwyck. I suspect the bitterness of their last days in Durinburg has fouled the sweetness of their memories from the rest of their days in that land. There is greater opportunity for them in Stanwyck. It would be best for them to remain where they are. As for my mother, I would not wish to subject her to such a harsh and uncomfortable journey. She and Mrs. Bergman have become good friends during their short time together. I would encourage her to remain in Stanwyck as well. Regarding Cynthia and Alexander, there is no sound reason for them to make the journey, either. Alexander and Steven have become great friends and Stanwyck, if not Buckington, will provide them with many adventures to share as they grow into men. I will extend the invitation, but I will not encourage them to accept it."

"Robert DuFay spent his life living in debauchery and it was not until the last hours of his life that he repented of his sins and was given the gift of salvation," Reverend Vendici said, addressing Andrew. "There is no man who is immune to the attacks of Satan. God gave us the armor to fend off those attacks, but unless we are dedicated to constant study of the Word and hearing the preaching of the Word, we are prone to shedding that armor. Have you given thought as to how you will fill that need in your court?"

"I have," Andrew replied. "It is my intention to invite Luther Muire to be our pastor and to shepherd us, if that would meet with your approval."

"I can think of no other man who would be better for the task," the reverend replied, smiling. "I will speak with him in the morning." He looked at those around the table. "It appears you have a strong start in filling your court, Your Majesty. You have your Chief Advisor, whom I believe can also serve quite well as the Court Jester. You have your Military Advisor. I believe Lady Talbot would make an excellent Chamberlain. You will have your Pastor, assuming Luther accepts the position. While I have not had the pleasure of becoming more than briefly acquainted with Victoria, from what I know she would be an excellent choice to serve as your Royal Bodyguard, or perhaps a diplomat of a clandestine nature."

"You mean a spy," Lawrence said. The reverend just smiled.

"I have one objection to your recommendations, Reverend," Victoria said. "While I do believe Marie would make an excellent Chamberlain, I do not believe such a position would be utilizing her skills and, dare I say, desires, to their fullest. There is another position for which she would be better suited and would be of greater benefit to Durinburg. The challenge will be in convincing her and the king to see what is plain to the rest of us."

"And just what would that position be?" Marie asked, puzzled. "I would be honored to be the manager of the royal household."

"That is what makes this other position so fitting for you," Victoria replied. "You could also, and knowing you, you would, be manager of the royal household."

"I see where this is heading," Lawrence said, not able to hold back a look of amusement. "This should be interesting."

"I still do not understand," Marie said, genuinely confused.

"My dear, there is only one place for you in Durinburg. That is at the king's side, at Andrew's side."

"What?" Marie asked, her eyes wide open. "You do not mean…"

"Of course that is what she means," Lawrence said. "There is no denying the magnetism between the two of you. Ever since Andrew brought you into his confidence, or rather you inserted yourself into his business, the two of you have been more than just partners in this quest. Even your bickering shows your connection. You should see the way the two of you look at each other."

"They are right," Angus agreed. "I have known you for your entire life. I have known Andrew for less than a year and confess that for most of that time, I did not consider him in a positive manner. However, I have seen the type of man he truly is, and he has my respect and admiration. The two of you are truly an ideal match if I have ever seen one."

"I believe all of you are being positively presumptuous," Marie replied defensively. "I have certainly never expressed or given indication of any such attraction or interest in Andrew or for that matter, any man."

"Come now," Victoria replied. "If your best friend, Heather, were here in this room, I venture she would have a different tale to tell. Besides, anybody who was in that tent at Sedgwick and saw how Andrew spoke to you, and how you responded, knows the truth."

Marie looked at everybody around the table, afraid to admit to them, or herself, her true feelings. Her entire life had been about her independence, making her own decisions, and what they were suggesting was a direct contrast to the type of life she had envisioned for herself. She looked at Andrew, who had yet to participate in the current conversation. His neutral expression did not betray what he was thinking.

"Andrew?" she asked, almost pleadingly. "You have not said a single word during this entire conversation, or rather interrogation if you must. Do you not believe these friends of yours are being more than a little intrusive if not offensive in their speculations?"

Andrew did not immediately answer, but took a moment to consider the situation, his new position and responsibilities, and his unvoiced but undeniable feelings for Marie.

"My intention is to return to Durinburg and work to rebuild the country to what it was when Reginald DuFay reigned over three hundred and fifty years ago," he finally responded, "a land where

God is first and foremost, where all people seek to put on the full armor of God every day. At the same time, I will work towards creating a system whereby the people govern themselves through elected representatives and not be ruled by a person simply because of a family name or a line of descendancy. People will choose their leaders and not have leaders imposed upon them. When the governing system is ready it will be implemented, I will relinquish the crown, and the current monarchy system shall come to an end. Durinburg will be a republic."

"That does not answer the question," Marie chided him.

"Reverend Vendici expressed the importance of a king surrounding himself with advisors who can offer wise and wholesome counsel," Andrew continued. "I believe such people to be seated at this table and I cannot dispute anything that has been said, though I greatly question the timing of their comments and the broaching of the subject," he said with a bit of a rebuking tone.

"I have yet to meet two people as stubborn as the two of you," Lawrence retorted. "If we did not speak up, neither of you would have the courage to broach the subject yourselves and believe us, it needed to be broached."

"Silence, Royal Jester," Andrew commanded, throwing an irritated glare at Lawrence. He returned his attention to Marie.

"When I first met you and your two friends, Heather and Elizabeth, even though you stood behind them you stood out among them. As we spent more time together, I could sense what Lawrence referred to as a magnetism between us, a connection. Our exploration of the bowels of Durinburg Castle was exciting to me not just in the mystery of what we might find, but in your being there with me. When Martin kidnapped you, there arose an anger within me such that no mountain or man could prevent me from rescuing you."

"Ahem," Lawrence cleared this throat, "if you will remember, it was Donald, Luis and I who actually accomplished her rescue while you baby-sat the prisoners."

"Reverend, does the church keep muzzles around for blasphemers?" Andrew asked rhetorically. Again, he looked back at Marie. "When we argued about going to Buckington and continuing the search for the DuFay Armor, I knew you were right, but I would not admit it. Believing you to be angry with me was one of the worst feelings I had experienced in a long time. Victoria mentioned the conversation we had in Sedgwick. I did not send you back here just to protect the armor. I sent you back here to protect YOU. I could not bear the thought of harm coming to you.

"I have expressed on several occasions that I desire nothing more in life than to have land and a family of my own, that power and prestige hold no interest to me. My new position and responsibilities have not changed that goal. I have more land than I could ever make use of in this life. But it will be nothing more than just that, land, without a family with which I can share it. Marie, you are head-strong, opinionated, and stubborn. You are also exceedingly intelligent, and curious, and creative, and kind, and gracious, and witty, and adventurous. I cannot imagine someone I could more greatly desire to be by my side as we work to rebuild Durinburg."

The room fell into silence as Andrew finished speaking. All eyes turned to Marie. She kept her eyes on Andrew. Her expression changed from astonishment to challenging.

"That is it?" she asked contemptuously. "First you insult me, then you try to compliment me, then you say you cannot imagine someone you could more greatly desire to be by your side as you work to rebuild Durinburg? Absolutely, Your Majesty, I shall be honored to be by your side, Your Highness. I shall fetch you wine and make sure your crown is polished to a high shine as you entertain nobles and dignitaries while I entertain you with my wit."

"Andrew, it continues to amaze me at how you can begin a train of thought with such eloquence and such promise, only to end in such disappointment," Victoria said, shaking her head.

"You did not let me finish," Andrew responded defensively, still unsure of how to say what he wanted to say. "Marie, I do not want you by my side as an entertainer, or as a steward, or as someone to shine my crown. I want you by my side as my queen, as the woman with whom I can build not just a country, but more importantly, a strong, faithful family. Will you, Marie Talbot, be my queen, my wife, my helpmeet in building a country and family?"

All eyes turned to Marie.

"Andrew, you are arrogant, stubborn, pushy, and not as funny as you believe yourself to be," she replied. "Yet, you are a man of wisdom, and discernment, and intelligence, and compassion, and generosity. You are a selfless man, and a man of strong faith. I cannot imagine someone whose side I could more greatly desire to be by in building a country, and a family. Yes, Andrew MacLean, I will be your queen, your wife, your helpmeet."

"Excellent!" Lawrence proclaimed. "You do not know how happy this makes me. I was afraid we were going to miss a great excuse for yet another celebration full of food, wine and ale!" He looked at Reverend Vendici. "In moderation, of course."

Reverend Vendici smiled.

"Of course," he replied to Lawrence. He looked at Andrew and Marie. "If you thought finding the DuFay Armor was difficult, wait until you try to plan a royal wedding."

Epilogue

He looked over the men, women and children who filled the massive auditorium. There were easily four hundred people packed into the building and every eye was on him, every ear anxiously awaiting his words. He had given numerous speeches over the past five years but this one would be the most momentous, the most consequential, of them all. And it would be his last as king. Andrew MacLean had rehearsed this speech a thousand times since the crown had been placed on his head, never wavering in his ultimate goal of getting to this moment in time. And now it was here. He glanced to his right at his queen. Marie gave a nod of approval, and Andrew turned back to the throng. All murmurings, all movement ceased. He knew that he had never heard such silence in his life.

"Two hundred years ago, a legend was born," Andrew started. "A legend of a man, a legend of a spirit, a legend of armor. The legend all but mutated into a prophecy, and many believe that prophecy to have been fulfilled when, five years ago, this crown was placed upon my head." He paused for effect. "I do not believe in fairy tales," he stated plainly. "The legend surrounding the armor of Reginald DuFay was just that, a fairy tale. There were no spirits placed in the six pieces of armor created for and in honor of Reginald DuFay. The 'spirit' of Reginald DuFay has not been waiting two centuries for his heir to take possession of the legendary pieces of armor in order to arise, retake the throne, and lead the kingdom and world to peace and prosperity the likes of which it has never known.

Reginald DuFay died three hundred and fifty years ago and his spirit, his soul, is far from here. Robert DuFay, the last DuFay to sit on the throne in this very land, died two hundred years ago and his soul likewise is far from here. But what Reginald DuFay believed, and what Robert DuFay came to believe in the last hours of his life, is still here, and will never perish or fade.

"What they believed was that spiritual warfare was far more essential to peace and prosperity than men slaughtering each other on the battlefield with swords and pikes and maces. Victories in spiritual warfare could make physical warfare obsolete. Defeats in spiritual warfare would lead to the horrors of the battlefield. They knew the importance of putting on the full armor of God, as we are told to do in the Holy Scriptures. For the battle we fight is a spiritual battle, not a physical battle, and we must be armed to engage in such warfare and to be able to not only defend against the attacks of Satan, but to attack with power and drive-back the enemy until he is ultimately defeated.

"The six pieces of armor that were created for Reginald DuFay, physical representations of the armor of God, stand on display in this auditorium, in front of this platform, as a reminder to you, the people, and those you choose to govern your land from this very building, of the importance of putting on the full armor of God every day. Teach your children to put on the full armor of God every day. When you elect your representatives to uphold the laws of the land, to settle disputes, to govern your kingdom, and to be representatives to other countries, ensure that they are men who put on the full armor of God every day.

"It was never my desire to rise to this level of royalty, to have a crown on my head, to lead a country. I did what I could to flee such responsibilities, but I could not run away from what God had foreordained for me. Ten years ago, I was sent on a journey to find an heir which put my life on a path which I could never have imagined. Five years ago, I found him. I found myself, and again this discovery put my life on a path which I could never have imagined. Today, I am yet again turning my feet to a different path, and this one is the one that I have always imagined.

"For the past five years, we have worked diligently to create a system of government where the people hold the power and not one man. We have created the Charter of Durinburg, which embodies the form of this new government along with the rights of the people. Power and leadership are no longer attained through blood lines or names, but through being chosen by the people to lead. Gone are the days of tyrants and dictators making and breaking laws at their whim, with virtually no accountability. You will have men, chosen from amongst yourselves, to ensure that righteous laws are created and upheld, and that no one man has ultimate power. But let this be a warning to you: All of us are fallen creatures, sinful, and subject to the temptations thrown at us not only by Satan, but by our own desires. While a king can become a tyrant, so can an elected assembly. That is why it is vital that you choose men who put on the armor of God to be your representatives, your leaders, your governors. You must hold them accountable at all times. Do this, and you, your families, and your country will prosper. Do this not, and your children and children's children shall suffer the fate of Robert DuFay.

"Today is the last day that I stand in front of you as your king. Today, I shall remove the crown from my head and the responsibilities of leadership, and governance shall pass to those you have chosen to do so. You have chosen a prime minister to be the leader of your country, yet he shall not govern autonomously but always be accountable to members of Parliament. However, the true power that governs this land is held in your hands. Use that power with great wisdom and discernment, and with full deference to the Word of God. Do this, and you, your families, and your country will prosper. Do this not, and your children and children's children shall suffer greatly.

"It has been my honor to sit on the throne of Durinburg for the past five years, a throne for which I have never been worthy. It is with a great mixture of emotions that I relinquish this crown and step down from the throne. However, I am confident that this new direction for Durinburg shall result in great prosperity and great freedom for all, more than would be realized through the rein of one man. The future of this country is in this room, in each and every one of you. I look forward to experiencing this future with you and among you."

Andrew turned to Reverend Luther Muire, who was sitting behind him and to his left.

"Reverend, if you would, please dismiss this meeting with a prayer."

Reverend Muire stood and approached the podium as Andrew stepped backward and sat in the chair beside Marie. He looked at Marie, who gave him a smile of approval and took his hand in hers. A peace he had never known washed over Andrew, and more than ever he looked forward to the path in front of him.

The great hall of the new Parliament building was once again silent, as the throng that had filled it a few hours before had long vacated the building. Andrew, Marie and Lawrence stood on the raised platform where Andrew had given his speech.

"You would have made a fine prime minister," Lawrence said to Andrew. "There was an overwhelming push by the people for you to take that position. Are you certain there is no place in politics for Andrew MacLean in the future?"

"Extremely certain," Andrew replied emphatically. "I have served my tour of duty."

"He has other responsibilities now," Marie said. "They are named Robert and Stephanie and are sitting at home waiting for their father."

"Is your confidence in this new government system truly so strong?" Lawrence asked.

Andrew stepped down from the platform and stood in front of the six pieces of the DuFay Armor.

"As with any government or institution, it is ultimately a reflection of the people," Andrew replied. "People are far from perfect and unfortunately, we are all bombarded daily with the remnants of sin in our hearts. The success of any government, any country, will be dependent on whether or not people put on the armor of God. That is why we decided to put the DuFay Armor on display right here, for all to see, as reminders that we are constantly under attack and must protect ourselves and arm ourselves in order to win the spiritual battles."

"Let us hope the people do not forget," Marie said as she looked at each piece of armor and read the Scripture references listed beside them. Each piece also had a commentary posted giving more details and additional Scripture references. They were beyond magnificent, each having a beauty which would be difficult if even possible to replicate. She had examined each piece very carefully over the past five years, always gaining a new appreciation for them and renewing her dedication to putting on the armor of God every day. She had also directed a preservation team which had fully chronicled the secret room she and Andrew had discovered so long ago in the bowels of the castle and created a museum and library for the DuFay history to be on full display for all to appreciate. The trio reached the end of the display, and Marie paused in front of the sword. It rose above all the other pieces in beauty and significance and was truly her favorite. She could never grow tired of gazing at it. As she did so this time, something seemed off. She leaned closer to the sword and squinted her eyes. She looked at the sword from its hilt to its tip.

"Something is wrong," she said, turning her head to Andrew.

"What do you mean?" Andrew asked.

"This is not the DuFay Sword," she replied, turning her attention back to the sword.

"Of course it is," Andrew answered dismissively.

"No, I have examined every piece of the DuFay Armor over the years, more times than I could count, and this definitely is not the original DuFay Sword."

"I believe you are mistaken," Andrew said with confidence. "That is the DuFay Sword. As you will recall, I carried it around for well over five years. It is what started my journey to this very spot on this very day. It is what I spent so much effort protecting and, if you listen to the foolishness of certain people, my obsession. Trust me when I say that I, of all people, know the DuFay Sword better than anybody else."

"That may be so," Marie replied, "but while it is a very exquisite sword, there are enough subtle differences that I can say for certain that this is not the DuFay Sword."

Andrew looked at Marie, then at the sword. He stepped forward and leaned as close to the sword as possible, appearing to examine every fraction of an inch of the weapon. After a few minutes, he stepped back.

"You are mistaken," he said with a reassuring grin. "This is the DuFay Sword. Now, I am hungry. Let us go home and have a nice meal and be parents to our children."

"But Andrew," Marie started to argue, "with all due respect—" She did not get to finish, as Lawrence interjected.

"Marie, as Andrew said, he spent five years toting this sword around. It practically became a part of him, an extension of himself. He knows best. If he says that this is the DuFay Sword, then who are we to argue? It is the DuFay Sword."

Marie looked at Lawrence, then back to Andrew. There was something in the shadows of the conversation that she could not quite see. It gnawed at her for a moment, but she quickly found the missing piece of the puzzle.

"You did not..." she began with a tone that bordered on rebuke. Instead of answering her, Andrew gave her a smile that almost bordered on a confession, then looked at Lawrence.

"My friend, why do you not join us for a fine meal? I am sure Robert and Stephanie would love a visit from their favorite, and only, uncle."

"It would be my pleasure," Lawrence replied and followed Andrew as he turned and walked toward the exit. Marie stood in silence for a moment, looking after the two men. Her look of confusion quickly transformed into a look of admonishment.

"Andrew MacLean!" she called out as though rebuking one of her children, hurrying after her husband.

www.ingramcontent.com/pod-product-compliance
Lightning Source LLC
Chambersburg PA
CBHW030229120726
47903CB00005B/1419